Getting c
situation,
by a han
delivered
thing. But it's another when
your hero won't let you go…
especially when all you really
want is to stay in his arms!

HER
RESCUER

Two fantastic, bestselling authors
deliver two page-turning novels.

HER
RESCUER

Michael's Temptation
EILEEN WILKS

Egan Cassidy's Kid
BEVERLY BARTON

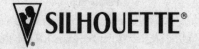 SILHOUETTE®

Silhouette Books, Eton House, 18-24 Paradise Road,
Richmond, Surrey TW9 1SR

HER RESCUER © Harlequin Books S.A. 2006

The publisher acknowledges the copyright holders of the
individual works, which have already been published in the UK in
single, separate volumes, as follows:

Michael's Temptation © Eileen Wilks 2001
Egan Cassidy's Kid © Beverly Beaver 2000

ISBN 0 373 60407 6

064-0506

Printed and bound in Spain
by Litografia Rosés S.A., Barcelona

Michael's Temptation

EILEEN WILKS

EILEEN WILKS

is a fifth-generation Texan. Her great-great-grandmother came to Texas shortly after the end of the Civil War. But she's not a full-blooded Texan. Right after another war, her Texan father fell for a Yankee woman. This obviously mismatched pair proceeded to travel to nine cities in three countries in the first twenty years of their marriage, raising two kids and innumerable dogs and cats along the way. For the next twenty years they stayed put, back home in Texas again—and still together.

Eileen believes her professional career matches her nomadic upbringing, since she has tried everything from draughting to a brief stint as a ranch hand. Not until she started writing did she 'stay put', because that's when she knew she'd come home. Readers can write to her at PO Box 4612, Midland, TX 79704-4612, USA.

This one's for Glenda,
who wanted to read about a woman minister
who didn't fit the stereotypes, with special
thanks to my editor, Mary-Theresa Hussey,
and to Joan Marlow Golan,
for making it possible.

Prologue

The sky growled. Lightning shattered the darkness, flashing an image of heavy wood and wet stone. The gargoyle flanking the door leered at him in the brief burst of light as he fitted his key to the lock.

Rain and darkness suited the old house, Michael thought as he swung the door open. Suited his mood, too.

The only light in the foyer came from a Christmas tree winking at him merrily from one corner. The wide stairwell was dark, and no light came from the hall that led to his brother's office.

Jacob wouldn't be in bed yet. The playroom, maybe. Michael's boots squeaked on the marble floor, reminding him that he was dripping wet.

Ada wouldn't thank him for tracking water all over. He stopped by a high-backed wooden chair that resembled a throne and pulled off his boots and leather jacket. Before tossing the jacket on the chair, he pulled a thick envelope from an inner pocket.

His steps were soundless now as he made his way to the back of the house. He paused in the doorway to the play-room.

The lights were off. A fire burned in the fireplace, hot and bright, tossing shadows along the walls. The windows were bare to the night, rain-washed, and the limb of one young elm tapped against the glass like fretful fingers. Jacob sat in the wing chair beside the fireplace, his legs outstretched, his face turned to the fire. He held a brandy snifter in one hand.

Michael smiled. "Snob. That expensive French stuff doesn't taste any better than what I can get at the grocery store for $12.95 a bottle."

If he'd startled his brother, it didn't show. Very little did, with Jacob. The face he turned to Michael revealed neither pleasure nor surprise, but the welcome was there, in his voice. "I have a palate. You drink like a teenager, purely for the effect."

"True." Michael moved into the room.

It was furnished in a haphazard way at odds with the el-egance of the rest of the house. Every time their father had taken a wife, the new Mrs. West had redecorated. Michael and his brothers had gotten in the habit of stashing their fa-vorite pieces here. The playroom had become a haven for castoffs in more ways than one.

There was a library table that had once been the property of a Spanish viceroy of Mexico. It made him think of his brother Luke and countless games of poker—which Luke had usually won. Michael's second-oldest brother might seem reckless, but he had always been good at calculating the odds. Luke was almost as at home with a deck of cards as he was on the back of a horse.

A chessboard with jade and jet pieces sat on the table now. Michael paused there to pick up the jet king and turn it over and over in the hand that wasn't holding the thick envelope. Chess had always been Jacob's game. The patience and planning of it had suited him when they were young, just as his careful accumulation of wealth did now.

Michael sighed and put the chess piece down. It was hard to ask, but worse not to know. "How's Ada?"

"Mean as ever." Jacob stood. He was a big man, Michael's oldest brother. Big all over, and four inches taller than Michael's six feet. His hair was short and thick, a brown so dark it almost matched Michael's black hair; his shirt, too, was dark, with the subtle sheen of silk. "She's doing well, Michael. The treatments are working."

The breath he hadn't realized he was holding came out in a dizzy rush. He cleared his throat. "Good. That's good."

"You here for a while?"

"I'll have to leave in the morning. I've been..." He glanced at the envelope still in his hand. "Taking care of business. You have anything to drink other than that fancy cologne you're sipping?"

"I think I can find something cheap enough to please you." Jacob moved over to the bar. "How much of an effect are you after?"

"More than that," Michael said when his brother paused after pouring two fingers of bourbon.

Jacob handed him the glass. "You can start with this. You won't be here long enough to nurse a hangover."

"I'll nurse it on the plane." He let his restless feet carry him to the pinball machine in the corner.

Pinball—that had been his game back when they all lived here. Flash and speed, he thought, and swallowed cheap fire, grimacing at the taste but relishing the burn. He'd been drawn to both back then. Lacking Jacob's patience and Luke's athleticism, he'd settled for the gifts he did have—a certain quickness of hand, eye and body.

He couldn't complain. Agility was an asset for a man who lived the way he did. So was a clear mind...but tonight he preferred to be thoroughly fuzzed. He tossed back the rest of the liquor.

Jacob's eyebrow lifted. "In a hurry?"

He shrugged and went over to the bar to refill his glass. What he'd done—what he intended to do—was for Ada, and therefore worth the sacrifice. Without the treatments administered by a Swiss clinic, she would die. But the treatments were experimental and very, very expensive.

There had been only one way for the West brothers to raise the money to keep Ada alive. The trust, the be-damned trust their father had left his fortune tied up in, could be dissolved and they could claim the inheritance none of them had wanted to touch...once they fulfilled the conditions.

Luke had already done his part. Michael intended to do his—that's why he was here. Jacob wouldn't be far behind...all three of them dancing to the old man's piping at last, five years after burying him.

Jacob set his snifter on the bar. "Pour me some more while you're at it. I'm not interested in a hangover, but I'll keep you company. What's the occasion?"

"What else?" He tossed the envelope on the bar. "That's a copy of the prenuptial agreement your lawyer drew up for me, duly signed and notarized."

"I see. Found someone already, have you?"

Michael lifted his glass, empty now, in a mocking salute. "Congratulate me. I'm getting married as soon as I get back from this mission. So tonight, I'm going to get very, very drunk."

One

Were they coming for her?

She sat bolt upright, thrust from sleep into wakefulness. The bed ropes creaked beneath her. The taste of fear was thick and dry in her mouth. *Dan,* she thought. *Dan, why aren't you here?*

There was, of course, no answer.

If it had been a sound that awakened her, she heard nothing now except the rhythmic rasp of Sister Maria Elena's breathing in the bed beside her. Darkness pressed against her staring eyes, the unrelieved blackness only possible far from the artificial glow of civilization.

Automatically her gaze flickered toward the door. She couldn't see a thing.

Thank God. Her sigh eased a single hard knot of fear. If they came for her at night—and they might—they would have to bring a light. She'd be able to see it shining around the edges of the door.

Her gaze drifted to the outside wall where whispers of

starlight bled through cracks between the boards, smudging the darkness. Soldiers had hammered those boards over the window when they'd first locked her in this room last week.

One week. When morning came, she would have been here a full seven days. Waiting for the man they called *El Jefe* to return and decide if she were to live or die...or, if the taunts of her guards were true, what form that death would take.

He would decide Sister Maria Elena's fate, too, she reminded herself, and wished the fear didn't always come first, hardest, for herself. But while the sister was a *religioso,* she was also a native of San Christóbal, not a representative of the nation *El Jefe* hated even more than he hated organized religion. She was old and ill. He might spare her.

A.J. pushed back the thin blanket, careful not to wake the nun, and swung her legs to the floor. Her knees were rubbery. Her breath came quick and shallow, and her hands and feet were chilled.

She ignored the physical symptoms of terror as best she could, making her way by touch and memory to the boarded-up window. There she folded her long legs to sit on the cool, dirty floor. Spaces between the boards let in fresh air—chilly, this far up in the mountains, but welcome. She smelled dampness and dirt, the wild green aroma of growing things, the heavier perfume of flowers. Even now, in the dry season, there were flowers here.

Wherever "here" was. She didn't know where the soldiers had brought her when they'd raided La Paloma, the sleepy village where she'd been working. San Christóbal had a lot of mountains.

The boards let in slices of sky along with air. And if the sky was clear...yes, when she leaned close she could see a single star. The sight eased her.

The night wasn't truly silent. Inside, there was the labored breathing of the feverish nun. Outside, frogs set up a staccato chorus, and the soft whirring of wings announced the hunt of some night-flying bird. Somewhere not too far away, a man cried out a greeting in Spanish and was answered. The distant scream of a puma rattled the night. Then there was only the sighing of wind through trees.

So many trees. Even without boards, without soldiers and fear, it had been hard sometimes to find enough sky here to feed a soul used to the open plains of west Texas.

A.J. tried not to regret coming to San Christóbal. That, too, was hard. Her eyes stayed open while her lips moved in a soundless prayer.

It shamed her, how deep and terrible her fear was. It weakened her, too, and she would need strength to get through whatever was to come. So she would pray and wait here, wait and watch as her slivers of sky brightened. In the daylight, she could remember who she was. There was Sister Maria Elena to care for then, and birdsong and monkey chatter to listen to. In the daylight, the slices of sky between the cracks would turn brilliantly blue. She could steady herself against those snatches of life.

But at night, locked into the darkness, she felt alone, lost, forgotten. In the darkness, she missed Dan intensely—and blamed him, too, as foolish as that was. In the darkness, the fear came back, rolling in like the tide of a polluted ocean. Sooner or later, *he* would be back. The one they called *El Jefe*. He would finish killing people elsewhere and return to his headquarters.

Being left alone was a good thing, she reminded herself. *El Jefe* was a man who believed in killing for his cause— but he didn't condone rape. Neither she nor Sister Maria Elena had been harmed in that way. A.J. watched her star and murmured a prayer of thanks.

If she hadn't been sitting with her head almost touching the boards, she wouldn't have heard the sound. Softer than a whisper, so soft she couldn't say what made it—save that it came from outside. From the other side of the window.

Her breath stopped up in her throat. Her eyes widened.

Something blacked out her star.

"Reverend? Are you there?" The voice was male and scarcely louder than her heartbeat. It came from only inches away. "Reverend Kelleher?"

It was also American.

Dizziness hit. If she had been standing, she would have fallen. "Yes," she whispered, and had to swallow. "Yes, I'm here."

A pause. "I'm going to kill Scopes," that wonderful voice whispered.

"Wh-what?"

"I was expecting a baritone, not a soprano." There was a hint of drawl in the whisper, a deliciously familiar echo of Texas. "Lieutenant Michael West, ma'am. Special Forces. I've come to get you out of here."

"Thank God." The prayer was heartfelt.

"How old are you?"

"Thirty-two." She bit back the urge to ask him how old *he* was.

"Are you injured?"

"No, I—"

"On a scale of couch potato to superjock, how fit are you?"

Oh—he needed to know if she would be able to keep up. "I'm in good shape, Lieutenant. But Sister Maria Elena is over sixty, and her leg—"

"Who?" The word came out sharp and a little louder.

"Sister Maria Elena," she repeated, confused. "She was injured when the soldiers overran the village. I'm afraid she won't be able to…Lieutenant?"

He'd begun to curse, fluently and almost soundlessly. "This nun—is she a U.S. citizen?"

"No, but surely that doesn't matter."

"The U.S. can't rescue every native endangered by a bunch of Che Guevara wannabes. And what would I do with her? Guatemala and Honduras aren't accepting refugees from San Christóbal, and Nicaragua is still pissed at the U.S. over the carrier incident last spring. They wouldn't let us land a military helicopter.''

''But—but you can't just leave her here!''

''Reverend, getting you out is going to be tricky enough.''

A.J. leaned her forehead against one rough board and swallowed hope. It lumped up sick and cold in her stomach. ''Then I'm sorry,'' she whispered. ''I can't go with you.''

There was a beat of silence. ''Do you have any idea what *El Jefe* will do to you if you're still here when he gets back?''

''I hope you aren't planning to give me any gruesome details. It won't help. I can't leave Sister Maria Elena.'' Her voice wobbled. ''She's feverish. It started with a cut on her foot that got infected. Sh-she'll die without care.''

''Lady, she's going to die whether you stay or go.''

She wanted desperately to go with him. She couldn't. ''I can't leave her.''

Another, longer silence. ''Do you know anything about the truck parked beside the barracks?''

She shook her head, trying to keep up with the odd jumps his mind made. ''I don't know. They brought me here in a truck. A flatbed truck with metal sides that smells like a chicken coop.''

''That's the one. It was running last week?''

She nodded, then felt foolish. He couldn't see her. ''Yes.''

''Okay. Get your things together. Wait here—I'll be back.''

She nearly choked on a giggle, afraid that if she started laughing she wouldn't be able to stop. ''Sure. I'm not going anywhere.''

The moon was a skimpy sliver, casting barely enough light to mark the boundaries between shadows. Michael waited in a puddle of deeper darkness, his back pressed to the cement blocks of *El Jefe*'s house. A sentry passed fifteen feet away.

The sentries didn't worry him. He had a pair of Uncle Sam's best night goggles, while the sentries had to rely on whatever night vision came naturally. He also had his weapons—a SIG Sauer and the CAR 16 slung over his shoulder—but hoped like hell he wouldn't have to use them. Shooting was likely to attract attention. If he had to silence one of the sentries, he'd rather use one of the darts in his vest pocket. They were loaded with a nifty knockout drug.

El Jefe's headquarters was like the rest of his military efforts—military in style but inadequate. The self-styled liberator should have stayed a guerrilla leader, relying on sneak attacks. He lacked the training to hold what he'd taken. In Michael's not-so-humble opinion, San Christóbal's government would have to screw up mightily to lose this nasty little war. In a week or two, government troops should be battling their way up the slope *El Jefe*'s house perched on.

But what the guerrilla leader lacked in military training he made up for in sheer, bloody fanaticism. A week would be too late for the soft-voiced woman Michael had just left.

What was the fool woman doing here? His mouth tightened. Maybe she was no more foolish than the three U.S. biologists they'd already picked up, who were waiting nervously aboard the chopper. But she was female, damn it.

One sentry rounded the west corner of the house. The other had almost reached the end of his patrol. Michael bent and made his way quickly and silently across the cleared slope separating the compound from the forest. Then he paused to scan the area behind him. The goggles rendered everything in grays, some areas sharp, others fuzzy. Out in the open, though, where the sentry moved, visibility was excellent. Michael waited patiently as the man passed the boarded-up window. He wouldn't move on until he was sure he wouldn't lead anyone to the rendezvous.

He was definitely going to kill Scopes.

It was Scopes who'd passed on word from a villager about some do-gooder missionary who'd been captured by *El Jefe*'s troops. He must have known the minister was a woman, damn him. Andrew Scopes was going to strangle on his twisted sense of humor this time, Michael promised himself.

Maybe the minister's sex shouldn't make a difference. But it did.

He remembered the way her voice had shaken when she'd whispered that she couldn't go with him. She'd probably been crying. He hated a woman's tears, and resented that he'd heard hers.

She was scared out of her mind. But she wasn't budging, not without her nun.

A nun. God almighty. Michael started winding through the trunks of the giants that held up the forest canopy. Even with the goggles the light was poor here, murky and indistinct, but he could see well enough to avoid running into anything.

Why did there have to be a nun?

Since he'd joined the service, he'd had more than one hard decision to make. Some of them haunted him late at night when ghosts come calling. But a *nun!* He shook his head. His memories of St. Vincent's Academy weren't all pleasant, but they were vivid. Especially his memories of Sister Mary Agnes. She'd reminded him of Ada. Mean as a lioness with PMS if you hadn't done your homework, and twice as fierce in defense of one of her kids.

Dammit to hell. This was supposed to have been a simple mission. Simple, at least, for Michael's team. His men were good. True, Crowe was new, but so far he'd proved steady. But gathering intelligence on the deadly spat brewing between *El Jefe* and the government of San Christóbal, rounding up a few terrified biologists on the side, was a far cry from snatching captives from a quasi-military compound.

Still, the compound wasn't heavily guarded, and the soldiers left behind when *El Jefe* left to take the mountain road weren't well trained or equipped. Michael and his men had watched the place for two days and a night; he knew what they were up against. No floodlights, thank God, and the forest provided great cover. Once they got their target out,

they had three miles to cover to reach the clearing where the
Cobra waited with its cargo of nervous biologists. An easy
run—unless you were carrying an injured nun with fifteen
armed soldiers in hot pursuit.

But *El Jefe* had thoughtfully left a truck behind. And, according to the Reverend, it had been running a week ago,
when they brought her here. There was a good chance it was
in working order.

If the truck ran…

She'd giggled. When he'd told her to wait there—meaning
for her to wait by the window so she would hear him when
he returned—she'd answered with one silly, stifled giggle.
That sound clung to him like cobwebs, in sticky strands that
couldn't be brushed off. He crossed a narrow stream in the
darkness of that foreign forest, his CAR 16 slung over his
back and memories of Popsicles melting in the summer sun
filling his mind.

Her giggle made him think of the first time he'd kissed a
girl. The taste of grape Nehi, and long-ago mornings when
dew had glistened on the grass like every unbroken promise
ever made.

There was no innocence in him, not anymore. But he could
still recognize it. He could still be moved by it.

He could knock the Reverend out. It would be the sensible
thing to do. Downright considerate, even, since then she'd be
able to blame him instead of herself for the nun's fate.

Of course, he'd blame himself, too.

When was he going to grow up and get over his rescue-
the-maiden complex? It was going to get him killed one of
these days. And, dammit, he couldn't get killed now. He had
to get married.

That wasn't the best way to talk himself out of playing
hero.

He'd reached the fallen tree that was his goal. He stopped
and whistled—one low, throbbing note that mimicked a bird
call. A second later, three men melted out of the trees. Even

with his goggles, he hadn't spotted them until they moved. His men were good. The best. Even Scopes, though Michael still intended to ream him a new one for his little joke.

He sighed and accepted the decision he'd already made, however much he'd tried to argue himself out of it. He couldn't leave the Reverend to *El Jefe*'s untender mercy. Or the nun.

The Colonel was going to gut him for sure this time.

The wheeling of the earth had taken A.J.'s star out of sight. Now there was only darkness between the slits in the boards.

Getting her things together had been easy. They hadn't let her bring any of her possessions, not her Bible, not even a change of underwear. She had a comb and a toothbrush tucked in her pocket, given to her a few days ago by a guard who still possessed a trace of compassion. Of course, he probably expected to get them back when she was killed. Still, she asked God to bless the impulse that had moved him to offer her those tokens of shared humanity.

Waiting was hard.

He was coming back. Surely he was. And if he did…*when* he did, he would take her and the sister away with him. He had to.

She touched the place between her breasts where her cross used to hang and wished she knew how long she'd been waiting. How long she still had to wait. If the sun rose and he hadn't returned…oh, she didn't want to give up hope. Painful as it was, she didn't want to give it up.

Time was strange. So elastic. Events and emotions could compress it, wad up the moments so tightly that hours sped by at breakneck speed. Or it could be stretched so thin that one second oozed into the next with boggy reluctance. *Slow as molasses,* she thought. Into her mind drifted an image of her grandfather's freckled hand, the knuckles swollen, holding a jar of molasses, pouring it over a stack of her mother's buttermilk pancakes….

"Hey, Rev."

Though the whisper was so soft it blended with the breeze, she jolted. "Yes." It came out too loud, snatching the breath from her lungs. "I'm here."

"In a few minutes there will be an explosion at the east end of the compound. Are you familiar with the setup?"

An explosion? Her heart thudded. "I didn't see much when I was brought here, and I've been kept in this room ever since. Are you going to…Sister Maria Elena, will you…?"

"Yeah." He sighed. "We'll take the sister. You ready? Got your things?"

"There's nothing." Her hand went to the place her cross used to hang. A soldier with pocked skin and a missing tooth had yanked it off her neck. "Just Sister Maria Elena."

"Is she ready to go?"

"She doesn't hear well. I didn't want to wake her to tell her what was going on. I would have had to speak too loudly."

"Explanations will have to wait, then. The sentries are taken care of, but there might be other guards inside the house."

The sentries were "taken care of"? What did that mean? She shivered. "Why an explosion? Wouldn't it be better to sneak out?"

"We need a distraction. One of my men is going to blow up the barracks at the other end of the compound. When it goes—"

"No." In her distress she rose to her knees, putting her hands against the boards as if she could reach him through them. "No, the soldiers—they're sleeping. You can't kill them when they're sleeping."

"It's a shaped charge, just a little boom. Noisy enough to get their attention, but most of the force will be dispersed upward, taking out the roof. It probably won't kill anyone."

He sounded matter-of-fact, almost indifferent. As if death—killing—meant little to him. "Probably?"

"Keep your voice down," he whispered. "Look, this is war. A small one, but the rules aren't the ones you're used to. These men would shoot you and the sister without blinking. That's if you're lucky. They've done worse."

A.J. swallowed. The area where she'd been working had been peaceful at first. She wouldn't have come to San Christóbal if she'd known...but after she'd arrived, she'd heard rumors of atrocities in the mountains. Men shot, tortured, villages burned. In Carracruz, the capital city, they blamed outlaws. In the rural villages, they whispered of rebels. Of *El Jefe*.

"Maybe so. That doesn't make it right to kill them in their beds."

"You worry about right and wrong, Rev. I'll worry about getting us out of here. Here's the plan. There's a helicopter waiting three miles away. While the *soldados* are busy worrying about the explosion, we get you and the sister out of here and run like hell. There's a trail that runs into the road about half a mile from the compound. We'll meet the truck there."

"What truck?"

"The one my men will liberate. It will get us to the copter. If everything goes well, we'll be airborne about fifteen minutes after Scopes's bomb goes off. Got it?"

It sounded good. It sounded so good she was terrified all over again at the sheer, dizzying possibility of escape. "Got it."

"One more thing. From this point on, I'm the voice of God to you."

"That's blasphemous."

"It's necessary. You have the right to risk your own life, but you don't have the right to endanger my men. You do what I say, when I say. No arguing, no questions. If I say jump, I don't want to hear any nonsense about how high. Just jump. Understood?''

''I'm not good at following orders blindly.''

''You'd better learn fast, or I'll knock you out and make my job easier.''

She swallowed. She didn't have any trouble believing Lieutenant Michael West would knock her out if he considered it necessary. ''You're supposed to be one of the good guys.''

''They don't make good guys like they used to, honey.''

''A.J.''

''What?''

''You've called me Reverend, Rev, lady, and now honey. My name's A.J.''

''Sounds more like—''

It was like being inside a clap of thunder—end-of-the-world loud, floor-shaking, ear-bursting loud.

His ''little boom'' had gone off.

Two

Michael had the first board popped off before his ears stopped ringing. He'd brought a tire iron for that chore, borrowed from the shed that held the truck Scopes and Trace were stealing at this very moment. He worked quickly, his SIG Sauer in its holster, the CAR 16 on the ground. He'd drugged the closest sentry before approaching the window; he could count on Hammond to take care of the other one.

The nun had let out a screech when the bomb went off. The Reverend was explaining things to her now—loudly.

A voice that was all bone-rumbling bass sounded behind him. "Do I get the one that's yellin'?"

"Nope." Michael pried off the last board and stepped back. "You get the one that screamed when Scopes's toy went boom. In you go."

"She'll start screamin' again when she sees me," Hammond said gloomily. The team's electronics expert did look like the Terminator's bigger, blacker brother, especially in camouflage with night goggles. He sighed and eased his six-feet-six inches of muscle through the small window.

Michael tossed down the tire iron and picked up his CAR 16, keeping his back to the window as he kept watch. He heard Hammond's low rumble assuring the Reverend she could trust him with the sister; seconds later, he heard the Reverend climbing out the window. He slid her one quick glance, then jerked his gaze back to the clearing and the trees.

She sure as hell didn't look like any minister he'd ever seen.

That momentary glimpse hadn't given him a lot details, and his goggles robbed the scene of color. But he'd noticed a slim, long-fingered hand that shook slightly. A tangled wreck of curls that hung below her shoulders. A wide mouth in an angular face, and big eyes fixed on the weapon he cradled. And about six feet of legs.

Lord, she must be nearly as tall as he was. And ninety percent of her was legs.

What color were her eyes?

Hammond was at the window, ready to pass out a blanket-wrapped bundle. Michael traded a CAR 16 for an armful of old woman.

Even through the blanket and the material of her habit, he felt the heat from her fever. She was tiny, so light Hammond could probably cradle her in one arm and still handle his weapon. She'd lost her wimple. Her hair was thin, short and plastered to her skull. Her face was small and round and wrinkled...and smiling.

She looked nothing like Sister Mary Agnes. Michael smiled back at her, told her in Spanish that they would take good care of her, then passed her to Hammond.

The scream of automatic fire shattered the night, coming from the other end of the compound. Good. The others were keeping the soldiers busy. His quick glance took in the preacher's pallor and shocked eyes. He didn't know if it was the gunfire that spooked her, or if she could see the huddled shape of the sentries a few feet away.

He didn't have time to coddle her. "We'll go single file. Reverend, you're the meat in the sandwich. Hammond and I can see where we're going. You can't, so hook your hand in my utility belt. We'll be moving fast."

"A.J. My name is A.J."

He turned away. "Hang on tight." As soon as he felt her hand seize the webbed belt at the small of his back, he moved out.

They crossed the clearing at a dead run and didn't slow much when they hit the forest. The ground was rough, and the night must have been completely black to her, but she didn't hold them up. A couple of times she stumbled, but her grip on his belt kept her upright, and she kept moving.

Good for her. He blessed her long legs as he wove among the trees, listening to the diminishing blast of gunfire behind them.

"Where are we going?"

"This trail intersects the road. We'll meet the truck there. There's a log here you'll have to jump." He leaped it.

She followed awkwardly but without falling. "This is a trail? Are you sure?"

He grinned, pleased with the trace of humor he heard in her voice. "Trust me. It's here." He'd found and followed it last night. Fortunately, the canopy wasn't as thick here as it was in some places—part of this forest was second-growth. But that meant that there was more underbrush.

"Hammond," he said. "Anything?"

"No sign of pursuit, Mick."

Everything was going according to plan. It made Michael uneasy. Yeah, it was a good plan, implemented by good men. Problem was, he'd never yet been on a job where everything went according to plan. The truck might not start, or any of a dozen things could go wrong with getting it out.

When they reached the road Michael's pessimism was rewarded. The truck wasn't there. A fistful of soldiers were. And they were coming *up* the road, not down it from the compound.

One second A.J. was running a step behind her rescuer, her hand locked for dear life in the webbing of his belt while plants tried to trip her. The next, he stopped so suddenly she slammed into him.

He didn't even wobble. Just spun, shoved her down and hit the ground beside her.

She couldn't see a thing. Her hip throbbed from her rough landing in the dirt. A stick was poking her shoulder, and she didn't know where Sister Maria Elena was. The other soldier, the one with the face of a comic book villain and the Mr. Universe body, wasn't beside them. When A.J. lifted her head to see what had happened to him, a large hand pushed it back down so fast she got dirt in her mouth.

He kept his hand on her neck. She felt breath on her hair, warm and close to her ear. His whisper was so soft she barely heard it. "Soldiers coming up the road. Not the ones from the compound."

Oh, God. More soldiers. Now that she'd stopped running, she felt cold. So cold. Or maybe it was his thumb, moving idly on her nape, that made goose bumps pop out on her shivery flesh. Or fear. She tried to keep her whisper as nearly soundless as his had been. "The truck?"

"Listen."

She heard it now—a motor laboring, moving toward them. And from the other direction, voices of the soldiers he'd seen, coming up the rough dirt road. How could they have gotten in front of the truck?

No, she realized, these soldiers weren't from the compound. They must be some of *El Jefe*'s other troops. Was *El Jefe* himself with them? Fear, sour and brackish, mixed with the flavor of dirt in her mouth. She tried to breathe slowly, to calm her racing heart.

Headlights! They splashed color against the dense black backdrop of trees just up the road as the truck rounded a curve.

"We'll have a few seconds before they realize the truck isn't part of their team anymore." His hand left her nape, and she felt him move, crouching beside her, his weapon ready. "I've signaled Hammond. When he moves, you follow. Head for the back of the truck."

The truck was closing the distance rapidly. Its headlights picked out three men on the road ahead—ragged, but unmistakably soldiers.

"I'll lay covering fire if needed, then—hell! *Damn* that Crowe!"

Shots—machine-gun fast and deafeningly loud—came from the truck. One of the soldiers jerked and fell. The rest scattered, leaping for cover. And firing back.

The gunfire hurled her back in time, to a place and moment she never wanted to see again—past blurring the present with horror and blood. Her ears rang. Terror spurted through her like flames chasing gasoline.

Someone yelled—it was him, Michael, the lieutenant—but she had no idea what he was yelling. He waved his arm and the other soldier leaped right over her, huge and dark and graceful. Then he was running toward the truck, the sister in his arms, with the roar and hammer of gunfire exploding everywhere.

The truck had slowed, but it hadn't come to a complete stop. The soldier leaped again and landed in the back of the rolling truck, the sister still in his arms. Oh, God, it was still moving. It would pass them by. She had to get up, had to run—but noise and terror, gunfire and memory smothered her, pressing her flat in the dirt.

The lieutenant grabbed her arm and jerked her to her knees. *"Run!"*

She gulped and shoved to her feet. A shadowy form loomed suddenly up out of the darkness. Moonlight gleamed on the barrel of his gun—pointed right at them.

Gunfire exploded beside her. The shadowy form jerked, fell. Someone screamed—was it her? Shots burst out all over, seeming to come from every direction. Dirt sprayed up near her feet.

He seized her hand and dragged her after him at a dead run—into the forest.

Away from the truck.

She pulled against his grip and tried to make him let her go. Maybe she cried out those words, *let me go, let me go to the truck*—but he dragged her after him, into the forest. She stumbled, tripped, crashing into the loamy ground. He jerked her to her feet and growled, "Run like the fires of hell are after you. They are."

She heard renewed gunfire. And she ran.

What followed was a nightmare of darkness and noise. The soldiers came after them. She heard them crashing through the underbrush, heard them calling to one another. And she heard their guns. Once, bark chips flew from a tree, cutting her cheek, when a bullet came too close.

They ran and ran. The lieutenant gripped her hand as if she might try to get away, but she no longer wanted to, no longer thought she *could* let go. She ran as if her feet knew the ground her eyes couldn't see, trusting him because she had no choice, relying on him to steer them both through the trees. She ran, images of death following her, of the man he'd shot to save them both—the body jerking, falling. Images of another man, shot under bright lights, not in darkness. Images of blood.

She ran, grieving for the truck and the lost chance of escape, fleeing ever deeper into the forest instead of being in the truck rolling rapidly away from guns and blood and bullets. After a while her entire being focused on running, on the dire importance of not falling, on the need to drag in

enough breath to fuel her. There was only flight and the
strong, hard hand that held hers. Pounding feet and a pounding heart and the sound and feel of him, so close to her,
running with her.

Gradually, she realized she could see the black bulks of
the trees and the vague outline of the man who ran with her.
There were grays now as well as blacks, and dimness between the trees instead of complete darkness. She had an urge
to look up, a sudden hunger for the sky. If she could see a
star, just one—receive the sweet kiss of the moon, or glimpse
the power of the sun pushing back the night...

He was slowing. As he did, the fear came rushing back,
making her want to run and run, to run forever. She made
herself slow along with him. And stop.

They stood in the gray light, motionless except for their
heaving chests. The sound of her breathing shocked her. It
was so loud, so labored. How long had they been running?
Where were they?

Then she heard something else. A distant, mechanical
thrumming. Coming from above? From the sky? A *helicopter,* she thought with all the wonder of renewed hope.

She turned to him, seeking the paler blur of his face. "Is—
that—yours?" She was badly winded, making it hard to get
the words out.

"They're looking for us. We have to get out from under
these trees." He gave her hand a squeeze. "C'mon. Unless
I'm lost, the trees end up ahead."

The air lightened around them. And it was lightest in the
direction they were headed, as if they were walking toward
morning. Another sound replaced the whir of the helicopter—
the thrumming roar of water falling. She smelled it, too, the
wild liquid scent of water.

So suddenly it shocked, they left the trees behind.

The air shimmered with morning and mist. The sky was
slate fading to pearl in the east. There was dampness on her
face, and she could see the ground she walked on, the spear-

ing shapes of trees behind her, and the bulk of rocks—a short, blunted cliff—rising off to her left.

And she could see *him*. Not with much detail, but at last she could see the man who had rescued her. He was tall and straight and carried his gun on his back. His face was partly hidden by the goggles that had let him lead their flight through the trees.

The sight of him, which should have reassured her, made her feel more lost. Fleeing through darkness with only his hand to guide her, she'd felt somehow connected, as if she knew him in some deep, visceral way. The reality of him, so straight and military and unknown, shattered that illusion.

The water-noise was very loud now. In the muted grays of predawn she saw it falling from the top of the cliff. Her breath caught as her feet stopped.

A yard away the ground ended, sheared off neatly as if cut by a giant's knife. And below—far below—was the destination of the falling water, dark and loud.

A river. Which one? She tried to summon a mental map of the country, but her weary brain refused to make pictures for her. Whatever the river's name, it was hearty, swollen with rain from the recently-ended wet season. Hemmed in by stone banks, water churned and rushed far below.

"Where are we?" she asked.

Maybe he didn't hear her over the noise of the waterfall. He was scanning the sky, the goggles pushed down. Was it getting too light to use them? Biting her lip, she looked at the sky, too, but didn't spot the longed-for shape of a helicopter.

"Come on, Dave," the man beside her muttered. "Where else would I be but—*yes!*"

She looked where he was looking and saw it—a dark shape flying low, coming out from behind the trees well down the river. Heading their way. She laughed, releasing his hand at last, wanting to jump up and down.

Safety was flying up the river toward them.

A.J. had excellent hearing. Her other senses were no better than ordinary, but her hearing was unusually keen. It was she who heard the shout over the racket the waterfall made.

She spun. There—coming out of the trees—a soldier. No, *soldiers*. She gasped and grabbed the lieutenant.

He was already in motion, turning, his gun lifting.

Again, the impossibly loud sound of gunfire. Bullets spitting up dust at her feet—the soldiers fading back into the trees, save for one, who lay still on the ground. And hands at her waist, digging in, jerking her off her feet—

Throwing her off the cliff.

She fell. And fell. And fell. It seemed to go on forever, or maybe it was only an instant before the water slapped her— a giant's slap, stunning and vicious. Water closed over her head so quickly she had no time to get a good breath, though instinct closed her mouth as she plummeted, expecting rocks that would crush and break, tumbled by the water until up and down were lost.

But one foot hit the bottom, mushy with silt. She pushed off, her lungs straining. The current was strong, but she kicked and clawed her way up, up, and at last her head broke the surface. She gulped in air.

Stony walls rushed past. The river moved even faster than she'd realized, and it took all her energy to keep her head above the churning water—but not all her thought. Where was he? She could see little but the dark rush of water. A rock loomed ahead, and she struck out with legs and arms, trying to avoid it. It clipped her hip as she tumbled by, but speed, chill and adrenaline kept her from noticing the blow.

Where was he? He'd thrown her from the cliff—and she would have fought him if she'd had time to understand what he was doing, but he'd known. All along, he'd known what to do. Somewhere in the back of her mind, while the rest of her fought the current, fought to breathe and stay afloat, she knew why he'd done it. The two of them had been out in the open, nowhere to go to escape the bullets spitting around them.

Nowhere but down.

So he'd thrown her off the cliff—but where was *he?* Had he made it over the edge, too? Or was he lying back in the clearing, bleeding and dying?

Again, it was her ears that gave her answers. Faintly over the noise of the water she heard her name. She opened her mouth, swallowed water, choked and finally managed to cry out, "Here! Over here!"

But the torrent didn't allow her a glimpse of him until it slowed, until the stony banks gave way to dirt and the river widened and her arms and legs ached with the fierce burn of muscles used beyond their limits. The sun had finished pulling itself up over the edge of the world by then. She glimpsed his head, some distance farther downriver from her. She called out again.

He answered. She couldn't make out the words, but he answered.

That quickly, the energy that had carried her was gone. Her legs and arms went from aching to trembling. Weakness sped through her like a drug, and she wanted, badly, to let the water carry her to him, let him do the rest.

Stupid, stupid. Did she want to drown them both? She struck out for the nearest shore, her limbs sluggish and weak.

At last her foot struck mud when she kicked. Silty, slimy, wonderful mud. She tried to stand, and couldn't. So she crawled on hands and knees, feeling each inch won free of the water as a victory worthy of bands and trumpets and parades.

The bank was narrow, a stretch of mud, twigs and rotting vegetation. She dragged herself onto it. And collapsed.

For long minutes she lay there and breathed, her muscles twitching and jumping. Never had she enjoyed breathing more. Birds had woken with the dawn, and their songs, cries and scoldings made a varied chorus, punctuated by the chatter and screech of monkeys.

He *had* made it to shore, hadn't he?

She had to look for him. Groaning, she pushed herself onto her side, raising herself on an arm that felt like cooked spaghetti, preparing for the work of standing up.

And saw him, for the first time, in the full light of day.

He sat four feet away with one knee up, his arm propped across it. Water dripped from short black hair and from the wet fatigues that clung to muscular arms and thighs. He wore an odd-looking vest with lots of pockets over his brown-and-green shirt. His face was oval, the skin tanned and taut and shadowed by beard stubble; the nose was pure Anglo, but the cheekbones and dark, liquid eyes looked Latin. His mouth was solemn, unsmiling. The upper lip was a match for the lower. It bowed in a perfect dip beneath that aristocratic nose.

Her heart gave an uncomfortable lurch. The stranger watching her was the most beautiful man she'd ever seen. And he was looking her over. His gaze moved from her feet to her legs, from belly to breasts, finally reaching her face.

"Basketball?" he asked.

Three

A.J. blinked. Maybe the vision of male beauty had taken a blow to the head? "I, ah, didn't bring a ball."

He grinned. "I must have swallowed more river water than I thought. No, I haven't taken leave of my senses. I was thinking of your legs. I thought I'd lost you…" His grin faded as his mouth tightened. "The current was rough. I couldn't get to you, and I didn't think you'd be able to make it on your own, not after the run we'd just put in. But obviously you use those legs of yours for more than kneeling."

"Oh." She processed the sentence backward to his original question, and answered it. "Track in college, baseball for fun, running for exercise, swimming sometimes."

"When you said you were fit, you meant it. Which relieves my mind considerably. We have a long walk ahead of us, Rev."

Annoyance flicked a little more life back into her. She pulled her weary body upright. "I've asked you not to call me that."

"Yeah, I know. The thing is, if I stop calling you Reverend, I'm apt to start paying attention to the wrong things, like those world-class legs of yours. They look great wet, by the way."

It occurred to her that her legs weren't the only part of her that was soaked. She glanced down—and quickly pulled her shirt out so it didn't plaster itself against her breasts. Heat rose in her cheeks. "Then you can call me Reverend Kelleher, and I'll call you Lieutenant West."

He shook his head. "I'll do better to think of you as one of my men for the next few days. We don't lean toward much formality on the team, so you need to be either Rev or Legs. I'm better off with Rev, I think." He reached for a canvas kit that hung from his belt. "Especially since the next thing we have to do is take off our clothes."

She stiffened. "I don't think so."

"You're cute when your mouth gets all prim."

"Refusing to strip for a man I don't know isn't prim. It's common sense. And a man who would ask me to—"

"Whoa." He held both hands up. "I might tease, but you're completely, one hundred percent safe with me. No offense, but you're the last type of woman I'd make a play for."

"Good." She might be superficial enough to react to his looks, but that was all it was—a silly, superficial reaction. It would fade. He was a man of war. Nothing like Dan.

He nodded and unhooked the kit. "Okay, now that we've got that straight…you'll find that I don't give a lot of orders. And never without a reason. When I do give one, though, you'd do well to follow it. And that was an order, Rev. Take off your shirt and pants."

"I'm not jumping without an explanation this time."

"Visual scan," he said briskly. "We need to check each other out for scrapes, scratches, anyplace the skin is broken. After being tumbled around in the river, we might not notice a small scratch, and between infection and parasites, even the smallest cut is dangerous.''

She thought of Sister Maria Elena's foot. He made sense...unfortunately. ''You first.

''I can wait.''

She inhaled slowly and prayed for patience. It was not a virtue that came naturally to her. ''What will happen to me if your misguided sense of chivalry kills you off before we get out of here?''

He didn't respond at first. His eyes were dark, steady and unreadable. Finally he pulled a small first aid kit out of his kit and handed it to her. ''Use the ointment—it's antibacterial. You'd better take care of my leg first.''

''Your leg?''

He nodded and unfastened his belt.

She tried not to gawk as he levered his hips up so he could pull his pants down. She was a grown woman. A widow. She'd seen male legs before. And her reason for looking at this particular pair of legs was strictly medical, so— ''Oh, dear Lord.''

''A bullet clipped me when I made my swan dive off the cliff.'' He bent to look at the long, nasty gouge dug into the flesh of his upper thigh. It was still oozing blood. ''Doesn't look too bad. The way it's been burning, I was a little worried.''

It looked bad enough to A.J. She dug out the tube of antibiotic cream. ''I don't see peroxide or rubbing alcohol to clean the wound.''

''Chances are it bled itself clean.''

They would have to hope so, it seemed. She uncapped the ointment and squeezed out a generous portion.

''Hey—be stingy with that. We don't have any more.''

''Shut up. Just shut up.'' Grimly she bent over his leg. ''I have no patience with blind, stubborn machismo. I can't believe you were going to let this wait while you looked for scratches I don't have.''

"A man has to take his pleasures where…" His breath caught when she stroked ointment into the shallow end of the wound. "Where he finds them. I expect I'll enjoy looking for your scratches more than what you're doing now. I don't suppose you were part of a medical mission?"

"Teaching." She bit her lip. She'd had little experience with nursing, and not much aptitude for it. Too much empathy. Her hands were already a little shaky. "You might want to start praying. Or cursing. Whatever works."

His muscles quivered when she pulled the torn flesh apart so she could get the dressing into the deepest part of the wound. His breath hissed out. But if he did any cursing or praying, he kept it to himself. "Nice hands. I don't see a wedding ring."

"I'm a widow."

"Pity."

What did he mean by that? "Okay. That's the best I can do." She sat back on her heels. "It needs to be bandaged, but the gauze is damp."

"Damned kit's supposed to be waterproof." He grimaced. "So was my radio, but I lost it and my CAR 16 in the river. Use the gauze. It won't be sterile, but it's better than letting flies lay eggs in my leg."

She bit her lip. "There's this plant…the villagers I worked with called it *bálsamo de Maria.* Mary's balm. I think it's a mild antibiotic. I don't see any nearby, but if I could find some, we could make a pad of the leaves."

"We don't have time to look for leaves." He grabbed the first aid kit, pulled out the gauze and began winding it around his leg. His mouth was tight, bracketed by pain lines.

"Here, let me."

Those dark eyes flicked to her. He handed her the roll of gauze.

His boots were on, and his pants were bunched up around his ankles. He should have looked silly. That he didn't might have had something to do with his briefs, which were undoubtedly white when they weren't soaked. At the moment they were more skin-toned. As she wound the gauze around his thigh, she could feel the heat from his body—and a slow, insidious heat in her own.

It was embarrassing but only natural, she told herself. She was a healthy woman with normal instincts. And he was so very male. "I think that will hold." She tied off the gauze and hoped she didn't sound breathless. "I'll check out the back of your legs now. If you could stretch out on your side…?"

He was remarkably obedient, moving as she'd suggested. The gleam in his eyes suggested he'd picked up on her discomfort, though. And the reason for it.

Oh, he knew he was beautiful. "Peacock," she muttered under her breath, and set herself to her task.

His legs were muscular, the hair dark and coarse. No cuts marred his calves, or the tender pocket behind his knees, or the stretch of skin over the strong muscles of his thighs. She did her best not to notice the curve of his buttocks, so poorly hidden by his shirttail and the wet cotton of his briefs.

Dan's thighs had been thicker than this, she thought, the muscles more bunchy, not as sleek. Hairier, too. Oh, he'd been hairy all over, her big, red giant of a man. And his calves had been freckled from the days when he'd worn shorts and let the sun scatter spots on his pale Irish skin, not dark like this man's was….

He looked over his shoulder at her. "Enjoying yourself?"

She jerked back. "I'm finished. No cuts."

He rolled into a sitting position. Levering his hips off the ground, he pulled his pants up. If the movement hurt, it didn't show. "Lighten up, Rev. I told you, you don't have to worry about me jumping you."

"I'm not." Automatically reaching for comfort, she started to touch her cross. But it, like Dan, was gone.

His fingers unfastened the many-pocketed vest. His eyes stayed on her face. "Something's wrong."

"Nothing that concerns you." Annoyed—with him for noticing, with herself for tripping once more over the past—she blinked back the dampness and the memories. "Do you have any idea what we do next?"

"Start walking." He tossed the vest aside and began unbuttoning his shirt. "I scraped my shoulder. You'd better have a look."

He was sleek all over. Not slim—his shoulders were broad, the skin a darker copper than on his legs—but sleek, like an otter or a cat. His stomach was a work of art, all washboard ripples, and his chest was smooth, the nipples very dark. Her mouth went dry.

She moved behind him. There was a scrape along his left shoulder blade, and in spite of the protection of his shirt, the skin was broken. "I'll have to use some ointment." She squeezed some onto her fingers. "Where do we walk?"

"Over the mountains, I'm afraid. To Honduras."

"Honduras?" She frowned as she touched her fingertips to his lacerated skin, applying the ointment as gently as possible. "I haven't known where I was since they took me and Sister Maria Elena out of La Paloma, but I thought we were closer to the coast."

"The river we just body-surfed down is the Tampuru. I'm guessing we're about forty miles upstream of the point where it joins the Rio Maño."

She wasn't as familiar with the mountainous middle and north of the country as she was with the south. Still... "Shouldn't we follow the river downstream, then? The government is in control of the lowlands, and Santo Pedro is on the Rio Maño." Santo Pedro was a district capital, so it must be a fair-sized city. *Telephones,* she thought. Water you didn't have to boil. And doctors, for his wound.

"Too much risk of running into *El Jefe*'s troops. Last I heard, there was fighting around Santo Pedro. If the government is successful—and I think it will be—the rebels will be pushed back. They're likely to retreat this way."

She shivered. "And if the government isn't successful, we can't wander into Santo Pedro looking for help." At least *she* couldn't. He might be able to, though. "You could probably pass for a native. None of the soldiers saw your face, and from what I heard, your Spanish is good."

"Wrong accent." He shrugged back into his wet shirt. "As soon as I opened my mouth I'd blend in about as well as an Aussie in Alabama. We're going to have to do this the hard way."

She sighed. "I'm sure we'll run across a village sooner or later. This area is primitive but not uninhabited."

"We probably will, but we can't stop at any of them."

"But we don't have any food! No tent, no blankets—nothing!"

"We'll eat. Not well, but I can keep us from starving. We can't risk being seen. Some villagers will be loyal to *El Jefe*. Most are afraid of him. Someone might carry word of our presence to him."

"Even if they did, why would he care? He has better things to do than chase us. Especially if his campaign is going badly."

"If it is, he and his ragtag army may be headed this way. And he won't be in a good mood. Do you want to risk having him punish a whole village for helping us?"

That silenced her.

"Your turn. Take off your shirt, Rev."

Her lips tightened. "If you want me to follow orders like a good little soldier, you're going to have to call me by name. And my name is *not* Rev."

Unexpectedly, he grinned—a crooked, very human grin that broke the beautiful symmetry of his face into something less perfect. And a good deal more dangerous. "Stubborn, aren't you? All right, A.J. Strip."

There was a path away from the river. It wasn't much, just an animal trail, and not meant to accommodate six feet of human male, but it was the only way into the dense growth near the river. Michael found a sturdy branch he could use as a walking stick—and to knock bugs or snakes from overhanging greenery.

At first, neither of them spoke. It took too much energy to shove their way through the brush and branches. Soon they were moving slowly up a steep, tangled slope.

A machete would have been nice, Michael thought as he bent to fit through a green, brambled tunnel. Hacking his way with one of those long blades couldn't have been much noisier than the progress they made without one. He had his knife, but it was too short for trail-blazing. It was also too important to their survival for him to risk dulling the edge, so he made do with his walking stick.

His leg hurt like the devil.

He'd really done it this time, hadn't he? He should never have complicated the operation in order to rescue a native. Even if she *was* a nun.

But Michael remembered the round, wrinkled face smiling up at him, and sighed. Stupid or not, there was no way he could have left Sister Maria Elena in the hands of a madman who made war on innocents.

His white-knight complex had put him in one hell of a bad spot, though. He hadn't exaggerated the danger of seeking help in a village. They wouldn't have to encounter *El Jefe* himself to be in big trouble. This area was smack dab in the middle of the easiest line of retreat for *El Jefe*'s troops if the action at Santo Pedro went against them, and soldiers on the losing side of a war were notoriously apt to turn vicious. The rebels already had a name for brutality. If *El Jefe* was defeated, his control over the worst of his men would be gone, leaving only one thing standing between the pretty minister and rape, probably followed by death: Michael.

And he was wounded.

He pushed a vine aside, set the end of his stick into the

spongy ground and kept moving. Already he was leaning more heavily on the stick than when they'd first set out.

His lips tightened. Pain could slow him down, but it wasn't a major problem. The real worry was infection, and there was damned little he could do about it. When the Reverend had made a fuss about treating him first he'd let her have her way, but that had been for her sake. She needed to feel useful, to feel in control of something. The few minutes' difference in getting his leg treated wouldn't have mattered. Not after his long soak in the river.

"Watch out for the branch," he said, ducking beneath an overhanging limb.

"Tell me, Lieutenant," said a disgruntled voice behind him. "Do you have any idea where you're going?"

In spite of his mood, Michael felt a grin tug at his mouth. He knew why he'd been demoted to a title. Her legs had looked every bit as delicious bare as he'd hoped. Better. He'd enjoyed looking them over—enjoyed it enough to make the first part of their hike uncomfortable in a way that had nothing to do with his leg.

That kind of discomfort he didn't mind. "I'm looking for high ground so I can figure out where we are and plan a route."

"How?"

"I've got eyes, a map, a compass and a GPS device." If he had to be saddled with a civilian, at least he'd drawn one with guts and stamina. She didn't complain, didn't insist on meaningless reassurances. She just kept going.

Couldn't ask for more than that. "What does A.J. stand for?"

"Alyssa Jean. I'm not fluent in acronym. What does GPS mean?"

"Global Positioning System." His brother Jacob had given him the gadget for his birthday, saying that this way Michael would know where he was, even if no one else did. "It talks to satellites and fixes my location on a digital map."

"Is that the thing you were fiddling with back at the river?"

"Yeah." He'd set the first waypoint after checking her out for scratches. He smiled. Man, those were great legs.

"I hope it's more watertight than your first aid kit."

"Seems to be. Why do you go by A.J.? Alyssa's a pretty name."

"First-grade trauma," she said, her voice wry and slightly winded, "combined with stubbornness. There were three Alyssas in my class. I didn't want to share my name, so I became A.J. It suited me. I was something of a tomboy as a kid."

"How does a tomboy end up a minister?" A minister with long, silky legs and small, high breasts...and blue eyes. That had surprised him. Somehow he'd thought they'd be brown, a gentle, sensible color. But they were blue. Sunny-sky blue.

"Same way anyone else does, I guess. I felt called to the ministry, so after college I enrolled in seminary." There was a scuffling sound, and what sounded suspiciously like a muffled curse. He paused, glancing over his shoulder.

She was climbing to her feet. "A root got me. Maybe I need a stick like yours."

"I'll keep my eye out for one." They were near the top of the hill. Maybe he would let himself rest for a few minutes while he plugged in the new waypoint. His thigh was throbbing like a mother.

"How's your leg?"

"Not bad." He ducked under a hanging vine, grabbed the limb of a small tree to pull himself up a particularly steep section, straightened—and froze, his breath catching.

A small, scared whisper came from behind him. "What is it?"

In answer, he moved aside, gesturing for her to come up beside him.

The pocket-size clearing in front of them was coated in

blue. Fluttering blue, brighter-than-sky blue, bits of sunny
ocean floating free, their wings sorting air currents lazily.

Butterflies. What seemed like hundreds of butterflies
flooded the little clearing, many with wingspans as large as
his two hands.

A.J.'s shoulder brushed his. A second later, the butterflies
rose—a dipping, curling cloud of blue swimming up, up
through the air, lifting above the surrounding trees. Then
gone.

"Ooh…"

Her soft exclamation was filled with all the wordless awe
he felt. He turned to look at her. "Yeah," he said, because
he had no words for what they'd just seen…or what he saw
now in her shining eyes.

Blue eyes. Not as bright as the butterfly cloud, maybe, but
clear and lovely.

A smile broke over her face, big as dawn. "I've never
seen anything like that."

He hadn't, either. A child's delight on a woman's
face…was there anything more lovely? Without thinking, he
touched her cheek. "You've got a spot of dried mud here."

Her smiled faded. "I've got dried mud in a lot of places."

"Brown's a good color on you." He rubbed lightly at the
spot on her cheek. Surely the butterflies' wings couldn't have
been any softer than her skin. His fingers spread to cup her
face, and rested there while he looked for something in her
eyes. Permission, maybe.

"Michael…" Her throat moved in a nervous swallow.

"I'm going to kiss you." At that moment, it sounded
wholly reasonable to him. "Just a kiss, no big deal."

"Bad idea." Her eyes were wide and wary. "Very bad
idea." But she didn't move away.

"Don't worry. I don't let my—ah, my body do my thinking for me." He bent closer to her pretty lips.

One kiss couldn't hurt, could it?

He kept it simple, the most basic of connections—no more

than the gentle press of one mouth to another. No big deal. Her lips were smooth and warm, her taste was salt and subtle spice. Her eyes stayed open. So did his.

And his hand trembled.

He straightened. The hand that had cupped her cheek dropped to his side. He stared down into eyes as wide with shock as his own.

What had he done? What the hell had he just done to himself?

Four

The sun was high in the sky, and it was hot. Headachy-hot, the kind of sullen heat that drains the body and dulls the mind. They moved among brush, oak and *ocotino* pines now, not true rain forest. Here, sunlight speckled the shade. Parrots screeched, monkeys chattered, and insects scuttled in the decaying vegetation underfoot. Sweat stung A.J.'s eyes and the scrape on her hand, picked up while scrambling over rocks earlier.

Like they say, it's not the heat, she told herself as she skidded downslope after Michael. *It's the blasted humidity.* Or maybe it was exhaustion making her head throb. Or hunger. Or dehydration. Her mouth and throat were scratchy-dry.

Best not to think about that.

At least the rainy season was over. The mercury dipped slightly during the wet months, but the increase in humidity more than made up for that small drop. Afternoons became steam baths. Daily rains turned every dip into a puddle and roads into mud baths, and the mosquitoes bred like crazy.

Not that roads were a consideration, she thought wistfully. They hadn't seen any. They'd followed a shallow stream for a while, and that had made the going easier. It had also made her thirsty enough to drink her own sweat.

She paused to wipe the perspiration from her face. Probably she should ask for Michael's water bag, a reinforced plastic sack from one of his many pockets.

Without a pot they couldn't boil water to make it safe to drink, but he had iodine. He'd assured her it disinfected water as well as wounds, and he had treated water from the stream with it. Unfortunately, it tasted as nasty as it looked. She hadn't been able to force down as much as she probably needed.

He was angling to the left now, moving across the slope instead of straight down. With a sigh, she followed.

His leg had to be hurting like a rotting tooth. He'd grown awfully quiet, too. Worried, she let her attention stray from the endless business of finding her footing to the man in front of her.

The back of his neck was shiny with sweat; his hair clung there in damp curls. She wanted to touch those curls. To taste the salt on his skin. She wanted—oh, she wanted to stop thinking of that kiss.

Why had she let it happen? One kiss shouldn't complicate things so much…but it did. It left her hungry, needy, too aware of him. She didn't want to come to life now—not here, not with this man. Oh, be honest, she told herself. The thought of becoming involved with anyone scared her silly. Such a coward she'd become! Dan would have hated that.

Of course, the soldier in front of her hadn't been thinking of getting involved in a relationship when he kissed her. He'd been thinking of sex, pure and simple. She was making too much of it.

Yet she remembered the look in his eyes when he'd raised his head. Maybe it hadn't been simple for him, either. And maybe, she thought as she skirted the trunk of a fallen giant, it wasn't pain that had kept him quiet ever since he kissed her.

Tired of her thoughts, she spoke. "How's your leg?"

"It's holding up." He glanced over his shoulder. "How about you? You've been quiet."

The echo of her thoughts about him made her smile. "Keeping my mouth shut is one way to avoid whining."

"Do you whine, then? You haven't so far. Maybe you're saving it for when things become difficult?"

"As opposed to merely miserable, you mean?" The path widened, letting her move up beside him instead of trailing behind. "Whining is an energy-sapper, and I don't have any of that to spare. And I don't really have any business complaining. When I compare where I am now to where I was yesterday, my calves almost stop hurting."

"I guess a minister would be into counting blessings. Like, for example, not having stepped on a snake."

"Or into a fire ant bed," she agreed. The bite of the tiny red forest ants hurt worst than a bee sting. "Then there's the size of these mountains. We could have been stuck in the Andes—"

"Not in San Christóbal, we couldn't."

She grinned. "The point is that these aren't terribly high. Compared to the Rockies back home, these are mere foothills."

"Are the Rockies home for you?"

"No, I'm from West Texas—the little town of Andrews originally, and San Antonio most recently. I'm not used to all this up and down. It is gorgeous here, though—when I look at something other than the ground. Dirt looks like dirt everywhere."

"So it does. What brings you to this particular patch of dirt?"

"I signed up for a year's service with UCA."

"Now you're the one speaking in acronyms."

"UCA is the United Churches Agency. It's a nondenominational organization that sends teaching missions to undeveloped countries in Central and South America."

"So you're a teacher as well as a preacher. What made you decide to give a year of your life to San Christóbal?"

"A promise." It had come out without thinking. Her forehead wrinkled. "You're deceptively easy to talk to."

"Better than the monkeys, at any rate. They interrupt too much. What kind of a promise?"

"One I made to my husband. After he died." She slid him a look, daring him to call her foolish.

He didn't answer at all, just kept walking. Something in his silence made her want to go on, to speak of things she'd kept wrapped up tightly inside. "He was killed in a convenience store holdup two years ago. We'd stopped to pick up some milk." The sheer freakishness of Dan's death clogged her throat. "It was senseless. So horribly senseless."

"Death seldom makes sense to the living."

"I suppose not." She'd revisited that night too often in her mind, in her dreams. Rewriting the script. Fixing things so that they didn't need milk, or went to the grocery store instead. She didn't want to go back there again. "So, what brought you to this patch of dirt?"

"War."

Well, that closed off one topic nicely. "And what made you choose war as your career?"

His eyebrows lifted. "You do have claws, I see."

His amusement mortified her more than her sarcasm. "I shouldn't have said that."

He shrugged. "I poked at your sore places. No surprise if you take a jab back. Believe it or not, I didn't choose the army because I enjoy war."

They were angling down again. She had to watch her footing, but her conscience wouldn't let her give it all her attention. "You wanted to be of service," she said after a moment. "That's what they call it, isn't it? The armed services. Serving in the army. You felt called to serve."

"I also liked to make things go boom. Here, watch out for the ant bed." He took her hand.

His palm was hard and calloused. Hers tingled. "I didn't—wait a minute." She peered down through the trees. "Look! Isn't that a road?"

"Yeah." He dropped her hand and stopped. "Looks like one."

It wasn't much, just a pair of muddy ruts twining up the little valley—but those ruts promised much easier going than they'd had so far. She sent a quick prayer of gratitude and started to move ahead of him.

He took her arm. "No. If any of *El Jefe*'s *soldados* are around, that's where we'll find them."

Impatient, she shook him off. "We're more likely to run across a bored *carbonero* who'd be glad to share his cooking fire. And your leg—"

"Isn't a consideration."

"Of course it is. Ignoring the wound won't make it go away."

"I'm not ignoring it. But I'd rather limp than get a bullet in my head because I tried to stop five or ten men from raping you."

Nausea rose in her belly, and the blood drained from her head. "Don't you dare. Don't even think about playing the hero, about—I'd rather be raped, you understand? I won't see it happen again. I won't!" The trembling hit then, a flood of weakness she despised and couldn't stop.

The tight grip on her arm turned gentle. So did his voice. "Is that how he died, Alyssa? Your husband? Was he trying to protect you?"

Unable to speak, she nodded.

He slipped his arm around her waist. Casually, as if they were strolling in a park, he guided her down the slope.

It took her a minute to get her voice back, and when she did, it wobbled. "I thought you didn't want to take the road."

"You're right about my leg. It's slowing us down."

"But…"

"Don't worry. If a horde of bloodthirsty bandits shows up, I'll let them have their way with you."

She nearly choked on a laugh. "That's awful. Promise?"

"On my honor as a graduate of St. Vincent's. Of course, I didn't quite manage to graduate. And I wasn't exactly their star student. But when they asked me to leave, at least one of the nuns still had hopes that I would avoid prison."

This time her laugh was freer, more real. She pulled away from the seductive warmth of his supporting arm. "You went to parochial school?" She shook her head. "You definitely don't seem the type."

"My mother's Catholic. It mattered to her, and my father didn't care."

She sensed layers of meaning in that last statement. *Later,* she thought, too tired to sort it out now. Later she'd find out what he meant.

They'd reached the road, what there was of it. "This is a good time to take a reading," he said, and pulled his GPS gadget out of a pocket. While he pushed the buttons on the tiny pad, he asked casually, "What was his name?"

"Who?"

"Your husband."

"Oh. Dan. The Reverend Daniel Kelleher."

"Good G—grief. He was a minister, too?"

She smiled. "You don't have to edit your language because I'm a minister. I'm hard to shock."

"I don't do it because you're a minister. You're also a lady."

That moved her. Flustered her. She was used to people—especially men—seeing the collar, not the woman.

"So how did you and Dan meet?"

"He was the youth minister at my church. He was great with the kids, and he loved working with them, but…this was his dream, you see. Missionary work. If he hadn't married me…"

"Pretty pointless to blame yourself for someone else's decision."

"I suppose. But we were married for three years, and for three years I put him off. Finally I agreed to take a year's sabbatical—soon." She'd been so sure, so arrogantly sure they had plenty of time. "If not for me, he would have been following his dream, not walking in on a holdup."

"And maybe died even younger. 'If only' is a dangerous game. You can play it forever and never win."

Her mouth crooked up wryly. "I'm wondering which of us is the preacher."

"Advice is always easier to give than to take." He slid the gadget back in the pocket of his vest. "Seems like he could have come on his own if it was that important to him."

"He didn't want to be separated for a year. Neither did I. But I was new to my ministry, just getting established…oh, I had all kinds of reasons we should wait. And then it was too late."

When he started forward, he seemed to be leaning more heavily on the staff. It worried her, but she knew better than to say anything. He'd just insist his leg was fine.

"I guess you came here for him."

"In a way…no," she corrected herself. "That's not true. I thought I did, but really I came for myself, looking for…I don't know. A way to stop grieving. To finish something left dangling. One thing about being a prisoner," she added wryly. "It gave me plenty of time to think."

"And you spent that time thinking about your dead husband."

She stopped. "Gee. For a couple of minutes there, I mistook you for a sensitive man."

"That was definitely a mistake. Look." He stopped, too, and ran a hand over his hair. "I'm not crazy about being jealous of a dead man, but there it is."

"No." She took a step back. "No, you can't be."

His smile came slow and brimming with suggestions. "Sure I can. You're a damned attractive woman, Alyssa."

"A.J.," she corrected him, distracted. "I'm not your type. You said so."

"I changed my mind."

"I haven't changed mine." She started walking. He found her attractive? The idea brought an insidious warmth, a subtle and frightening pleasure.

"Haven't you?" He caught up with her easily in spite of his limp. "Tell me that you aren't attracted to me. That you haven't been looking at me the way a woman watches a man she wants."

"I'm a big girl. I don't have to act on every impulse my hormones send my way."

"This is more than impulse." His fingers curled around her arm possessively. He moved close to her, crowding her. Making her aware of his body. "Were you raped?"

"What?" She shook her head. "Oh, you mean when— when Dan died. No. That's not…look, if I gave you the wrong idea earlier, I'm sorry. I'm not ready for a relationship, and I don't believe in flings or quickies."

"Quickies?" His mouth tilted in a wicked smile. "Naughty talk from a minister."

"Don't." She tugged her arm free. "Don't tease, don't smile like that, don't…hope. I'm not interested."

He was still smiling, but in his eyes she caught a glimpse of another man—the warrior who'd gotten her out of the compound, and killed at least one man doing it. "But I am," he said softly, and let go of his walking stick, thrust his hands into her hair—and kissed her.

This was no sweet sharing, but a wild ride. His mouth was hard, rough. Insistent. Her own mouth had dropped open in shock or to make some protest. He took immediate advantage, stroking his tongue deep.

Her mind blanked. Longing rose, swift and merciless, a blind need to touch and be touched. Her eyes closed. She clutched his arms, holding on, holding him, bringing the warmth and fierce life in his body nearer. And in the darkness behind her closed eyes she saw a man's form, shadowed by night, jerking as bullets tore into it.

Her eyes flew open. She made a small, distressed sound.

He lifted his head. His eyes were hot and hard. "You're interested."

Her head jerked back. Her heart was pounding madly. "When my eyes closed, I saw him. The soldier you shot back by the truck. Your mouth was on me, and I saw you killing him."

His hands fell away. His expression smoothed into blankness. Without a word he bent and picked up his walking stick, turned and started limping up the rutted road.

The water was cold, and his hand was growing numb. Michael waited, his bare arm submerged in the swiftly flowing water of the stream, his eyes fixed on the fish inches from his elbow.

They'd climbed back into true rain forest as the day wore on, leaving the scraggly undergrowth behind. The sun was sinking on the other side of the dense canopy overhead. The light was green and dim. Trees crowded close, but the ground was bare. Finding a campsite had been a problem, but finally they'd run across a spot where *carboneros* had felled a few trees to make charcoal.

Another fish was already on the stringer he'd fashioned from a length of string. Farther downstream, A.J. was scouting around for dry wood. He hoped she found some. He didn't relish raw fish for supper.

Supper. He was good for that, he supposed. She wouldn't object to his skill at killing when it came time to fill her belly.

And that, he knew, was unfair.

The fish drifted, lazy and unalarmed, around the bend in his arm. He waited.

She hadn't called him names, hadn't accused him of anything. She'd stated a fact: when he kissed her, she saw the image of the man he'd killed.

He could have argued with her. In his head, he had. For the next hour, walking in silence down the rutted road, he'd argued bitterly. Yes, he had killed—to save her life as well as his own. Would she rather be dead herself? Maybe she'd prefer to see him bleeding his life out in the dirt.

But in his heart, he'd known she was right. He had no business putting his hands on her. God, he'd kissed her right after she told him how her husband, the saint, had been killed—gunned down in front of her eyes.

Good move, he told himself savagely.

He was drawn to her. Powerfully drawn. He might be jealous of her dead husband, but he was fascinated by her loyalty to the man. If there was one virtue Michael believed in, it was loyalty.

Then there was her innocence. Oh, not sexual innocence. That was a fleeting quality, not especially interesting. But Alyssa was untouched in a deeper way, one possible only to those rare souls who truly believe in right and wrong. People who saw the line clearly—and didn't cross it.

He'd crossed too many lines in his life. Sometimes because that's what it took to prevent a greater wrong. And sometimes, when he was younger, he'd been so purely mad at the world he hadn't cared what he did. After a while, the line between right and wrong had blurred. After a while, he wasn't sure there was a line, just a gray no-man's land where you did whatever you had to do.

The fish poked along the streambed. Close now, very close, but on the wrong side of his hand. He waited.

No, he didn't have any business touching her. The sweetness that drew him was the very reason he couldn't have her. He knew it. And knew he would kill again to protect her, if he had to.

Now. A flash of silver, a quick movement—and his hand

closed around a slippery fish. He stood, holding on to the meal he would offer the woman he couldn't have, and headed for the stringer.

Technically, he was engaged. Technically, he had no business kissing anyone but his betrothed—a woman he'd never kissed, much less taken to bed. He didn't want Cami, didn't like her, didn't intend to have anything to do with her aside from the necessary legal transaction. And that wouldn't matter to Alyssa. If she knew about Cami, she'd think he was scum.

Maybe he was. The lines had blurred a long time ago.

Yeah, he'd keep his distance, he thought, threading the string through the fish's gills. But he didn't have to like it.

Five

"**W**hat else is in those magic pockets?" A.J. asked. She sat on a fairly dry patch of ground, her knees drawn up to her chin, her feet bare. Michael had insisted they remove their shoes and socks and dry them by the fire he was building, using matches he'd carried in a waterproof pouch in one of his pockets. "A color TV? Or an air mattress, maybe."

"Aside from my transporter, you mean?" A whisper of flame flickered along the shredded bark.

"I guess it would be cheating to use that."

"We don't want to take all the fun out of things."

The brief jungle twilight had closed in, erasing clarity, leaving them wrapped in dimness and sound. The frog chorus was in full swing, and a breeze rustled the leaves overhead. There were no walls, nothing between them and the animals whose home they had invaded....

An unearthly roar shattered the night.

She jumped. "What was that?"

"A howler monkey." He fed twigs into his small flame. "Surely you've heard them before."

"Of course. I've never heard one bellowing at night, that's all. I wasn't expecting it." She'd thought it was a jaguar or puma—or maybe a monster. Oh, but she was silly with exhaustion, her mind tumbling from thought to thought without the energy to connect them rationally. Everything ached. She would be in real pain tomorrow, she thought, after sleeping on the ground overnight.

Her gaze strayed to the bed she'd cleared while he was catching supper, picking out all the small stones and twigs to make the dirt as comfortable as possible. One of the treats from his magic pockets was a silvery "space blanket" that was supposed to trap body heat. They'd climbed enough that day that the night would be chilly. Already it was cool.

One blanket. One bed. It was the only reasonable way for them to sleep—and it made her itchy from the inside out. She jerked her gaze away.

He'd sharpened a stick with his knife earlier; now he thrust the stick through one of the fish and held it near the merry crackle of the fire. A.J. watched the flames and sighed.

She was accustomed to thinking of herself as rather athletic, but compared to the man who was cooking their supper she was a couch potato. Michael knew what to do and how to do it, while she knew nothing. She felt useless. That, too, was new and unwelcome.

She glanced around their small campsite, but everything was already done. "I should reapply the ointment on your wound."

"I'll take care of it."

So much for that idea. He took care of everything.

How had he managed to keep going with a bullet wound in his thigh? Sheer determination, she supposed, coupled with the extraordinary degree of fitness necessary to a young man whose career was war. "How old are you?" she asked suddenly.

He looked up. The fire painted his face in shadows and warmth. "Thirty. Why?"

She shrugged, embarrassed. So he was two years younger than she. It didn't matter. "Just wondered how long it had been since you and St. Vincent's parted ways."

"A long time." His voice was soft and a little sad. He turned the speared fish slowly. "I was fifteen and, according to a lot of people, bound for hell or jail. Whichever came first."

"Did you stay out of jail?"

"Yes and no." He grinned suddenly. "My father sent me to military school. Some would say it was a lot like prison."

"Good grief. Were you really such a hard case?"

"I had a problem with authority. My brother Jacob used to say he didn't know how I managed to stand upright with all that attitude weighing me down. If someone told me to go right, I'd break my neck turning left. I didn't want to be at St. Vincent's, didn't want to hang around with a bunch of rich preppie types, and I made sure everyone knew it."

"Ah." Her ready sympathy was engaged. "You felt like an outsider."

"I'm Mexican on my mother's side, and that made a difference to some. Mostly, though, I made my own trouble. I didn't like snotty-nosed rich boys." He chuckled. "Probably because I *was* a snotty-nosed rich boy."

He came from money? She blinked, her picture of him doing a sudden one-eighty. "I was a Goody Two-shoes up through high school," she admitted. "Straight A's, teacher's pet."

"Never colored outside the lines, or took a walk on the wild side with a bad boy?"

"Heavens, no." She grinned. "But like a lot of good girls, I liked to look, as long as they didn't catch me at it. I didn't cut loose until college."

"Somehow I doubt you cut loose then," he said dryly. "Unless you call having a beer on Saturday night getting down and dirty. Here, hold out your plate. Your fish is ready.''

She held out the huge leaf she'd rinsed off in the stream earlier. He eased the fish off the stick. The meat flaked apart at his touch. ''It's hot,'' he warned her.

''Good.'' Her stomach growled. ''And thank you for feeding me first, before I embarrassed myself and started gnawing on your arm. I won't make any cracks about chivalry this time. I'm too hungry.''

She made herself eat slowly while he punched the stick in the other fish and held it near the flames. The flavor was strong and smoky and delicious.

''I really did get a little wild in college,'' she said between bites. ''All that freedom went to my head. My parents had me late in life—I was an only child and had been pretty hemmed in until then. This is incredibly good,'' she said, licking her fingers. ''Either you're the best cook on the face of the planet, or what they say about hunger being the best spice is true. What do your folks think about you being in the army? Do they worry?''

''My father died a couple years ago, but it's safe to say he was greatly relieved when I decided I liked the service. Surprised as hell, but relieved. My mother…'' He shrugged. ''She's not always in close touch with reality. Too much self-medicating. Liquor, mostly.''

''Oh.'' Her hands fell to her lap. ''I'm sorry. Is she depressive? Bipolar?''

He gave her a funny look. ''You know the lingo.''

''My bachelor's degree is in sociology. Before I decided to go to seminary, I was planning on being a therapist.''

He grunted—one of those all-purpose male grunts that can mean anything—and slid his fish off onto his leaf-plate. ''The water bag is right next to you. Drink. You need at least a gallon of water a day.''

She made a face, but picked up the bag and swallowed quickly.

Darkness had closed in while they ate and talked. The cheerful dance of their little fire was the only light now, and the air felt chilly after the day's heat. She hugged her knees closer and wished she didn't like him so much. Wanting him was bad enough. Discovering she liked him, too, made her feel even more of a fool.

At least he was talking to her again. He'd been silent for hours after that kiss. Not that she blamed him. He'd saved her life at great risk to his own, and she'd all but called him a killer.

He wasn't a killer, not in the sense most people meant the word. Yet he had killed. And that bothered her—no, it went deeper than that. It troubled her soul. Why? He'd done it to save her life, and his...

Oh, she thought. Oh, yes. Because of her, a man was dead. He'd died at Michael's hand. Michael was the link between her and violent death. Just like Dan, who had died because of her...no, what was she thinking? He'd died because he'd been in the wrong place at the wrong time. Hadn't she worked that out for herself slowly, painfully, over the last two years?

Nothing made sense. Not her thoughts, not her feelings. Maybe she shouldn't try to sort things out, anyway. A relationship with Michael could go nowhere, and she couldn't indulge in a brief physical relationship. Of course, no one would ever know....

The whispery thought shamed her but wasn't hard to answer. *She* would know. She tried to pray, to seek guidance, but couldn't hold her thoughts together. They were scattering, drifting away....

"Hey. You're falling asleep sitting up. Better make a trip to the bushes before you nod off."

A.J.'s head jerked up. She blinked. "Right."

She didn't go far. The night was dark, the rustlings in the bushes scary. When she came back, he had his pants down and was spreading ointment on his leg. She averted her eyes quickly, moving to their bed. "How's your leg?"

"It'll feel better when I've been off it a few hours." He rewound the bandage. "Go ahead and lie down. I'll take care of the fire when I get back."

He took his gun with him. She didn't think it was a conscious decision; keeping his gun handy was automatic.

How different they were. How totally, unbridgeably different.

A.J. stretched out with a sigh, fully dressed except for her shoes and socks. Probably, she thought, if she weren't so tired she'd be vastly uncomfortable. As it was, her eyelids drifted down the moment she was horizontal.

She barely woke when he joined her. His body curved around hers, big and warm and solid. He pulled the lightweight cover over them both, and rested his arm on her waist. She breathed in his scent, feeling safe, mildly aroused. And guilty.

Her eyes opened onto the darkness. "Michael?"

"Yes?"

"I'm sorry."

She was nearly asleep again before she heard him whisper, "So am I."

The ground was hard. The woman he held was soft. Between the fire in his leg and the one in his groin, Michael didn't hold out much hope of sleep.

But she was asleep. Soundly, peacefully asleep. That baffled him. The exertions of the last day and night had been enough to make stone feel as comfortable as a feather bed...but she'd curled into him so trustingly. That's what didn't make sense.

He'd made it clear he wanted her. She'd made it clear she didn't want him. Oh, on a physical level, she did. He wished he could take some satisfaction from that truth, but he couldn't. Not when it was *him* she rejected—his actions, his choices, his career. His life.

Yet she was snuggled up as warm and cozy as if they'd slept together for years. As if she trusted him completely. What was a man supposed to make of that?

Women were always a mystery on some level, he supposed. Maybe it was the estrogen-testosterone thing—one flavor of hormones produced a vastly different chemical cocktail from the other.

Still, for all her mysterious femaleness, Alyssa would have made a good soldier, he thought, trying to find a comfortable position for his throbbing leg. She had what it took—dedication, compassion, humor. And guts. A woman with the sheer, ballsy courage it had taken to refuse to be rescued unless they took the nun with them wouldn't flinch at other unpleasant necessities, like sharing a blanket with him.

But courage didn't banish fear. It might triumph over it, but couldn't erase it. And there was no fear in the warm body he held.

The night was black and restless, filled with small sounds. Brush rustled. A breeze plucked at the leaves overhead, and from off in the distance came the howl of some night-roamer. The pain in his leg was strong, a vicious red presence dulling his mind. The woman in his arms slept on, her breathing easy and slow. Her hair tickled his chin. It smelled good, he thought fuzzily. She smelled good.

Funny how soothing it was to breathe in her scent as his eyes closed...did she like the way he smelled? Pheromones, he thought fuzzily. Maybe there were trust pheromones as well as sexual pheromones, some mysterious alchemy of scent that could make a woman fall peacefully asleep in the arms of a man whose kiss repelled her.

He was still puzzling over that when exhaustion dragged him gently into oblivion.

Shortly before dawn, it started to rain.

It was Alyssa who remembered their footwear. She bolted upright and dashed to the extinct campfire.

"How wet are they?" he asked, holding the blanket up so she could climb under it again with his boots, her shoes and their socks.

"Not bad."

She sounded a bit breathless. Maybe that was because of her sudden movement. Or maybe she was noticing all the things he was noticing, like how perfectly they fit, snuggled close together beneath the silver cover. And how much his body appreciated the round shape of her rump, tucked up against him.

The leafy canopy overhead filtered the rain; it reached them only in stray drops, a cold trickle here and there. She shifted. Her movement had an immediate and enthusiastic effect on his body—which he didn't think she could have missed.

"Luke 12: 6 and 7," she said in a disgruntled voice.

He stiffened. "And your meaning is?"

"He keeps track of every sparrow—but He doesn't promise to keep them dry."

His laugh surprised him almost as much as she had. "We'll dry off eventually," he said. "Once it stops raining."

The rain faded to a drizzle about the time the road petered out into a trail, and dried up completely by midmorning. It was dim and green and warm beneath the canopy, an enormous plant-womb brimming with life. The rain forest was supposed to be home to sloths, anteaters, tapirs, armadillos, peccaries, and deer. The only wildlife they saw that morning had six or eight legs.

They didn't find any fruit, either. A.J. was feeling hollow all the way to her toes when they spotted the village at noon.

"I will not let you steal from those people," she whispered fiercely.

About one hundred meters below them, barely visible through the trunks of giant trees, lay a ragged cluster of huts in a narrow valley. The five huts probably belonged to *colonos* who, desperate for land, had chopped down or burned off enough of the forest giants to clear the small fields they worked communally. The soil beneath the rain forest was so thin and poor that in a year or two they'd have to move and do it all again…and more of the rain forest would die. It was slash-and-burn agriculture at its worst, but it was the only way they knew to survive.

A.J. and Michael had been arguing ever since they'd spotted the huts and he'd dragged her off the trail and up this hill.

So far, she was losing.

"Yeah?" he said. "How do you plan to stop me?"

"They have so little—anything we take could make the difference between survival and starvation."

"And you see our situation as being different in what way?" He shifted impatiently. "I'll leave them some money, more than the few things I take will be worth. I just want a couple of blankets, a little food, a cookpot."

"Taking things without permission is stealing."

"Give your overactive conscience a rest, Rev. Money is rare for these people. They'll be glad to get it."

She bit her lip. "If you're caught—"

"I won't be."

Maybe not. If everyone was in the fields, he might manage to slip in and out without being seen. But if he did, he wouldn't get any help for his leg—which was one reason she wanted to deal with the villagers, not steal from them. Not that she'd used that argument. He wouldn't admit his leg was worse. "You're being paranoid."

"That's one way of looking at it. From my point of view, you're dangerously naive."

She turned her head to study him. There were lines of strain along his mouth, and he was leaning against the smooth trunk of one tree. He'd been limping heavily for the last hour. "Your leg—"

"Don't worry about my leg," he said curtly. "It might slow me, but I can still move quietly."

Maybe so, but he needed to stay off of it. Since he couldn't, he needed *something,* some kind of help, and some of the folk remedies she'd run across while living in La Paloma were surprisingly effective. Of course, there might not be anyone down there who could help, even with folk medicine. It wasn't much of a village.

A. J. tried one last time. "These people don't care about politics, and they aren't going to spare an able-bodied man to carry word of our existence to *El Jefe* on the off chance he might care."

"They won't have to, if any of *El Jefe*'s troops are in the area. And trust me—*El Jefe* would definitely care about getting his hands on a U.S. officer who carried out an assault on his headquarters."

Cold touched the base of her spine. "We haven't seen any of his troops."

He shrugged. "We haven't seen anyone at all until we came to this village. Doesn't mean no one's around. Look, I'm going. You can sound the alarm on me, I guess—that would stop me. But since they usually chop off the hands of thieves, I hope you'll decide to wait up here."

She was angry, scared, hating what he was going to do— and unable to stop him. Or help him. "You'll be careful?"

He nodded, checking the strap that held his gun at his waist.

"You won't need that."

He shot her a hard look. "Don't worry. I'm not going to shoot anyone over a blanket. Over a steak, maybe, but only if it came with a side of fried potatoes and onions."

She shook her head, impatient with them both. "I know that. Michael…" She took his arm. His sleeves were rolled up, so her fingers closed around bare skin. "You're burning up!"

"Your hands are just cold." He shook her off.

Her hands were cold, cold with fear for him. And yet...maybe it was because she'd slept with him the night before, however chastely. Maybe it was because he was the only other person in her world right now, and so much depended on him. Whatever the reason, she'd been acutely conscious of him all morning, as if some subtle thread connected them. She'd found herself noticing the way his hair curled up at his nape, and the dark hairs on his forearms. The shape of his hands, and the signs of strain around his eyes. All morning, she'd been aware of the sheer physical presence of the man, strong and sure and warm.

But not this warm. She was sure of it. "You've got a fever."

"I'm fine." He picked up his walking stick. "Stay here and stay quiet. If I'm not back in an hour, you should..." He stopped, frowning, looking down at the village.

She looked, too.

Something was going on. People were running—the women and children, she realized. They were fleeing into the jungle. The men stayed in the fields, but they weren't working. They were watching the trail.

She didn't realize she'd clutched Michael's arm again until he moved away. His face was closed, his attention wholly on what was happening below them. Her hand fell to her side. "You can't still intend to go down there now. They're alerted. They'll see you."

"Something spooked them. I need to know what. Information can be more important than food." His smile was probably meant to be reassuring. "I shouldn't be long. Twenty minutes, maybe. Don't worry, okay?"

Don't worry?

He was right. Wound or no wound, he could still move silently. She watched him melt into the trees, moving slowly but surely. And she didn't hear him at all.

*   *   *

Going down the hill had hurt. Coming back up was a bitch.

Michael paused halfway up, breathing hard. Entirely too hard for such minor exertion.

Yeah, he had a fever. He wasn't sure why he'd denied it, except that he couldn't stand the thought of being fussed over. And he hadn't realized he was feverish at first. He'd been hot all morning, but they were in the tropics, weren't they? His wound had seemed explanation enough for his growing weakness. Finally, though, he'd had to accept that his temperature was climbing faster than the trail. He'd wanted to curse the air blue, but he'd kept moving. Not much else he could do. The aspirin in his kit had been contaminated by the river.

On a scale of one to dead, his fever rated around seven. What he'd just learned was worse. It wasn't on the same scale.

He glanced up the hill. She'd be worrying. He'd stayed away longer than he'd told her he would—first so he could get into position. Then to make a decision.

Not about grabbing blankets and food. That possibility had gone out the window as soon as he'd verified that the arrivals in the village were *El Jefe*'s men. He'd overheard enough to know that the self-styled leader had suffered some major reversals. Professionally, that pleased Michael. San Christóbal's current government wasn't great. There was corruption, inefficiency, plenty of problems. But it was democratically elected, and it was making an effort to observe basic human rights. *El Jefe* would be a hundred times worse.

Personally, though, the news stunk. Adding what he'd heard to the implications, he came up with an unpleasant sum. *El Jefe* was getting desperate. To survive, he would have to gather more support quickly. He thought he'd found a way to do that.

Alyssa had some more worrying to do, he thought grimly

as he started uphill again. Oh, he'd offer her a choice. That was only right. But he was pretty sure which way she'd jump.

Alyssa Jean Kelleher. The Reverend Kelleher. She wasn't what he'd expected, that was for sure. In her own way, she was as tough as they came. Tenderhearted, though. And she didn't know squat about how to move through hostile territory—hell, she barely realized she was in hostile territory. She didn't know how to get by with a knife, a map, a length of string and a few other odds and ends when she had mountains to cross.

Which was why he'd made the decision he had before starting back up this blasted hill. He just hoped like hell he'd chosen right.

"Of course I'm staying with you."

Michael shook his head. Hadn't he known she'd say that? Still, he had to make sure she knew what she was risking. "You do understand? *El Jefe*'s soldiers are after me, not you. He wants to embarrass the U.S. and drum up support from his neighbors. Without it, he doesn't stand a chance, and he knows that. He plans to use me to make it look like their *Norteamericano* Big Brother has been interfering in little brother's business again, and there are some who will back him, based on that."

Her brow pleated. "Does he have to take you prisoner to do that? I mean, he can say whatever he wants. And probably will."

"Without me to display, he has no credibility."

"Then you can't afford to be caught."

No, he couldn't. Though he doubted she understood what that meant. "The point is, if we split up they'll probably ignore you. You could stop in the next village we come to, send word to the authorities in the capital. Sooner or later, someone would come for you."

"And you'll probably die of that infection you insist you don't have."

"You going to lay on hands and cure me, Rev? If not, I can probably move faster without you. And my best hope of getting treated is to get the hell out of this country."

Her cheeks lost some of their color. "Oh. I…hadn't thought of that. Of course. If you could let me have some of the matches, and maybe—no, you'll need the knife." She did a good job of keeping her voice even, but the fear fairly screamed from those big blue eyes.

Damn. Why was he swiping at her? He ran a hand over his hair. "I'm not trying to ditch you. I haven't gone to this much trouble to get you out just so I could jump ship. But I want you to make your decision based on what's best for you, not on my goddamned leg."

For some stupid reason she smiled. "God didn't damn your leg, Michael. A bullet did the damage, and a man pulled the trigger on the gun that put it there. I'll be better off with you, I think."

Relief swelled in him. He ignored it. "Then we won't have to decide who gets this." He reached behind him and retrieved the one thing he'd brought back from his scouting trip—a battered five-pound coffee can. "Our new cooking pot. Don't say I never gave you anything."

They made camp early, well before dark. This time he let her help, directing her in laying the fire, showing her how to make their bed.

She knew why. His fever was up, his cheekbones sharp and flushed. He was too weary to do everything himself— and he was planning ahead. If he died before they got to safety, he wanted her to have some idea of how to go on without him.

The thought made everything inside her tighten. She wasn't going to let him die. Though what she could do…oh, she'd do something, she vowed. She'd find a way.

God, please don't let him die. Show me what to do.

They ate fish again. Her share tasted wonderful but didn't fill her up. He must have been even hungrier than she was, but he insisted on splitting the catch evenly.

Maybe tomorrow they'd find some fruit or see some kind of game. A.J. wasn't comfortable with the thought of killing an animal, but she wasn't foolish enough to pay attention to her squeamishness. Her stay in La Paloma had begun her education in that respect. Animals of all kinds went into stew-pots there, and the process wasn't clean or pretty.

Survival was a messy business, she was learning, and seldom kind.

At least they'd been able to boil water. She hadn't needed to be nagged into drinking her share, and she'd watched to make sure he drank plenty, too. His fever would have dehydrated him.

When twilight hit she made a trip to the bushes, just like last night. And, just as before, when she came back he was redressing the wound on his leg. She frowned. He'd waited until she was out of sight—again. She didn't think his timing had anything to do with modesty.

This time she walked up to him. "How bad is it?"

He kept right on winding the worn gauze around the wound. "I'll be okay."

"Dammit, don't treat me like a child who needs to be reassured!"

He looked at her, brows lifted. "Cursing, Rev?"

"You only call me 'Rev' when you want me to back off."

"Yeah? And your point is…?"

"That you should level with me about what shape you're in. I might be able to help. I'm not a nurse or doctor, but I have had some first aid training."

"So have I." He went back to his bandaging, tying off the dirty, tattered gauze. "Save those nurturing instincts for your congregation. I prefer to take care of myself."

"I figured that out." She clenched her hands in frustration.

"What happens if you become too sick to go on? Will you hold me off at gunpoint rather than let me help you?"

"Depends on whether I've shot anyone that day or not. I wouldn't want to bag over my limit." He jerked his pants up and levered himself to his feet with his stick. "I'm going to get some sleep. Feel free to stay up and work on your sermon some more. It's a little rough."

A.J. stood in the deepening dusk and watched him hobble the few steps to their makeshift bed, her fists still clenched.

She'd always thought the fable about the mouse taking the thorn from the lion's paw was unrealistic. A great, proud beast like that was a lot more likely to swipe the mouse into oblivion with one huge paw, lashing out against its own help-lessness.

Good thing she wasn't a mouse, she decided.

Her fists relaxed and she moved to join him, settling be-neath the thin blanket without speaking. His body was as hard and reassuring as it had been the night before. It was also warm. Much warmer than last night.

A.J. stared out at the gathering darkness, listening to the frogs' serenade, the calls of the other night creatures, and the steady breathing of the man whose body heated hers like a furnace. He'd fallen asleep almost immediately.

She didn't. Long after exhaustion should have dragged her down, she lay there sorting her options, wondering, worrying. Praying.

She shouldn't have pushed. The harder she tried to make him admit he needed help, the harder he was going to shove her away. Some people were like that. Accepting help made them feel vulnerable, and they couldn't handle it. She wasn't sure why she'd tried to force things earlier—except that it had hurt. It had hurt a great deal more than it should that he wouldn't let her help, wouldn't let her *in*.

Well, she'd have to get over that. She wasn't doing either of them any good by trying to force a level of intimacy and trust he didn't want. And he had no reason to trust her, she reminded herself. They didn't really know each other...if it seemed as if they did, that was due to their situation.

But whether he wanted to admit it or not, Michael needed her. He was ill, injured, and he was going to have to depend on her, just as she depended on him. Or neither of them would make it out of this jungle alive.

Six

"**M**y temperature's down this morning," Michael said when she returned from brushing her teeth at the creek.

Fortunately, Michael's magic pockets had held a toothbrush for him and a small tube of toothpaste, and she still had the toothbrush the guard had given her. The small ritual of brushing her teeth possessed amazing restorative power, as did being able to comb her hair. She felt more like herself when she was done.

Michael sat on a rock, tying the laces of his boots. He did look better. Less flushed, and his eyes were clear. Of course, fevers often went down in the morning, only to climb during the course of the day. It didn't mean he was well.

But there was a spark of relief in his eyes. She wouldn't take that away from him. "That's good," she said, folding their blanket, smoothing the air out and refolding it until it would fit in the pocket of his vest once more. "A good night's sleep must have helped."

Not that he'd slept well the first part of the night. He'd

been restless, moving often enough to wake her. Some time before dawn, though, she thought he'd fallen more deeply asleep.

"I'm not used to being sick." He picked up his stick and straightened. "I can't remember the last time I was. Probably when I was a snot-nosed kid."

"If that's your roundabout way of apologizing for acting like a cranky child last night, apology accepted."

"A cranky child, huh?" He grinned.

And she was in trouble all over again.

She was falling for him. It was temporary, she was sure— the product of isolation, danger, the fact that he'd rescued her...and her unfortunate susceptibility to male beauty. She'd been down that path in college, tumbling into one hormone-driven infatuation after another. She knew better now. She'd get over this.

But oh, how the world lit up when he grinned at her.

His fever came back by noon.

Michael didn't try to deny the growing heat and weakness this time. He cursed silently for a few hundred yards, then stopped for rest sooner than he wanted to, when they ran across a stream. He sent Alyssa to gather wood for a fire so he could boil more water.

He was going to need extra fluids.

She didn't nag, didn't ask annoying questions about how he was feeling. Quietly, efficiently, she did as instructed. Perversely, that irritated him, too.

While she scrounged for wood, he pulled out his topographic map. He'd entered their campsite in the GPS device last night and checked it against the topo map, so he knew where he was: about thirty miles from the border, another thirty from the nearest Guatelmalan town.

Those miles translated into a lot of mountain. If he'd been in good shape, he could have made the pass he was aiming for in a couple of days, and the town in another two or three. As it was…he refolded the map carefully.

As it was, he'd be lucky to make it at all.

A shiver went through him. He didn't want to die. Not like this, with so much left undone… What would happen to Ada if he died here? Would Jacob and Luke still be able to dissolve the trust? Michael had no idea what the legal ramifications would be if he died unwed…*Luke is already married,* he thought, *and I wasn't there to see Jacob's face when he learned who Luke had wed—Maggie, the woman Jacob had been dating. And Jacob…he might be married, too, by now. He'd sure been taking dead aim at that gorgeous new assistant of his…*

No, he didn't want to die from some stupid fever that made him sick and weak, unable to take care of himself, much less the woman he was supposed to be rescuing.

Some rescue. Quite the hero, wasn't he? Maybe he should have let her think she was slowing him down. She would have agreed to split up if she'd thought she was endangering him.

But he still didn't believe she could make it on her own. He'd just have to push himself. The fever wasn't that bad, and he was strong. His body might yet throw it off. He could keep moving. He had to.

"I couldn't find much," she said cheerfully. "Is this enough?"

Alyssa stood there, a small armload of sticks distributing a fresh serving of dirt on her already-grungy shirt. Her face was smudged, and her chinos were beyond dirty. Her abundant mess of curls was tied back with a scrap of cloth torn from the sleeve of her shirt. And she was smiling.

"You should have seen this bird," she said. "I only caught a glimpse of it before it flew away, but it was gorgeous—bright red, with long yellow feathers in the tail."

Something stirred inside him he couldn't name, something

odd and warm and disturbing. "Let's see if you remember your fire-building lessons."

What would happen to Alyssa if he died before getting her to safety?

He heaved himself to his feet, leaning heavily on his walking stick. "I'll fill the water bag."

"You should stay off your leg. I can get it."

A black rage descended out of nowhere. "Dammit to hell, would you quit arguing with everything I say? I'll do it."

The fury faded almost as quickly as it had hit, but the black feeling remained, clinging like cobwebs. She was right. He knew that even as he limped toward the thin trickle of the stream. If she'd been one of his men, he would have sent her for the water without a second thought. She was more fit than he was right now.

Only he couldn't stand being so damned weak. Depending on her. It made him want to claw the bark off the nearest tree and howl.

When he came back she had the twigs and small branches in place, ready for his matches. He took a deep breath, let it out. "I'm sorry."

She gave him a smooth, hard-to read glance. "We've both got a lot to learn, I guess. What do you think of my fire-building?"

It wasn't perfect, but it would do. They didn't have to worry about the smoke showing—the forest canopy would dissipate that. He showed her again how to light it, then forced himself to rest while she boiled water in the coffee can. And while the water was cooling, he showed her how to use the GPS device and topo map. Just in case.

They made camp at another little stream, stopping well before dark. Supper was simple and not very filling. Earlier they'd run across a mango tree, which A.J. had climbed, leaving Michael white-lipped on the ground. The fruit was green but edible, and they had a couple of mangos apiece left to go with the *plátanos* they'd found later. The thick, rather bready bananas were usually fried, but turned out okay when baked on hot rocks near the fire.

Before they ate, A.J. had taken Michael's shirt downstream and washed it as best she could. He needed to use the sleeves for bandaging; the gauze could still serve as a pad, but was too worn to work alone. She'd washed herself, too, and her panties and bra, though the stream was so shallow it was mostly a sponge bath.

Michael had said it was too shallow for fish. That was probably true. A.J. thought it was also true that his hand wasn't steady enough for fishing.

"It's a good thing it's December," she said after swallowing the last mouthful of *plátano*. "We wouldn't find as many streams in the dry season."

Michael grunted. She looked up, biting her lip.

He didn't look good. Fever glittered in his eyes and flushed his cheekbones, but there was a gray, pallid look to his skin otherwise. His hair clung damply to his forehead and nape and gleamed on his shoulders—his *bare* shoulders. He was using his knife to cut the sleeves off of his shirt.

She leaned back on her heels. "Hot compresses."

He glanced up. "What?"

"For your leg. I don't know why I didn't think of it before. We'll use part of your shirt and hot water. The heat should draw out some of the infection."

He hesitated, then handed her one of the sleeves. "It can't hurt. No, I take that back. It's going to hurt like hell, but maybe it will do some good."

"The water's simmering now. Are you ready for me to do this?"

He grimaced, nodded and unfastened his pants.

She looked away. By now she should have been used to him casually stripping in front of her. She wasn't. Using the hem of her shirt as a hot pad, she picked up the coffee can and poured some of the steaming water over the flat rock they'd cooked on, cleaning it as best she could. Then she folded the sleeve into a pad and poured more hot water over it. "It needs to cool a bit. The water was almost boiling."

"It needs to be hot to do any good." He reached over, picked up the pad and held it briefly as if testing the temperature. Then laid it on the red, angry wound in his thigh.

His lips peeled back. The breath hissed out between his teeth. "Mother Mary and all the saints. That ought to do something. Remove a few layers of skin, if nothing else. Keep the water hot. We'll need to repeat it."

There was a lot of skin showing right now. Michael was wearing briefs and a small pad of cloth, and nothing else. "Here." She handed him the silvery blanket. "This may help hold the heat in."

He spread the blanket over his legs while she moved the coffee can next to the fire. "You sound very Catholic when you're trying not to curse," she said as lightly as she could.

"You can take the boy out of the parochial school, but you can't take the parochial school out of the boy." He reached for the water bag. "Talk to me. I could use the distraction."

"You've pried all my best stories out of me already." He'd kept her talking most of the afternoon, probably for the same reason he'd given now. It helped take his mind off the pain. "Except for the tales of my misdeeds in college, and I'm not about to spill those."

"I'll bet I can top them. C'mon, let's trade—you tell me one of your deepest, darkest secrets, and I'll tell you one of mine."

A.J. looked at him thoughtfully. "You don't think I have any deep, dark secrets, do you?"

"You said you were a Goody Two-shoes."

"That was in high school. I made my share of mistakes in college."

He gave her a lazy, disbelieving grin. "Right." He tipped the water bag to his mouth.

"When I was a freshman, I lost my virginity in the men's locker room."

Water sputtered out of his mouth. "The hell you say."

She grinned. "I was dating the captain of the basketball team, and he had a key. I'd always wondered if their facilities were better than ours—I think I mentioned that I was in track? Well…" She spread her hands. "Late one night, he showed me around."

Amusement glinted in his eyes now, along with the fever. "And did you enjoy checking out the facilities?"

"Um…" She busied herself rolling up the leaf "plate" she'd used, tossing it into the trees and wishing she'd resisted the urge to shock him. "I've told you a secret. It's your turn."

"I was more traditional than you. I lost my virginity at seventeen in the back seat of my Jag."

What kind of a hell-raiser waited until he was seventeen to lose his virginity? Certainly he wouldn't have lacked for opportunity. She opened her mouth to tease him about that, but at the last second common sense stepped in. Enough talk about sex. "You had a Jaguar at seventeen?" She shook her head. "You did say you were a rich boy."

"Jacob gave it to me—my oldest brother. It was a bribe so I'd stick it out when my dad gave up and shipped me off to military school. Jacob bought the Jag used and rebuilt the engine while I was learning the joys of close-order drill." He moved the blanket aside and lifted the pad from his thigh. "Better hit me again. It's cooled off." He handed the cloth to her.

His big brother had bought him his first car after his father gave up on him? A rapid, dangerous softening in the vicinity of her heart made A.J. look away and tested the water with her fingertip. Hot, but not scalding. "Your brother rebuilt the engine himself? I'm impressed."

"Jacob's second passion is old cars. He gets off on grease and lug nuts."

"What's his first passion?" She wrung out the pad, put it on the stone and poured water over it again.

"The money game. He plays it well, and plays to win. Not that different from Luke, really, for all that they use a different set of counters for success. Luke—" He stopped, hissing as she put the pad on his leg. "That wasn't as hot as the first time."

"Hot enough. Second-degree burns won't speed the healing process. Who's Luke? Another brother?"

Michael nodded. "He's an athlete. Picked up a gold at the Olympics for three-day eventing before he settled down to train horses."

"Sounds like you come from a family of overachievers."

His mouth turned up. "Two out of three of us, at least. I'm the ordinary one."

A.J. stared at him. "Amazing. You can say that with a straight face while sitting there with hole in your leg and a fever burning you up after spending the last few days keeping both of us alive in a jungle while being hunted by an army."

His gaze flickered away. "This is what I'm trained for. If I were like my brothers, I'd be—oh, at least a captain by now."

The light was going, dimming from shadowy green to the hush of twilight. The silvery blanket across his legs seemed to glow in the half light. Michael himself seemed to grow darker, his coppery skin blending with the deepening dusk. His expression was lost to her in the fading light, but there was tension in the stillness of his body.

This was important to him, she realized. For some reason, he had no clue what a remarkable man he was. For some reason, she couldn't stand that. She leaned forward, determined to make him listen. "You play to win, too, Michael. Just like your brothers. Only you play for higher stakes than they do—lives, freedom, the precarious balance that passes for peace. Definitely an overachiever. You are," she finished softly, "one of the two most extraordinary men I've ever known. Real heroes are rare."

His head jerked around to face her. He was scowling. "Don't expect me to believe that. I've heard enough about Daniel Kelleher today to know you thought he was some kind of saint. And I know what you think of me."

No, he didn't. She wasn't sure herself, except that her ideas—of him, of a lot of things—were changing. "Daniel was hardly a saint." It was surprisingly easy to smile. "He was always late. He could be self-absorbed, and he had a lousy memory for anything that didn't interest him. I can't tell you how many times I'd ask him to pick up something on the way home, and he'd forget. That's how—" Her breath caught. "That's how we wound up at that convenience store that night. He'd forgotten to pick up the milk earlier."

Michael seemed to study her for a long moment, though she couldn't make out his expression. Then he pulled back the blanket. "This has cooled off again." He handed her the pad.

Hurt rushed in, making her as silent as he had been earlier. She took the cloth and turned away. Apparently she'd said too much, gotten too close to some invisible boundary, and he intended to pretend she hadn't spoken.

The fire had died down some, and the water wasn't as hot as it needed to be. She moved the can closer to the flames, hugged her knees closer to her chest and waited.

Long moments later, he spoke. "When my father died, he was a week away from marrying his sixth wife."

That pulled her head around to look at him. "He was married six times?"

"Seven, actually, to six women. He married Luke's mother twice." Michael grimaced. "I don't know what to say to you. I can tell that you had a real marriage. Solid. To me, that's like walking on the moon. I know some people have done it, but it doesn't have much to do with me. It's not something I'll ever experience. My mother was Dad's fourth wife. I had three stepmoms before he died, and that doesn't count the women who hung around between marriages. I can't imagine what it was like for you to lose someone you'd built a real marriage with.''

"Michael." She got that far, then stopped and swallowed. Now she was the one who didn't know what to say. Her eyes stung, and she wanted to believe it was the smoke from the fire making them burn, but she knew better. Nor was it anything as unselfish as sympathy. "I, uh, think the water's hot now."

She bit her lip as she prepared the compress, getting herself back under control. When she turned to hand him the pad, she thought she had her expression evened out.

Their fingers brushed when she handed him the pad. "Damn. You got it hot enough this—'' He broke off when he put the pad on his leg. His head tipped back and the cords in his neck stood out. For a few seconds he just sat there and breathed hard, riding out the shock of pain.

When he continued, his voice was lower, slightly husky. "The real heroes are the men like your Dan, you know. The ones who know how to handle the daily stuff. The ones you can count on, day in and day out. That takes a kind of guts I don't have or understand.''

Her heart was pumping hard, as if she'd rounded a familiar corner and found herself face-to-whiskers with a tiger. "Are you by any chance warning me?''

The ghost of his usual grin touched his mouth. "Why would I do that? You're not crazy enough to fall for a man like me. But if you change your mind about taking that walk on the wild side you missed out on when you were a teen—''

"Never mind." Suddenly she pushed to her feet. "I'm going to wash my face and make a trip into the bushes before it gets any darker.''

Michael was asleep when she got back. Not pretending sleep—though he might have done that to save them both embarrassment, he would have put the fire out first. She took care of that chore, then lay down next to him.

He was lying on his back. He hadn't put his pants or vest back on. He was all but naked, and his skin was dry and hot. Fear was becoming as familiar as aching calves and thighs, but the furnace of his body notched it up another level. She curled around him protectively.

Why had she kept him awake so long? Such a pointless conversation, too. She'd been doing it again—probing, trying to create an intimacy he didn't want. She was angry with herself for putting them both through that.

He *had* been warning her, however carelessly he'd denied it. And he'd been right to do so. And if she'd hadn't been so crazy with worry for him right now, she would have been horribly embarrassed. He'd picked up on her emotions before she'd let herself acknowledge them…and had gently let her know how hopeless those mute, newborn longings were.

She closed her eyes, too tired for the tears that had threatened earlier. Somewhere along the line, she'd come to realize that they weren't as different as she'd thought. They were both hopeless idealists. Oh, he chased his ideals differently, with guns and a capacity for violence that dismayed her. But his choices were as shaped by ideals as hers were.

He was an extraordinary man, just as she'd said—a weary knight in tarnished armor. He was also damaged. Wise enough to know the damage existed, and kind enough to warn her about it.

They were more alike than she'd realized, yes. And still so far apart in so many ways. He came from wealth, from a family fractured so many times she could scarcely imagine it. She came from loving if overly protective parents, the placid normalcy of Saturday Little League, Sunday pot roasts and a budget that only occasionally stretched to a vacation to someplace exotic…like Six Flags.

And she ached for him anyway. Lying on the hard ground,

surrounded by night and its creatures, with his ill, feverish body in her arms, she ached with desire for him.

She sighed and stroked the damp hair back from his face. He didn't stir. Michael was as wrong for her as she was for him, but he was a man who needed and deserved to be loved. After this was over, when she went back to her safe, ordinary life and he went on to find other dragons to slay, she might find the strength to pray that he found a woman who could give him everything she didn't dare.

But right now he slept beside her, gripped by the twin fists of fever and pain. Right now—however temporarily—he was hers.

It was around noon two days later that A.J. admitted the truth.

Barring a miracle, they weren't going to make it.

For two more days they'd tried. The hot compresses seemed to help his wound—the angry red streaks had retreated slightly—but the infection must have already been systemic. His fever didn't go away. At night it climbed alarmingly. For two more nights, A.J. had slept next to him as he burned, tossed and turned before falling into a deep, exhausted sleep that scared her worse than his restlessness.

She was hungry. Gut-gnawingly hungry in a way she'd never experienced. They'd found some more fruit—guavas last night, small and green and hard—but Michael hadn't let her eat much of it. An all-fruit diet, especially when the fruit was green, was likely to throw their digestive systems into revolt. Diarrhea and dehydration were more immediate dangers than hunger.

Earlier today, they'd seen a small deer, and A.J., who still cried when the hunters killed Bambi's mother, had been eager for venison. But Michael's hand had been shaking too badly to get a shot off. He'd stood there afterward, his head down, cursing the air blue.

She didn't know how he could still be moving, putting one

foot in front of the other. She didn't think his temperature
had been below a hundred since yesterday morning, and they
were still at least a day's journey from the border, farther
than that from the tiny Guatemalan town he'd said was their
goal.

A.J. was scared all the way down to her toes. And trying
desperately not to let it show, because the last thing Michael
needed was to have her fears to deal with as well as his own.
However much he pretended he wasn't scared spitless, he
had to be.

Overhead, in the hidden sky, clouds must have moved in.
The light was dim. She thought it might be around noon.
This part of the trail was narrow and steep and frequently
obstructed by vines, shrubs and roots. They were high now,
entering the range where conifers dominated, though the
leaves of encina oaks still mixed with the knots of feathery
needles on the towering ocote pines.

Michael was in the lead. He had the gun, the map and the
know-how, even if he was wobbly and fuzzy with fever.
Sweat lent a slick sheen to his skin. He wore only his vest,
unbuttoned, and his camouflage pants; two nights ago he'd
fashioned his stick into a crude crutch, lashing a second
branch to it with vines and using his shirt to pad the top.

He was moving very slowly.

She wanted to prop him up, to let him use some of her
strength. Tired and sore and hungry as she was, she still was
in better shape than he. But she'd already offered the use of
her shoulder, and received a polite refusal—along with a look
of such flat fury that she hadn't mentioned it again.

If the only thing keeping him going was stupid, stubborn
pride, she wouldn't kick that crutch out from under him.

He stopped. She kept going, closing the distance between
them, thinking dully that he'd paused to get his breath—
something he'd been doing fairly often today.

But he didn't start moving again. Something in his stillness
alarmed her. "What is it?" she whispered.

He shook his head and turned slightly so she could move up beside him. She stopped with a whisper of space between them and put her hand on his shoulder.

Dear Lord, he was hot.

Over his shoulder she saw that the path dropped off all at once, winding down precipitously. They'd run across one of the little hidden valleys again—and this one held a village.

A *real* village. Thirty huts, maybe. She could see cleared fields and people in those fields, moving between the huts. A shout drifted up to them, vague and wordless at this distance, but sounding so human, so cheerful and ordinary that her eyes abruptly filled.

"It's remote," he said abruptly. "*El Jefe*'s men may not come this far, and if they do, they probably won't be looking for you. This is your best chance."

Her insides skittered unpleasantly, like nails on a chalkboard. "*Our* best chance," she corrected him.

"I can't risk it."

"You'll risk more by not getting help." She grabbed his shoulders, willing him to be sensible. His eyes didn't glitter now, but were dulled by illness. Hunger had dug hollows beneath his cheekbones. "You can't go on like this. You need rest, food, whatever help these people are willing to give."

He jerked himself away, turning his back to her. And he wobbled, damn him. "I'll be okay. I can move faster once I know you're taken care of."

He could barely move at all! She gritted her teeth against frustration. Or despair. He had to face the truth. "Michael, you're going to die if you don't get help."

"If I go on alone, I'm only risking myself. If I go into the village, I risk falling into *El Jefe*'s hands. I can't let that happen."

He knew. Oh, God, he knew he wasn't likely to make it, yet he still intended to go on alone. "This place is so remote—you said so yourself. No roads in or out, no reason to think *El Jefe* even knows about this place, or cares."

"I can't risk it."

She blinked furiously, trying to keep the tears in. He'd said he couldn't let himself be captured, but she hadn't realized what he meant—that he wouldn't take any chance of that happening. No matter what. A.J. tried to care about all those nameless, faceless people who would be hurt if *El Jefe* found a way to drag the war out. She wanted to care. She couldn't. Not enough to sacrifice Michael for them.

Michael cared. He cared enough to die, if necessary, for people who would never know his name. Was there any truer definition of *hero?*

In that moment, something small and simple and complete fell into place inside her, quietly and without fuss. She took a deep breath, balanced between painful calm and near hysteria.

What a moment to realize all her sensible decisions had been as effective as the sand walls children build to hold back the ocean. It was too late for fears, reasonable or otherwise. She was in love with him.

"All right," she said after a moment. "You know your duty better than I do. If you can't risk it, you can't. Do we take a break now, or keep going?"

He turned. His eyes narrowed. "*We* don't do anything. You go down there, make friendly with the natives."

"No."

Michael fought dirty. He told her he didn't want or need her tagging after him. She was a burden. She was more likely to get him killed than she was to help him.

"I don't think so," she said calmly. "And I don't care what you want. I'm going with you."

He dragged a hand over his hair. "Look, if you come with me, we'll probably both die. You want me to die knowing I caused your death?"

"You gave me some good advice a couple days ago.

There's nothing more useless than blaming yourself for someone else's decision. This is my choice, not yours.''

Finally, his eyes bleak and wild, he turned and started moving—back up the path. Away from the village.

A.J. followed.

Her decision had been quite simple, really. If she left him, he would die. Oh, he'd keep going as long as he could, and she didn't doubt his will, his drive. He wouldn't give up until the breath left his body.

But will and drive weren't always enough.

He might die anyway, of course. Her knowledge and skills were limited. But she'd do everything she could, and if it wasn't enough...if it wasn't enough, she thought, swallowing hard, she could at least be sure he didn't die alone.

Seven

Heat. Pain. Both beat at him, throbbed through him. Fire raged in his leg and pulsed through his body. His head and heart pounded in rhythm with the furnace. He tried to take a step with every beat. But it was growing darker.

Damned sun, he thought. Hiding behind a cloud when he needed to see. Couldn't trip. If he went down, he wasn't sure he'd be able to get up.

Unless…maybe it was night?

That seductive thought made him stop. He contemplated darkness, swaying and blinking at the sweat stinging his eyes. Night meant peace, rest. Lying down with Alyssa. Her hand on his skin, her body curled around him…

"It's not dark yet," he muttered, clenching his hand on the crutch-stick that held him upright.

"No, not yet," her soft voice agreed. And then she was taking his stick from him, lifting his arm. She put it over her shoulder, tucking her own shoulder under his arm. "Come on, soldier."

That's right. He was a soldier. He had to keep going, keep away from the village…keep Alyssa safe. But she was supposed to have stayed in the village. Safer for her there. "You're supposed to be back there," he said, trying to focus on her face. "In the village."

"I decided to stay with you." Her voice was so soothing. "Can you go a little farther, Michael? If we can find a stream, I can bathe you, maybe get the fever down."

A stream. Yes, that was good. They needed water.

He started moving again. It was a little easier now, with her shoulder supporting him on one side.

The first time he went down, she helped him stand. The second time, she begged him to stay where he was. He didn't curse or argue. He didn't have the energy. It took everything he had to get to his feet. Then walk. Keep moving. If he stopped…he was no longer sure what would happen if he stopped. Something terrible. His world narrowed until all that remained was heat, pain, the necessity of putting one foot in front of the other.

After some brief eternity, his knees buckled. She was right there—lowering him to the ground.

"Have to rest," he muttered, closing his eyes. "Be okay in a minute."

"That's right. You rest."

Something settled on top of him. His eyelids lifted slightly—the blanket. "Is it night? Time to camp?"

"Close enough." Her voice sounded funny. "You sleep, Michael. I'll be back soon."

Back? His hand shot out, capturing her wrist more by instinct than aim. "Where are you going?"

"To the village." Her hand was cool on his forehead, smoothing back his hair. "I'll be back as soon as I can."

She was going. Leaving him. That was what he'd wanted—wasn't it? For her to go to the village, where she'd be safe… "You aren't coming back."

"Yes, I am. I will." Her face was a fuzzy oval, but her voice was clear. And her hand was blessedly cool on his skin…he didn't want her to go. He needed her.

No. No, he couldn't need… "Don't come back."

"I'm sorry. I know you have your duty. I have to follow my own conscience. Or maybe I'm just not as strong as you are. I can't let you die because there's a *chance* you would be captured. Maybe you wouldn't be. Maybe…oh," she said, hurrying over the words, "I'm not putting this well, and you're too sick to know what I'm saying. Rest." Her hand again, stroking him, soothing him. "Sleep. I'll be back."

Then the comforting hand and the soothing voice were gone.

He almost cried out. But he remembered that she was supposed to go, to be safe…and that he shouldn't be heard, seen, found.

Couldn't be seen…but he was in the middle of the trail. That was wrong. He heaved himself onto his hands and knees. His head spun. *Keep moving,* he told himself, and crawled until he saw a great, spreading bush. He dropped to his stomach and rolled, aiming to get under those sheltering branches, and bumped his injured thigh.

The pain was fierce and violent. *Don't cry out.*

After a moment his breathing steadied. He would rest. He would lie here and rest until he had some of his strength back. Then he'd keep moving.

Keep moving…

"Mikey, can't you move any faster?"

"I don't want to go." He sat on his bed, his mouth sulky, his jaw stubborn. "Why do we have to go?"

"Because your father will be home soon. I have to get away. He's swallowing me. I—oh, you're just a kid. You can't understand. Never mind, honey." His mother smiled, but her lips trembled. "Be a good boy and put your things in the suitcase. I'll explain…oh, I forgot my necklace. I'll be back,'' she said, already moving. ''Pack your things, there's my good boy.'' She whirled out of his room on jasmine-scented air.

Michael sat beside the open suitcase she'd put on his bed. He wanted to cry, but he couldn't. He wasn't a little kid anymore.

He didn't pack. It made his insides knot up to disobey, but he didn't want to leave his father, his brothers. Where would they go? Who would take care of his mom if they left? The tears almost won when he thought about that, about having to take care of her by himself.

He wasn't a little kid anymore, but he wasn't really big, either. Not big like Jacob, or even Luke. Luke was eight, four years older than him. And Jacob was really big, thirteen and awfully bossy, but he always seemed to know what to do. And Ada...he sniffed. He really, really wanted Ada.

But his brothers were at school, and Ada was at the store. Michael was home alone with his mom.

He didn't know what to do.

''Mikey?'' She was back. ''Oh, Mikey, you haven't *moved*. We have to go *now*.''

''I don't want to go. My brothers are here. If you don't like Dad anymore, you can just stay away from him.'' His brothers would help him take care of her. She might be just their stepmom, but they loved her, too. He could count on them to help—if he and his mom stayed here.

''It's not that simple, sweetheart. Here, you'll want your new jeans, won't you?'' She began folding his clothes, her movements jerky.

''It's a big house. You could move into the yellow bedroom, the one in the east wing. You like yellow.''

''Oh, Mikey.'' Her hand trembled when she stopped moving, the small, telltale tremor he knew too well. She'd be drinking soon. ''How selfish I am. I understand, sweetheart.'' Swiftly she bent and kissed him.

She always moved fast when she was like this, as if there was too much of her crammed inside her skin and she was trying to get away from herself. "You stay here, sweetheart. He's not a bad father, and you'll have Jacob and Luke and Ada...you'll be better off here. Lord knows I'm not—not—" Her breath hitched and she straightened. "I'll come see you soon, all right? I just have to—to pull myself together. I'll be better soon," she said, spinning and heading for the door. "When I'm away from *him*."

"Mama?" He shot off the bed. "Mama, you can't go without me!"

"It's for the best." She picked up her suitcase, stretching her mouth in a too-bright smile. "You'll see, darling. I love you so much...tell Jacob and Luke I love them, too, will you? I don't like leaving without seeing them, but I have to go. I'll be better soon," she promised, turning and walking quickly down the hall. "You'll see. Everything will be better soon."

"Mama?" He ran after her. "Mama, don't go! Mama..."

Don't go. Don't... Michael's eyes jerked open.

Leaves. There were leaves above him, ground below. And pain, terrible pain in his leg and his head. The light was dim, but it wasn't night...the rain forest. He remembered now. He'd been hurt, shot, and Alyssa had left him. She'd gone back to the village.

He was alone. And he was dying.

No! He struggled, got his elbow under him, levered himself up—not sitting, not quite, but it was a start. Only the effort made him pant, made his head spin. Darkness fluttered, frothy and inviting, at the edges of his vision. He collapsed onto the dirt once more.

He had to keep moving....

Where? How? *God,* he thought, but couldn't think of what to pray for, except for life. He wanted to live so badly.

Alyssa, he thought, or maybe he said it. She'd said she would be back.... Alyssa of the gentle hands, incredible legs and soothing voice. If only he could hear her voice again…funny. He couldn't hear her, but he could see her…the awe on her face when she'd seen the butterflies. The smudge of dirt on her cheek. The single, sweaty curl that kept straggling into her face in spite of the way she kept shoving it back…

She wasn't here. He knew that. She'd left him, yet he could still see her. Wasn't that strange?

Keep her safe, he thought, and let the darkness have him.

"We're almost there," A.J. said in Spanish, scrambling up a short, steep slope.

How had Michael made it up this part of the trail? Her own heart was hammering so hard she barely heard the murmured reply from behind her. That, too, was in Spanish, but the dialect was so thick she caught only some of the words. The tone, though, was clear—comfort, reassurance.

She made herself slow down. Sister Andrew might seem sturdy, with her broad face, shoulders and hips, but she had to be at least sixty. Señor Pasquez, the village's *tepec,* or headman, was even older. He looked like a strong gust of wind would blow him away.

At the top of the rise, A.J. looked around frantically. Here. She was sure she'd left Michael here. So where…? "Oh," she cried, hurrying to grab the silver material snagged on a branch. Their blanket. She'd covered him with it before she left.

Where was he?

She didn't realize she'd spoken aloud until Señor Pasquez answered in his colloquial Spanish. "Your man was out of his head, you said. He's moved a little, maybe. He won't be far. We will find him."

She flashed him a worried smile. "Yes. Yes, of course. He—I see him!"

He was several feet off the trail, half hidden beneath a bush. What instinct had prompted him to crawl under there, to hide? She hurried to his side, pushing the branches back. Sister Andrew went with her; Señor Pasquez and his donkey followed more slowly.

He was so still. But his chest moved. Life still breathed in him. "Michael." A.J. forced a calm she didn't feel into her voice, stroking his hair. He was very hot. "Michael, I've brought help."

Slowly, his eyes drifted open. He smiled up at her. "Hey." His voice was weak. "How about that. I can hear you now, too."

Then he passed out again.

Hands pulled at him. Michael roused from the dark ocean to fight.

"Shh, it's all right. We have to move you, Michael. Señor Pasquez's donkey can pull you once we get you on the travois."

Alyssa's voice? She wanted him to move. Yes, he remembered now. He was supposed to keep moving.

He tried. His wounded leg wasn't working, but he managed to push with the other one. Strong hands gripped him under his arms and dragged him. It hurt. He gritted his teeth. Did he still have to be silent? He couldn't remember. "Alyssa?"

"Here," she said. "Right beside you. It will take a while to get you back to the village, and I'm afraid you'll be bounced around. But they've got penicillin." She sounded excited. "Sister Andrew has had some medical training, too, and she knows the local remedies. She'll help you."

But the nun was named Sister Elena, not Andrew. Andrew was Scopes's first name. Was Scopes here?

No, that was silly. His eyes closed again. If he was going to hallucinate, he wished he'd dream up a soft bed and air-conditioning, not this hard jolting. It hurt. It hurt so much....

At some point the jolting stopped. There were people, voices—but he couldn't make the sounds break up into words. Children? Did he hear children's high, piping voices? Where was he?

He tried to focus, but everything blurred—people, light, movement. But Alyssa was there. She was holding his hand while other hands and arms lifted him, carried him... darkness. Something smooth beneath his back. A hand behind his head, and a cup held to his lips. He drank—cool, sweet water.

Another voice. A woman, but not Alyssa. She spoke English with a thick Irish brogue, which made no sense. Scopes had a touch of brogue in his speech...but Scopes wasn't here. Wherever *here* was.

Michael frowned. Hands tugged at the top of his pants. He struggled to sort the whirl of images, sensations, thoughts...

"Why?"

"The sister needs to look at your wound," Alyssa said.

"No..." He shook his head weakly. "Why did you come back?"

"I couldn't leave you. And it will be okay, Michael, you'll see. These are good people. They insisted on bringing you here so the sister could take care of you." Her lips pressed a blessing to his forehead. "You're going to be all right now. You'll see."

Somehow that's when he knew. She wasn't a hallucination. None of this was. Alyssa was really there with him— in a hut. In the village. She'd done exactly what he'd told her not to do, jeopardizing his mission.

She'd come back. And they were safe.

Relief crashed in, a huge wave that swept him back out into that black ocean.

Eight

The water was waist-high and cool. Dirt squished between her toes. A.J. scooped soft soap out of the wooden bowl, luxuriating in the clean, slippery feel of it. She hummed as she rubbed the soap into her hair. The air was alive with birdsong, with the coppery tang of the river and the blended smells of earth and green, growing things. Trees leaned out over the water, but there was a long strip of unobstructed sky above the river, as blue as every promise ever made—and kept.

She looked up at that strip of sky, breathed it in and thought of Michael.

His fever had broken yesterday. Last night, though, it had peaked. He'd been delirious, and he'd babbled about many things. *Not all promises are kept,* she thought sadly. And when promises made to a child are broken the pieces can't always be put back together again.

She dunked beneath the water, then surfaced. Water streamed from her face, hair and shoulders.

"You look very clean now, *señora,*" a polite young voice said in Spanish.

A.J. smiled at the fourteen-year-old girl who'd accompanied her to the river. It wasn't considered safe or seemly to bathe alone. "Yes, I'm clean now."

"You certainly do enjoy bathing." Pilar handed her the length of cloth that would serve as a towel.

"It's considered very important where I come from."

A.J. dressed quickly. The air was warm, but she wasn't used to being outside in the nude, though they were screened by trees from the homes and fields.

Pilar chattered happily as they headed back to Cuautepec. The girl was as tolerant of A.J.'s oddities as the rest of the villagers. A.J.'s passion for frequent baths was only one of her peculiarities; more baffling was her status. Who had ever heard of a woman priest? She wasn't a holy woman like the sisters, nor was she like the priests who came to marry, baptize and offer communion every couple of years. The villagers didn't know what to make of her, so they called her Señora Kelleher.

Widowhood, they understood all too well.

She and Pilar parted by the well. A.J. unfastened the peg, let the bucket drop and heard it splash. It was certainly nice not to have to boil the water anymore. Or dose it with iodine, as Michael had done that first day.

Michael.

Love ached in her so strongly she rubbed her chest, trying to ease the pain. After their adventure was over, they'd never see each other again. A.J. knew that. Accepted it.

But oh, how scary and hard and beautiful it was to be in love.

She thought of the names he'd called out when he was feverish—his brothers, mostly. Jacob and Luke. He'd talked to someone named Ada, too. She frowned as she winched the bucket back up. Who was Ada? Someone important, she thought, pouring the water into one of her buckets. A stepmother? Aunt?

Girlfriend?

He hadn't cried out for his parents. But he had cried. The fever had sent him back in time at one point, way back, to when he'd been a little boy, crying for a mother who had left him. Other times, he'd spoken to one or another of his brothers about the need to take care of his mother.

"¿Su novio, il esta mejor hoy?"

A.J. blinked back to the present. An older woman, her black hair covered by a faded red cloth, her eyes kind and curious, waited patiently to take her turn at the well. A.J. flushed, embarrassed at being caught drifting off into her thoughts. She'd done that a lot the last two days. *"Perdone me, Señora Valenzuela. Si, il esta mucho mejor."*

Novio meant fiancé. The rural people of San Christóbal were relaxed about sexual matters; still, a woman, even a widow, didn't travel alone with a man who wasn't a relative. Therefore, Michael was A.J.'s *novio*. Sister Andrew had gently suggested that A.J. not argue with the assumption, which was at least partly a polite fiction.

A.J. emptied the water into her other bucket. "He isn't used to being sick, though," she went on in Spanish, "and he's restless. He thinks he should be well overnight."

The older woman chuckled. "Men. They are such babies about sickness. And so much trouble! Do this, fetch that. But how we miss them when we don't have them underfoot!" She shook her head.

Señora Valenzuela had a husband and a grown son that she longed to have underfoot once more, A.J. knew. "Perhaps Rualdo will be able to return for a visit soon."

She shrugged. "God willing. My girls work hard, but they haven't a man's muscles. If only…ah, well. Complaining doesn't make the pot boil faster." She took her place at the well.

A.J. positioned herself beneath the yoke that balanced the

water buckets across her shoulders. They were heavy when full. Straightening, she headed back to the biggest building in Cuautepec—the orphanage.

She and Michael had drawn more than their share of luck when they ran across this particular village three days ago. Compared to others in the impoverished north, little Cuautepec was prosperous. The fields produced crops regularly, due in part to a system that let the villagers dam a small river annually, flooding the fields and depositing valuable sediment. Many of the villagers had goats or chickens; there was good, clean drinking water from a well and even a crude sawmill, though it wasn't in use now.

The reason for all this prosperity was twofold: Sister Andrew and Sister Constancia. The two nuns had established the small orphanage fifteen years ago. That hadn't been enough to keep them busy, however. Over the years they'd done much to improve the lot of the villagers.

The one thing the village sorely lacked was able-bodied men. Many of the younger men traditionally left the village for a few months each year to work on a coffee plantation on the other side of the ridge. Then *El Jefe* had started "recruiting" by force, and several of the village men had been impressed into his army. Some had managed to return. Some—like Señora Valenzuela's husband—hadn't.

She exchanged greetings with three children, an old man, a goat and two more women before reaching the orphanage.

The small building that housed the nuns and their charges possessed many advantages, too. The roof was tin, the floors cement, and the exterior walls were cement blocks. There were four rooms. One took up half the building, and in it cooking, eating, work, play, prayer and lessons took place. The other half was divided into bedrooms for the children— one for the boys, one for the girls—and a tiny room at the back shared by the sisters.

A.J. went around back, stepping up on the plank porch, where a pretty girl with a missing front tooth flashed her a smile, then went back to grinding corn with a stone mortar and pestle. Inside, a six-year-old girl was shelling beans while two boys argued over whose turn it was to bring in firewood. A smaller boy sat on a stool in one corner, his back to the room, his shoulders slumped in dejection.

Manuel. A.J. smiled. The boy had enough energy and curiosity for an entire schoolroom. Unfortunately, he hadn't developed think-ahead skills yet. His curiosity often landed him in trouble.

"You don't have to get the water," Sister Andrew scolded in her lilting English. "We have many hands and backs for such chores."

"I drink it," A.J. said, bending at the knees until the buckets sat on the floor. "I should take a turn fetching it."

In the far corner, Michael sat on his pallet, whittling at something with that long, lethal knife of his. He wore his vest and pants. His chest looked hard and strong. The muscles in his arms shifted as he plied the knife.

He looked up when she spoke.

His skin still had the drawn look of illness, but his eyes—oh, his eyes. Why did he keep looking at her that way? Had he guessed how she felt? Flustered, A.J. bent her attention to unhooking the buckets from the yoke. "Looks like our patient found something to do."

Sister Andrew smiled. "He promised that if we let him work with his knife he wouldn't try to chop firewood."

"Firewood?" A.J. straightened, giving Michael a hard look. "He'd better not."

A smile played over his mouth. His eyes never left her. "I'm behaving. Come feel my forehead and see if I'm too warm."

"I should help with supper."

"Nonsense," Sister Andrew said. "The girls don't need help to cook beans."

"Sister Constancia—"

"Doesn't need any help teaching the little ones their catechism, either. Go, spoil your man for a few minutes."

Pressed, she did as she'd been told, pausing long enough to dip him a cup of water.

His pallet consisted of two blankets folded lengthwise to cushion the hard floor. Two more blankets, folded more compactly, waited against the wall. They were what A.J. slept on—next to him. When she could sleep.

Even when he'd been sick, he'd aroused her. Now…well, now she no longer slept snuggled up to him, but it didn't seem to matter. Lying beside him, even without touching, made her ache. But she wouldn't act on her feelings. Just thinking about it—about him, about caring and intimacy—made her stomach constrict in a sick, nervous knot.

When she reached him, he smiled and put down the wood and his knife so he could take the wooden cup from her. "Thanks."

She sat next to him on the folded blankets, keeping several inches between them. Her foolish body ignored that, reacting as if she'd done what her palms itched to do and stroked the firm muscles of his arm. "It's nice to see your hands steady again. What are you making?"

"It's supposed to be a bowl. Sister Andrew is indulging me by pretending she needs one." He finished the water and set the cup down. "I see you've been scandalizing the villagers by bathing again."

She felt her cheeks warm. "What gave me away? The fact that I'm several shades lighter now?"

He touched her hair. "Your hair is damp. And it shines like polished copper."

"I wish you wouldn't flirt."

"Why? Don't ministers flirt?"

She gave him a wary glance. Before, when he'd referred to her calling, he'd used it as a way to put walls between them. Now he was plainly, gently teasing. "It makes me uncomfortable."

"That isn't why you're uncomfortable, Alyssa. I can't do anything about the real problem. Yet."

Uh-oh. She was *not* having this conversation in a room with one nun and three children. "I need to get more water." She started to get up.

He caught her wrist and pulled her back down. "I'll behave. Promise."

His eyes were laughing at her. It annoyed her. "You and I have different ideas about what constitutes behaving."

"Your mouth sure is sexy when you prim it up like that."

She didn't mean to laugh. It just slipped out. "Keep it up and you'll have an opportunity to tell me I'm beautiful when I'm angry, too."

He smiled and picked up the lump of wood he'd been shaping. "Did I tell you that when I was feverish I thought Sister Andrew was Scopes?"

"No, you didn't." She relaxed slightly. "Who's Scopes— one of your men? You were ordering him around something fierce that first night we got here, when your fever was so high."

"Was I?" He frowned. "Did I babble a lot?"

"Some." He'd said more than he would want her to know, she felt sure. "So why did you think the sister was Scopes?"

"He's half Irish with a trace of brogue, and his first name is Andrew. I was afraid he'd suffered some terrible transformation." He chuckled.

A.J. smiled and smoothed their silvery blanket, which lay on top of the others. "The sisters have been good to us. The whole village has. I can hardly believe how lucky we were to stumble across them."

"Was it luck?"

"I'd call it God's grace, but I thought you might prefer to think in terms of luck."

"I'm not a complete disbeliever, even if I'm not sure what to believe in." He picked up his knife and started digging at the wood. "I'm worried about the trouble our presence could cause these people."

"Me, too." A chill touched her at the sight of that long, wicked knife in his hands—a foolish reaction. A knife was just a tool, and he'd used it often enough on the trail.

Had he ever used it to kill?

She shook her head, trying to shake off the morbid thoughts. "Sister Andrew was determined to help as soon as I told her about you. She's like that. The other villagers have been amazingly generous, considering how little they have."

"I'll see that they don't suffer for having helped us." A long wood curl spiraled off his knife. "I should be strong enough to move on in another two or three days. Are you going to go with me or stay here?"

Two or three days? Her heart gave a funny little hop in her chest. It was so soon. Too soon. And yet, hadn't she expected him to want to leave even faster?

Once he began to mend she'd expected all sorts of reactions from him that she'd hadn't seen, though. Anger, because she'd brought him here against his wishes. Maybe some gratitude mixed in with it. The one thing she'd been sure of was that he'd be antsy, anxious to leave.

He hadn't been angry. Or antsy, as far as she could tell. He just watched her all the time with those calm, intent eyes. Hunter's eyes.

He was confusing the heck out of her.

"Hey." He used his thumb to smooth her forehead. "What's the frown for?"

"I thought you'd try to leave as soon as your fever went down, even if you had to crawl. Instead you sound content to wait around."

"I was out of my head with fever when I insisted on continuing instead of getting help," he said mildly. "Now that we're here, I'd be foolish to leave before I'm strong enough."

He'd been so determined to avoid coming here that he'd

nearly killed himself—and now he was okay with staying a few more days? "So you're not going to try to slink away before your wound is healed?"

"I can't wait until it's fully healed, but I won't be doing any slinking." His knife stroked another long curl out of the center of the wood. "What about you, Alyssa? What do you want?"

You. The word echoed so strongly in her mind she had to pause before answering. "Why are you calling me Alyssa?"

"Why not?"

"I'm used to A.J."

He started another curl of wood with his knife. "It's human nature to hang on to whatever we're used to. When the Allied armies liberated the concentration camps, some of the prisoners walked out the gates, then turned around and walked back in. They weren't used to freedom anymore."

"You make it sound as if wanting to be called by my own name is like living in a concentration camp."

He paused and touched her arm lightly with the hand that held the knife. "But your name *is* Alyssa."

She moved her arm away.

"The knife bothers you?" He pulled it back, his eyes steady on hers. "I won't pretend to be other than what I am."

"I'm not asking you to. But I can't pretend it doesn't trouble me."

He nodded. "Fair enough. Honesty is a good starting point."

Hope and heat fluttered inside her. So did fear. "We're not starting anything, Michael."

"I think we already have. Doesn't anyone call you Alyssa?"

"My mother." Thinking of that warm, busy woman made her smile. "When I told her I wanted to be called A.J., she hugged me and said that was fine—but she liked the name she'd given me."

"What about your father? What does he call you?"

"Oh, I'm A.J. to Dad." Affection and memory chased each other, making her chuckle. "Since he didn't have any sons, he was delighted when I turned out to be a tomboy he could teach to pitch, bat and field a fly ball."

"A baseball fan, I take it."

"An addict." They would be so worried about her. They must know she'd been taken prisoner. Would they be told about the attempted rescue? Restless, anxious over what she couldn't change, she rose to her feet. "I need to get more water."

"Alyssa."

She paused, looking over her shoulder at him.

"Did your husband call you A.J.?"

Her brows knit in a quick, warning frown. "Yes."

He nodded and went back to his whittling. "That's what I thought."

She was all grace and light. Michael watched Alyssa as she helped the others put their simple supper together that night. She paused to wipe a child's dirty face, then to admire the pretty rock another had found.

He knew he made her uneasy. He wanted to. He wanted— needed—for her to be aware of him.

She might not know it yet, but the rules had changed for both of them. *Everything* had changed. He was feeling his way in this new landscape, unsure of a great many things— but very sure of his goal.

When the others were gathered at the big table near the fireplace where the cooking was done, Michael pushed to his feet. He still used his walking stick, but every day he needed it less.

Sister Constancia said the blessing. The two oldest girls served. One—Pilar? Yes, that was it—brought the beans to the foot of the table, where he sat as guest of honor. She was a pretty girl, clear-skinned, with a gap between two of her teeth that gave her smile a certain lopsided charm. At fourteen, she was ready to practice beguiling whatever male moved into range. She set the beans in front of him with a ducked head, shy smile and sideways glance. He thanked her gravely, took a portion and passed the bowl to his right.

Alyssa sat there. Their fingers brushed when she took the bowl. She glanced at him. Her smile came and went too quickly.

She didn't trust him. He knew that and he hated it, but he understood. She had no reason to trust. She had saved his life, while he had very nearly cost her hers.

He should never have let her go on with him after they'd seen this village. If it had taken him longer to collapse, she might have died, too, lost in a wilderness she didn't have the skills to cope with. But she'd been determined to stay with him. When he'd been out of his head with fever and unable to do either of them any good, she'd stayed. Then she'd left...but she'd come back. And changed everything.

Michael shifted on the hard bench. His leg ached. He'd used it more than anyone except himself had thought wise today. But he knew his limits, and he hadn't done any damage. He had to get his strength back. He couldn't stay here much longer.

In truth, he should have already left.

He glanced at the woman on his right. She hadn't said if she was going to leave with him. And he wasn't leaving without her.

"¿Señor West?" a small voice to his left said, going on in rapid-fire Spanish as soon as Michael turned his head, "Will you tell me about the television again, where the pictures move? And the electricity that makes this happen, and makes the lights work?"

He smiled at Manuel, who always had questions—especially about the marvels found in that mythical land, the U.S. It occurred to Michael that if he lived, he would soon be a very rich man.

Funny. He'd never cared about the money, never counted

on it. His father's bizarre will had come as a nasty surprise, but not because he was interested in wealth. There would be advantages to having money, though, he thought as he tried to explain the mysteries of electricity to a six-year-old. A boy as bright and inquisitive as Manual deserved a chance to soak up all the learning he could.

One of the girls chided Manual for not letting their guest eat. The boy reluctantly returned his attention to his supper, giving Michael a chance to scoop up beans with one of the soft tortillas they used in lieu of silverware.

"You're good with him," Alyssa said quietly in English.

"I like kids. You do, too, from what I've seen."

She nodded, looking down at her bowl. "That's another thing I put off. Having children. It made sense at the time, since we intended to put in at least one year of missionary work."

"Regrets?" He captured her hand. "You can still have children, you know." *My children.* The thought startled him. And aroused him. Yes, he thought as another part of this new landscape became clear. He wanted to see her big with his child.

Awareness flashed through her eyes, sharp and hot. She pulled her hand away. "You'd better eat," she said lightly. "Seconds only go to those who finish their first helping quickly."

Michael obeyed with an easy docility that would have warned his brothers to keep an eye on him. He'd gotten what he wanted—for now. She was aware of him.

Alyssa was going to be his. She just didn't know it yet.

There was a great deal of laughing and bickering while the table was cleared and dishes were washed. Michael joined the friendly chaos, insisting he was well enough to scrub the bean pot. Pilar looked shocked. Manuel wanted to know why he would wash a pot when there were girls to do such things. He told the boy that a real man always did his share of the work. Since he wasn't fit enough to chop wood yet, he would wash pots.

Finally, after Sister Andrew had dressed his wound again, the children were sent to bed and the sisters went to their own room. By the time Michael returned from a trip to the facilities behind the building, the fire had burned low in the fireplace. The room was warm and dark, and he had Alyssa to himself.

She leaned out the window near the front door, pulling the crude shutters closed. Someone had given her a nightgown. The yards of much-washed cotton nearly swallowed her.

"How's your leg?" she asked when she turned around. "You've been using it a lot today."

"Sore, but mending." He propped his stick against the wall and lowered himself onto his pallet.

"Thank God for penicillin. When I think of how ill you were..." She shook her head and knelt to unfold her blankets. "It's a miracle."

"Close enough. Of course, it helps that I'm so tough."

She chuckled. He settled on his side, his head propped on one hand. He loved watching her by firelight. The hints and shadows, the shapes shifting as she moved, the whisper of fabric and the quiet intimacy of bare feet—it all fascinated him. Aroused him. "Do you realize I'd never seen you indoors until we came here?"

"What a strange thought." Quickly, competently, she spread her blankets a foot away from his. "We haven't known each other very long, have we? Though it seems..." She shook her head, lay down and smoothed one blanket over her. "I was indoors when you found me at *El Jefe*'s compound."

"I wasn't. And I didn't see you until you came out the window."

Their eyes caught. Held. "I've wondered about Sister Maria Elena and your men. If they made it out okay."

"I'd put money on it. They're good men." Her eyes were

luminous in the dim light, her shape more sensed than seen. There was an easy intimacy to lying side by side this way. There was also a foot of space between their blankets. "I liked it better when you slept tucked up against me."

She looked away. Her fingers plucked nervously at the blanket. "That was necessary on the trail. It isn't necessary now."

He wondered if her pulse was pounding as wildly as his. It would be easy to find out—all he had to do was stretch out a hand and touch the smooth skin of her throat.

He sighed. She'd probably jump up and move her blankets to the other side of the room. "Do you only do what's necessary, Alyssa Jean?"

"Oh." Her laugh was shaky. "I haven't heard that in ages. My mother only called me Alyssa Jean when I was in trouble."

He smiled at her through the deepening darkness. The fire was down to coals now. "I don't think I remind you of your mother."

For a long moment she didn't answer. "No. Which is why I'm over here and you're over there, and it's going to stay that way."

He could have told her that his intentions were honorable, but that was only partly true. And she would probably have scurried over to the other side of the room anyway. Yet she could do that now, couldn't she? He no longer needed a nurse in the middle of the night.

She stayed near because she wanted to. Frustration, keen and sexual, gnawed at Michael, but satisfaction was stronger. "How about a picnic tomorrow?"

"What?"

"You know—dirt and ants. Finger food. Eating outdoors."

Her voice was low and amused. "We've done plenty of that."

"I'm trying to be good, but I'm bored out of my mind. I thought a little walk tomorrow might let me exercise my leg without straining anything. I need to see how well I can manage. And I'd like some company."

"Oh…well, okay. I guess."

She sounded dubious. He smiled at the darkness. Her instincts were good. If she'd known how right she was to be wary of his invitation, she'd never have accepted it. "Good. I'll arrange it in the morning. Good night, Alyssa."

Her answering "good night" was soft and, whether she knew it or not, a little wistful.

It was funny, he thought as he rolled onto his back. A week ago, he would have sworn that he liked women. He'd been sure he'd gotten over the confusion his childhood had created about the female half of the species.

But you couldn't tell a man who had never seen the sun what light was like. Trust was the same, he'd learned. He hadn't known he was missing something until he'd been forced to depend on a woman—and learned what it was to trust her. Wholly, but without blinders. The same way he trusted the men on his team, or his brothers. He knew them well, understood their flaws, and knew he could count on them anyway.

He couldn't have guessed it would matter so much to trust a woman.

Until now, Michael had snorted at the idea of men and women being friends. Friendly, yeah—he liked a lot of women. But Alyssa was different. Like his brothers, like the men on the team, she was someone he could count on. She was a real friend.

Of course, she was a friend he wanted to have sex with. Badly.

Time was short and the stakes were high. For the first time since he'd put on his uniform, Michael was putting something ahead of duty. He had no business hanging around this village even one more day, but he would. Even though his leg was probably strong enough to carry him out of here now.

Probably wasn't good enough. Not when he had every intention of taking Alyssa with him. He had to be sure he was fit enough to keep her safe. Tension tightened the muscles across his shoulders.

He meant to have her. To keep her. But he wasn't underestimating the problems ahead. First and largest loomed her beloved ghost, Daniel Kelleher. She mourned him still and would resist taking another man in his place—especially a man like Michael, trained for war and death instead of healing and peace.

But Dan was dead. Michael was alive, and so was she. That was his biggest advantage.

There was also the matter of the woman back in Dallas who expected Michael to marry her upon his return.

Michael was used to walking in the blurred grays, where right and wrong were vague directions instead of sure and certain guides. Alyssa wasn't. She would never let herself become involved with a man who was engaged to another woman, no matter what the circumstances were. And if he explained those circumstances, she'd think he wanted to marry her to get his hands on the trust. She might sympathize with his motives, but she'd never agree to marry him.

She would want to be loved. Unease tightened the muscles at the base of his spine. He could offer her a lot, but love? The kind of strong, healthy love she'd known with her husband? Michael had never seen that kind of love, never come close enough to touch or smell it. How could he build something he'd never seen? All he knew of love was the destruction it wreaked when it was bent, twisted, when two people got their needs tangled up so tight they nearly choked the life out of each other.

He heard his mother's thin, shady voice in his mind… *I'm sorry, Mikey. I tried to stop loving him, but it never worked. Nothing worked*….

She'd swallowed a medicine cabinet's worth of pills out of love—or what she called love—that time. Then she'd called Michael to say goodbye.

He'd been fourteen. His father had been on a business trip and Jacob had been in his last year of college, but Luke had been home. He'd gotten Michael there in time, though for the last few blocks the flashing lights and siren of a police car had screamed up the street after them. Not surprising, considering their speed and the red lights Luke had run.

The cop had come in handy. He'd radioed for an ambulance.

They'd pumped Felicia's stomach and she'd spent the next year in a quiet place down by Houston with grassy lawns and flowers twining up the high iron fences. His father had paid for it. He'd paid for all of his fourth wife's medical care, never grudging the money. In some ways, Randolph West had been an admirable man—a disaster as a husband, but a steady friend, generous with his money, if not his time.

The psychiatrist had told Michael that she'd called him because part of her still wanted to live. She'd unconsciously cast Michael in the role of rescuer because her love for him had kept her alive in the past.

Maybe so. Sometimes, though…sometimes when he was growing up, he'd hated her. Now she mostly made him feel sad and tired.

Michael closed his eyes and shut the door on the past. It was a trick he'd gotten good at over the years. The present was what counted. And the future.

He wanted to spend that future with Alyssa. Friendship, he thought—he could give her that. He knew how to be a friend. Then there was sex. Oh, yeah, he thought, shifting slightly to ease the way his pants constricted his arousal. He could handle that part, too.

With luck, Alyssa would never know about his fiancée. All Cami really wanted was the money guaranteed her by the prenuptial agreement they'd signed. Once he gave her that, she'd slink off to spend it happily enough.

He would make it work. Somehow. Life called to life, and Alyssa wanted him. She didn't like it, didn't intend to act on her desire, but it was there, simmering beneath the surface of everything she said, everything she did. He could use that.

For a woman like Alyssa, bed and marriage went together.

Michael didn't have time to persuade her to trust him, to ease her into a relationship slowly and gently. He had to move fast, and, yeah, he had to be ruthless or he was going to lose her. That was unacceptable.

He'd use whatever he had to. That's the kind of man he was—not her kind, and they both knew it. So he'd use sex to get to her. Then he'd persuade her to marry him.

Nine

Village time was different. Smoother than civilized time, it flowed and eddied without the jerky pace imposed by clocks and daily planners. Still, A.J. was shocked when she realized it was only twelve days until Christmas.

Twelve days until Christmas, and she was walking through a rain forest, not a shopping mall, on her way to a picnic breakfast with a man she loved and couldn't have. A.J. shifted the sack that held fruit, goat cheese and a round of coarse bread rather like a thick, nutty tortilla.

"You're quiet this morning."

She glanced at Michael. They'd followed the cheerful flow of the river for several minutes after leaving the village, then veered off on a path cut into the tangled growth. Vegetation was fierce here, with vines, plants, saplings and larger trees competing for space. The light was warm and green. "I was thinking about snow and shopping malls."

"Having a seasonal moment?" Michael still used his walking stick, but it seemed more of a prop than a necessity as he moved easily beside her. "How would you celebrate the holiday if you were home?"

"Usually I don't get to go home for Christmas. Not home to my parents' house, that is. They live in Andrews, and my church is in San Antonio, about seven hours away."

"I guess your duties keep you busy at this time of year."

She chuckled. "You could say that. There are a lot of church functions, of course, and the season is hard on people who are depressed or alone." For the last two years, she'd had to try to minister to those fighting grief, loneliness and depression while enduring the same battles herself. "My folks drive down to spend Christmas with me sometimes."

The last two years, they'd made a point of being there. Because she'd lost Dan, and they knew what she went through when the holidays approached.

Yet here she was, walking beside another man, one who made her heart pound and her body ache. A man who wore a gun on a holster at his waist. Yearning and fear twisted together. What was she doing? How could she be in love again? It was too soon. Too sudden, too—everything. Quickly she asked, "What do you do to celebrate?"

"Pretty much the usual. Get together with family, open presents, eat too much." He smiled. "Ada likes to stuff my brothers and me so full of turkey and fixings we can't do much except groan, then complain if we miss a speck when we clean up her kitchen afterward."

"Ada? You mentioned her when you were feverish. I wondered who she was."

"She used to be my father's housekeeper. When he died, Jacob wanted the house and Luke and I didn't, so he lives there now. Ada takes care of the place for him."

"A housekeeper?" Surprise lifted her voice and her eyebrows. The woman seemed like an important piece in the puzzle that was Michael. "Ada sounded important when you spoke about her. I thought she was a girlfriend or a relative."

His glance was cool and measuring. "She *is* important. She's also a housekeeper."

"I'm not criticizing her. My aunt Margaret was a house-keeper for thirty years. None of the families she worked for ever cleaned up the kitchen for her, though, on Christmas or any other day."

He chuckled. "It isn't as if Ada gives us a choice. Hey— I think we've arrived."

A.J. followed him into the tiny clearing—and stopped. "This is the place Señor Pasquez told you about?" she asked softly.

"Yeah." His voice, like hers, was quiet. "It's special, isn't it?"

Like a cathedral, the tiny clearing called for hushed voices and awe, but this was reverence on an intimate scale. The green wall of the forest breathed all around. There was a tiny trickle of a stream, so small and perfect in its tumble over stones that it seemed placed there for effect. Grass, a rarity in the poor soil and perpetual shade of the rain forest, carpeted the ground. And there were flowers. An orchid bloomed in singular splendor on a branch overhanging the little stream, and tiny blue-white flowers nodded on short stalks here and there. A foot-long lizard, green as spring, stared at them unblinkingly from a rock, then vanished in an emerald streak.

And there was sun. The canopy was broken overhead and sunshine fell, warm and mellow, on the grassy patch. She laughed in delight. "Oh, this is wonderful. A fairy grotto."

He smiled and spread a blanket on the ground.

They sprawled on the blanket, spread the cheese on the nutty bread, and talked. About anything and nothing—everything except war and passion and the choices that loomed in front of them.

She'd been humiliated by a D in English her third year in high school. He'd gotten D's in everything until he went to military school and discovered what it meant to have a goal.

He liked rock music. She preferred country western. They both liked fast cars, which made him raise his eyebrows and ask what other weaknesses she had. She laughed and admitted she loved dancing—two-step, square dancing, ballroom dancing, anything that got her moving to music. He claimed to have two left feet, which made her snort. "No one who moves the way you do would have any problem on the dance floor."

"You like my moves?" He waggled both eyebrows at her. "Want to see my etchings?"

She laughed again and leaned back on both elbows, tilting her head so she could breathe in the sky. "It's good to see blue overhead. All this green is beautiful, but I start feeling hemmed in."

"You'd have been used to wide open spaces in Andrews. San Antonio has plenty of green, though. It's a fascinating city."

"You've been there?" The idea pleased her.

"Went to visit Stephanie there once, before she married a politician and moved to Tennessee."

"Ah—who's Stephanie? An old flame?" She sat up and reached for one of the guavas they'd brought for dessert.

He chuckled. "Hardly. Stephanie is Luke's mom. She's the one who married Dad twice, poor woman. Put in nine years altogether as Mrs. Randolph West. A record."

"You must have had a good relationship with her if you went to see her after she and your father were divorced." Maybe, she thought, he'd found someone to mother him. From what she'd been able to piece together from his ramblings when his fever was high, his own mother had been in and out of treatment centers and hospitals for years.

He shrugged. "Stephanie's okay. Not exactly Mom material, as she says herself, but a friendly sort. Very tolerant. She had to be," he added wryly. "She was around during my wild days. In fact, it was her idea to send me to military school. That's one reason I went to see her later. I was mad as hell at her at the time, and I wanted to let her know it had worked out.''

She looked down, turning the guava over in her hands. It was green and about the size of a plum. ''Did you and your brothers all have different mothers?''

''Yeah. Here, let me dig out the pit for you.'' He took the fruit from her and pulled his knife from the scabbard at his waist. He'd set his gun down on the blanket earlier, but she'd noticed that the knife didn't leave his side. ''We weren't exactly the Cleavers, but I think you're imagining all sorts of traumas that weren't part of the picture.'' He handed her the halved fruit and dug into the sack for another. ''I had my brothers. We're pretty tight. And I had Ada.''

Ada again. She bit into the fruit. Green or not, it was tart and tasty. She finished both halves and reached for another one.

A twig cracked loudly.

He moved so fast her mind scarcely registered the motion. One moment they were eating. The next he was crouched, handgun ready, scanning the wall of green surrounding them.

She hadn't even seen him retrieve the weapon.

A flurry of birds took off from the tree to her right. Otherwise, there was silence—then the shrill complaints of capuchin monkeys somewhere off to their left.

Something was out there. The second guava rolled, unnoticed, out of her limp hand.

Then she heard a squeal followed by thrashing noises and furious grunting from many throats. Animal throats. A.J. remembered to breathe. ''Peccaries,'' she said with relief.

''Mmm-hmm.'' He didn't put his gun down or stop watching the forest.

''I think they're moving away. Unless you want to hunt them down and shoot one for supper, you won't be needing your gun.''

''Probably not.'' His voice was soft. ''But something could have spooked the peccaries.''

She swallowed. "Jaguars hunt at night. I can't think of anything else big enough to be a threat to a bunch of bad-tempered pigs."

"Men hunt day or night."

"Come on, Michael. How likely is it that some bandit or renegade soldier is out there?"

"Not likely. I wouldn't have brought you here if I thought there was much danger. But *unlikely* and *impossible* are not the same." He studied the trees a moment longer, then slipped his gun back in its holster. His smile lacked humor. "Kind of spoiled the mood, didn't I?"

She took a steadying breath. "You never completely relax, do you?"

"Not on a mission."

She'd forgotten. She was a mission, wasn't she? Or part of one. A disastrous last-minute addition to his real mission here, which she assumed involved gathering data. He hadn't even known who he was rescuing when he'd shown up at her window. He'd thought Reverend Kelleher was a man.

How long ago was that? It seemed another life, but it was…she counted back. Nine days? Only nine days.

Surely she couldn't fall in love in nine days. It had to be infatuation.

"Look," he said, sitting down beside her. "I think we'd better talk about this."

"This?" She shook her head, disoriented. "About what?"

"The way you feel about my gun, my training. My career as a soldier."

"I don't see the need," she said stiffly.

"Yeah, well, you haven't seen the look on your face every time I handle a weapon."

Guilt made her bite her lip. "I'm sorry. I don't mean to…I'm not used to guns. To any of this."

One of the guavas had rolled near his foot. He picked it up. "I think it's more than that. Your husband was shot to death in front of you. Seems like that would give you a pretty powerful hatred for guns. Maybe for men who use them, too.''

"No! No, I don't feel that way about you. Truly." In her need to convince him, she made a big mistake. She touched him.

Her heart began a slow, hard pounding.

He knew. He felt it, too, for his eyes darkened, his voice deepened. "How do you feel about me, Alyssa?" He covered her hand with his. "Do you ache for me the way I ache for you?"

Her mouth went dry. Her heart thudded. "This is too fast for me. Much too fast."

"Fast, maybe, but not sudden." He took her hand from his arm and carried it to his mouth, and pressed a kiss to the center of her palm. "This has been growing between us from the first."

"It can't. We can't." She was near panic, yet couldn't bring herself to pull her hand away and lose the sweet touch of his mouth. "There's nowhere for us to go with—with what we're feeling."

Wickedness lit his eyes, curving his mouth in the shape of sin. "I can think of someplace I'd very much like to go with you."

She grabbed for sense, for reason—for all those reasons that seemed so important when he wasn't touching her. He made her feel so alive.

He made her feel too much. "I don't believe in flings."

"I know that." He released her hand, only to thread his fingers through her hair. "How about kisses, Alyssa? Do you believe in kisses?"

Yes. Her body shouted it while her heart quivered, small and aching and frightened, longing to hide. And still she didn't move, didn't pull away.

His smile faded. With utmost seriousness, as if the simple act of bringing his mouth to hers called for his entire attention, he laced his other hand on the right side of her head, tilting her face just so. And he kissed her.

Soft. The lips she'd seen tight with pain, curved in pleasure, hard with determination and—just now—tilted with wicked suggestions, were amazingly soft.

For a moment—just for a moment—she would let herself savor that surprise, and the warm delight of his mouth.

Her breath sighed out. When she inhaled, she breathed him in.

He smelled like Michael, like closeness and warmth in the night, teasing and companionship by day. And when his lips parted, urging hers open, he tasted like the fruit they'd both eaten. Tart, tangy…and living. The vivid male heat of him flashed through her, calling to everything female and alive in her. And it was sweet, so sweet, to feel her body sing with desire.

She'd forgotten how intimate a kiss could be. How it could blend two people, so that their needs touched, parted, and joined again, just as their mouths did.

Deeper this time. Hotter. He made a noise low in his throat and thrust his tongue inside—and broke through the sweetness, cracking open the need.

Oh, yes, she needed this, needed him. Her hands searched for the places on him she didn't yet know—the smooth skin on his cheek, the muscles taut beneath. His neck, and the pulse that pounded there. The flex of his shoulders as he slid his arms around her, drawing her close.

And his body. He eased her down onto the blanket, holding her close, and he was warm and hard against her. His leg slid between hers as he kissed her and kissed her—not pressing aggressively up against the juncture of her thighs, just resting there, his body and hers finding a fit.

His hand moved to her breast and kneaded it. She was the one who made a sound this time, a low croon of pleasure and approval.

At the back of her mind, a voice cried out warnings. There

was a reason, a very good reason, she couldn't do this…but this was what she'd dreamed of every night. Waking dreams that kept her from the comfort of sleep, kept her aching and aware…though this was better than dreams, better than anything she'd felt or imagined since…

Since Dan died.

The thought shot through her, stiffening her body, bringing a rush of feelings too huge and tangled to grasp. They swept through her, making her moan. And she put a hand between them to push him away.

"Shh," he murmured, his hands gentling now, caressing her breast, her throat. "Shh. It's all right. He wouldn't want you to mourn forever."

Whatever it was she felt, it wasn't guilt. "Michael," she whispered, confused. "I'm not ready for this."

"Who is?"

He sounded wry, even whimsical, but his eyes held darkness, a need so vivid and real she felt it lapping at her, a private ocean spilling from his shores to hers. Moved, she touched his cheek.

His jaw tensed—and he crushed his mouth to hers.

Huge, swelling chords of emotion and sensation made her body thrum and her heart yearn. She slid her tongue inside his mouth, seeking…and in the taste and scent and feel of him, she lost something. And found something else. Her shoulders relaxed.

It was all the signal he needed. His mouth left hers, but only to journey over cheeks, throat. He murmured to her, low, encouraging words about how good she felt, how right.

Yes. This was right. She wove her fingers into his hair, the rhythm of her breath breaking as he slid his hand inside her shirt and found her breast. He teased the tip, quick, feathery brushes of fingers, then squeezed it. The muscles of her thighs tensed as desire shot its electric arc from breast to belly to groin.

More. She needed more—of his skin, his taste. She needed

his muscles shifting, straining, as he answered the wild call drumming in her blood. Her fingers fumbled at the front of his vest, shoving it aside so she could explore his chest, his stomach. His muscles jumped at her touch.

When his mouth came back to hers this time, there was no wooing, no gentle soothing. On his part, or hers.

She tore her mouth from his and ran her hands down his sides. "You walk around in this damned vest...you've got the sexiest stomach. Did you know that?" she demanded, bending to press a kiss to his hard, flat stomach. "Did you guess how often I've thought of doing this?"

He groaned, his hands fisting in her hair. "If you've thought of it as often as I have..." When her tongue wandered from belly button to the smooth, tight muscles of his chest, pausing to circle one flat nipple, he jerked her head away.

"My turn." His voice was hoarse. "Let me show you what I've been thinking of doing to you. Dreaming of doing."

"Clothes," she said, tugging at his vest. "Clothes first."

Her shirt, his vest, her bra. Her shoes, his boots—oh, footwear made a foolish pause in the midst of such heated action, a time-out in the bottom of the ninth with the bases loaded. Sanity should have caught up with her then. But when her laces defied her and doubts nibbled at her mind, she pushed the thoughts away.

He got his boots and pants off while she still struggled with knotted shoelaces. She made the mistake of looking at him then, and forgot her shoes, her doubts, everything.

He was magnificent.

She'd seen his body before, but only in parts. Every time she'd tended his wound she'd seen the power in his thighs. Following him on the trail she'd been aware of the fluid strength of his back and shoulders. His hands had fascinated her from the first.

Now she saw all of him. Naked. And aroused.

He didn't wait around to let her admire him. As soon as he tossed his pants aside, he knelt and yanked off her still-tied shoes, then her socks—and then he kissed her foot. His tongue flicked the tender arch of her sole. She gasped.

He smiled a dark, pleased smile, hooked his fingers in the waist of her pants and tugged them, and her panties, down.

Naked was better. She had his skin against hers, sweat-slick and hot. The hard male shape of him pressed against her, the wall of his chest eased the ache in her breasts, and she had his whole body to explore.

He would have slowed down then. She wasn't having it. She wanted the haste and the heat and no room for thought. But he wouldn't be rushed too much. He had to lick here, touch there, press a kiss to the tender place beneath each breast.

At last, he rose over her, his upper body propped up by one arm, his other hand guiding him to her opening. She wrapped her legs around him, welcoming him, urging him to come in, into her.

He stopped at the very threshold. She felt him there, pulsing against her. The pupils of his eyes were huge, the lids heavy. Strain drew grooves along his cheeks.

"Marry me," he said. And began to sink slowly home.

Her eyes went wide. He hadn't said that. He couldn't have—oh, he was stretching her, entering so slowly, yet still she could barely take him in. He was big, so hard and thick.

And it had been so long. "What?" she gasped, her fingers digging into his shoulders.

He shoved, one short, hard thrust, and was fully seated.

She moaned, her muscles contracting around him. "Michael, what did you *say?*"

"*Querida,*" he murmured, and bent and kissed her gently as he started to move. "Beautiful Alyssa. Wise, strong A.J. Marry me."

She shook her head, refusing to hear, to believe—and met his movement with her own. Slow motion at first, as they found each other's rhythm—hips rising, falling, hands gripping, sweetness and sweat rolling over them both. Body, heart, hands and lips, she rejoiced in the ancient dance, the sound of flesh meeting flesh, the rolling, rocking motion of the sweetest union this side of heaven.

And her mind stayed locked. Blank.

The slow motion didn't last. They were both too close, too eager, near the edge from the moment of joining. Heat and haste overtook her even as his thrusts grew harder, faster, until she cried out—one thin, high cry—and body, mind, world, contracted in a single knot of pleasure. And burst.

Ten

Michael lay on his side with his arms around her, her head pillowed on his arm, his chest heaving, his sex wet from her body. And cursed silently.

It had gone wrong, all wrong. Oh, not the sex. *Incredible* didn't begin to describe that.

She'd surprised him. Amazed him. He hadn't expected shyness, but neither had he expected such earthy appreciation. When she'd licked her way up his stomach…desire stirred, waking what he'd thought was down for the count for the time being, a fresh current binding them.

His arms tightened around her. Alyssa was right for him…but he was going to have a helluva time convincing her he could be right for her, too. Especially after the way he'd just screwed up.

God knows it wasn't the way he'd planned to propose. He'd meant to ask her afterward, when she was sated and happy. When his brain was functioning, dammit. Instead, he'd just blurted it out. And seen her eyes go blank with shock.

He'd tried. With everything in him, he'd tried to hold back, to gather his mind so he could give her words. Women needed words, and he thought Alyssa in particular would need coaxing, persuasion. Reasons. But he'd been inside her. She'd been pulsing around him, the fit perfect, her scent in his nostrils and her taste on his lips.

He couldn't have stopped then if *El Jefe* had jumped out of the bushes and held a gun to his head.

She hadn't spoken. Hadn't said a word since he'd asked her to marry him.

How was she going to play it? Would she pretend he hadn't asked her to marry him? Give him a kiss, maybe, a smile, then get dressed as if nothing had happened except a quick, hot romp? Or maybe she'd just continue to lie there, silent, her body so intimately his...every other part of her distant.

Not if he could help it.

He didn't know what to say, though, so he pressed a kiss to her hair. She stirred, then turned in his arms. Her hand came up to touch his cheek, then trace his lips. Her expression was calm.

Her eyes weren't. "Michael," she said sadly, "I can't marry you."

The pain was unexpectedly strong. He'd known what her answer was. Still, it hurt like blazes to hear it, to see the look on her face as she rejected him. So calm...as if she had regrets but no real doubts. "I need a little more than that. Like a reason." *Give me a reason so I'll know what I'm up against.*

"I'm not ready."

"You didn't think you were ready for this, either." He ran his hand down her side, curving over her hip, her bottom. "You were wrong about that."

He saw the flicker of heat in her eyes. And the way her

lips tightened. "You don't want an explanation. You want a hook to hang an argument on." She pulled out of his arms, pushed to her feet and grabbed her clothes.

Dammit to hell. "So that's it? That's all you're going to tell me—you're not ready?"

She moved over to the little stream, and bent down to wash him off. She wanted to wash away the stickiness of their joining, and as reasonable as that was, it made him furious. He pushed to his feet. "I just asked you to marry me, dammit! I want to know why you won't."

"Don't curse at me." She yanked her panties on, then reached for her pants. Her hand was shaking.

Good move, West. Yell at her enough and she's sure to agree. Michael lowered his head and stood quietly, struggling to get a grip on things he couldn't close his hands around. Finally he exhaled, turned his back to her and began dressing.

When he had everything back in place, from boots to SIG Sauer, he faced her again. She was dressed and shod, but fumbling with her buttons. He went to her and pushed her hands away.

She looked up. Her eyes were swimming with tears.

"Oh, hell." He sighed, put his arms around her and pulled her to him. "Seems like I should be the weepy one here."

She sniffed. "Right. When's the last time you cried, soldier?"

"I might be a little out of practice," he conceded, and sighed. "You were right. I do want to change your mind. But I also deserve to know why you gave yourself to me if you don't want me."

"I don't know!" She pushed out of his arms. Her shirt hung open, and her hair was wild. So were her eyes. "I've got reasons. All sorts of good, logical reasons. Practical reasons. Only there are too many of them, and they don't make sense. Nothing does." She jammed a hand into her hair as if trying to tame it, then winced as she hit a tangle. "God, I'm a mess. In more ways than one."

He reached into his pocket, pulled out his small black comb and held it out.

She stared at the comb as if he'd tried to hand her a snake. Then she laughed. It was shaky, rueful, but it seemed to smooth some of her other tangles.

"Thanks," she said, taking the comb. Instead of using it, though, she turned it over in her hands. "You're a good man, Michael. One of the best I've ever known. And I do want you. I guess I proved that, didn't I? But this has all happened so fast. I can't imagine…" She sighed and started working the comb through her hair.

He reached for her shirt. She jumped.

"Hey, I'm trying to have a meaningful conversation here. Can't do that when your breasts are peeking out at me." He pulled the sides together and tucked a button into its buttonhole. "So what can't you imagine?"

She was yanking the comb through her hair as if she was going to be graded on how fast she finished. "I can't picture you attending ninety-nine church potluck suppers a year. Or living in the cozy brick house that goes with my church. Or—ouch." She grimaced and plied the comb a little more carefully. "This—this whatever it is between us—how much is it a product of everything we've been through? I've got another world waiting for me back home, one that doesn't—Michael? What is it?"

He'd gone still, his hands stopping halfway up her shirt.

Then he heard it again—a low, throbbing bird call.

"My God," he said, and meant it. A grin broke out. He stepped back, cupped his hand around his mouth and returned the call.

Two men wearing grungy fatigues, with wicked-looking guns slung over their shoulders, stepped out of the bushes that marked the entrance to the grotto.

Alyssa gasped—then her hands flew to the job that had been interrupted. Hastily she fastened the last two buttons.

"You've been one hard son of a bitch to find, Lieutenant,"

the taller and darker of the two men said in the crisp tones
of upper-class Boston. He nodded at Alyssa. "Good to see
you're all right, ma'am."

"Jeez, Mick." The red-headed one shook his head mourn-
fully as the two men came into the clearing. His accent was
peculiar—Deep South touched by a hint of old-country
brogue. "Here I've been picturing you neck-deep in all sorts
of calamities. Instead, looks like we interrupted a little R and
R. Sorry about that."

"Scopes," Michael said, "put a sock in it."

It could have been worse, A.J. told herself. Michael's men
might have found them when she had a lot more unfastened
than a couple of buttons.

Still, it was mortifying. Michael took her hand when he
introduced her to his men, and she pretended she had no idea
what they were thinking. Banner—the tall black man—made
that easy with his gentle courtesy. Scopes was another matter.
Though his grin was good-natured, it was obvious he intended to give his lieutenant a hard time about his "R and
R."

The three men were obviously close. Tight, Michael would
say. She listened to their easy banter and tried not to mind
the way the sunlight dimmed when they left the little clearing, Banner in front, Michael and her in the middle, Scopes
in the rear.

Michael still held her hand. She was too dizzied by everything that had happened to know if that was wrong or right.
Probably foolish, she decided—and left her hand in his.

What was one more folly after what she'd done?

Apparently Scopes and Banner had been looking for Michael all along. Their colonel had feared the same kind of
repercussions Michael had if he were taken prisoner—at
least, that's what she assumed, reading between the lines of
Banner's brief explanation.

Scopes put it more colorfully. "You know what a skinflint

the Colonel is. Worries about every penny as if it was his own. He wasn't about to let you wander around playing tourist on Uncle Sam's ticket. 'Fetch me that idiot,' he told me—''

"That's not quite the way I remember it," Banner broke in dryly.

Scopes ignored that. "So off we went. Been wandering around this godforsaken jungle—pardon, ma'am—so long my toes have grown mossy. That's when Banner wasn't scaring me silly in his damned chopper. I'd have found you a lot sooner if they'd given me a *real* pilot."

Banner snorted. "Or if you could read a map."

A.J. broke in. "Pardon me, but—I've wondered for so long about Sister Maria Elena. The nun who was with me. Is she all right?"

Banner glanced over his shoulder at her. He was a long, narrow man with a basketball player's big hands and a bass voice that would have had her choir director salivating. His eyes were the same shade of brown as his skin, and as kind as they were curious. "Just fine, ma'am. Treated and released at the base hospital, they told me. I think she went to a convent in Guatemala."

A load lifted from her heart. "Oh, good," she murmured. "That's wonderful."

"How did you find me?" Michael said. "Especially if Scopes was navigating. I'm surprised you didn't end up in Costa Rica with him handling the map."

"Hey, I can read a map," Scopes protested. "We'd have found you a lot sooner if you hadn't stopped off to do a little sightseeing at a village so small it wasn't *on* the map." He chuckled. "Boise is gonna be so pi—ah, ticked off. He bet me a century he'd find you first."

"He drew a rough section to search," Banner pointed out in his rumbly bass. "Been a lot of fighting by Santo Pedro."

"What's going on?" Michael asked sharply. "Has the government retaken the main road into the north yet?"

"Better than that, boyo." Scopes's voice was gleeful. "*El Jefe* got his butt kicked, big time. Broke his so-called army into little pieces."

A.J. listened with half an ear while they passed on details of the battle—which Banner refused to dignify by that name, saying it had been a pathetic excuse for a fight—and argued about whose fault it was that they hadn't located their lieutenant sooner.

She was amazed they'd found him at all, in several hundred square miles of jungle. They'd guessed Michael would head for the border, and had divided into pairs to search. Scopes and Banner had been quartering their section by chopper, stopping frequently to question the natives when they found a village or settlement. They'd almost missed Cuautepec, but Scopes had seen a flash of light—sunlight reflecting from the orphanage's tin roof, probably—and they'd decided to check it out.

She was thankful. She really was, especially for the news about *El Jefe*. She just wished…A.J. sighed. Her wish list was absurdly long, and lamentably contradictory. She wished Michael's men had found them sooner, before she lost her mind and made love with him. Only she wouldn't give up the memory of their union in that clearing for anything, so she wished they'd come a few minutes later.

She wished—oh, if only she knew what to wish for, she might be able to get somewhere in sorting out the jumble of thoughts and feelings.

She'd made love with him. After all the times she'd assured herself she wouldn't let her attraction take her farther than she could afford to go, she'd let him kiss her—no, she'd welcomed his kiss.

From kissing to lovemaking had been one short, hard fall.

How could she have done it?

She glanced down at their joined hands. There were calluses on his palm. She could barely feel them now, but when he'd drawn that palm along her inner thighs…

Who was she trying to fool? She knew why she'd made love with Michael. She was in love with him, and she'd craved him, pure and simple.

Only she *couldn't* be. How could she love a man she'd only known nine days? Lust might hit that fast, or infatuation, but love didn't work like that.

Though she'd never before experienced anything like the last nine days. Or anyone like the man she'd spent them with.

She thought of him on the trail—the humor in spite of pain, the determination. Then she thought of the way he'd offered her his comb such a short time ago, and tears stung her eyes. She'd said she was a mess. He hadn't argued, had just given her what he could—a comb to untangle her hair. In that second, she'd had a flash of what it might be like to be married to him. He'd tackle leaky toilets and snarled schedules with the same step-by-step determination he used to cross a jungle, she thought.

He was a good man. An incredible man. And she'd hurt him, she was sure of that. Though he hadn't said anything about love…a cramping ache around her heart made her bite her lip. *Be fair,* she told herself. She hadn't exactly encouraged him to speak of love.

Soon, very soon now, they would be flying back to their real lives. The ones they lived in different cities.

Would she ever see him again?

Did she want to? Yes.

No.

Great. She was in love with him, but she wasn't sure she wanted to see him again. What kind of sense did that make?

It was his career that made her so uncertain, she thought. He might be an honorable killer, but still he killed. She was repulsed by his capacity for violence. No, not repulsed…bothered? Upset? Oh, she didn't know what she was. She needed time. Time to figure out what was wrong with her. Time…if he came to see her in San Antonio, maybe…but would he? She'd just turned down his proposal.

Dammit, he'd rushed her. Relationships took time. She couldn't just jump into one the way she might dive into a pool and swim laps. She'd known Dan for nearly a year before they even went out together, and they'd been dating for six months when he proposed.

Dan. A sudden shaft of feelings tore through her—guilt, sorrow, and an odd flutter of panic unlike the hasty fear she'd felt a moment ago, when she thought of never seeing Michael again. This felt as if she'd already lost something, an important piece of her that was gone now, forever gone. But that made no sense. She'd lost Dan more than two years ago, so what—

"I'd offer you a penny for them, but I'm low on cash. Do you give credit?"

She looked up, startled, into Michael's eyes. They'd reached the river, and his men had moved slightly ahead. Scopes was talking on a radio or walkie-talkie of some kind.

"None of my thoughts are worth going a penny in debt for right now."

"Say something stupid, then."

In spite of herself, she chuckled. "What are you trying to do—spoil a good brood?"

"If it takes that expression off your face, yes." He ran his thumb back and forth in her palm. "Why so unhappy? We're going home."

Just that. Just that simple, intimate brush of his thumb on her palm, and she wanted him again. Still. A.J. lowered her eyes, hoping to shield her reaction. "And what happens next?"

"Banner flies you out of here."

She stopped. "But what about you?"

"We don't have the Cobra here—the big helicopter," he explained. "They've been using a recon helicopter because it's smaller, lighter, covers a lot more territory without having to refuel. Sets down in a lot of places the Cobra can't, too. But it's strictly a two-man bird." He chuckled. "One-and-a-half men, according to Scopes. The passenger seat is directly behind the pilot, and it's cramped."

She bit her lip. "And…when I get home?"

"What happens with us, you mean?" He framed her face with both hands, smiling that wicked smile. The one that ought to come with a warning label. "Well, I'll probably propose again."

Her heart leaped—and that horrid flutter of panic came back. She swallowed. "Before we go any further, there's something I need to know."

He drew his hands down to her shoulders. "Okay. Shoot."

"What…" She couldn't say it. Couldn't come out and ask what he felt about her. "Why do you want to marry me?"

"At last I get a chance to speak my piece." His thumbs circled under her jaw, lightly, as if he couldn't just touch. He had to savor. "I had this great proposal all worked up. Forgot the whole thing when you seduced me."

"Me?" She tried to look indignant, but a smile slipped out. "I didn't—"

"Hey, Mick." Scopes was headed back toward them, his expression for once serious. "Just heard from Boise. The Colonel's had him and Smiley tracking the largest splinter that's left of *El Jefe*'s forces—some of the real bad asses. His signal was breaking up pretty bad, but I think I got the gist of it."

Michael frowned. "And?"

"They're headed this way, and they're not happy campers. Damned maniacs, sounds like." He shook his head, looking sour. "If there's anything I hate, it's a bunch of damned wannabes doing the rape-and-pillage thing. Gives us real soldiers a bad name."

Michael had gone very still. "How far away are they?"

"They just hit a village about twenty miles away, horizontally. Not that anything is horizontal around here. It didn't have much for them to loot, which made 'em—" He glanced at A.J. and cleared his throat. "Anyway, if the natives of this flyspot have someplace they can hide out awhile, they might want to head there. Quick.''

Choices and chances. Life was full of both, Michael thought as he left the *tepec*'s hut, his stride long and impatient. But sometimes the only choices were between the bad and the unbearable. And all too often, the chances only came once.

It looked as if his chance with Alyssa had already passed.

All around him, people hurried—women calling instructions to children, children chasing livestock into the jungle. Women and children and a few—a very few—men, most of them over fifty.

El Jefe's men were coming—without *El Jefe*.

As soon as they'd returned to the village, Michael had sent Banner up in the copter, high enough that the mountains wouldn't interfere with the radio reception. He'd gotten a more complete report on the portion of the broken rebel army that was headed this way.

Bad asses indeed. About forty men who had taken too large a part in some of the worst of *El Jefe*'s activities, men who couldn't go home again. Men with nothing to lose—not even their humanity. Considering what they'd done at the last village they'd encountered, that was already lost.

He'd told Señor Pasquez and the village elders. They'd chosen to evacuate, to head for the plantation where some of their men worked. The plantation had guards and weapons. More important, it was foreign-owned so the government would be forced to send troops if there was trouble. San Christóbal couldn't afford to lose foreign investors.

But it would take the villagers two days to get there, and there was a good chance the plantation was the renegades' goal, too. It was the only place between here and the border worth looting.

Michael spotted his quarry—Andrew Scopes's rangy figure, bent to help an old woman adjust the sling holding a sleepy baby on her back. "You've got what you'll need?" he asked tersely when he reached the sergeant.

"I'm good to go. You?"

"I will be once I've talked to Banner. He's by the copter?"

Scopes nodded. His shrewd blue eyes studied Michael. "You still intend to send the copter back to the base?"

"Yes." For several reasons—some of them tactical, one not. Michael felt another wave of doubt hit, tinged by guilt. "Are you sure—"

"If you ask me again, I'm gonna be offended." Scopes spat to one side. "Fine opinion of me you seem to have."

Michael didn't argue. There wasn't time. "I'll meet you at the head of the trail, then, in fifteen minutes."

Scopes glanced around. "Think they'll be ready to go that quick?"

"They have to be," Michael said grimly. "The renegades are less than two hours away." He turned away.

The copter waited in a field at the other end of the village. Michael increased his pace to an easy jog. Time was short, but he wasn't leaving without telling Alyssa goodbye.

She was going with Banner. Michael and Scopes were staying with the villagers, who didn't have a hope in hell of making it without them if the renegades headed for the plantation. Their chances weren't great, even with two soldiers guarding their rear. Two armed men against forty-five weren't good odds.

As for Michael's chances…

Choices and chances, he thought again. He couldn't choose any differently than he had. At least she would be safe. Knowing that made his other choices bearable.

Eleven

"**W**hat the hell is this crap you gave Banner about not going with him?" Michael stood in the doorway to the girls' room, hands on hips.

"Sounds like you got my message. Now, please step out of the way or else help me pack." A.J. spoke more calmly than she felt. She looked around, biting her lips. "What am I forgetting?" Something. Undoubtedly she'd forgotten several important things, but there was so little time…

"Alyssa." A pair of hard hands landed on her shoulders, turning her to face him. "Banner is waiting for you at the chopper. There's no time to debate the subject. You're leaving now."

"I'm ready." She hoped she was. "But I'm not going with Banner. I'm going with Sister Andrew, Sister Constancia and the children. They need me."

"No, they don't. They've been taking care of those kids for years without you."

"Michael." A hint of amusement filtered through the pervasive urgency. "It's obvious you've never traveled with children. There are thirteen of them, and Sister Constancia is fifty-seven, Sister Andrew even older. I can help."

"This isn't a blasted car trip to see the Grand Canyon!"

"It's not a forced march with trained infantry, either. My skills will be needed as much as yours will."

"Dammit, you are not—"

"Keep your voice down. You're frightening the children."

The nuns and most of the children were in the main room, packing food. Two of the smallest children had followed A.J. into the girls' bedroom and watched with big, bewildered eyes while she grabbed blankets and clothes and tried to shape them into packs the older children could carry. One— little Rosita—started to cry, more in confusion than real distress.

"There, sweetheart." A.J. stroked the toddler's head but didn't stop to pick her up. There was too much to do, and too little time. She met Michael's eyes. "You're doing what you feel you have to do. So am I."

Michael cursed under his breath. Then he kissed her once, hard. His eyes were bleak. "Forget the rest of the stuff. We're moving out *now*."

Two hours and five minutes after Scopes first told him about the rebel soldiers, Michael had his ragged troop moving down the trail. They'd done well, extraordinarily well, to move as quickly as they had, he thought. Especially since the thirty-some adults were responsible for three times that many babies, children and adolescents.

Manuel had nearly managed to be left behind. He'd been very disappointed when A.J. found him hiding in the big mango tree at the start of the trail.

A smile touched Michael's mouth. Alyssa had been right. This wasn't going to be like any forced march he'd ever been on.

His smile didn't last. They might have pulled off the evacuation faster than he'd expected, but they were still cutting it close. Too close. Soldiers could move a lot faster than the villagers. Even if they amused themselves for a couple of hours by torching huts and killing livestock, they'd still catch up with the villagers before nightfall.

So the bastards had to be slowed down, or diverted entirely.

Fifteen minutes after the last of his charges had vanished around a bend in the trail, Michael uncoiled from his position next to a pine that leaned out over a deeply cut gully, where he'd been watching for any sign of the rebels. He shouldered the CAR 16 that Banner had left with him and moved a little farther up the trail.

"How's it coming?" he asked Scopes.

"She's ready," the smaller man said, straightening. "Didn't have time to put her deep, but she'll do the trick. Bring down plenty of dirt."

Scopes always referred to explosives as female, for what he claimed were obvious reasons. "We don't want half the mountain falling on the trail," Michael warned. "The villagers will need to be able to clear it when they come back."

Scopes gave him a wounded look.

"All right, all right. You know what you're doing." Michael looked at the setup one last time. On one side of the trail was a small chasm crammed to the top with trees, saplings and brush. It would take many hours of machete work to hack a path through that. On the other side was a rough, steep hillside that climbed into a stubby peak—even more impassable.

Scopes had dug into the loose dirt where the slope was steepest, setting a charge that should take a bite out of the mountain. What was up would come down. And cover the trail.

If they were lucky, the renegade soldiers would never know how much trouble he'd gone to on their behalf. If their goal was to make straight for the border, they'd use the trail to the west of the village and never see the avalanche Scopes dumped on this one.

Michael believed in luck. He courted it. He didn't rely on it.

Scopes was laying the fuse. "Don't make it too short," Michael said. "I know you like to watch your babies go off, but I'd like fifteen minutes between us and whatever goes flying."

Scopes sighed and reeled out a little more fuse. "You got it."

A minute later they were moving up the winding trail, the fuse burning merrily behind them. They didn't run, just kept a good, steady pace, walking quickly enough to catch up with the villagers.

"I still think you shoulda let Banner do a few fly-bys," Scopes said. "Let him open up the guns on his bird a few times, and those sons of bitches would think twice about making trouble."

"Try to remember that we're assisting in the peaceful evacuation of civilians—a deviation from our original orders, but one that doesn't put egg on Uncle Sam's face. Strafing a bunch of former soldiers on the losing side of a war is another story."

Scopes's assessment of those "former soldiers" was obscene, and one Michael agreed with. "Think the Colonel will let Banner bring back the big bird?"

"I heard a rumor once that the Colonel does have a heart."

Scopes snorted. "Can't believe everything you hear. But those kids…"

Michael nodded. However much trouble he and Scopes might be in for expanding on their orders so drastically, they could still hope the Colonel would agree to provide nonaggressive emergency backup—for the children. The Cobra was big enough to lift most of them if things went south—and if it got here in time. "He's going to be plenty unhappy with you and me, though."

"Yeah, yeah. You gave me the pitch already. So maybe I lose my stripes. Wouldn't be the first time. I'll get 'em back." He glanced at Michael. "Colonel's gonna come down harder on you than me, anyway."

"That's the price I pay for getting to wear those pretty silver bars on my dress blues."

"I know how much you like looking pretty for the ladies. Speaking of which…" He cleared his throat. "You were putting out some pretty strong signals about the Reverend."

"I knew you could take a hint." Since Scopes's idea of subtlety meant substituting PG-rated equivalents for the obscene part of his vocabulary, Michael's "hint" had consisted of threatening to tie Scopes's tongue around his throat if he gave A.J. a hard time.

"Yeah, well…I just wondered if you and she were, like, a permanent thing."

"Thinking of trying your luck?"

"No, no, nothing like that. Though she is a looker. I just never saw you get all touchy about a woman before."

"I plan to marry her."

Shock held the other man silent for a few minutes. "You set the date?"

"Not yet. She turned me down."

"Well, hell."

"Yeah." Michael stopped, looking back. "Shouldn't the charge have gone off by now?"

"Pretty quick. So, she got someone waiting back home for her or something?"

Michael supposed he should be flattered that Scopes thought the only reason a woman would turn him down was a previous involvement. "No, she's a widow whose husband was shot to death in front of her. She's got a problem with guns." There was a good chance that she'd see him use his again, soon. If Scopes's boom didn't close the trail off as thoroughly as they were hoping… Michael's lips tightened. "How long was that fuse?"

Scopes grinned. "Hey, I'm good, Mick. Watch this. Five, four, three…"

The ground walked. Sound slapped his ears. On the other side of the mountain, dust rose into the air.

"No, no, *niñita,* that wasn't devils after us," A.J. bent to comfort the little girl who'd run to her, screaming. "Remember? Señor West told us how his big boom would make the earth shake."

The little girl sniffed and nodded.

Several other children had crowded close to A.J. and Sister Andrew. Most were looking back along the trail, where the dust thrown up by the explosion was slowly settling, falling out of sight behind the mountain's shoulder.

"I wish I could have seen it," Manuel said sadly.

She suppressed a grin. The boy had certainly tried. Good thing Sister Andrew had insisted on a head count. "Then maybe it would have been you flying up in the air, not just some dirt." She straightened. "Come on. Let's keep moving."

The villagers directly ahead had stopped, too, exclaiming over the explosion. Gradually, those in front started moving again, and A.J. and the children could, too. They were among the last in the long, winding stream of people.

There were only two donkeys. An old man with a bad leg rode on one up near the head of the caravan. The other donkey dragged a travois carrying a woman too ill to walk. On that animal's back were strapped Señor Pasquez's precious record books; as the *tepec,* he acted as a sort of justice of the peace and county clerk combined. Births, deaths, marriages—all became official when they were recorded in his books.

Everyone else walked at the pace of the slowest among them.

Trees grew right up to the edge of the left side of the trail, a crowded vertical weave of trunk and limb. To the right was a slope so rocky and lacking in soil that it was nearly bare, a rare emptiness in the forest that allowed a trail to grow instead of trees. On that side, sunshine shone down on rocks and small, tough plants, including a scattering of the tiny blue-white flowers she'd seen in the clearing that morning.

A.J.'s heart stumbled when she thought of the clearing and Michael and what had happened between them. She wanted to climb that rocky slope and bathe her head in the sunshine. She wanted to stop right here and wait for Michael to catch up because her heart was already hungry for the sight of him. And she wanted to hide from him.

Most of all, she thought wryly, she wanted to make her mind stop racing around and around and biting itself from behind.

Sister Andrew, who walked just behind, must have noticed her agitation. "There is no point in rushing the first part of our journey," the old nun said kindly, using English. "It would only tire some too much to continue later."

"My mind knows that, but my feet keep wanting to hurry."

"Mmm. You are afraid of the soldiers?"

"Aren't you?"

"Time enough for fear if I see them coming. Right now, there's just the sunshine, the children, the way my bunion aches." Her eyes were merry in their nest of wrinkles. "When you get to be my age, you have to conserve your energy. Borrowing troubles before they appear tires a person."

"I suppose so, but I don't know how to stop. My mind's doing the hamster thing—you know, circling round and round the same thoughts, going nowhere."

The sister studied her face a moment. "Thoughts of the soldiers?"

"Not entirely." A.J. hesitated. She was sorely in need of counsel, but didn't know how to bring the subject up. "Sister...you know that Michael isn't really my *novio?*"

She chuckled. "If there is one thing that can chase thoughts of many dangerous men from a woman's mind, it is one particular man. Yes, I'd guessed you two weren't engaged. But I think you have feelings for him."

"I'm in love with him." Saying the words out loud, she discovered, was a relief. "But…"

"Why do we always find 'buts' to stick on love?" She shook her head. "Never mind. I interrupt too much. Go on."

"I don't know. There's this great, big 'but' hanging over me like a dark cloud, but I don't know what it is. He asked me to marry him," she confessed in a low voice. "I said no. I thought it was his…well, his violence that bothered me, but—"

"His what?" The sister rolled her eyes like a teenager. "Oh, I expected better of you. No, no, don't color up. Old women have silly expectations."

"I don't think Michael is like the soldiers we're escaping, or anything like that. I just…" She bit her lip. "I saw him shoot a man—a man who was going to kill us. He did what he had to do. I know that, only I can't seem to get that image out of my head." *The man falling, dying…*

"Hmm." They walked on in silence for a minute before the sister continued. "I am used to dealing with children, so forgive me if I shape my advice into a silly game. I want you to imagine something for me. Imagine that you have a gun in your hands right now—feel the weight of it, the cold metal. Now, what if one of those soldiers came out from behind that tree—oh! Right there!" She pointed, acting out alarm so realistically that A.J. jolted and looked. "And he has a gun. He's pointing it at little Manuel. No—at me. What do you do?"

"I—I guess I'd point my gun at him, tell him to stop."

"And if he didn't? If you saw that he was going to kill someone, and the only way you could stop him would be to shoot him?"

A.J. swallowed. The sister's game didn't feel silly at all. "I'd shoot."

"You would accept that stain in order to prevent another evil. But what if you didn't see him before he shot? What if he killed me, left me bleeding at your feet—but then you pointed your gun at him. It's a much bigger gun, and he is afraid. He drops his gun and surrenders. What do you do? Do you still shoot him?"

"I…" A.J. took a shaky breath. *Gunfire—harsh, unbearably loud. Blood. Dan's blood, splattering her, the wall, the floor…and rage.* Blind, consuming rage. "Oh, God. Dear God."

"What is it, child?"

"My husband. Two years ago, he was shot. Killed. I watched him—saw him fall. His blood…I think, if I'd had a gun then, when that man shot him, I might have—I would have—"

The nun stopped and put her arm around A.J., turning them both gently away from the children. "My dear, I'm so sorry. When I played my little game, I had no idea you had such horrors in your memory."

"It's…all right. I just…" Only then did A.J. realize she was crying. "I didn't know. I never let myself think—" She hiccupped. "Think about it. I didn't want to know. I—oh, I hate to cry."

"We hate to have splinters removed, too, but we're the better for it." Callused fingers wiped the tears gently from Alyssa's cheek. "You are all right now?"

She nodded, unable to speak. It was so obvious now. She wasn't repulsed by Michael's violence. She was repulsed by the echo it set up in her, the festering fear that she was capable of much worse than what he'd done. That she might be able to kill—not in defense, but out of the blind need to strike back.

She hadn't wanted to see her own ugliness, hadn't wanted to taste again the desperate hate that had exploded in her when Dan was killed. Now that she had...she drew a shaky breath. "I'm okay. I'm better." Wobbly, with a sourness in the pit of her stomach, but better for having faced what she'd tried so hard not to know. "I need to think about...all this."

The nun smiled. "Children give us little opportunity for reflection, I'm afraid, but there are moments between wiping noses and—ah, look. Here comes your young man."

So he was. Michael and his sergeant had rounded the nearest curve in the trail and were less then fifteen feet away.

He moved so beautifully, with the easy, ground-eating pace of a man who refuses to waste energy he would need later. A man with the strength and stamina to keep going long after others had flagged or failed. Her heart swelled at the sight of him.

He was frowning. "What's wrong?"

Belatedly she realized her face must show the effects of her tears. Well, no point in pretending her cheeks weren't wet. She dried them unselfconsciously. "Nothing. We heard the explosion. Did it go okay?"

"The lieutenant wouldn't let me stay to watch," Scopes said sadly.

Michael's frown didn't waver. "The rest of you had better catch up with the others. Alyssa and I will be along in a minute." Then he waited, obviously expecting to be obeyed.

He was. A.J. tried to ignore Scopes's smirk as he and the sister moved on ahead. "You do the 'officer in charge' thing very well," she said.

"You should see me when I have a whole troop to order around instead of a few dozen women and children. Now— tell me what's wrong."

"I'm okay. Really," she insisted. "Sister Andrew was just...removing a splinter."

"If you've got an open wound—"

She smiled. "A spiritual splinter. I'll tell you about it later." This wasn't the time. She needed to think, to absorb and understand what she'd learned. And he didn't need his attention divided right now. Still... "I'm glad to see you," she said, and impulsively stretched up to place a soft kiss on his mouth.

That startled him—but surprise didn't keep him from sliding an arm around her waist, drawing her closer and returning her kiss. When he lifted his head, pleasure had replaced surprise in his eyes—a deep pleasure, which hinted at more than the simple flare of desire.

Though that was there, too. "I'm glad to see you, too." He brushed her lips lightly one more time, then slid his hand down to grasp her hand. "Come on. I'm on duty. We'd better catch up with the others."

She liked, very much, knowing she could make him smile that way. They started walking together, and it felt rather like their first days together. And very different. "Good idea. Who knows what Manuel has decided to investigate?"

"Hmm. Think I should warn Scopes to make sure Manuel doesn't get into his pockets? He keeps a different set of goodies on hand than I do—fuses, wire, explosive caps."

Her eyes widened in alarm. "Michael, you don't think—"

"Hey, I'm just kidding." He frowned. "Mostly kidding."

"He was really fascinated by the explosion."

They exchanged a glance and, in unspoken agreement, walked faster.

Twelve

For the next couple of hours, Michael coursed up and down his ragged column like a sheepdog with a big, unruly flock, his walking stick in his left hand, his CAR 16 slung over his shoulder. And fought the desire to drag Alyssa off into the bushes and take her, hard and fast.

The degree of his desire—and his frustration—baffled him. Sure, danger could be an aphrodisiac, but there wasn't much to do right now but walk and wait, with none of the adrenaline-drenched rush of action. Yet he went right on wanting her with a deep, dragging ache.

Something had changed.

He couldn't put his finger on what was different. He just knew something was. The change was there in the way she smiled at him every time he passed her while checking out the rear. It had been there in her kiss.

Her kiss. He shook his head slightly, trying to clear it.

He'd just conferred with Pasquez again. The *tepec* assured him his people could keep up this pace—such as it was.

They'd discussed the route in more detail. They should reach a river in an hour or so, and could make good time once they forded it; the northern bank was rocky and bare for the most part. They'd continue along the river for about three miles before the trail parted ways with the water, winding up to a narrow pass. The climb there was steep, and the pass was going to be one hell of a bottleneck, but there was a small meadow on the other side where the villagers could camp…while Michael and Scopes took positions at the pass.

Michael was headed for the rear now, hoping Scopes had returned. As expected, they'd lost radio contact with Boise and Smiley, so Michael had sent his sergeant to reconnoiter their back trail, see if there were any signs of followers. There shouldn't be. Not yet. It ought to take the renegades at least half a day to either dig out the trail or hack a new one through the gully—but Michael didn't like depending on what *ought* to be true.

He rounded a curve in the path, working his way upstream through the flow of people, and saw Scopes moving toward him. Scopes saw him and gave a quick hand signal—all clear. Michael breathed a little easier.

The two of them moved as far to the side as possible, letting the others flow around them. "No sign of 'em," Scopes said.

"Good." Michael took out his map and brought Scopes up to date on their route. "We have to make that pass before nightfall." Michael refolded the map. "There's a steep drop on one side."

"Couldn't take it in the dark, then. Not with the kids."

"The renegades could. If they're feeling hasty."

They exchanged a glance. "Guess we'll be seeing some night duty, then."

"Yeah." He shifted the strap of the CAR 16. "I'm going to the rear, make sure we don't have any stragglers."

The sergeant chuckled. "Is that what you're doing? And here I thought you wanted to see A.J."

Michael's brows lifted. "Her name's Alyssa."

"She said to call her A.J. Real nice woman, even if she is a preacher," he said tolerantly. "Got a pair of legs on her that won't quit, doesn't she?"

Michael sighed. "What did you say to her?"

"Don't get all bent out of shape. I know how to be respectful. You go on back and tell her hi, and if you'll take my advice—"

"I don't want your advice."

"Sweet talk her off into the bushes. You're wound about as tight as a man can get without snapping something, and nothing relaxes a man like a good—" The look on Michael's face must have been hint enough for once, because he stopped, frowned, then went on testily, "I wasn't being disrespectful. She could probably use—ah, a little relaxation, too. She smiled real cheery and all, but she's bound to be getting frazzled, the way those kids hang all over her."

Michael started to snap something about minding his own business—then closed his mouth. Scopes was right about one thing. He was wound tight. Normally he wouldn't get bent out of shape by his sergeant's decidedly casual notions of what constituted respect. "After I see Alyssa, I'll check the back trail."

"Sure thing. Look, if you're too shy to take her off in the bushes, just drop back behind the rest. Hold her hand and look at each other all moony-eyed awhile." He winked. "Ain't as good as the other, but it might help."

He sighed. "You've got the column for now, Sergeant."

Scopes tossed him a cocky salute. "You say hi to your lady for me. And don't hurry back."

Michael wished, as he made his way past babies being carried, older children bickering or playing, young women and older women, that Scopes had kept his mouth shut for once. Taking Alyssa—into the bushes, or anywhere else—was on his mind too much already.

Then he rounded a curve in the trail and saw her. Scopes

had been right. She was a child-magnet. A toddler was in her arms; Manuel walked alongside her, no doubt peppering her with questions, while two older girls followed, obviously including her in their conversation.

Then she looked up and saw him, and her face lit up. And his focus narrowed to her. Only her.

When he joined her, though, the children were too delighted with the novelty of his presence to let him talk to Alyssa. He took the toddler from Alyssa to give her arms a rest, dissolved the two girls in giggles with a couple of compliments, and patiently explained to Manuel why some things burned and others exploded when touched by fire.

His eyes met Alyssa's. Some things, he thought, could do both—burn and explode, over and over again. Maybe Scopes had been right about two things. He wanted time with her alone. Not long. A few minutes...what could it hurt? "Think the sisters could handle the kids for a few minutes?" he asked causally in Spanish. "I'd like to talk to you."

"Well..." She glanced behind her.

Sister Constancia was nearest; she made a shooing motion, smiling. "I'll take the little one for a while," she said, and Michael transferred the sleepy toddler to the nun's soft, strong arms.

Then he took Alyssa's hand and started walking back down the trail, away from the others.

"Is something wrong?" she asked, her forehead creasing.

"No. I just wanted to be with you."

"Oh." That pleased her. Color rose in her cheeks and her eyes glowed. She pushed her hair behind her ear. "How's your leg holding up? It's still got a hole in it."

"Not such a big hole." In truth, it ached, but the muscle hadn't been damaged as badly as he'd feared. It had been infection rather than the wound itself that had crippled him; with that cleared up, he had almost normal use of the leg again. "How are you holding up? If you've been carrying that little girl for long, your arms must be tired."

She chuckled. "Think cooked spaghetti, and you'll have the idea. I thought I was in good shape until recently, you know."

"You are." He stopped. They'd rounded a curve in the trail, and the others were out of sight. "In damned good shape, I mean."

She slid him a teasing glance. "So are you."

The invitation he read in that glance couldn't be there. Not now, not here. But his unruly body didn't care about the time and place. *Down, boy.* He took her other hand to keep himself from grabbing anything he shouldn't. "You seem…different. Almost lighthearted." Which was a damned silly thing to say, considering their circumstances.

"I do feel lighter. I told you that Sister Andrew removed a spiritual splinter…that's part of it. Then, too, I've been trying to follow her advice about living in the moment, not borrowing trouble." She grimaced. "Easier said than done, of course. Especially…" She paused. Her chin came up a fraction, and she finished calmly, "Especially when the man I love has a habit of getting himself shot while protecting everyone but himself."

There was a roaring in his ears. Weakness in his legs. A dippy, dizzy swirling in his mind, and a terrible hunger in his gut. "Alyssa?" He groped for sense, or at least for words, but came up empty. Except for her name. "Alyssa."

Her fingers tightened on his. She looked a little pale, but met his eyes steadily. "You must have guessed. After the way I gave myself to you, you must have guessed."

"I…" He wanted to hear her say the words, say them directly to him. He needed that—but how could he tell her? How could he ask, just come out and ask, if she was sure—if she really *loved* him—he groaned, grabbed her face in both hands, and kissed her.

She opened to him. Molded her body up against his in instant welcome, and all he could think was *more*. He needed more, needed all of her. He ran his hands over her, back to waist, hips to buttocks, and groaned.

A.J. had never felt anything like the storm of need that raged inside Michael, spilling over onto her with every sweep of his hands. Where had this come from, this raw, shaking power? Had she truly loosed it by letting him know she was in love with him? Now, drawn into the center of the storm with him, she could only gasp for air, and shudder in reaction when his fingers dug into her hips and he ground himself against her.

He tore his mouth away. "I need...let me have you, Alyssa." His mouth quested over her face, her throat, somewhere between plea and demand in its urgency. "Will you let me?"

He said "let me." She heard "love me." Silently she gave—comfort, with the sweep of her hands along his back. Permission, with the press of her lips. And love, with everything in her.

He shuddered. Went still, as if struggling to contain the storm—but it broke, crashing over them both.

His hands raced over her, finding buttons, snaps. His mouth followed. By the time he backed her around a tree and up against its smooth bark, her shirt hung open and her breasts were wet from his mouth. And she was on fire.

Her own hands trembled, then tore at the stiff, stubborn button above his zipper. He cupped her with one hand, kissing her, thrusting his tongue deep in taunting mimicry of what they wanted. Needed. The low sound that came from her throat sounded suspiciously like a growl. He jerked her zipper down.

His gun slid from his shoulder, thumping against her arm. He froze.

The gun didn't matter, not the way it had before. Not the way she'd made him think it mattered. She had to be sure he knew, so she took the strap and eased it off his arm herself, her eyes meeting his.

Something wild surged in his eyes. Quickly he set the

weapon on the ground, then held her face in both hands, and kissed her.

The buttonhole on his pants finally gave up its button, but she couldn't get to his zipper—he was dragging her pants and panties down. Her heart pounded, her blood rushed. *Now,* it beat. Now, now, now. Cloth bunched awkwardly at her feet. *Shoes,* she thought—stupid, blasted, in-the-way shoes—but he solved the problem by jerking the material over one shoe, and off that leg.

She tugged down his zipper, took him into her hands. He groaned, his neck going rigid, then slid his hands beneath her bottom, lifting her. His easy strength sent another tremor of hunger through her. The trunk was hard and round against her back. Her bare leg came up automatically, hooking itself around him as he lifted and positioned her—and thrust inside.

The suddenness jolted her. "Michael?" She scattered kisses over his face, his neck, whatever she could reach, and with her hands tried to slow him, to soothe them both.

He groaned and began to move. Quick, hard thrusts—but the position didn't let him come deeply enough inside. She moaned in frustration, trying to shift, to find a way for him to penetrate deeper. Already his thrusts were quickening, the tempo building, and she was ready, so ready—but couldn't get the pressure *there,* where she needed it. She hung on the very edge of explosion—then his hands moved, shifting to her thighs, opening her legs more fully, and when he slammed against her this time, it was right. Perfect.

She cried out, her body bucking with the force of the climax. He thrust one more time, his head thrown back, and she felt the hot spurt of him deep inside. The world went blank.

Birdsong. That was the first thing she noticed in the slow, languid return of sense. Then the deep, shuddering breath he drew as they sank, together, to the earth, stopping when he reached his knees, so that she straddled his lap. His head dropped forward, his forehead resting on her shoulder. His chest heaved as if he'd just finished a marathon.

She leaned her head against his. How silly they must look, she thought, smiling. Her pants and panties were still bunched up around one ankle; his were around his knees. Passion was such an undignified business, glorious and messy.

She stroked his hair, cherishing him, feeling a deep calm descend now that the storm had passed. He'd needed her so badly, and that need had taken the shape of passion. But it wasn't only her body he'd needed. She was sure of it.

She spoke very softly. "I love you."

He wrapped his arms around her and held on tight. And said nothing at all.

He'd taken her up against a tree. A tree, for Pete's sake. Michael couldn't believe he'd dragged her off the trail and taken her up against a tree.

God, it had been wonderful. He was grinning as he tucked in his shirt and zipped his pants. He draped an arm over her shoulder, watching with interest as she fastened her pants, then pulled her shirt together. "Need any help with those buttons?"

"What buttons?" she muttered, head down as she fastened her shirt "You popped half of them off."

"Uh-oh." He ought to regret that. He should at least make an effort to stop grinning like a fool.

She slid him a reproachful glance. "Everyone is going to guess what happened to my buttons."

"Hmm." Since he couldn't think of anything reasonable to say, he opted for silence.

She loved him. It was still sinking in. Of course, she still hadn't said she was going to marry him—but if she loved him, surely that would be the next step.

It took only a couple of steps to be back on the trail. He shook his head, amazed all over again at himself. At least they were well behind the others. No one would have seen or heard...but there were those buttons. The missing ones.

For some reason that made him grin again. Primitive and

base as it might be, he liked the idea of everyone knowing she was his. He glanced at her, his arm tightening slightly on her shoulders.

Her eyes were heavy-lidded, nearly closed. Compunction struck him. "Tired?"

"Shh. I'm enjoying a bath fantasy. It involves a deep, deep tub filled to the brim with hot water and bubbles. Lots and lots of bubbles."

"I wish I could give you that bath, and the time and safety to enjoy it." He wanted to give her everything she wanted, everything she needed. And had so little to offer…

"Oh, the fantasy will do for now." But her eyes opened, smiling with amusement into his. "At least my fantasies are harmless. Manuel has started fantasizing about explosions."

His brows drew down. "Is it fantasy, or trauma?"

She chuckled. "Oh, fantasy in this case, I'm sure. He's so fascinated by explosives that he thinks every cloud of dust he sees is another of your big booms."

Her words settled uneasily in his mind. "Every cloud of dust…Alyssa. When did he see another cloud of dust?"

"I guess it was about thirty minutes ago. Not long before you joined me, actually. That's what he was telling me about. I was trying to convince him it couldn't have been another explosion he'd seen, since you'd only set off that one, but he…what is it?"

Half an hour ago, Scopes would have been on his way back, having nearly caught up with the "column" once more. Michael himself would have just left Pasquez about then. He hadn't seen any telltale rise of dust, but the terrain could have hidden it. "Dammit to hell! I didn't think of it. Not once did it occur to me."

"What? Michael, what is it?"

"They could have had explosives, too. The renegades."

He questioned Manuel, and the others who had been in about the same location at the time. Two others—a ten-year-old girl and an older woman—reported seeing a sudden, dirty

haze rise into the air over the shoulder of the mountain. He
hurried to find Scopes.

His sergeant greeted him with a grin. He was chewing on
a twig—an old campaigner's trick to keep the mouth from
drying out when you couldn't stop to drink. "Hey, you don't
look relaxed. Didn't you—" He cut himself off, his tone
changing completely. "What's up, Mick?"

"If the bastards behind us tried to clear the trail using
explosives, would we have heard the blast?"

His teeth clamped down suddenly on the twig, snapping it
in two. He spat out the piece in his mouth. "Depends on
how far away we were, whether they buried the charges, how
deep, what they used."

"Half an hour ago, Manuel and a couple of others saw
dirt rise in the air back toward the village."

"Hell."

That about summed it up.

They reached the river quickly, urgency lending energy to
even the oldest and youngest among them. The children
didn't understand what was wrong, but they knew their mothers were frightened and kept up the newly quickened pace
for the next hour.

But inevitably, some began to flag, and the pace slowed.
Michael tried to get Pasquez to speak to his people, persuade
them they *had* to hurry, especially here where the going was
relatively easy. But this time the old man set his jaw stub-
bornly. "We don't know those devil men are on this trail. A
cloud of dust—what does that mean? Anything. Nothing.
You are young," he said, and sighed. "Young and impatient.
Old legs cannot keep up with yours. The worst of the trail is
still ahead, when we climb up to the pass. The little ones and
the old ones like me must save our strength for that."

Michael had to bow to the old man's greater knowledge
of his own resources. Logic said the *tepec* could be right
about the dust cloud, too—but Michael's instincts were shrill-
ing.

He'd cursed himself once, briefly, for having sent the helicopter off. If he'd kept it near, he could at least have stayed in radio contact with Boise, known for sure what was happening back at the village. He'd cursed himself, too, for not having considered the possibility the rebels might have explosives, but not for long. It was a waste of time and energy to indulge in regrets. And realistically, he'd had no reason to think a bunch of ragtag rebels might have explosives. His sergeant might never leave home without them, but Scopes was the exception to a number of rules.

He could only hope the rebels didn't have anyone as knowledgeable as Scopes. A poorly planned blast could have made matters worse instead of better. Otherwise…well, at least he had some experts at praying on his side.

Three of those experts were just ahead of him. Alyssa looked relaxed. She was holding little Rosita again, talking and smiling with three boys. Every now and then she glanced over her shoulder to say something to one of the nuns, who walking slightly behind her.

And every time she did, her gaze strayed farther back. Checking out the trail behind them.

She looked up as he approached, her lips curving in a smile much too saucy for a minister. "Hi there, soldier."

"Hi, babe. Got a minute for a lonely man in uniform?"

She chuckled. One of the boys grabbed Michael's hand, asking to be carried. He looked tired and fretful, poor kid. Michael lifted the youngster, tucking him on his hip the way he'd seen the women do. The little boy made a surprisingly warm and comfortable burden.

What would it be like to have a child of his own?

Quickly he shut the thought off. Until they got through this, he couldn't afford to think about the future. The odds were against him having one.

"I saw you looking over your shoulder," he said quietly to Alyssa, using English so the children wouldn't understand. "Don't worry. No one will get past Scopes without us knowing about it."

He'd sent Scopes behind to play rear guard. It was a position he would rather have taken himself, but his sergeant's pithy comments about the weakness in Michael leg having seeped into his head had made him agree that Scopes was more fit for that duty.

Alyssa shifted Rosita. The little girl had fallen asleep, and her cheek was damp and sweaty where it had been cushioned by Alyssa's breasts.

His burden, too, was drowsy, laying his head on Michael's shoulder. He really ought to put the boy down. He needed to keep his arms free…in a minute he would, he promised himself. There was a surprising comfort in the small burden.

"How far back do you think they are?" she asked, low-voiced.

"Maybe still at the village."

"Don't coddle me."

It had been a pretty feeble effort, but dammit, there was so little he could do for her. "We can't know for sure. It depends on how well their blast cleared the trail and how much of a hurry they're in. We've been making about two miles an hour. Chances are they'll make three miles an hour. Could be more," he admitted. "If they have some reason to hurry."

"And how far do we still have to go?"

"The pass is only about four miles from here…horizontally. Unfortunately, a lot of that distance is up a steep slope. Pasquez says we should reach it around five."

She was silent. He figured she was doing the math. Five o'clock might be too late. "They have no reason to hurt us," she said at last. "If their goal is the plantation and they're in a hurry, messing with us would just slow them down, make them waste ammunition."

He nodded. He could at least give her that hope—and it wasn't unreasonable, given what she didn't know about what had happened at the other village. And wasn't going to know, if he had anything to say about it.

Nausea touched Michael's gut. It wasn't an unfamiliar

EILEEN WILKS   163

feeling, before battle or after one. Death was never pretty. But the way some of those people had died…his arm tightened on the small, drowsy boy he held.

"Michael?" She touched his arm. "You okay?"

He shook himself mentally. "I was having a little tactical chat with myself. Nothing important."

"I've got some tactics to suggest, if we ever make it to a bed."

She made him smile—which was just what she'd had in mind, he could tell. Her own smile widened, her gaze playing come-hither with his. So he flirted back and walked a little farther with the young boy in his arms, stealing these few moments. Finally, though, he had to bend and put the boy down. *"Lo siento,"* he murmured at the boy's protest.

He straightened. "I have to keep my arms free. And I really should drop back. The rear guard is supposed to march at the rear, not wander along chatting."

She glanced at the gun slung on his back and nodded. No protests. No begging him to be careful. Whatever fear she felt, she kept to herself.

Gallant. That was the word for her. "Have I told you that you're a lot like one of my men? Only prettier, of course. And a helluva lot sexier."

She pushed her tangled hair behind her ear and grimaced. "You aren't picky, are you, Lieutenant?"

"Yes, I am," he said softly, drawing a fingertip along her cheek. He would make sure she made it home to savor that bubble bath she'd fantasized about, and sleep safely in her bed. Even if he wasn't there to share it with her. "Very picky. About some things."

Thirteen

She'd thought she was tired before. Three hours later, A.J. knew the full meaning of the word. She was hot, dirty, sweaty—and sticky between her thighs from that glorious, hasty coupling against a tree.

The thought of it made her smile, but her smile faded quickly. He hadn't said he loved her, but he'd made it clear he needed her, that she was special to him. That was enough…wasn't it?

A.J. shifted her arms, adjusting the weight of the child on her back in a futile effort to find a way to ease the strain. She hurt. Back, shoulders, arms—they'd gone from aching to trembling, with occasional sharp, stabbing pains. No surprise. Sister Constancia had taken Rosita from her when they stopped at the river for a short break so A.J. could carry four-year-old Sarita. Sister Andrew was carrying little Carlos. Dimly, that worried A.J.; the grade was steep here, and while the nuns might be used to hard work, they were twice A.J.'s age.

But there wasn't anything she could do about it, so she concentrated on putting one foot in front of the other. Since they'd started climbing, her thighs and calves had joined the mass of aches that made up her body. She'd be lucky if she could stand upright tomorrow.

Assuming she made it to morning. A.J. glanced over her shoulder and saw nothing—nothing except the sisters, some of the older children, and green. That all-pervasive, choking green. When she faced forward again she saw more green, along with the broad back of Señora Valenzuela, who had come to the rear to help with the children, bless her.

She didn't see Michael, hadn't seen him since the all-too-brief rest by the river when he'd nearly caused a mutiny by insisting everyone lighten their loads before tackling the steep slope. Since the bulk of what they'd brought was food, and everything else was essential, they'd refused.

Even the nuns had resisted the idea. A.J. had told them quietly that they must trust God to provide—but that He wouldn't provide earthly food for dead children. Sister Andrew had nodded grimly and instructed the older children to abandon their packs so they could carry the little ones.

Michael hadn't wasted time arguing. Instead, he'd started going through their packs, throwing food into the river—and he'd very nearly been attacked by the people he was trying to save. Then Señor Pasquez had joined him, calmly tossing corn, flour, beans and dried fruit onto the ground.

There had been some grumbling, but the example of their *tepec* had encouraged the rest to lighten their packs. Maybe they were glad now, she thought, catching at a tree trunk to help her up a particularly steep bit.

Since then, Michael had dropped farther back, out of sight. Guarding their rear. She was so afraid for him....

Up ahead, someone exclaimed loudly. Others began chattering up, but A.J.'s Spanish wasn't good enough to sort out what had them all excited. "What is it?" she asked Señora Valenzuela. "Can you hear?"

"Shh…" The older woman was badly out of breath, so she stopped, listening. "Ah, praise God! They have reached the pass, those at the front." She beamed at A.J. "We are nearly there, and no devil-men."

The news heartened them all. A.J.'s muscles didn't stop aching, but she found it easier to ignore the pain and press on.

The pass didn't mean safety for Michael. For the rest of them, yes. The pass was narrow. Two men with automatic weapons like those Michael and his sergeant carried could hold off forty men there, if need be.

But eventually, those two men would run out of bullets.

Maybe the rebels wouldn't come. Maybe their blast had gone wrong, and they'd never even started down this trail. And if they did come, surely they'd give up when they saw how lethally the pass was defended, long before Michael ran out of ammunition. Surely the—

Gunfire screamed, shattering her thoughts, making her stumble. *Michael!* Instinctively she started to turn.

"Go!" Sister Andrew's hand at her back wasn't gentle. "Go and go quickly, unless you want to take the baby on your back into the middle of *that!*"

She went. Tears came. She ignored them as well as her screaming heart, scrambling up and up—toward the shouts of the others, the crying of children, a woman's scream of fear. Little Sarita was sobbing with terror in her ear, her legs clenched tight, her arms nearly strangling A.J.

And from behind, gunfire. A sharp burst, several individual shots, another burst—from a different spot?

Scopes is back there, too, she reminded herself. Michael isn't alone. God, please God, keep him safe, keep them both safe….

So suddenly it was like stepping outside from a crowded room, the trees ended. Rocks surrounded her now on both sides, towering high on the left and well above her head on the right. Rocks and dirt slid beneath her feet and she nearly fell, nearly lost the precious burden on her back, catching Sarita at the last moment as she slipped, her poor little legs unable to hold on. She made herself slow down. The breath heaved in her chest.

And she heard it. Disoriented, she couldn't identify the sound, though she'd heard it before—a thrumming, mechanical noise, getting louder by the second. Coming from—the sky?

She looked up. And a great, army-green helicopter flew into view over the tops of the rocks on her left—heading toward the shooting.

Thank you, thank you, thank you!

"Praise God," Sister Andrew murmured, adding more practically, "Keep moving. They're still shooting."

The trail leveled then sauntered down, an easy slope now, widening as it descended. A.J. was still moving quickly, with rocks high on either side, when gunfire erupted again—this time a huge, steady stream of it, coming from the air.

The copter. It must be firing on the rebels. A.J.'s breath hitched. The safety she'd prayed for had come in the shape of death—for some.

The fusillade cut off as suddenly as it had started. Behind her, Sister Andrew was murmuring a prayer in Spanish for the souls of those killed by that hail of bullets.

A.J. drew a deep breath. Death had been dealt back there— for whom? How many? Michael was all right, she told herself. He had to be. And life lay on the other side of these rocks.

The rocks led them into a wide, grassy clearing surrounded by towering pines. People flooded into it ahead of A.J., most of them hurrying, a few pausing to look over their shoulders. Some crossed themselves. Children cried, and everyone clustered together, seeking comfort in closeness.

Confusion reigned. No one knew what to do.

Then the helicopter appeared over the ridge. It hovered just above the clearing, impossibly loud, the wind from its blades huge, alien. People scattered.

As soon as it had a clear space, it set down. The big doors in the side opened and men spilled out. Men in uniform, government troops—but not the U.S. Army. They wore San Christóbal's brown uniforms, and they hit the ground running, heading back toward the pass.

The cavalry had come to the rescue.

Michael had plenty of reason to bless whatever luck or foresight had moved him to send the helicopter back to the base. Banner had gone straight to the Colonel, ready to plead his case. Rather to his astonishment, the Colonel had nodded, told him to get the big Cobra ready—and then he'd gotten on the phone.

Seems the San Christóbal government had urgently requested U.S. support in rounding up the strays from *El Jefe*'s army, but the brass at the top couldn't get a green light from the president. They had, however, been authorized to provide limited technical support.

The Colonel had decided that flying a squad of San Christóbal troops right to the spot where the biggest bunch of rebels were known to be qualified as damned fine technical support. The U.S. had the helicopter and the knowledge of the rebels' whereabouts—that was the technical part. The natives could supply the troops. He'd called his counterpart in the San Christóbal army and set it up.

Michael couldn't help thinking it would have been nice if the troops had arrived about ten minutes earlier.

His bearers nearly tipped him out of the stretcher on the steepest part of the climb to the pass. White-hot fire exploded in his shoulder. As soon as he could breathe again, he started cursing.

"Might want to tone it down," Scopes said from beside him. "Here comes your lady."

Alyssa. He managed to lift his head and saw his sweet,

gentle Alyssa nearly mow down two of the soldiers in front
of his stretcher, getting to him. "Michael! Oh, God, they told
me you'd been shot."

"Hey, I'm okay."

She shuddered. Scopes dropped back before she could
shove him out of the way, too, and the men carrying him
started moving again. He reached for her with his left hand—
his right arm was strapped to his side—and she took it, walking alongside the stretcher.

He let his head fall back as he drank in the sight of her—
huge eyes, dirty cheeks and all. There were smears in the
dirt. She'd been crying. Over him?

"You are *not* okay, damn it," she said fiercely.

"I will be," he said. "But you're a mess."

Her laugh broke in the middle. "Not half as much of a
mess as you are." Her gaze skittered over his shoulder—
which, he knew, did look pretty bad, with all the blood.
"When the soldier who told me you were hurt said you
wanted to see me—he said to *hurry*." She gulped.

Dammit, the idiot had made it sound like he was on his
deathbed. He stretched out his free hand. She took it. "I
asked them to bring you so I could propose again."

She stared at him blankly. "Now?"

The pain in his shoulder was getting worse. Hard to see
how that could be, but it was. "I told them they couldn't
load me on the copter until you married me."

"You what?" She glanced around frantically, as if looking
for someone with the authority to override him. Scopes just
shrugged. So she spoke quickly in Spanish to the men carrying him, telling them not to listen to the idiot on the
stretcher—get him to medical help, and do it *now*.

They looked uncomfortable, and apologized.

"I'm afraid I'm the hero of the moment," Michael said.
"They don't want to go against my wishes."

One of the men, who may have understood some English,
broke in then in Spanish, urging her to do as the *Americano*

teniente wished—and quickly, please, before he lost any more blood.

What little color she'd regained fled from her face.

"I'm not dying," he said as firmly as he could—though it came out more breathless than he would have liked. "I just want to get married. Now." She shook her head, but more because she was dazed than in refusal, he thought. "I'm sorry I don't have a ring, but…" He had to stop and catch his breath when the angle shifted as they moved downhill. That hurt. "I asked the corporal to find someone else, too. If he…good. Here he is."

Señor Pasquez joined them, huffing and puffing. "I hurried," he said, "but I may have to perform the ceremony sitting down. My legs…ah," he sighed, and smiled. "The bride is here. Good."

"You have your book, to make it legal?" Michael asked.

"I will write it in the register," the old man promised. "Now, you are ready?"

Michael looked at her and waited. She'd said she loved him. He was pushing her hard, but he *had* to. When that copter had lifted up over the peak that held the pass, he'd been down, his gun arm useless, with blood running out of him like water from a burst pipe.

Now that he had tomorrow back, he meant to spend it with Alyssa. No waiting around, giving life a chance to throw more surprises at him. There were going to be some problems…a few of them swam dizzily through his mind. He blinked, realizing he'd faded out for a moment.

Hell. Get married first, sort things out later. His hand tightened on hers. "Alyssa?"

She took a deep breath. "Yes. All right. I'm ready."

He made it through the simple ceremony, though toward the end black dots were dancing in front of his eyes. He stayed conscious when they carried him to the helicopter, though his head was swimming by then. Before they lifted his stretcher onto the floor of the copter, though, he very sensibly passed out.

A.J. spent the first two hours after her wedding with sound battering her eardrums. The chopper was very loud, even with the earplugs Banner had handed her.

She couldn't hold Michael's hand because the corpsman attending him and the IV needed to be there. She stayed close, but he wouldn't know that. He didn't regain consciousness. When they landed in Panama at the small base that was their destination, he was still out cold.

Four hours later she was airborne again—this time in a DC-9. This time Michael had a paramedic and a nurse with him, and a lot more equipment—a full hospital bed that clamped to the side and deck of the plane. Oxygen. A heart-rate monitor. And the IV, of course.

He did wake long enough to insist she call his brothers. He gave her his brother Jacob's phone number, then he slipped away again.

The copilot put the call through for her. She sat on the jumpseat behind the pilot, headphones on her ears and lights blinking at her from the bewildering console and listened to a phone ringing in Dallas, Texas.

"Yes?" a female voice said.

"I—is this Ada?" For a moment, curiosity swamped everything else.

"Yes. Do I know you?"

She had to smile at the tart inquiry. "No. I need to speak to Jacob West, please."

"You and everybody else today. All right, just a minute while I fool with these buttons. Don't know why they needed to put in such a fancy phone," the woman muttered. "Here. I think this one will—"

Silence. She was just beginning to think she'd been cut off when a deep, masculine voice said, "West here."

"Jacob West?" Her heart was pounding. She tucked her

fingernails into her palm, squeezing, fighting to stay in control. She had to deliver the news calmly.

"Yes."

"This is Reverend Kelleher." No, that wasn't right, not anymore—but she'd sort all that out later. Right now she had to tell this man… "I'm calling about your brother Michael. He's been…hurt."

His quick, indrawn breath was barely audible. His voice remained cool and steady. "How bad?"

She squeezed her hand tighter, the nails digging in. "His condition is stable. He's being flown to Houston for surgery."

"What kind of surgery? Dammit, tell me what's wrong with him. Now."

In spite of everything she could do, the tears were starting. "He was shot. The bullet did—they say it did very little damage on entry. They think it might have been a ricochet." *Get it said*, she ordered herself. Tears or no tears, she had to say it. "But it lodged near his spine. Th-there's danger of paralysis. That's why they didn't want to operate at the base in Panama. He wants you and Luke to be there."

A.J. stood by the window in the nearly empty surgical waiting room, holding her elbows, keeping her arms locked tight to her body. She had the silly idea that if she let her arms hang loose, something inside her would break free and she'd come apart.

The glass was dark, though she could see lights. Lots and lots of lights. After so many nights when the only light came from the moon and stars, Houston, with its noise, crowds and millions of artificial lights, was a little overwhelming.

But then, she was easily overwhelmed right now.

She'd called her parents shortly after they wheeled Michael into surgery. They'd been overjoyed to hear from her and would be here as soon as possible, but it might be a couple of days. They'd both come down with the flu. Her father had been ready to jump in the car anyway, but A.J. had told him firmly she didn't need their germs, knowing that would work better than any pleas to wait until they were up to traveling.

It was lonely, though, waiting by herself....

"Reverend Kelleher?" a man's voice said.

She turned slowly, still hugging her arms close. "Not exactly."

Four people were crossing the room, heading for her—two men and two women. One man looked like a male model, only better. There was too much charm in those easy, perfect features for such a plastic profession. The other man was taller, older, with a face that might have been shaped by a hatchet, not an artist's chisel. One of the women was older, a tiny, skinny woman in baggy jeans, with a frizz of unlikely yellow hair around her leathery face. The other was flat-out beautiful.

"Try to be exact," the hard-featured man snapped. "The nurse said you were the minister who arrived with my brother Michael. Are you or not?"

"Jacob." The beautiful woman put a hand on his arm.

So this was Michael's oldest brother, the one he thought so much of. He was a big man, well over six feet, broad through the shoulders and chest. "I used to be Reverend Kelleher. I just remarried. I'm not used to my new name yet."

"Pleased to meet you, Reverend," the tiny woman with yellow hair said. "Now, tell us about Michael."

"He's in surgery." And had been for what seemed endless hours, though the clock assured her only fifty minutes had passed.

"Excuse me, but you look about to fall down." The woman with Jacob West put her hand on Alyssa's arm. "Have you been with him all this time?"

She looked polite but puzzled, as if she wasn't sure why Michael might have—or want—a personal chaplain in attendance. It made A.J. smile. "Yes, I was there when—when—my, but you're gorgeous." The inappropriate comment made her flush. "Excuse me. I'm not thinking straight."

The woman laughed. "That's perfectly all right. Oh—we haven't introduced ourselves, have we? I'm Claire, Jacob's fiancée. This good-looking reprobate is Luke, his brother. And this is Ada." Her smile indicated the yellow-haired woman, who was studying A.J. with a frown on her face.

"You do look all done in, honey," Luke said kindly. "Maybe you should sit down awhile."

Honey? A.J. shook her head, trying to clear it. She knew she looked worse than "all done in." Someone—she couldn't remember who—had given her a fatigue shirt to replace the one she'd worn for so long. The one with the missing buttons. Tears stung her eyes. "So you're Luke."

"Yeah." He tipped his head to one side thoughtfully. "You're not here as a minister, are—"

"I am going to have to sit down," a soft, breathy voice said. "I just can't stand hospitals. Never could. The energy here is terribly distressin'—all those sick people."

Jacob turned, frowning. "What kept you?"

"Cami had to stop off in the ladies' room," the younger, smaller of the two women who'd just entered said. She had a round, friendly face, a trim figure clad in jeans and a purple top—and an incredibly bright green cast on her wrist. She was half supporting the other woman, a pretty blonde with big curls, big eyes and a simple little silk dress that had probably cost several hundred dollars.

"I swear," the blonde said in that little-girl voice, "a faintness comes over me every time I set foot in a hospital. I have always been sensitive that way. But I had to come. I just had to."

The woman with her wrist in a cast rolled her eyes but kept her voice soothing. "Sit down for a few minutes and you'll feel better."

"I have to know how he is first. Poor Michael. If he should

be paralyzed—oh, it just doesn't bear thinkin' of, does it?" She sniffed delicately. "I do assure y'all, I will still marry him, even if he never walks again."

"I'm sure you will," Ada said tartly.

Heat, then cold, chased over Alyssa's body. She heard herself speak as if from a great distance. "What did you say?" She started toward the blonde. "Who *are* you?"

The woman blinked very fine, thick eyelashes. "Why, I'm Cami Porter, Michael's fiancée. And you are…?"

Alyssa licked her suddenly dry lips. "Alyssa Kelleher…West. His wife."

"Calling Cami with the news was not one of my better ideas," Jacob admitted, shoving his hands in his pockets.

"I'm damned if I can see why you did it," Michael snapped.

"I wasn't thinking straight. Why else would I have called your fiancée to let her know you were undergoing major surgery?"

Michael had run out of breath before he'd run out of curses after learning about the scene in the waiting room yesterday. He rubbed his chest gingerly now. Breathing hurt. Everything hurt. Getting kicked by a mule would have to feel a lot better than he did right now.

But they'd gotten the bullet out, and without doing any lasting damage. He was sure he would feel really good about that…eventually. When his life wasn't totally screwed up.

"It was quite a scene," Luke said reminiscently. "One thing you have to say for Cami—she does know how to wring every ounce of drama from a situation."

"Don't worry about her threat to call her lawyer," Jacob said. "My lawyer will handle that. The prenuptial agreement is tight. She's not entitled to a penny unless you marry her—which, obviously, you won't be doing now."

"I don't give a damn about Cami, her lawyer or the money! Alyssa…" God, what she must be thinking, feeling...his left hand tightened into a fist. She had to give him a chance to talk to her. To explain.

"She waited," Luke pointed out. "Stuck it out the whole time, waited until you were in recovery before she let Jacob whisk her off to a hotel to get some rest."

"She would." It didn't mean anything, except that Alyssa wasn't the sort to run out on a man when he was down—even one she must think had used her. "Hasn't been back since, though, has she?"

Luke and Jacob exchanged uneasy glances. Alyssa had left the hospital yesterday morning shortly after dawn, when Michael was moved to recovery. None of them had seen or spoken with her since.

"I explained to her about the will," Jacob muttered. "When I was driving her to the hotel."

"I'm sure *that* helped." She must think he'd married her because of the trust, that devil-inspired, thrice-damned trust.

"She probably slept the clock around," Luke said. "By the time the surgeon came out to tell us you'd made it through okay, she looked worse than you do right now."

"Yeah. Maybe. Look—"

The door to his room opened, and hope burst, full-blown and painful, in Michael's heart. But the woman who came in wasn't Alyssa.

Ada set the plant she'd brought on the dresser opposite the bed, then put her hands on her hips, sharing her frown with each of them equally. "All right, you can all clear out now. I'm going to talk to Michael."

Luke and Jacob protested, but neither could stand against Ada when she was in a mood. And she was definitely in a mood.

"You will remember that he's convalescing?" Jacob said from the door, scowling in a way that had been known to send investors scurrying for cover.

"I'm not going to beat him up," she said tartly. "Now, go on, get out of here."

As soon as the door closed behind them she turned to Michael, her hands on her hips, and shook her head. "Maybe now you'll be ready to give up all that gallivanting around you do, playing with guns and trying to save the world."

"Maybe." He felt too weary to pick up their usual argument.

She made a *tch* sound and came up to the bed. "You scared the bejabbers out of me, boy," she said gruffly, and touched his cheek once, lightly.

A measure of peace entered along with her touch. Ada wasn't a hugger, wasn't one to stroke or nurture in the usual ways. But she'd always been there, she'd always cared, and he and his brothers had always known that. "Sorry about that. I'll try not to do it again."

"Well." She nodded once. "Enough of that. Time to straighten out this mess you've made. Of all the lamebrained, idiotic—proposing to that Cami creature has to be the stupidest thing I've ever seen you do. And you've done some damned stupid things," she added darkly.

"It seemed like a good idea at the time." He couldn't explain, not without giving away why he and his brothers were marrying in such haste—and Ada wasn't supposed to know what they were doing for her.

She propped her hands on her skinny hips. "I suppose you're just as stupid as Jacob and Luke, thinking I don't know what's going on."

"Ah—"

"Oh, I'm used to male stupidity—have to be, after all those years with your father. But I don't know what I've ever done to make the three of you believe *I've* got beans for brains. How any one of you could think I wouldn't figure out why you all three suddenly developed this overwhelming yen for matrimony, I will never know."

He opened his mouth, realized he had nothing to say, and shut it again.

She gave another sharp nod. "Good for you. Not much

point in trying to make yourself sound like anything but a fool. Of course, I have to give you and your brothers credit—once you decided to do the thing, you found some powerful women to tie the knot with.'' She smiled smugly. ''What little sense you do have, you got from me, not your father.''

At last she'd said something he knew how to respond to. ''True.''

''Now,'' she said, dragging over a chair and sitting next to his bed. ''We had better figure out how you're going to keep that pretty thing you married from running the other direction when she hears your name.''

''I've screwed it up,'' he said quietly. ''Worse than my father ever did, I think.''

''Oh, not worse. First thing is, you have to tell me if you love her or not.'' She gave him a sharp look. ''I'm guessing you do.''

The word sent up strange shock waves inside him. ''I...does it matter? Even if I manage to convince her I care, love doesn't fix anything, cure anything. How many women did my father love over the years?''

''Too many.'' Her voice was uncharacteristically soft, a little sad.

''Love is...'' He didn't know what it was. That was the problem. ''It complicates things.''

Now she snorted. ''No, love is simple. Everything else is complicated. You start out with love, you've got something simple and strong to return to when life gets messy. I'll say one thing for your father—the old fool did get that part right. Only problem was, every time things got complicated, he started all over again with another woman instead of sticking it out, building on the love that was already there. He never could get it through his thick head that you can't close a circle if you start drawing it all over again every time you get confused.''

He shook his head, smiling at her fondly. He had no idea what her circles had to do with the mess he'd made of his own life—he and Alyssa hadn't even gotten started in their marriage before everything fell apart. "Well, my mind's going in circles. Does that count?"

"You're paying attention to the complications, not the important stuff." She stood. "When you see Alyssa again, pay attention to what you feel, not what you think. Your biggest problem right now isn't the way your wife and your fiancée tripped over each other yesterday. It's the fact that you can't say out loud, even now, that you're in love with your wife."

There was a soft tap at the door. It swung open. "Hi," Alyssa said quietly. "Jacob told me you had company, but I thought you might not mind a little more."

"I'm on my way out," Ada said. She paused, patted his hand once—a little awkward, as usual, with the gesture of affection—and left.

Alyssa stood near the doorway, her eyes uncertain. She was wearing a dress. That came as a small shock. He'd never seen her in anything but the pants and shirt she'd worn in San Christóbal. The dress was a simple knit, narrow and belted at the waist, in a sunny sky blue that matched her eyes. Her hair was different, too. The curls had been partially tamed by being pinned into a chignon, but some of them were escaping, frisking around her face. He cleared his throat. "You clean up pretty good." *Beautiful,* he thought. She looked so beautiful to him.

Her mouth crooked up on one side and she moved a farther into the room. "I guess this is the cleanest you've ever seen me. I think," she said, smoothing a nervous hand down her skirt, "this is when I'm supposed to ask how you're feeling. For old time's sake, tell me about your leg first."

He smiled, but it hurt. Old time's sake? That's what you said to someone you hadn't seen in a long time, someone who wasn't part of your life. "I haven't noticed any problems with my leg since I got the new hole in my chest. Alyssa…"

She turned to study the plants and flowers set in a row

along the dresser. "My, you have quite a garden started here. I'm afraid I didn't bring anything."

She wasn't going to make it easy on him. Well, why should she? "I'm sorry," he said simply.

She didn't turn. Her shoulders were stiff. "I remember when you told me you deserved an explanation. I do, too."

"Jacob said he told you about the trust, and why…why I thought I had to marry quickly."

"Oh, that part's been explained." She turned suddenly, her eyes flashing. "The part I want to hear from you is why you never mentioned it. Why you never mentioned *Cami.*"

"You wouldn't have married me if I had." His chest was hurting. Bad. He pushed the button that made his bed lift anyway. He didn't like being flat on his back, and he needed to see her face better. "I never wanted her. From the first time we kissed after seeing the butterflies, there was only you."

She swallowed. "And after I told you I loved you? You didn't think I deserved to know about a little detail like a fiancée then?"

"There wasn't much time for explanations." He started to lift a hand toward her, winced and let his arm drop. "And I didn't want you to think I'd married you to dissolve the trust. I didn't…that's not why."

She looked away, then down, both hands smoothing the unwrinkled surface of her dress. When she met his eyes again, hers held a hint of—amusement? Surely he was mistaking that gleam.

"I know that," she said. "Jacob told me that if you'd wanted to throw a spanner in the works, you went about things just right. He isn't sure if our marriage is even legal, which could make dissolving the trust tricky. Especially if Cami sues for breach of promise the way she's threatening to do."

"God save me from helpful brothers," he muttered.

"Look, I'm holding you to it. Our marriage. I don't care what the courts say—you're mine, and I'm not letting you go."

"Michael." She sounded—exasperated? Not angry, not hurt—but rather like Ada when she was lecturing him. Now she came over to the bed. "I believe you, you know. I…when I first heard, I was shocked, hurt…but I knew you hadn't lied to me. Not with your words, not with your actions."

She believed him. Believed *in* him. For one terrible instant, his eyes stung. He swallowed, fighting to get himself under control. "I'm not like your Dan," he managed to say. "I can't be the kind of man he was, the kind of husband he was."

"No, you can't." She sighed. "One of the hardest things for me has been letting go. I didn't want to be anyone other than the woman who had loved Dan, the woman he'd loved. But his death changed me. Time changed me. I had trouble admitting that." She took his hand then, and smiled at him. "You aren't like Dan. You're wonderful just as you are—exactly the kind of man I need in my life now."

He could swear his heart started beating again at that instant. Whatever it had been doing before hadn't done the job right, apparently, because only now did oxygen and life flow through his body again.

"We'll marry again, if that's necessary for legal reasons. But…but there's something you haven't said. Something important." She hesitated. "I need the words, Michael."

"I…I've never said them to a woman. Maybe not to anyone," he admitted. He couldn't remember. Had he ever told his father he loved him? His brothers? His mother? Maybe, when he was very small…. "I don't know about love," he said a little desperately. "I don't know if I can do it right."

She said nothing, just stood there, her hand warm and comforting in his, her gaze steady. Waiting.

"Hell," he muttered. All right, he could do this. "I love you, all right?"

Her hand tightened suddenly on his. "Was that so hard?"

"Yes. No," he corrected himself immediately. There was an odd warmth, a looseness, in his chest. "No, it was really…kind of simple, wasn't it?" The warmth spread, reaching his neck, his jaw, widening his mouth into a smile. "I love you," he repeated, the smile stretching into a big, silly grin.

She made a sound between a laugh and a sob, bent and took his face in her hands, and kissed him. "I love you, too."

This time he managed to get his arm to work. He had to, had to feel her hair, touch the silky skin along her throat. "We'll work the rest of it out. All the details." They had the basics, the place to start from—love.

"Sure we will. First things first, though." She lifted her head, her eyes wicked and happy. "You'd better get yourself well as soon as possible, because you owe me a wedding night, soldier—with a bed. I insist on having a bed this time."

He laughed.

Epilogue

Christmas Day, at the West mansion

"Mmm." Michael pressed a kiss to the side of her neck. "Have I told you how sexy you look in those robes, Reverend?"

Alyssa laughed. "And I'm staying in them, too. There are twenty people downstairs, waiting for me to marry your brother."

"He's too late." He'd tugged the robe to one side and was bending his attention to the sensitive place where her neck met her shoulder. "I already married you."

She turned in his arms, looping hers around his neck. "So you did. Twice." And gave herself up, for the moment, to his kiss.

On the advice of Jacob's attorney, they'd gone through a second ceremony as soon as he was released from the hospital to make sure there wouldn't be any problems with the trust. Cami had ceased to be a problem as soon as Michael signed over a portion of the money he would soon inherit to her—an action that had disgusted Jacob, but neither Michael nor Alyssa wanted to drag things out. Nor did they care about the money. Cami might be walking away with a small fortune, but Michael, it turned out, was going to have a large fortune. Very large.

Large enough to do a lot of things more important than taking his ex-fiancée to court. The village of Cuautepec was going to have a new school, for example, complete with a teacher. They'd already received the goats and chickens. And Sister Andrew was looking into establishing a pottery, using clay from the river and the kiln and supplies Michael had promised.

And that would put only a small dent in the money.

Someone pounded on the bedroom door. "Hey, you two—stop necking," Luke called. "We need to get Jacob married before he starts gnawing on the woodwork. Or the guests."

Reluctantly, Michael lifted his head. "I intend to finish this discussion later. In bed."

She grinned. That tree along the trail would always hold a special place in her heart, but there was no denying that beds were more comfortable.

He picked up his cane and started for the door. Luke had given him the handsome ebony walking stick topped by the snarling head of a wolf for Christmas. In another couple of months, he probably wouldn't need it anymore.

When he was medically cleared, he might rejoin his team. Or he might not. He hadn't decided, and she wasn't pressuring him. They both still had a lot of adjustments to make, a lot of decisions about how to shape their life together.

It would work out, she thought as they went into the hall. They were very different people—in some ways. But both wanted to live lives in service to others, however differently they'd chosen to serve. And they loved each other.

Sometimes it really could be that simple.

"There you are." Luke spoke from the stairs, relief and humor in his voice. "Jacob is driving us all crazy."

"The ceremony isn't scheduled to begin for another fifteen minutes," Alyssa said mildly.

"Tell my brother that. He wants to get married, and he wants to do it *now*."

She exchanged a smile with Michael. That had been his approach, too.

Her parents were there, as were the parents of Luke's wife, Maggie, and Claire's mother and stepfather. Luke and Maggie had arrived early that morning with the boy they were planning to adopt so they could stage a massive paper-tearing spree. Luke had been an extravagant Santa—which, from what she'd learned from Maggie, was a miracle all by itself. He'd brought dozens of gifts for Maggie and the boy, and several for the rest of them, too.

Alyssa and Michael had exchanged a single present—the rings they'd bought each other, two simple gold bands. And Ada had given them all a wonderful present when she'd returned from her latest treatment—a glowing bill of health from the doctor, along with her threat to "be around long enough to tell all of your children the truth about you."

"Have I mentioned that this is a very odd house?" Alyssa asked as they started down the stairs. The finial at the bottom was shaped like a snarling lion, and that was the least of the house's peculiarities.

"Most people think so," Michael said cheerfully. "Uh-oh. Battle stations. There's Jacob."

He certainly was. The cool, controlled man she'd met at the hospital, the businessman whose icy control and acute sense of timing might eventually make him richer than his father had been, looked ready to jump out of his skin.

She told herself that ministers weren't allowed to giggle.

"At last," Jacob said, heaving a sigh of relief. "Everyone is ready."

"Claire isn't going to vanish if you don't marry her in the next five minutes," Michael said, amused.

"I know, but—" He reached up to jerk at the knot of his tie. "I just want to get it done."

He'd twisted the tie crooked. Luke chuckled and straightened it for him. "If I'd known how much fun it would be to watch you come apart like this, I'd have encouraged you to get married years ago."

"Wouldn't have done you any good. I didn't know Claire then," Jacob said simply.

A few minutes later, Alyssa stood in front of friends and family, both new and old, and opened the book. Snow was sifting down lightly outside; it would probably melt as soon as it touched down, for the weather wasn't cold. A Christmas tree glowed merrily at the other end of the room. A scrap of red ribbon, missed in the hasty cleanup, dangled from the chandelier.

It was that bit of red ribbon that undid her. After all she'd been through, all these others had been through, to have arrived safely to this day—miracles still happen, she thought, and sniffed.

Oh, dear, she thought, blinking rapidly. Claire and Jacob didn't want to be married by a weepy minister.

Alyssa's mother sat at the piano, playing the old, familiar music as the bride started her slow walk on her stepfather's arm. Claire was certainly a beautiful woman—but her physical beauty was secondary now, eclipsed by the radiance of a bride who walks forward to join the man she loves.

She stopped in front of Alyssa and took Jacob's hand.

Oh, my. Alyssa struggled to blink away the happy tears filling her eyes. Ada was already crying, she saw. And a couple of others were, too. Then her gaze met Michael's.

She smiled. *Miracles call for a few tears,* she thought. "Dearly beloved," she began, tears blurring the words, but her voice clear and firm. "We are gathered here today…"

*　*　*　*　*

Egan Cassidy's Kid

BEVERLY BARTON

BEVERLY BARTON

has been in love with romance since her grandfather gave her an illustrated book of *Beauty and the Beast*. An avid reader since childhood, Beverly wrote her first book at the age of nine. After marriage to her own 'hero' and the births of her daughter and son, Beverly chose to be a full-time homemaker, aka wife, mother, friend and volunteer. The author of over thirty books, Beverly is a member of Romance Writers of America and helped found the Heart of Dixie chapter in Alabama. She has won numerous awards and made several bestseller lists.

To Billy Ray Beaver, DG Hatch
and every man and woman who served their
country during the Vietnam war years.
And to their families.

Special thanks to Malaina for permitting
me to use her heartfelt poetry that so
beautifully expresses the emotions shared
by many veterans.

Prologue

After all these years, he finally had what he wanted—the perfect ammunition to use against his worst enemy. At long last, he could make Egan Cassidy pay. All he had to do to bring Cassidy to his knees was kidnap Bent Douglas.

General Grant Cullen, the supreme leader of the Ultimate Survivalists, leaned back in his swivel chair and grinned. Revenge was sweet. Hell, just the contemplation of revenge was sweet.

He had waited nearly thirty years for this day and he was going to savor every minute of it.

"I want champagne," Cullen told his right-hand man, Winn Sherman. "Send one of the boys to the wine cellar. This is a celebration!"

"Then your phone call was the news you've been waiting for?" Winn asked.

"Oh, yes." Grant rubbed his hands together gleefully. "I've been searching a lifetime to find a way to destroy Egan Cassidy. I knew that sooner or later the way in which

I could inflict great suffering on him would be revealed to me.''

"And the way has been revealed, sir?''

Grant laughed. "Mmm-mmm…" He licked his lips and sighed. "I could have killed Cassidy years ago, but I wanted more. I need to see him suffer, to see him lose everything, the way I did. And now it's going to happen.''

"I thought you'd told me that Cassidy had nothing to lose, except his life.''

"Ah, but that's the joy of it. He does have more to lose—much more—and he doesn't even know it,'' Cullen said.

"Then this last private detective uncovered something you can use against Cassidy?''

"Indeed he did. He came upon some information that none of the other idiots I hired ever discovered.''

Grant couldn't remember when he'd felt more alive. More exhilarated. Pure pleasure wound its way through his mind and body as he fantasized about the moment he would rip out Cassidy's heart.

"It seems that for the past fourteen years Cassidy has paid for flowers to be placed on the grave of Bentley Tyson III, a former Vietnam vet, from some Podunk little town in Alabama,'' Grant explained. "When I learned that bit of information, I knew that Tyson had meant something to Cassidy. So I had my detective investigate a little further. Seems Tyson saved Cassidy's life in Nam.''

Winn frowned. "I'm afraid I don't understand. What good is this information if Tyson is dead?''

"Tyson had a younger sister.''

"I see, sir. What significance—?''

"Maggie Tyson Douglas has a fourteen-year-old son.''

"I don't follow you, sir,'' Winn admitted sheepishly.

''Tyson's sister and nephew wouldn't mean anything to Cassidy, would they?''

''Oh, yes, but they do, my friend. They do. They mean more to him than he realizes. Especially the boy.'' Euphoria unlike any he had ever known suffused Cullen's very soul. ''After we've arranged to bring Bent Douglas here for a little visit, I plan to telephone Cassidy and tell him just how important Maggie Douglas's child is to him.''

''I'm confused, sir.'' Winn's cheeks flushed with embarrassment. ''You're inviting this boy here to the fort?''

Cullen shot to his feet, clamped his hand down on Winn's shoulder and smiled broadly. ''We're going to insist the young man come for a visit. You see, Colonel Sherman, Bent Douglas is Egan Cassidy's kid and the man doesn't even know it.''

Chapter 1

"Don't eat so fast," Maggie Douglas scolded. "We aren't running late this morning. We have plenty of time to get you to school early for your student council meeting."

"I'm hungry, Mama," Bent replied, his mouth half-full of cereal. "Is my grilled cheese sandwich ready, yet?"

Using a metal spatula, Maggie sliced the sandwich in two, then lifted it from the electric skillet and laid it on her son's plate. For the past six months the boy had been eating her out of house and home. No matter how much he ate, he remained famished. She smiled, remembering how her father had teased her brother when he'd gone through his ravenous period at about the same age Bent was now.

Maggie wanted to ruffle her son's hair, the way she'd done when he was younger. But another change that had occurred in the past few months was Bent's obsession with his hair and clothes. He wore his silky black hair in the latest style: short, moussed and sticking straight up. And his baggy jeans and oversize shirt looked as if they'd been purchased at a secondhand store, despite their hefty price tags.

Bent lifted a sandwich half and stuck it into his mouth. His gaze met Maggie's just as she rolled her eyes heavenward. He munched on the grilled cheese, swallowed and then washed it all down with a large glass of orange juice.

Bent wiped his mouth with the back of his hand. "Go ahead and ask me."

"Ask you what?"

"Ask me if my legs are hollow." Laughing, Bent shoved back his chair and stood. "You know you said Grandfather used to tell Uncle Bentley that he ate so much his legs had to be hollow."

"I don't need to ask you. I've come to the conclusion that all teenage boys have hollow legs and sometimes—" she reached up and pecked the top of his head "—hollow noggins, too."

"Ah, gee, Mama, don't start that again. Just because I want to go to Florida with the guys this summer doesn't mean I'm stupid."

Maggie looked up at her six-foot son and a shudder rippled along her nerve endings. Dear Lord, the older he got, the more he resembled his father. And the stronger the wild streak in him grew. A yearning for adventure and excitement that was alien to Maggie. She'd always preferred safety and serenity.

"You're too young to go off with a bunch of other boys, without a chaperone." She and Bent had been batting this argument back and forth for weeks now. She had no intention of allowing her fourteen-year-old child to spend a week in Florida with five other boys, ranging in age from fourteen to eighteen.

"Chris's big brother is going along to chaperone us."

Bent picked up his clear vinyl book bag from the kitchen counter.

"And how old is Chris's big brother?" Maggie downed the last drops of lukewarm coffee in her mug, set the mug aside and grabbed her purse off the table.

"He's twenty," Bent said, as if twenty were an age of great wisdom and responsibility.

Maggie snatched up her car keys and headed toward the back door. "Let's go. If I have to drop you off a block from the school, then we'd better head out now so you'll have time to walk that extra block."

Bent grabbed Maggie's shoulder, then leaned over and kissed her cheek. "You're the absolute best mom. Some mothers wouldn't understand why a guy my age would be embarrassed to have his mommy drive him to school every day."

Maggie caressed her kissed cheek. Those sweet moments of little-boy affection were few and far between these days. Her only child was growing up—fast. Each day she noted some small change, some almost indiscernible way he had transformed from a boy into a young man.

"Buttering me up won't work, you know." She opened the kitchen door and shooed him outside. "You aren't going to Florida this summer, unless you go with me."

Bent shrugged. "If you say so."

He let the subject drop, but Maggie knew the issue was far from dead. Her son was a good kid, who'd given her very little trouble over the years, but she knew that the wanderlust in him would sooner or later break her heart. She could protect him, now, while he was still underage, but what would happen once he reached eighteen?

Ten minutes later, Maggie pulled her Cadillac over to the curb, one block from Parsons City High School. "Do you need any money?"

Bent flung open the door, glanced over his shoulders and smiled. Even his smile reminded her of his father's.

"Got plenty," Bent said. "You just gave me twenty Monday, remember?"

Maggie nodded. "Have a good one. And don't be late this afternoon. You're getting fitted for your tux at four-thirty so you need to meet me at the bookstore by four."

He slid out of the car, then leaned over and peered inside, his smile unwavering. "I'll meet you at the bookstore no later than four." With that said, he slammed the door and walked down the sidewalk.

Maggie watched him for a few minutes, then eased the car away from the curb and out into traffic. Another perfectly ordinary day, she thought, then sighed contentedly. Perhaps her life wasn't perfect, but it was good. Maybe she didn't have a special man in her life and hadn't had anyone since her divorce from Gil Douglas four years ago, but she was content. She had the most wonderful child in the whole world, a job she loved, enough money for Bent's college as well as her old age and both she and Bent were blessed with excellent health. What more could a woman want?

A sudden, unexpected memory flashed through her mind. Her heartbeat accelerated. Heat flushed her body. Why had she thought about *him?* she wondered. She had tried to forget, tried not to ever think about that week they'd spent together and the way she had felt when she was with him. Fifteen years was a long time. Long enough for her to have gotten over her infatuation. So, why had she been thinking about Egan Cassidy so often lately? Was it because Bent had grown up to be a carbon copy of him?

She couldn't help wondering where Egan was now. Was he even alive? Considering his profession, he could have been killed years ago. Emotion lodged in her throat. Despite the fact that a part of her hated him, she couldn't bear the thought that he might be dead. As surely as she hated him, she still cared. After all, he was Bent's father.

"Psst... Hey, kid, are you Bentley Tyson Douglas?" a deep, masculine voice asked.

Bent jerked his head around, seeking the man who had called out to him. "Who wants to know?"

A big, burly guy wearing faded jeans and an army fatigue shirt stepped out from behind a car in the parking lot at Bent's right. "I'm a friend of a friend of your old man's."

Bent inspected the rather unsavory-looking character, from his shaggy dark beard to his scuffed leather boots. Bent very seriously doubted that this man was a friend of anyone Gil Douglas referred to as even an acquaintance. His adoptive father was one of the biggest snobs in the world. He probably wouldn't let a guy who looked like this man did walk his dog.

"So? What do you want?" Bent asked.

"I got a kid fixing to start school here next year," the man said, easing closer and closer. "Thought maybe you could tell me about the teachers and stuff like that."

Bent glanced into the mostly empty parking lot. It'd be another twenty minutes or so before the majority of his fellow students would start arriving. The only cars already here belonged to a few teachers on early duty and the other student council members. But right this minute, he didn't see another soul around. Instinct warned him not to trust this man. Maybe he was selling dope. Or maybe he was just a nutcase. Whatever, there was something all wrong about him.

Across the street, on the school grounds, Bent noticed a couple of students entering the building, but they were too far away to hear him if he yelled.

What are you afraid of, Douglas? he asked himself.

You're not some little kid. You're a pretty big guy, so if this man tries anything funny, you can handle him, can't you?

"Look, I haven't got time to talk," Bent said, taking several steps backward until he eased off the sidewalk and into the street.

The man grinned. Bent didn't like that sinister smirk. Just as he started to turn and make a mad dash toward the schoolyard, he heard the roar of a car's engine. Before he had a chance to run, the big man moved in on him. Tires screeched. Someone grabbed him from behind. A hand holding a foul-smelling rag clamped down over his nose and mouth. With expert ease, the two men lifted him and tossed him into the back of the car.

The last thing Bent remembered was the car speeding away down the street.

"So how does mama bear feel about her cub going to his first prom?" Janice Deweese stacked the tattered books into a neat pile, being careful not to crease any of the loose pages. "And with an older woman!"

"Grace Felton is only two years older than Bent," Maggie corrected. "She's hardly an older woman. Besides, I've known Grace's parents all my life and—"

"She's quite suitable for Bent."

"Lord, did I sound that snobbish?" Maggie stood perched on a tall, wooden ladder placed against the floor-to-ceiling bookshelves at the back of the room.

"I did hear a hint of Gil Douglas in that comment." Janice eyed the books in front of her. "Should I start on these today or wait until tomorrow? Repairing all eight of them will require a great deal of patience."

Maggie checked her wristwatch. "Since it's nearly four, why don't you wait and get started on that job first thing in the morning. Bent should be here soon and I'll need you to close up shop for me today.''

"Have you two settled your trip-to-Florida argument?" Janice slid off the stool behind the checkout counter and stretched to her full five-foot height.

"As far as I'm concerned it's settled." One by one, Maggie placed the recent shipment of books, which were collections of first-person Civil War accounts, into their appropriate slots on the shelves. "Bent is too young to go off to Florida with a bunch of other teenage boys. He'll have time enough to indulge his adventurous streak after he turns eighteen.''

"Bent's a great kid, you know. I don't think you need to worry too much about him. You've done a wonderful job of raising him without a father," Janice said.

"But Bent has a father who—"

"Who wasn't much of a parent, even before you two got a divorce. Let's face it, Maggie, you've brought up your son with practically no help from Gil Douglas.''

"Gil tried.'' Maggie wished she could have loved Gil the way a woman should love her husband. Perhaps if she had, Gil might have been a better father to Bent. In the beginning, he had made a valiant effort, had even adopted Bent. But a man like Gil Douglas just wasn't cut out to raise another man's son.

"Face the truth, Maggie. Gil couldn't get past the fact that you were engaged to him when you had your little fling with Egan Cassidy.''

Maggie tensed. "I've asked you not to mention his name.''

"Sorry. I didn't mean to dredge up bad memories.''

That was the problem, Maggie thought. The memories weren't bad. They were bittersweet, but not bad. Nothing had prepared her for an affair with a man like Egan. She had been swept away by a passion unlike anything she'd known—before or since.

"It's all right," Maggie said. "Just try not to forget again."

The bell over the front door jingled as a customer entered. Both Janice and Maggie glanced at the entrance. Mrs. Newsom, a regular patron who collected first editions and had a passion for books of every kind, waved and smiled.

"You two just keep on doing whatever you're doing," Mrs. Newsom said, her sweet grin deepening the laugh lines around her mouth. "I just came to browse. I haven't been by in several days and I'm having withdrawal symptoms." Her girlish laughter belied the fact that she was seventy.

Maggie climbed down the ladder, shoved it to the end of the stacks and emerged from the dark cavern of high bookshelves into the airy lightness at the front of the store, where the shelves were low and spaced farther apart. She checked her watch again. Four o'clock exactly. Bent should arrive any minute now. Her son was always punctual. A trait he had either inherited or learned from her.

Bent regained consciousness slowly, his mind fuzzy, his body decidedly uncomfortable. Where was he? What had happened? He attempted to move, but found himself unable to do more than twitch. Someone had bound his hands and feet. He tried to call out and suddenly realized that he'd also been gagged.

The guy in the school parking lot and someone who'd come up from behind had drugged him and tossed him into a car.

Bent looked all around and saw total darkness. But he felt the steady rotation of tires on blacktop and heard the hum of an engine. He was still in a car, only now he was inside the trunk.

Obviously he'd been kidnapped. But why? Who were these guys and what did they want with him? His mother's finances were healthy enough for her to be considered wealthy by some standards, but he knew for a fact that her net worth was less than a million. Her bookstore, which specialized in rare and out-of-print books, barely broke even, so she relied on interest and dividends from her investments for her livelihood. So why would anyone kidnap him when there were kids out there whose parents were multimillionaires? It just didn't make sense.

Bent had heard about young boys and girls being kidnapped and sold on the black market, so he couldn't help wondering if his abductors planned to ship him overseas. The thought of winding up on an auction block and being sold to the highest bidder soured Bent's stomach. Or he could end up in some seedy brothel, a plaything for dirty old men. A shiver racked his body. He'd rather die first!

But he had no intention of dying or of being used as a sex slave. He'd find a way to get out of this mess. He wasn't going to give up without one hell of a fight!

"I can't understand where Bent is," Maggie said, checking her watch again. "It's ten after five. He always calls if he's running late and he hasn't called."

Janice grasped Maggie's trembling hands into her steady ones and squeezed tightly. "He's all right. Maybe he forgot. Or he could be goofing off with the guys or—"

Maggie jerked her hands free. "Something's wrong. He's been in an accident or... Oh, God, where is he?"

"Do you want me to check the hospital? I can call the ER."

"If he'd been in an accident, the police would have contacted me by now, wouldn't they?"

"I think so. Yes, of course they would have."

Maggie paced the floor, her soft leather shoes quiet against the wood's shiny patina. "I'm going to call some of his friends, first, before I panic. He usually catches a ride with Chris or Mark or sometimes Jarred."

"So call their houses and find out if maybe he's with one of them. And if he just forgot about calling you, don't give him a hard time."

"Oh, I won't give him a hard time," Maggie said. "I'll just wring his neck for worrying me to death."

Setting her rear end on the edge of her desk in the office alcove, separated from the bookstore by a pair of brocade curtains, Maggie lifted the telephone and dialed Chris McWilliams's number first.

Fifteen minutes and six calls later, Maggie knew what she had to do. Janice stood at her side, a true friend, desperate to help in any way she could. With moisture glazing her eyes, Maggie exchanged a resigned look with Janice, then lifted the receiver and dialed one final number.

Paul Spencer, Parsons City's chief of police answered. "Spencer here."

"Yes, this is Maggie Douglas. I'd like to report a missing child."

"Whose child is missing?" he asked.

"Mine."

"Bent's missing?" Paul, who'd gone to high school with Maggie, asked, a note of genuine concern in his voice.

"I've contacted all his friends and even talked to Mr. Wellborn, the school principal. Although I dropped him at school this morning—early—for a student council meeting, he never arrived. No one has seen him all day. Oh, God, Paul...help me."

"Are you at home or at the shop?"

"I'm still downtown at the shop."

"Stay where you are. I'll be right over. As soon as you fill out the N.C.I.C form, we'll get it entered into the computer. But I'll go ahead and have a couple of men start checking around to see what they can find."

"Thank you." The receiver dangled from Maggie's fingers. Every nerve in her body screamed. This couldn't be happening. Not to her child. Not to Bent, the boy she loved more than life itself.

Janice took the telephone from Maggie and returned the receiver to its cradle, then she wrapped her arms around her best friend. Maggie hugged Janice fiercely as she tried to control her frazzled emotions. This was a parent's worst nightmare. A missing child. She kept picturing Bent hurt and alone, crying for help. Then that scenario passed from her mind and another quickly took its place. Bent kidnapped and abused—perhaps even killed.

Maggie clenched her teeth tightly in an effort not to scream aloud.

Egan Cassidy poured himself a glass of *Grand cru* Chablis as he watched the salmon steak sizzling on the indoor grill. As a general rule, he dined alone, as he did tonight. Occasionally he had beer and a sandwich at a local bar with another Dundee agent. And once in a blue moon he actually took a woman out to dinner. But as he grew older, he found his penchant for solitude strengthening.

He liked most of his fellow Dundee agents, but except for two or three, they were younger than he. Perhaps the age difference was the reason he had very little in common with most of the other employees of the premiere private security and investigation firm in the Southeast, some said in the entire United States.

And as for the ladies—he'd never been a womanizer, not even in his youth. There had been special women, of course, and a few minor flirtations. But it had been years since he'd dated anyone on a regular basis. He had found that most of the women close to his age, those within a ten-year-span older or younger, were often bitter from a divorce or desperate because they'd never married. And he found younger women, especially those in their twenties, a breed unto themselves. Whenever he dated a woman under thirty, he somehow felt as if he were dating his daughter's best friend. Of course, he didn't have a daughter, but the fact was that at the ripe old age of forty-seven he easily could have a twenty-five-year-old daughter.

Egan turned the salmon steak out onto a plate, then carried the plate and the wine to the table in his kitchen. Although the kitchen in his Atlanta home was ultramodern, his table and chairs were antiques that he'd brought here from his apartment in Memphis. Over the years, while he'd traveled the world as a soldier of fortune, he had always returned to the States, so he'd maintained a place in his old hometown. But two years ago, after joining the Dundee Agency, he'd bought a home in Atlanta and moved his furniture, many priceless antiques, into his newly purchased two-story town house.

The salmon flaked to the touch of his fork and melted like butter when he put it into his mouth. He ate slowly, savoring every bite. He enjoyed cooking and had found that he was a rather good chef.

Egan poured himself more Chablis, then stood, picked up the bowl of fresh raspberries on the counter and headed for the living room. He could clean up later, before bedtime, he thought. As he entered the twenty-by-twenty room, he punched a button on the CD player and the strains of the incomparable Stan Getz's saxophone rendition of

"Body and Soul" filled the room. The stereo system he and his friend and fellow Dundee agent, Hunter Whitelaw, had installed was state-of-the-art. The best money could buy. Everything Egan owned was the best.

Easing down into the soft, lush leather chair, he sighed and closed his eyes, savoring the good music as he had savored the good food. Maybe growing up on the mean streets of Memphis, with no one except an alcoholic father for family, had whetted Egan's appetite for the good things in life. And maybe his lack of a decent upbringing and his brief tenure in Vietnam when he'd been barely eighteen had predisposed him for the occupation to which he had devoted himself for twenty-five years. He'd made a lot of money as a mercenary and had invested wisely, turning his ill-gained earnings into quite a tidy sum. He had more than enough money, so if he chose to never work again, he could maintain his current lifestyle as long as he lived.

Two hours later, the kitchen cleaned and the bottle of Chablis half-empty, Egan made his way into his small home office. The bookshelves and furniture were a light oak and the walls a soft cream. The only color in the room was the dark green, tufted-back leather chair behind his desk. This was the one room in the town house that his decorator hadn't touched. He smiled when he remembered Heather Sims. She'd been interested—very interested. And if he had chosen to pursue a relationship with her, she would have been only too happy to have filled his lonely hours with idle chitchat and hot sex. Three dates, one night of vigorous lovemaking and they had parted as friends.

Egan sat, then opened his notebook and picked up a pen. No one knew that he wrote poetry. Not that he was ashamed, just that to him it was such a private endeavor. At first, it had been a catharsis, and perhaps even now it still was.

With pen in hand, he wrote.

because he was eighteen
he was considered
man enough to fight old men's wars...

The ringing telephone jarred him from his memories,
from a time long ago when he'd lived a nightmare—a boy
trapped in the politicians' war, a boy who became a man
the hard way.

Egan lifted the receiver. "Cassidy here."

"Well, well, well. Hello, old friend."

Egan's blood ran cold. He hadn't heard that voice in
years. The last time he'd run into Grant Cullen, they'd both
been in the Middle East, both doing nasty little jobs for
nasty little men. When had that been, six years ago? No,
more like eight.

"What do you want, Cullen?"

"Now, is that any way to talk to an old friend?"

"We were never friends."

Cullen laughed and the sound of his laughter chilled
Egan to the bone. Something was wrong. Bad wrong. His
gut instincts warned him that this phone call meant big
trouble.

"You're right," Grant Cullen agreed. "Neither of us has
ever had many friends, have we?"

Cullen was playing some sort of game, Egan thought,
and he was enjoying himself too damn much. "You want
something. What is it?"

"Oh, just to talk over old times. You know, reminisce
about the good old days. Discuss how you screwed me over
in Nam and how I've been waiting nearly thirty years to
return the favor."

"You want me, you know where to find me," Egan said,
his voice deadly soft.

"Oh, I want you all right, but I want you to come to me."

"Now why the hell would I do that?"

"Because I've got something that belongs to you. Something you'll want back."

"I don't know what you're talking about." Egan clutched the phone tightly, his knuckles whitening from the strength of his grasp.

"Remember Bentley Tyson III, that good ol' boy from Alabama who saved your life back in Nam?"

"How the hell do you know about Bentley?"

"You've been paying for flowers to be put on his grave every year ever since he killed himself fifteen years ago."

"Get to the point," Egan snapped, highly agitated that a man like Cullen would even dare to say Bentley's name. Bentley, who'd been a good man destroyed by an evil war.

"The point is I know that when you paid your condolences to Tyson's little sister fifteen years ago, you stayed in Parsons City for a week. What were you doing, Cassidy, screwing Maggie Tyson?"

Egan saw red. Figuratively and literally. Rage boiled inside him like lava on the verge of erupting from a volcano. How did Cullen know about Maggie, about the fact that he'd spent a week in her home?

He's guessing about the affair you had with her, Egan assured himself. He wants to think Maggie meant something to you, that she still does.

"I don't know where you got your information," Egan said. "But you've got it all wrong. Bentley's little sister was engaged to a guy named Gil Douglas and they got married a few months after Bentley's funeral."

"Oh, I know sweet Maggie was engaged, but she didn't marry Gil Douglas until five years later. What Maggie did a few months after Bentley's funeral—nine months to be exact—was give birth to a bouncing baby boy.''

Egan felt as if he'd been hit in the belly with a sledge-hammer. His heartbeat drummed in his ears. He broke out in a cold sweat. No, God, please, no! He'd spent his entire adult life looking over his shoulder, waiting for Grant Cullen to attack. He had denied himself the love and companionship of a wife and the pride and joy of children to protect them from the revenge Cullen would be sure to wreak on anyone who meant a damn thing to Egan.

''What's the matter, buddy boy, didn't sweet Maggie tell you that you have a son?''

''You're crazy! I don't have a son.'' *He couldn't have a child. God wouldn't be that cruel.*

''Oh, yes, you do. A fine boy of fourteen. Big, tall, handsome. Looks a whole hell of a lot like you did when you were eighteen and you and I were buddies in that POW camp.''

''I do not have a son,'' Egan repeated.

''Yes, Cassidy, you do. You and Maggie Tyson Douglas.''

Cullen laughed again, a sharp, maniacal sound that sliced flesh from Egan's bones.

''You're wrong,'' Egan said, his statement a plea to God as well as a denial to Cullen.

''Run a check. Your name is on his birth certificate. And one look at a photograph of Bentley Tyson Douglas will confirm the facts.''

''I don't believe anything you've told me. You're a lying son of a bitch!''

''Well, believe this, buddy boy. As we speak, your son is in my hands. I had him flown in from Alabama this afternoon. So just think about that for a while. And you have a good night. Bye now.''

Chapter 2

It couldn't be true. Maggie's child couldn't be his. She would never have kept the boy a secret from him all these years. Not Maggie. She would have come to him, told him, expected him to do *the right thing*.

Don't be an idiot, Cassidy, an inner voice chided. You ended things with her rather abruptly once you realized she was in love with you. You gave her a hundred and one reasons why a committed relationship between the two of you would never work. You broke her heart. Why would she have come to you if, later on, she'd discovered she was carrying your child? You had made it perfectly clear that you didn't love her or want her.

And there was another reason he couldn't be the father of Maggie's child—he had used condoms when he'd made love to her. He never had unprotected sex. The last thing he'd ever wanted was to father a child—someone Cullen could use against him.

His thoughts swirled through time to the week he'd spent

with Maggie Tyson. She had been in mourning, torn apart by Bentley's suicide. And she'd reached out to someone who had known and cared for her brother. Someone who had lived through the same hell, who understood why Bentley had been so tormented. She'd realized that Egan was on a first name basis with the same demons that had haunted her brother for so many years, had shared the same nightmares that finally had driven Bentley to take his own life. Maggie had reached out to Egan and, for the first time in his life, he had succumbed to the pleasure of giving and receiving comfort.

But the connection he and Maggie had shared quickly went beyond sympathy and understanding, beyond a mutual need to mourn a good man's untimely death. Passion had ignited between them like a lightning strike to summer-dry grass. An out-of-control blaze had swept them away.

Suddenly Egan remembered—he hadn't used protection the first time he made love to Maggie!

He paced the floor, calling himself all kinds of a fool and finally admitting that the only way to find out the truth was to telephone Maggie. *God help us all if her child is my son and Grant Cullen really has kidnapped him.*

Maggie escaped into the powder room, locking the door behind her. She needed a few quiet moments away from the crowd that had gathered at her house. All her friends, aunts, uncles and cousins meant well, as did Bent's friends and their parents, who were congregated in her living room. Paul Spencer had stopped by less than an hour ago to give her an update on the local manhunt for Bent. No one had seen the boy all day and there wasn't a trace of him or the book bag he'd been carrying. It was as if her son had dropped off the face of the earth.

The agony she'd felt earlier had intensified to such an

unbearable degree that she wondered how she was able to function at all. But somewhere between the moment she realized that Bent was missing and this very second, a blessed numbness had set in, allowing her to operate with robotic efficiency.

If only she could shut down her mind, stop all the horrific scenarios that kept repeating themselves over and over in her head.

She held on to the hope that Bent was still alive and unharmed. That any minute now he would walk through the front door with a perfectly good reason for where he'd been and why he had worried her so.

She could hang on to her sanity as long as she could believe that her son was all right. If anything happened to Bent…if she lost him…

Maggie rammed her fist against her mouth to silence a gut-wrenching cry as she doubled over in pain. No! No! her heart screamed. This wasn't right. This wasn't fair. Bent was all she had. He was her very life. If she lost him, she would have nothing.

Her son deserved to live and grow up to be the man she knew he could be. He had a right to go to college and get a job and find a girlfriend. To marry and have children. To live a normal life and die in his sleep when he was ninety.

As Maggie slumped to her knees in the small powder room, she prayed, trying to bargain with God. *Let him be all right. Let him live and have a long, happy life and you can take me. Take me now and I won't care. Just don't let my precious Bent suffer. Don't let him die.*

A loud tapping at the door startled Maggie. She'd been so far removed from the present moment that she had forgotten she had a houseful of concerned friends and relatives. The tapping turned into repeated knocks.

"Maggie, honey, there's a phone call for you," Janice

said. "I told him that now wasn't a good time for you, but he insisted. Mag, it's Egan Cassidy."

"What!"

"Do you want me to ask him to call back later?"

"No." Maggie lifted herself from the floor, stared into the mirror over the sink and groaned when she saw her pale face and red eyes. "I'll be there in a minute. I'll take the call in the den. Would you make sure no one else is in there."

"Sure thing."

Maggie turned on the faucet, cupped her hands to gather the cold water and then splashed her face. After drying her face and hands, she unlocked the door and stepped out into the hall. She made her way through the throng of loving, caring, wall-to-wall people, as she headed toward the den. Slowed down by hugs and words of encouragement, it took her quite some time to finally reach the small, cosy room that she considered a private sanctuary.

Janice waited by the mahogany secretary, the telephone in her hand. Maggie hesitated for a split second, then took the phone, breathed deeply and placed the receiver to her ear. Janice curled her fingers into a tiny waving motion as she started to leave the room, but Maggie shook her head and motioned for her friend to stay.

"This is Maggie Douglas." She was amazed by how calm her voice sounded.

"Hello, Maggie. It's Egan Cassidy."

"Yes, Janice told me."

"I know you're probably puzzled by this phone call."

"Yes, I am. After fifteen years, I never expected to hear from you." Why was he calling now? she asked herself. Today of all days?

"I need to ask you some questions," Egan said.

"About what?"

"About your son. You do have a son, don't you? A fourteen-year-old son named Bentley Tyson Douglas."

"What do you know about Bent?" She couldn't hide the hysteria in her voice. Had Egan found out that he had a son? Had he somehow talked Bent into going away with him? Was that why Egan was calling, to tell her that he had claimed his son?

"Then you do have a son?"

"Yes, I—is Bent with you? Did you find out that—"

"Bent isn't with me," Egan told her. "But your son is missing, isn't he?"

"If he isn't with you, then how do you know—"

"How long has he been missing?"

"Since this morning. I dropped him off at school and no one has seen him since."

"Damn!"

"Egan, please, tell me what's going on. How did you know about Bent and how did you find out he was missing?"

Long pause. Hard breathing. Although they were physically hundreds of miles apart, Maggie could feel the tension in Egan, could sense some sort of emotional struggle going on inside him.

"Egan, you're frightening me."

"I'm sorry," he said, his voice deep and low and the sentiment truly genuine. "Maggie, I need to know something and it's important that you tell me the truth."

The rush of blood pounded in her head. Her heartbeat accelerated rapidly. Adrenaline shot through her like a fast acting narcotic. "Ask me."

"Is Bent my son?"

Maggie closed her eyes. A tear escaped and trickled down her cheek. Janice rushed to her side and draped her arm around Maggie's waist.

"Are you all right?" Janice whispered. "Do you want me to talk to him?"

Maggie shook her head, then opened her eyes, her vision blurred by the sheen of moisture. "Yes, Bent is your son."

Egan groaned. Maggie bit down on her bottom lip. The sound from Egan that came through the telephone was that of a wounded animal. A ferocious hurt. An angry growl.

"Listen to me very carefully," Egan said. "I know what has happened to Bent—"

Maggie cried out.

"Don't panic. For now, he's safe. Do you hear me? He hasn't been harmed. But in order to keep him safe, you're going to have to let me handle things. Do you understand?"

"No," Maggie said. "No, I don't understand anything. Where is Bent? What's happened to him?"

Janice gasped. "He knows where Bent is?"

"Who's that?" Egan asked. "Who's there with you?"

"Janice Deweese. In case you've forgotten, Janice is my dearest friend and my assistant at Rare Finds."

"Then you can trust Janice?"

"Yes, of course I can trust her."

"With your life? With Bent's life?"

"Yes."

"I assume you've alerted the local authorities," Egan said. "But what I'm going to tell you, I want you to keep it to yourself. Or at least between you and Janice."

"God in heaven, Egan, will you just tell me what's going on?"

"Bent's life could depend on your following my instructions, on letting me handle things without involving any law enforcement other than the ones I chose to bring in on this."

"Bent's life could—" Maggie choked on the tears lodged in her throat. Her son's life was in danger and Egan

knew from what or from whom that danger came. How
was it possible that Egan was involved in Bent's disap-
pearance when he'd never been a part of Bent's life? She
didn't understand any of this. Nothing made sense. It was
as if she'd suddenly passed through some invisible barrier
straight into the Twilight Zone.

"Maggie!" Egan demanded her attention.

"I don't understand anything. None of this makes any
sense to me. Explain to me what's happening. Where is
Bent? Why…why—"

"Don't do anything. And don't speak to anyone else
tonight. If there are people in your house, get rid of them.
I'll fly into Parsons City tonight and I'll explain everything
to you when I get there."

"Egan, wait—"

"I'll get your son back for you, Maggie. I'll bring him
home. I promise you that."

"Egan!"

The mocking hum of the dial tone told Maggie that Egan
had hung up. She slumped down in the chair at the secretary, covered her face with her hands and moaned.

Janice knelt in front of Maggie, then pried Maggie's
hands from her face. "What's going on?"

"I'm not sure," Maggie admitted. "Somehow Egan
found out that Bent is his son and he knows that Bent is
missing. Egan said…he said that he knew what had happened to Bent and that he wanted me to let him handle
everything. He promised me that he'd bring Bent home."

"Is Bent with Egan?"

"No, I don't think so." Maggie stared straight through
Janice. "Egan is coming here tonight to tell me what happened to our son."

Bent glared at the plate of food his jailer had brought to
him several hours ago. He was hungry, but he hadn't

touched the fried chicken, mashed potatoes and green beans. He had no way of knowing whether or not his food had been poisoned. But why his captors would choose to poison him, he didn't know. They could easily have killed him a dozen different ways by now.

Although they had taken his book bag and his cellular phone, they hadn't robbed him of either his wallet or his wristwatch. And other than drugging him initially in order to kidnap him and keeping him bound and gagged in the car and then on the airplane, his abductors hadn't laid a finger on him. Of course, they had blindfolded him when they'd taken him off the plane.

He had heard one of them, the guy who'd approached him in the school parking lot, tell the other one, a younger, more clean-cut man, that *the general* didn't want the kid hurt.

"He's waiting for the kid's old man to show up first."

Bent didn't understand. What did his father have to do with his kidnapping? He hadn't seen Gil Douglas in over a year. And he hadn't spoken to him in three months. After his parents' divorce his relationship with his dad had slowly deteriorated. And it wasn't as if his father was rich. Gil spent every dime he made, as a chemical engineer, on his new wife and two-year-old daughter.

Nope, it didn't make any sense at all that his dad was involved in any way, shape, form or fashion with his kidnapping.

So what was going on? He had been abducted, flown across country to only God knew where and was being kept prisoner in a clean, neatly decorated bedroom and served a decent meal on a china plate.

Bent checked his watch. Fifteen after nine. He'd been missing for more than twelve hours. His mother must be out of her mind with worry. She'd probably called the police and had every friend and relative in Parsons City out scouring the countryside for him. And what had she done when no one had been able to find him? His mom would stay strong and hopeful. And she would go to her kitchen to think and plan. He could picture his mother now, in their big old kitchen, baking. For as long as he could remember, his mother had baked whenever she was upset, depressed or needed to make a decision.

Boy, what he'd give for some of her delicious tea cakes. And a glass of milk. And his own bed to sleep in tonight.

Eaten alive by frustration and an ever-increasing fear, Bent tried the door again. Still locked. Stupid! He scanned the room, searching for any means of escape. There were no bars on the two windows, both small rectangular slits near the ceiling. He shoved a chair against the wall, climbed onto the seat and peered out the windows. The moonlight afforded him a glimpse of the shadowy, enclosed courtyard below and the two men who seemed to be guarding the area. Scratch the idea of climbing out the windows.

He heard voices in the hallway, but couldn't make out the conversation. His heartbeat increased speed. Sweat dampened his palms. What if they were coming for him? What if—

Footsteps moved past the door. Silence. Was someone standing outside the door guarding him? Had another someone stopped by to issue orders?

Bent balled his hands into tight fists and beat on the door. "Let me out of here! Why are you doing this? What are you going to do with me?"

He pummeled the door until his fists turned red, until they ached something awful. And he hollered while he banged on the hard wooden surface—hollered until he was hoarse. But no one replied. No one released him. It was as if no one could hear him.

Anger boiled inside Bent, mingling with fear and frustration. He kicked the wall, denting the Sheetrock with his toe. Damn! He couldn't blast his way out of here. He was stuck, trapped, caught.

Bent flung himself down on the neatly made bed, shoved his crossed arms behind his head and glared up at the ceiling. He had to find a way to get out of here, to free himself from his captors. But how? He didn't know. But there had to be a way. He sure as hell wasn't going to give up! Not now. Not ever.

"Are you sure you don't want me to stay with you?" Janice asked as she stood on the front porch with Maggie. "I can spend the night."

"No, Egan said to clear the house. He doesn't want anyone here when he arrives." Maggie hugged her arms around her as she waited for her friend to leave.

"Why do you trust him? He's the man who ran out on you and left you pregnant."

"Egan never made me any promises."

"No, but he didn't have a problem taking advantage of you, did he? He sweet-talked his way into your bed, made you fall in love with him and then told you that he wasn't interested in a committed relationship."

"None of that matters now," Maggie said. "All that's important is that he knows what's happened to Bent and he's promised to bring my son home to me."

"And you believe him?"

"Yes, I do."

"Aren't you the least bit suspicious? You haven't heard from the guy in fifteen years and suddenly, on the very day

Bent disappears, he calls to tell you he knows Bent is his
son.''

"Yes, of course I'm suspicious. But I know—I know!—
that Egan is as concerned about Bent as I am. I could hear
it in his voice. He was in pain.'' Maggie looked out over
the front yard. Streetlights on either end of the block illuminated the manicured lawn and flower beds. She and Bent
did all the yard work themselves—a mother and son proj-
ect.

Janice gave Maggie a tight hug, then released her and
walked down the porch steps. ''I'm a phone call away. I
can be back here in five minutes.''

"Go on home and get some rest. Call me in the morning,
if you haven't heard from me before then.''

"Okay. And don't worry about the bookstore. I'll take
care of things there.''

Maggie remained on the porch until Janice backed her
car out of the driveway, then she turned and went inside
the house. In the foyer, the tick of the grandfather clock's
pendulum kept time with her heartbeat. As she made her
way through the living room and dining room and into the
kitchen, she found herself wishing Janice and the others
hadn't cleaned up after themselves. If they had left dirty
glasses and nasty ashtrays, at least she'd have something
to do, something to occupy her mind while she waited.

She had thought of nothing else for the past two hours
except the fact that Egan Cassidy knew what had happened
to Bent. She had gone over at least a dozen possibilities,
but not even one plot line was based in reality. Her mind
had run the gamut from Bent having left home to find his
biological father to someone from Egan's mercenary world
having kidnapped Bent to hold him for ransom.

Maggie found herself alone in the kitchen, her favorite
room of the house. All her life, since early childhood when

she had hovered at her grandmother's side and watched her beloved MaMa create mouthwatering meals, Maggie had found her greatest solace in this room.

She had redecorated the kitchen and the master bedroom shortly after her divorce, needing to wipe away any memories of Gil. Forgetting her five-year-marriage to her childhood friend had been easy enough, especially when he had remarried so quickly. In less than six months after their divorce was final. Even then, realizing that he'd probably been unfaithful to her for quite some time, she still couldn't blame him for the demise of the marriage. How could she hold him at fault when he had always known that he was her second choice, that Bent's father was the one man she had truly loved?

Rummaging in the cabinets for the ingredients to MaMa's tea cakes—Bent's favorite—Maggie let her mind drift back to the first time she ever saw Egan Cassidy. Oh, she'd heard about Egan for years. Bentley had talked about his old war buddy, when he was sober as well as when he was drinking. Her brother had admired and respected Egan in a way he had no other man. Several times over the years, Bentley had gone to Memphis to visit Egan, to share a few days of wine, women and song. But Egan had never come to Parsons City. Not until Bentley died.

Three weeks after Bentley's funeral she'd gone to the cemetery to put fresh flowers on the grave. Just as she rose from her knees, she noticed someone behind her. The stranger stood by the willow tree at the edge of the Tyson plot. He didn't say anything, didn't make a move to come toward her. But when she passed him, she looked into his intense dark eyes and saw the pain.

"Did you know my brother?" she asked.

"You're Maggie, aren't you?"

"Yes." She felt drawn to this man, as if he existed solely to comfort her.

"I'm Egan Cassidy. I didn't find out about Bentley until yesterday," he explained. "I've been out of the country on business."

"I called and left several messages. And when I didn't hear from you, I wrote."

"I'm sorry I wasn't here for the funeral."

"He killed himself." She heard her voice, heard her state the undeniable fact and yet she felt as if someone else were speaking. "He took his pistol, put it in his mouth and pulled—" She burst into tears.

Egan wrapped his arms around her and eased her up against his body, encompassing her in a tender, comforting embrace. "I should have been here for you. Bentley was the best friend I ever had. I owed him my life."

Maggie had clung to Egan, feeling safe and secure. And knowing that this man shared her grief. Bentley's Vietnam comrade understood as no one else did what it had been like for her brother. How he had used alcohol as a crutch to get him through each new day.

She had taken Egan Cassidy home with her and he had stayed for seven days. That had been almost fifteen years ago and she hadn't seen him since.

Maggie mixed the ingredients together with expert precision. She needed no recipe. Indeed, she could prepare these little cakes with her eyes closed. Eggs. Butter—real butter. Flour. Milk. And vanilla. She would make fresh coffee when Egan arrived and serve him tea cakes and coffee in the living room, just as she'd done that day, long ago, when she had opened her home and her heart to Bentley's friend.

At eleven o'clock, Maggie put away her cooking utensils, stored the tea cakes and the raisin-nut bread she had prepared and tidied up the kitchen. Just as she untied the strings on her apron, the doorbell rang. She jumped as if she'd been shot.

Calm down, she cautioned herself. It took every ounce of her willpower not to fall completely apart, not to scream and cry until she was totally insane. But she couldn't come unglued. She had to remain strong and in control. For her own sake and for Bent's sake.

Maggie hung the yellow gingham apron on the back of the Windsor chair at the table, squared her shoulders and marched hurriedly through the house. Before she reached the front door, the bell rang again. He was impatient, she thought. But then, he always had been.

Peering through the glass panes, she saw Egan Cassidy standing on her porch. Big. Tall. Lean. Just as he'd been fifteen years ago. She opened the door.

"Maggie." He studied her face as if he were trying to memorize it, as if he had forgotten how she looked and never wanted to forget again.

"Come in, Egan."

His short, jet-black hair was now laced with silver and he wore a neat, closely cropped beard and mustache that gave him a roguish appearance. An aging desperado. A renegade who lived by his own rules.

Khaki slacks covered his long legs, a brown tweed jacket clung to his broad shoulders and a navy blue cotton shirt covered his muscular chest. His appearance belied the dangerous warrior within him.

"Are you alone?" he asked.

"Yes, I'm alone," she told him. "I did as you asked and sent everyone home. Janice wanted to stay, but—"

Egan lunged toward Maggie, grabbed her shoulders and shoved her gently back into the foyer. He kicked the door closed with his foot. Maggie gasped when she looked up into his eyes and saw fear. Never in her wildest imagination could she have pictured Egan Cassidy afraid of anything or anyone. He was the type of man who put the fear of God into others. But he was invincible, wasn't he? He had not only survived Vietnam, but he had somehow managed to remain sane and return to warfare on an international level as a soldier of fortune.

What—or who—was Egan afraid of?

She trembled, her whole body convulsing in one long, uncontrollable shiver. If Egan was afraid, then she had reason to be terrified.

"Why didn't you tell me that I had a son?" he demanded.

"What?" She tried to pull free of his tenacious hold, but he held her fast.

"If I'd known about Bent, I could have found a way to protect him, to protect both of you!"

"I don't understand, dammit. What are you talking about? Why would Bent and I need protection?"

"Why didn't you tell me?" he asked again.

Maggie had never thought this day would come. Not really. Oh, she had once fantasized that Egan would learn about Bent and how he would come to her, profess his undying love and claim her and her son for his own. But those daydreams had died a slow, painful death. After waiting five years for Egan's return, she had finally agreed to marry Gil. Another monumental mistake she'd made.

"Why would I have told you? You'd made it perfectly clear that you and I had no future. You didn't want any type of commitments in your life. No wife. No children. That is what you said, isn't it?"

Egan released his grip on her shoulders, but quickly draped his arm around her and led her into the living room.

She went with him quite willingly, not having the strength to argue.

"God, Maggie, I'm so sorry." He stepped away from her and gazed into her eyes. "You'll never know how sorry I am. You're the last person on earth I'd want to hurt. I can't blame you for not telling me about Bent. But heaven help me, I wish you had."

"Would it have made a difference?"

"More than you know."

"More than—are you saying that you would have cared, that you would have wanted to be a part of our lives?"

"I'm saying that if I had known I had a child, I would have found a way to prevent what happened to Bent."

"What—what happened to Bent?"

"A man who hates me, a man with whom I endured months of hell in a Vietcong POW camp, a man who has spent over twenty-five years searching for a way to destroy me, has kidnapped our son."

Chapter 3

Maggie couldn't feel her body. Numbness claimed her from head to toe. She could hear the roar of Egan's words as he continued speaking, but she couldn't understand what he was saying. Suddenly the room began to spin around and around. Maggie reached out, grasping for Egan, but before she could grab him, she fainted dead away.

Egan caught her before she hit the floor, lifted her into his arms and carried her to the sofa. By the time he laid her down and placed a pillow under her head, she opened her eyes and moaned.

"Oh, God." She tried to sit up, but Egan placed his hand in the middle of her chest and forced her to lie still.

"Are you all right?" He hovered over her, wishing so damned hard that he didn't have to put her through the nightmare that lay ahead of them. It was unfair that Maggie was suffering because of him.

"I'm all right." When she looked into his eyes, she smiled weakly. "Really. I'm okay. I don't know what happened. I've never fainted before in my entire life. Not even when I was pregnant with— Oh, God! Bent!'' She reached up and grasped the front of Egan's shirt. ''Bent's been kidnapped by someone who wants to destroy you. This man knows…he knows that Bent is your son. But how?''

Egan helped Maggie to sit up, then eased his big, lanky frame down beside her on the tan-and-cream striped sofa. He ran his hand across the smooth silk fabric, but what he wanted to do was pull Maggie back into his arms. Comfort her. Tell her how sorry he was that this had happened. Beg her to forgive him.

''You put my name on your son's birth certificate,'' Egan said. ''Cullen got hold of a copy. And he also has pictures of Bent. He told me that the boy looks a lot like I did when I was eighteen.''

Maggie nodded. ''Bent does resemble you. He's only fourteen and already six feet tall. He has your gray eyes. Your black hair.'' Maggie's quivering hand lifted ever so slowly and reached out toward Egan's face. ''Why, Egan, why?''

They stared into each other's eyes, each seeking understanding, each sharing a realization that no parent should have to accept.

''He—he…this man you call Cullen, he's going to kill Bent, isn't he?''

Maggie's hand dropped to her side. She sat very still. Egan could hear the sound of her breathing. Silence hung between them like a heavy veil.

''I won't lie to you, Maggie.'' He had never lied to her. Never pretended to be anything other than what he was. Never made her promises he knew he couldn't keep. ''I'm sure that's Cullen's plan.''

Maggie gasped loudly and the agony on her face was

almost more than Egan could bear. For just a split second he had to close his eyes and shut out the sight of her.

"But Cullen won't harm Bent," Egan said. When Maggie's eyes cleared and she looked to him for hope, he amended his statement. "Not yet. He'll want me there. To watch."

Egan shot up off the sofa. How the hell had this happened? He'd been so careful all these years, making sure no woman became important to him, so that Cullen wouldn't have anyone to use against him. He had given up what most men wanted—a wife, children, a real home—in order to prevent this very thing from ever happening.

Pacing the floor, he forked his fingers through his hair and cursed under his breath. "I'll move heaven and earth to stop Cullen," Egan vowed as he halted his prowl and faced Maggie. "I'll find a way to save Bent."

Squaring her shoulders, Maggie lifted her chin and glared at Egan. "What did you do to this man to make him hate you so much? Can't you undo whatever it is you did?" Although she sat perfectly still, her hands folded primly in her lap, there was just a hint of hysteria in her voice. "You can't let him kill…kill my…" Tears glazed her soft, brown eyes.

Egan rushed to her, dropped down on one knee and grabbed her hands. "If I'd only known about Bent, I could have—"

Maggie jerked away from him, shoved him aside and rose to her feet. "Don't you dare blame me for this! You keep saying if only you'd known about Bent, as if it's my fault that he's been kidnapped by some lunatic who wants to punish you." She pointed directly at Egan, who rose from his knees to his full six-foot-three height.

"I didn't mean to imply that this is your fault."

"Then why don't you place the blame where it belongs," she glowered at him, anger and hatred gleaming in her eyes, turning them from brown to black. "You're the reason my son was kidnapped, the reason his life is in danger. You—" she jabbed her finger into the air, pointing it in his direction and then at herself "—not me."

"Maggie, let me explain." He held open his hands, the very act a plea for her understanding.

"Explain what? That you've lead such an unsavory life, such a wicked life, that you have evil men, capable of murder, searching for ways to punish you." Maggie flew toward him, her arms lifted, her hands cupped into taut fists. "The hard, cruel world you chose to live in, the ungodly way you chose to make a living is the reason Bent's life is in danger." Maggie hurled her fists into Egan's chest. "You've never cared about anyone—ever! You've lived only for yourself, never wanting or needing me or my child. You don't deserve to be a father!"

Her slender, white fists flayed him repeatedly. He barely felt the blows in a physical sense, but emotionally he felt as if Maggie had stripped him down to his bones, with one angry, cutting accusation after another.

He stood unmoving, allowing her to vent her frustration, to beat her fists against his chest until she was spent. He deserved her hatred. She was right. It *was* his fault that Cullen had kidnapped Bent.

When Maggie's blows lost their strength and she seemed barely able to raise her hands, Egan wrapped his arms around her. If only she would allow him to hold her, to comfort her, then perhaps he could find some small amount of comfort himself. Her head lay against his chest as she sucked in her breath, gasping for air. Uncertain how to proceed, Egan lifted one hand to her head and caressed her hair. He remembered how much he had loved Maggie's long, mahogany-red hair.

"I'm sorry," he whispered. "I'd give anything if I could have spared you."

As if suddenly realizing that the man who held her was the enemy, Maggie disengaged herself from his embrace and shoved him away. "I don't want your apologies. Saying I'm sorry now is too little, too late. All I want from you is for you to save Bent."

"I'm going to do everything—" Egan's cellular phone rang.

Maggie jumped. "Would he call you on your cell phone?"

"No. There's not any way he could get this number. All the phones issued to Dundee agents have restricted numbers and operate with a scrambling security frequency."

Maggie laughed, the sound harsh and brittle. "You're still in the cloak-and-dagger business, aren't you?"

"Look, I need to get this," Egan said, then removed his small cell phone from the clip on his belt. "Yeah?"

"Egan, I've called in our top six men," Ellen Denby, the CEO of the Dundee agency, said. "And I've put in a call to Sam to alert him that you're going to need not only manpower, but that he'll need to use all his connections to make sure we head up this operation and we get full cooperation from the FBI. By the way, are you already in Alabama?"

"Thanks for handling things for me," Egan said. "And, yes, I'm in Alabama, with the mother of my child."

"Any word from the kidnapper?"

"Not yet. But it's only a matter of time."

"I've already called in a few favors of my own," Ellen told him. "I'll have a dossier a foot thick on Grant Cullen by morning. I'll know what toothpaste he buys and how many times a day he uses the john."

"Have the men on standby," Egan said. "As soon as

we hear from Cullen, I want to move in quick and hit him hard.'' When Egan heard Maggie gasp, he glanced across the room at her and their gazes locked. ''My one and only objective is to rescue my son. Getting Cullen will be a bonus.'' Egan saw the startled look on Maggie's face, the shock in her eyes, the very minute she realized that in order to save Bent, Egan might have to annihilate his abductor.

''When you're ready to move, just let me know,'' Ellen said.

''You're the best, Denby.''

''Yeah, and don't you ever forget it.''

Egan hit the Off button and returned his cell phone to its nest on his hip. ''I work for a private security and investigation firm based in Atlanta,'' he explained to Maggie, who was staring at him questioningly. ''I've been with them for a couple of years now. Most of the agents are former special forces or former lawmen, all highly trained professionals. My boss has just called in the top six men at Dundee's to be ready to act on my command, once we hear from Cullen.''

''You're planning Bent's rescue as if it's a commando attack, as if this man Cullen is going to tell you where he has Bent and invite you to come and get him.'' Maggie flung her hands out on either side of her body in an are-you-insane? gesture. ''This is my child's life we're talking about. I'm going to call the FBI right now. I've had enough of this craziness.''

Maggie swerved around and headed toward the white and gold telephone sitting atop the chinoiserie cabinet positioned along the back wall. Egan reached her in three giant strides and grabbed her arm just as she lifted the receiver.

''Put the phone down.'' His voice brooked no refusal.

Maggie glared at him, hesitating to obey his command.

When he tightened his hold on her arm, she winced. "Why should I listen to you? Why should I do what you tell me to do?"

"Because handling this situation my way is the only chance we have of getting our son back alive."

Maggie continued staring at Egan, but she gradually lowered her arm and replaced the telephone receiver. "So, what do we do now?"

Egan released her and when she rubbed her arm, he realized he might have held her too tightly. "Did I hurt you?"

"No, not really. You just don't know your own strength."

"You've got to believe me, Maggie, I'd never intentionally hurt you."

"That's debatable," she told him. "But it isn't important. Not anymore. But you didn't answer my question, what do we do now?"

"We wait."

"Wait for what?"

"Wait for Grant Cullen to call us and give us his demands."

Grant Cullen strolled the grounds of his secluded Arizona camp, hidden away in the mountains southeast of Flagstaff. It had taken him years to build and stock his retreat and to man it with his own army. His troops, though few in number, were well-trained young men—schooled personally by him. Two dozen well-trained and obedient followers were worth more to him than a hundred ordinary men.

He had founded the Ultimate Survivalists thirteen years ago when he had realized that eventually he and other brave souls would have to defend themselves against an ever strengthening left-wing, liberal government. There were many men such as he who felt it their God given right to govern their own lives without interference from Uncle Sam. The time would come when chaos would reign and only those who had prepared themselves for the confrontation would survive. When martial law was declared and men were stripped of their rights and their weapons, he and his followers would be prepared to fight to the death.

He had spent a lifetime acquiring the means to secure land in the United States and create a hideaway where he could retreat after every mercenary mission. He and Egan had been in the same line of business, ever since they'd returned from Nam. The only difference was that he hadn't been choosy about the people who hired him. He had no allegiances to any country, not even his own. He hired out to the highest bidder and did whatever nasty little chore that needed to be done.

And all the while he had been planning and preparing, he had known this day would come. The day of reckoning. The day he would finally have the revenge that was long overdue.

His rottweilers, Patton and MacArthur, trotted on either side of him, two ever-alert canines with the same killer instincts he himself possessed. And like the men under his command, obedient unto death.

After sunset, even springtime in the mountains maintained winterlike temperatures and tonight was no exception. A cold north wind whipped around Grant's shoulders. He breathed deeply, dragging in as much fresh, crisp air as his lungs would hold. Invigorated by thoughts of triumph over his nemesis, he experienced a feeling of pure happiness that he hadn't known since before Nam. Before having been a POW. Before having had his promising military career destroyed by an eighteen-year-old recruit with a Boy Scout mentality.

Grant Cullen had been the son, grandson and great-grandson of West Point graduates and no one had been prouder than he the day his name was added to that family tradition. And no one had been more willing to serve his country than he. Everyone who knew him had been certain that he would one day be a great general, just as his heroes, George Patton and Douglas MacArthur had been.

But Egan Cassidy had ruined any chances he'd had of a distinguished military career. Once Cassidy had exposed him as a traitor, even his own father had turned against him. It had been his word against Cassidy's until that snot-nosed Vietcong major had been captured and had collaborated Cassidy's story.

Revenge had been a long time coming, but finally Cassidy was going to get what he deserved. He was going to learn what real suffering was all about.

Grant entered the two-story fortress through the wrought-iron gates that opened up into an outdoor foyer. Two guards, one outside the gate and one inside saluted him when he passed by. He marched into the interior entrance hall, the rottweilers at his heels.

"Winn! Winn!" Grant called loudly. "Where the hell are you?"

The stocky, hard-as-nails Winn Sherman, stormed down the long corridor that led from Grant's office and met his commander halfway. "Yes, sir!" He clicked his heels and saluted.

"Bring the boy to my office." Grant checked the time. "In exactly forty-eight minutes. I'll be making a phone call precisely at three o'clock and I want young Bent Douglas to say a few words to the folks at home."

The corners of Winn's thin lips curved into a smile.

Grant liked his protégé, a man who shared Grant's thoughts and beliefs. A man he trusted as he trusted few others.

"You will personally be in charge of Cassidy's son from now until…" Grant laughed heartily, as he contemplated the various ways he could kill the boy—slowly and painfully while his father and mother watched.

In her peripheral vision Maggie saw Egan down the last drops of his third cup of coffee and then set the Lenox cup on the saucer that rested on the silver serving tray. The grandfather clock in the foyer struck the half hour. Maggie lifted her head from where it rested on the curved extension of the wing chair. Instant calculations told her it was now two-thirty. Her muscles ached from tension. Her frazzled nerves kept her on the verge of tears at any given moment. And her heart ached with a burden almost too great to bear. No mother should ever have to endure what she was being forced to endure.

But she had never been a pessimist or a quitter or a whiner. She wouldn't—couldn't—give up hope. She had to trust Egan, had to believe that he could do what he had promised—save their son. But who did he think he was, some kind of superhero? Maybe he was a rough, tough, mean son of a bitch. Maybe he did know a hundred and one ways to kill a man. And maybe he did have an elite force of Dundee agents prepared to do battle with him. But did that mean he could rescue Bent?

She watched Egan as he treaded across the Persian rug centered in the middle of the living-room floor. Weariness sat on his broad shoulders like an invisible weight. He plopped down on the couch and tossed aside a white brocade throw pillow, which landed on its mate at the opposite end of the camelback sofa. Bending at the waist, he dangled his hands between his spread legs and gazed down at his feet. He repeatedly tapped his fingertips together and patted his right foot against the hardwood surface, just inches shy of the large, intricately patterned rug.

Her feminine instinct told Maggie that Egan was suffering in his own strong, silent way. He hadn't shed a tear. Hadn't shown much emotion at all, except anger. And he most certainly hadn't fainted, as she had. But she knew he was in pain. In some strange way she could feel his agony and understood that he probably could feel hers just as intensely.

Was he feeling guilty? she wondered. He should feel guilty! Because of something in his past, her son's life now depended upon the whims of a madman.

A part of Maggie hated Egan, more than she'd ever thought possible to hate anyone. But a part of her pitied him and shared his grief. And yet another part of her, a small, nagging emotion buried deep inside, still cared for him.

You fool! she chastised herself. This is the man who broke your heart. He left you and never looked back. He didn't want you and he wouldn't have wanted Bent. The only reason he wishes he'd known of his son's existence is so he could have figured out some way to have protected Bent from Grant Cullen.

Don't you ever forget what kind of man Egan is. You were naive enough once to think that your love could change him, could liberate him from the bonds of a lonely, unhappy existence.

"Would you like me to make some fresh coffee?" she asked.

Egan's head snapped up; his eyes focused on her. "Yeah, sure. And maybe something to eat, for both of us. I'll bet you haven't had a bite since lunch yesterday, have you?"

''I'll fix you something,'' she said. ''I don't think I could eat anything.''

''Why don't I go into the kitchen with you and we'll fix something together, and then I want you to try to eat something. You can't help Bent by making yourself sick.''

I can't help Bent at all, she felt like screaming. But she held herself in check, suppressing the urge to rant and rave.

Egan stood, walked over to her and held out his hand. She stared at his big hand, studying his wide, thick fingers, dusted with dark hair just below the knuckles. A tingling awareness spread through Maggie as she recalled exactly how hairy Egan was. Dark curls covered his muscular arms and long legs. Thick swirls of black hair coated his chest, narrowing into a V across his belly and widening again around his sex.

Sensual heat spread through Maggie, flushing her skin and warming her insides. *How could she be reacting to Egan sexually at a time like this?* her conscience taunted. What sort of power did this man have over her, that after fifteen years, she was still drawn to him in the same stomach-churning, femininity-clenching way?

Apparently tired of waiting for a response from her, Egan reached out, grasped her hand and hauled her to her feet. She wavered slightly, her legs weak, as she stood facing him, her gaze level with his neck. He had once teased her about being tall and leggy.

I'm a leg man, he had said. *And you, Maggie my love, fulfill all my fantasies.*

Without asking permission, Egan slipped his arms around her waist and held her, but didn't tug her up against him. ''You haven't changed much, Maggie. You're still... You're even more beautiful than you were the first time I saw you.''

She told herself to move away from him, to demand that

he release her and never touch her again. But she knew that all she had to do was slip out of his hold. His grip on her was tentative, featherlight and easily escaped.

Everything that was female within her longed to lean on him, to seek comfort and support in the power of his strong arms and big body. She was so alone and had been for what seemed like a lifetime. And who better than her son's father to give her the solace she so desperately needed at a time like this?

Don't succumb to this momentary weakness, to the seduction of Egan's powerful presence and manly strength, an inner voice warned. *If you do, you'll regret it.*

She lifted her gaze to meet Egan's and almost drowned in the gentle, concerned depths of his gunmetal-gray eyes. "I have changed," she told him. "I have very little in common with that starry-eyed, twenty-three-year-old girl who rushed into your arms…and into your bed, without a second thought."

"I was very fond of that girl." Regret edged Egan's voice.

Fond of. Fond of. The words rang out inside her head like a blast from a loudspeaker. Oh, yes, he had been *fond of* her. And she had *loved* him. Madly. Passionately. With every beat of her foolish, young heart.

Maggie eased out of his grasp. He let her go, making no move to detain her flight. When she turned and walked away, he followed her.

"You put on the coffee," she said, her back to him. "And I'll make a couple of sandwiches."

Egan went with her into the kitchen and although the room had been redecorated since his weeklong visit years ago, the warm hominess mixed quite well with the touch of elegance, just as the decor had back then. Creamy cabinetry, curtains and chairs contrasted sharply to the earth-brown walls, the brown-and-tan checkered chair cushions and dark oak of the wooden table.

He went over to the counter at the right of the sink and there, where she had always kept it, he found the coffee grinder. "You still keep the beans in the refrigerator?"

"Yes." She didn't glance his way. Instead she opened the refrigerator, retrieved the coffee beans and held them out to him, without once looking at him.

He grasped the jar, accepting her avoidance without comment, and pulled out a drawer, searching for a scoop. Then he asked her a question that had been bothering him. Tormenting him actually—ever since Cullen had told him that Maggie had married and divorced the man who had been her fiancé before Egan became her first lover.

"What happened with Gil Douglas?"

Maggie almost dropped the head of lettuce she held in her hand, but managed to grab the plastic container before it hit the floor. "Gil and I married when Bent was five." *After I'd given up all hope that you'd ever return to claim your son and me.* "Gil and I managed to hold things together for five years and then we divorced."

Beginning and end of story! Egan thought. Her meaning had been so clear that she might as well have made the statement.

"Gil adopted Bent?"

"Yes." Maggie retrieved the makings for their sandwiches and dumped the ingredients on the work island directly across from the refrigerator.

Where was Bent right now? her heart cried. Was he hungry? Was he hurt? Was he frightened? Did he know that the lunatic who had kidnapped him intended to murder him?

"Are Gil and Bent close?" Egan asked. "Do they have a good father-son relationship?" His feelings were torn between hoping Gil was such a great dad that his son didn't need him and wishing that he would have the opportunity to be a real father to Bent.

"Is Gil here, now, waiting with me, out of his mind with worry?" she asked, not the least bit of anger in her voice, only a sad resignation. "That should tell you what sort of relationship they have."

"I assume Bent knows Gil isn't his father." Egan waited for her to respond. She didn't. "Does he know…? Have you ever told him…? What I'm trying to say is—"

"He knows his father's name is Egan Cassidy. Like you said, your name is on his birth certificate." She opened the cellophane-wrapped loaf and pulled out four slices of wheat bread. "I'm afraid that I mixed truth with fiction when I told him about his conception." She unscrewed the mayonnaise jar. "I told him that you and I had loved each other, but that we had ended our affair before I knew I was pregnant."

Egan ground the coffee beans to a fine consistency, measured the correct amount, then dumped them into the filter. "What else did you tell him about me?"

Maggie searched a drawer in the island and brought out a knife, which she used to spread the mayonnaise on the bread. "I told him that you were a soldier of fortune who worked all over the world and that we had agreed there was no way a marriage between us would ever work."

Egan filled the coffee carafe from the jug of spring water that rested on a stand in front of one floor-to-ceiling window. "You were generous, Maggie. More generous than I deserved."

She washed the ripe tomato, placed it on the cutting board and sliced through the delicate skin. "I didn't lie for you, Egan. I lied for Bent's sake."

Bent, her precious baby boy, who was alone and afraid.

And probably asking why this had happened to him. Oh, God, where was he? And why hadn't Grant Cullen contacted Egan? What was he waiting for? But she knew, as did Egan, that the man was prolonging their torture, savoring each moment he could make Egan suffer.

"Will Bent hate me when we meet?"

"You mean *if* you meet, don't you?" Her hands trembled. The knife slipped and sliced into her finger. She cried out, startled by what she'd accidentally done to herself.

Egan rushed to her side, grabbed her hand and turned on the faucets of the island sink. Holding her injured finger under the cool running water, Egan said, "Cry, dammit, Maggie. Go ahead and cry!"

She snatched her hand from his and inspected the wound. Enough to require a bandage but not stitches, she surmised. "I'll just wrap a piece of paper towel around it to stop the blood flow. Later, I'll put a bandage on it."

He stood by and watched her as she doctored her own cut, all the while wishing she would allow him to do it for her.

"Bent is safe," Egan assured her. "And he'll remain safe until Cullen has me right where he wants me."

"Then don't go." Maggie shook her head, realizing how irrational her thoughts had become. "Don't listen to me. I don't know what I'm saying."

Tears glistened in Maggie's eyes. Egan wished to hell she'd just go ahead and break down. He'd rather see her screaming and throwing things than to see her like this. Deadly calm. Numb from pain.

If only she would let him hold her. But he knew better than to try again. Every time he got too close, she shoved him away. He was the one person on earth who could even begin to understand the agony she was experiencing, and yet he was the one person she wouldn't allow herself to turn to for comfort.

The telephone rang. Egan froze to the spot. Maggie cried out, the sound a shocked, mournful gasp.

Egan walked over to the wall-mounted, brown telephone that hung between two glass-globed, brass sconces. With his stomach tied in knots and his hand unsteady, he lifted the receiver. Maggie hurried to his side.

"Cassidy here."

Maggie grabbed his arm.

"Hello, buddy boy," Grant Cullen said. "I've got somebody here who wants to talk to his mama."

Chapter 4

Egan placed the receiver to Maggie's ear. Her inquiring gaze searched Egan's eyes, and then suddenly she heard the sweetest sound on earth.

"Mama."

"Bent!"

"I'm all right, Mama. They haven't hurt me. Don't worry—"

"Bent? Bent?"

Another voice, one she didn't want to hear, spoke to her. "Maggie, put Cassidy back on the phone."

"No, please, let me talk to Bent," Maggie said. "Whatever reason you have to hate Egan, don't take your revenge out on an innocent boy. Bent doesn't mean anything to Egan. They don't even know each other." Tears welled up in her eyes.

When Egan yanked the phone away from her, Maggie crumbled like a broken cookie, her nerves shattered. Before he returned the receiver to his ear, he grabbed her around the waist and hauled her to his side. Holding her securely, he spoke to Cullen.

"Name the time and the place," Egan said.

Cullen chuckled. Egan's stomach churned. Salty bile rose in his throat.

"Maggie seems a tad upset," Cullen said. "I suppose she's worried about her son. So, how does it feel, big man? I'm holding all the cards and there's no way you can win."

"Name your terms." Egan tried to keep his voice calm. The last thing he wanted was for Cullen to pick up on the panic he felt. The bastard fed off other people's misery.

"I could just kill the boy right now," Cullen said, every word laced with vindictive pleasure. "That way your son would be dead and your woman would hate you until her dying day."

"You want more than that, don't you, Cullen? I can't believe you'd be satisfied with such a paltry revenge."

Maggie's wide-eyed stare momentarily broke Egan's concentration. He realized that she was on the verge of losing it completely. She'd taken just about all she could stand. Without giving his actions a thought, he pressed his lips to her temple and kissed her tenderly. She melted against him, her arms clinging, her body shaking, as she buried her face against his chest.

"You know me too well, buddy boy," Cullen said. "After Nam my pretty little wife left me and took my kid with her. My father never spoke to me again and even disinherited me. I left the army in disgrace. And I owe all those good things to you." Cullen chuckled again. "Now, it's payback time. And payback is going to be a bitch."

"Just name your terms. What, where and when. And I'll be there."

"You and Maggie."

"No," Egan said. "Not Maggie. Just me."

Maggie lifted her head, puzzlement in her eyes. He shook his head, cautioning her to keep quiet.

"You bring your woman or there is no deal. I'll put a gun to your boy's head and blow his brains out. Do I make myself perfectly clear?"

"Perfectly." Egan narrowed his gaze, frowning at Maggie when he noticed she had opened her mouth to speak.

"You haven't done something stupid, like calling in the feds, have you?" Cullen asked.

"Maggie notified the local authorities, but no one else." He kept his gaze focused on her face. She had to keep quiet and let him handle things from here on out. She only suspected what they were up against with Grant Cullen, but he knew. God help them, he knew!

"Good. I figured you were too smart to screw up like that. As long as you keep using your brains and following orders, Bent stays alive. Screw with me and he's dead!"

Egan heard the snap of Cullen's fingers. His own heartbeat thumped an erratic *rat-a-tat-tat*, the sound humming in his ears.

"Your game, your rules," Egan said. He rubbed Maggie's back, trying to soothe her, but at his touch she tensed even more.

"Got that damn straight."

"What do I have to do?" Egan asked.

"All you have to do is come get your son. You want to see him, don't you? Flesh of your flesh. Bone of your bone. The fruit of your loins."

"Yeah, sure, I want to see him."

"Then why don't you and Maggie hop a plane and come on out to Arizona for a visit. It'd be nice if you could get here within forty-eight hours. That way the boy would still be alive when you get here."

"Forty-eight hours. I think that can be arranged."

Maggie glared at Egan and he understood she wanted to speak, wanted to ask questions, but wisely remained silent.

"Won't be as easy as you think, buddy boy," Cullen told him. "My place is rather secluded. Can't get here except on foot. Of course, I've got my own helicopter pad, but I don't want you flying in. You might bring company with you and we wouldn't want extra visitors showing up, now would we? If that were to happen, I'd have to execute your son immediately."

"I understand. So, where exactly are you located?"

"Fly into Flagstaff, then take Highway 40 southeast. When you come to a town called Minerva, go to Schmissrauter's Garage and ask for directions to the general's fort. You can take a Jeep part of the way in, then you'll have to switch to horseback. But I want you and Maggie to walk in, so leave your horses."

Instantly Egan began calculating the scenario, trying to figure out the best plan of action. But any way you looked at it, the chances of rescuing Bent and his getting Maggie and himself out alive were—with the aid of the Dundee agents—fifty-fifty. If he discounted himself, then the odds rose to maybe sixty-forty in their favor.

"Anything else I should know?" Egan asked.

"That's about it...except...I'm looking forward to meeting your son's mother. Figure I'll enjoy getting to know her and I'll make sure she enjoys getting to know me."

Egan clenched his teeth together. Even knowing what Cullen was doing, why he was taunting him with images of Maggie being raped, it took every ounce of Egan's willpower to keep from telling the slimy bastard to go straight to hell. At that precise moment, he knew that if he ever got his hands on Cullen, he would kill him.

The dial tone hummed in Egan's ear. He replaced the receiver, then turned and pulled Maggie into his embrace.

No one was going to hurt this woman more than she'd already been hurt. If he had to move heaven and earth to protect her and their son, then that's what he'd do. If it meant dying to save them, then he would gladly lay down his life.

Do you hear me, God? Are you listening? Do we have a bargain? My life for Maggie's life and Bent's?

Maybe he'd better improve the odds, he thought. More than likely his soul was going to burn in hell anyway, so maybe he should be making his bargain with Lucifer instead of the Almighty.

You want my soul, Old Scratch? I'm willing to make a bargain with you, too, if that's what it takes to save Maggie and Bent.

"Egan?" Maggie's voice rasped with emotion.

He looked down into her eyes, into those beautiful, warm brown eyes and his only thought was how dear and good and loving Maggie was.

His lips took hers in a breath-robbing kiss as his arms tightened around her. Equal parts of frustration and desire dictated the intensity of the kiss. As if her body had never forgotten the feel of his, Maggie responded. Her breasts pressed against his chest as she fitted herself snugly to him. When she opened her mouth to him, he accepted the invitation.

Egan kissed her until they were both breathless, then he laid his forehead against hers and whispered into her mouth, "I care, Maggie. I did then and I do now."

Turning her head so that she couldn't see the expression in his eyes, she hunched her shoulders and slid out of his embrace. "What about Bent? My son is the only thing that matters to me. I don't care about you or me or how either of us feels about the other."

How could he blame her for the way she felt? She was

a mother whose only child had been kidnapped by a psychotic son of a bitch who had every intention of killing the boy.

"I know where *our* son is," he told her. "And you and I are going to get him and bring him home."

Bent understood things a lot better now. Now that he knew when the man in charge said "your father," he wasn't talking about Gil Douglas. He was referring to Egan Cassidy, who was nothing more to Bent than a name on his birth certificate.

His being kidnapped was connected to some sort of grudge this man had against Egan Cassidy. Bent realized that he was simply a pawn in a game between two mercenaries. A prize to be won. Or lost.

While two burly guards flanked him on either side, Bent studied his abductor. Six feet. Maybe six-one. Somewhere in his early to mid-fifties and in great physical shape for an old guy. There was definitely a crazy look in his blue eyes, as if he were spaced out on speed. He laughed too much. And a nervous twitch pinched his left cheek and blinked his left eye from time to time.

He wore army fatigues and his men called him General. His grayish-brown hair had been cropped short like a GI from an old fifties movie. And he strutted around as if he were king of the world.

The general looked directly at Bent, then pointed his index finger at him. Bent swallowed hard. Show no fear, he told himself. Show no fear. But how the hell did he do that when he was so scared he was about to wet in his pants?

"Your old man's on his way here."

"I guess you're talking about Egan Cassidy, aren't you?" Bent asked.

"Yeah. So you know who your father is? What did your mother tell you about my old buddy, Cassidy?"

"Nothing," Bent said. "Just that he fought in Nam with my uncle Bentley and that he became a mercenary after the war."

"Then you don't know that your old man is one of the toughest sons of a bitch that ever lived. His own life never meant spit to him, so just killing him was never an option." The general approached Bent, a sick smile on his face. "I've waited over twenty-five years to find his Achilles' heel." The general jabbed his finger into Bent's chest. "And here you are, the answer to my prayers—Egan Cassidy's kid, all mine to do with what I will."

Bent lunged at the general, but before he could touch him, the two guards grabbed Bent and jerked him back away from their leader.

"If Egan Cassidy is the hard-ass you say he is, he'll storm this place and kick your butt!" Bent shouted.

The general laughed long and hard and loud. Then as his laughter died down, he clamped one large, hard hand over Bent's shoulder and looked him square in the eye.

"You're just like your old man. God, would he be proud of you."

Joe Ornelas answered the phone on the third ring. "Yeah, Ornelas here."

"Joe, this is Egan Cassidy. Has Ellen been in touch with you?"

"She called me about an hour ago. Hey, man, I'm really sorry about your kid."

"Thanks," Egan said. "Ellen is using the Dundee jet so we can be in Arizona as quickly as possible. Cullen's given us a forty-eight-hour deadline and the clock is ticking."

"I'm already packed," Joe told him. "Ellen and I figured you'd need somebody familiar with the lay of the land, who just happened to be a pretty good tracker."

"She explained to you why you can't go all the way in with Maggie and me, didn't she?"

"Sure did. All I'll do is get you there, then I'll join forces with our guys who'll be coming in by helicopter, within a few miles of Cullen's fort," Joe said. "Ellen put together Whitelaw, O'Brien, Parker and Wolfe for this operation."

"Counting you, that's only five men. I asked for six."

"You'll have six. Ellen's taking this one on personally."

"Why am I not surprised?"

Cassidy had never known a woman quite like Ellen Denby. She was equal parts femme fatale and highly trained commando. Every man who worked for Dundee liked and respected the CEO of the agency.

Although she was everybody's buddy in a social setting, she kept her private life strictly private. And if there was a man in her life, she kept him private, too.

"We'll all be aboard the jet when we pick up you and Ms. Douglas. We can work out our plan of attack and rescue on the way to Flagstaff. Ellen's already pulled in a few favors and gotten maps that pinpoint Cullen's fort, so we won't have to wait for directions in Minerva."

"I take it that somebody's been keeping tabs on Cullen," Egan said. "I assume Ellen didn't give away any secrets in order to acquire info."

"Nobody's going to get in our way," Joe assured him. "This is going to be our party, even though the feds have been invited along."

"If one thing goes wrong—"

"We'll get your kid out alive."

"Joe?"

"Yeah?"

"I don't factor into this rescue operation. Our only objective is to get Maggie and Bent to safety. You got that?"

"Yeah, sure. If it comes down to it, you're expendable."

"Make sure the others understand."

"Yeah. I will."

Maggie dug into the back of her closet, searching for a pair of old jeans that she used when she worked in the yard. Egan had told her she'd need an outfit to wear on the plane trip to Flagstaff and the Jeep ride to Minerva. Something comfortable and practical. Then she'd need jeans, shirt and jacket to change into for the horseback ride and final trek to Grant Cullen's hideaway.

"The last thing I want to do is take you with me," Egan had told her. "But your being with me is one of Cullen's demands. And for now, we have no choice but to play this game by his rules. Do you understand?"

She'd nodded her head and said yes, that she understood. She understood more than Egan realized. The two of them would walk into the lion's den alone and be taken captive by the man who was holding Bent. Their lives would depend on six Dundee agents who would storm the fort and, God willing, save them. Egan hadn't told her what their odds were, but she could guess. He hadn't explained any details or implied that there was even the remotest possibility that he and she and their son could all die, but she knew.

"Got any old boots?" Egan asked.

Gasping, Maggie jumped at the sound of his voice. She had left him downstairs to make a phone call ten minutes ago and his unexpected appearance in her bedroom unnerved her. It had been fifteen years since Egan had been in this room, but she could remember, as if it were yesterday, the long nights and sweet mornings they had shared in her bed.

Nothing in this room was the same, not even the bed. When she married Gil, she had redecorated before he had moved in with her and Bent. And then she'd redecorated again after her divorce. The bed she had shared with Egan was now stored in the attic.

"Boots?" she asked.

"Where we're heading we're going to run into some pretty rough territory. And in the mountains, it'll be cold at night. I want you to wear some heavy socks and some sturdy boots. If you don't have any, we'll have to find you some."

"I have hiking boots," she told him. "Bent and I go to the Smoky Mountains at least once a year to hike the trails. Twice a year, some years. We've done that ever since he was five. Of course, back then we took easy trails and I made it more of an adventure than a real hike."

At the thought that Bent and she might never hike together again, might never share another Smoky Mountain vacation, Maggie's stomach twisted into knots. Her gaze locked with Egan's and she realized he could read her thoughts. But what was he thinking? she wondered. About all the years he had missed with his son? Or that now he was aware of the fact he had a child, he might never get the chance to know him?

"Good," Egan said. "A pair of boots that have already been broken in will be a lot better for your feet."

"I'm almost finished packing." Maggie diverted her attention from the man in her bedroom to a search through her closet. "I'll have to dig the boots out. They're in the back here somewhere." She dove into the walk-in closet, down on her knees, scrambling around, searching through the boxes stored there.

Egan tried not to look at her, did his level best not to notice how curvaceous her hips were or how long her legs were. At thirty-eight, Maggie was a gorgeous woman. In some ways more beautiful than she'd been at twenty-three. Just the sight of her excited him, aroused him. And now, more than then, something about her brought out all his possessive, protective instincts. The primitive man within him recognized her as his mate—his woman.

He had known his share of women, but no one had ever touched his soul. Only Maggie. He supposed that was one of the reasons he had run from her fifteen years ago. Why he had cut their affair short. Because he'd known that he wanted more from her than a brief, no-strings-attached relationship. He could never have had what he'd wanted most—a lifetime with Maggie. He had walked away before it had been too late—before Cullen had learned about their relationship. He had thought that by leaving her, he was protecting her.

Why the hell hadn't he been honest with her back then? Why hadn't he told her about Cullen? If she had known the danger existed, she would have come to him when she'd found out she was carrying his child.

"Here they are." Maggie emerged from the closet, a pair of scuffed, well-worn boots held high, as if they were a prize catch. After tossing them into her unzipped overnight bag, she lifted her underwear and socks off the bed where she had laid them out and then stuffed them into a large side pocket.

"We're going to fly into Flagstaff on the Dundee jet," Egan said. "Six agents will be going with us, but only one—Joe Ornelas, a former Navajo policeman—will be making the trip to the fort with us."

"Aren't you concerned that Grant Cullen will somehow

learn about your plans to storm his fortress? Shouldn't we be more worried about secrecy?''

"Cullen will be expecting an attack," Egan told her. "There's not a chance in hell that we'll take him by surprise."

"I thought he told you that we had to come alone, that we couldn't involve anyone else."

"He did."

"Then I don't understand—"

"Just trust me, Maggie. Believe that I know what I'm doing."

"I'm trusting you with the most precious thing in the world to me. My son's life."

"Our son," Egan corrected. "I might have only known about Bent's existence for less than twenty-four hours, but that doesn't make him any less my son."

Maggie nodded agreement, but quickly whirled around and began searching inside her closet again. Egan wandered around the large, airy bedroom. A row of three tall windows, curtains drawn back, lined the back wall and overlooked the side yard. Early-morning sunlight slipped into the room and lightened the soft pink walls to a pale blush. A beige cotton throw hung over the arm of a floral-upholstered settee at the foot of the bed. This had been the room he had shared with Maggie, but that wasn't the bed. If not for the distinct architecture of the room itself, he wouldn't have recognized it. She had changed everything, including the furniture.

As Egan sauntered past a writing desk in front of the windows, he noticed several volumes held upright by fleur-de-lis brass bookends. Curious as to why these particular books warranted a special place atop her desk, in her bedroom, Egan removed one thin volume. For a split second his heart stopped.

I Remember. By Nage Styon.

One by one he removed, examined and then returned to its place each of the six volumes of poetry. Memories. Cries from the heart. The soul's torment. A vein opened and words were written in the author's blood.

He was the class of sixty-three
full of hopes, dreams, and ideas for his future
but returned with death, nightmares, horrors,
the blood of friends on his hands,
the smell of rot encrusted in his memory,
something in the jungle stalking his soul...

Did Maggie have any idea who the author was? Egan wondered. Or had she purchased these specific books and kept them close to her because they helped her understand her brother and the hell he had lived through in a faraway country when he'd been not much more than a boy and she only a small child? When a publisher had bought Egan's first volume of poetry, he had insisted on using a pseudonym. Had Maggie deciphered the thinly veiled transposition of letters that formed the name Egan Tyson? Although he wrote the poetry, he believed that the sentiments expressed came from Bentley's soul as well as his own, so he used both his name and his deceased friend's name.

"Have you ever read Nage Styon?" Maggie asked.

Egan almost dropped the book he held, but managed to clutch it to his chest. "Yes, I've read all these volumes. I see you have everything he's written."

"I ordered his first book twelve years ago, when it was first published and I've been a devoted fan ever since." Maggie folded her faded jeans and laid them alongside her boots inside the vinyl overnight bag. "Whenever I read his poetry, I cry," she admitted. "I think about Bentley. And

I think about you." She took a deep breath. "And all the other young men who had their lives forever changed by that war."

"All those young men, those who are still alive, are all old men now," Egan said, unable to discern whether or not Maggie knew the truth about the author. "Most of them are older than I am and not a one of them has ever forgotten. Grant Cullen sure never forgot what happened in that POW camp."

Egan could sense Maggie tense when he mentioned Cullen. He should tell her about those months he and Cullen had been together, prisoners of the Vietcong. She had a right to know why her son had been kidnapped, why Cullen planned to kill all three of them.

He had never told anyone the whole story and never would. Only in the deepest, darkest recesses of his soul did the complete memory of those months remain. But he could tell her the basic facts, the simple truth of why for the past twenty-eight years he had spent his life waiting, looking over his shoulder, wondering when and where Grant Cullen could attack. Never had he considered the possibility that Cullen's *day of reckoning* would involve Maggie and her child.

"Did the war mess up Cullen's mind?" Maggie asked, as she walked over to Egan and took the book of poetry from him. Her fingers touched his briefly during the exchange. A whisper touch. Fleeting, yet tremendously powerful.

"Cullen was pretty messed up before he ever went to Nam."

She placed the book with the others and straightened the row. "Why does he hate you?" she asked.

"Because I destroyed his military career. Cullen was a West Point graduate, just like his father and grandfather before him."

"How did you destroy his career?"

"Short and simple. During our detainment in a POW camp, Cullen betrayed his fellow soldiers and his country. And he did it to save his sorry hide and make his life in prison easier. He willingly traded information he possessed for favors and later on he exposed a planned escape. The only reason I wasn't killed along with the other men that day was because I was being *interrogated* at the time it happened."

"Oh, Egan." Maggie grasped the edge of the writing desk, her knuckles bleached from the pressure.

"Later, when we were free, I gave a full account of Cullen's actions to my CO. It was Cullen's word against mine, until a Vietcong major, one of the officers at the camp, was captured by our side and collaborated my account of the events."

"Cullen has hated you all these years," Maggie said. "He has wanted to pay you back because you told the truth about what he did."

"Yeah, and now he thinks he's found a way to exact revenge."

"By killing your son." Maggie's face paled.

"I won't let that happen." Every muscle in Egan's body tightened, every nerve tensed. He thought he knew what torture was, thought he had experienced the worst in that Vietcong POW camp. But he'd been wrong.

Maggie held out her unsteady hand, an offering of care and comfort and unity. Egan clasped her hand in his. With the newborn morning sun washing light and warmth over them, they stood together, their eyes speaking a silent language. The heart's language. A mother and a father praying for the strength and courage—and the chance—to save their son's life.

Chapter 5

The testosterone level aboard the Dundee jet was off the Richter scale. Maggie had never been surrounded by so much high-octane masculinity. As she watched Ellen Denby's total ease commanding these ultramacho guys, she envied her greatly. What gave a woman as beautiful as Ellen the ability to give-and-take with these men as if she were just one of the boys? There was not a trace of unease or unsureness in Ellen. Every one of the agents showed her the greatest respect and accepted her orders without blinking an eye. Despite the comradery and familiarity that existed among them, not one man treated Ellen like they would have any other woman. And Maggie figured that it wasn't easy for them, considering Ellen's obvious physical attributes. A to-die-for body and a face like an angel.

"Care for some coffee, Ms. Douglas?" Jack Parker approached, a mug of freshly made brew in his hand. "Sugar, no cream. Right?"

"Why, yes, thank you, Mr. Parker." Maggie accepted

the white mug that bore a gold-and-blue Dundee Agency emblem.

Jack sat beside her. "Call me Jack. And I can't take credit for remembering how you like your coffee, even though I fixed you a cup right after we first boarded. Egan reminded me to add the sugar."

Maggie glanced toward the table where Egan, Joe Ornelas and Ellen huddled over topographical maps of Arizona, taking special interest in the areas south and east of Flagstaff. She had heard them talking about mountains and gorges, about the Tonto National Forest, East Sunset Mountain, West Sunset Mountain, Clear Creek and something called the Mogollon Rim.

"Would you like a sandwich to go with that?" Jack asked.

Maggie smiled at the charming and attractive man who had undoubtedly been assigned the task of keeping an eye on her. He'd been quite attentive during the entire flight and she could see why he'd been chosen as her baby-sitter. Jack Parker possessed a magnetic personality. And he was good-looking in a rugged, John Wayne sort of way.

"Thanks, I'm not hungry. But you could do something else for me, if you would." She lifted the mug to her lips and took a sip of the strong, sweet coffee.

"Name it, lovely lady, and it's yours."

"Tell me something about yourself and these other Dundee agents who will be risking their lives to save my son."

Jack's broad smile vanished, replaced by a sadness in his golden eyes. "Not much to tell. I suppose Egan's already told you that we're a bunch of former government agents, military men and law enforcement officers. I can assure you that we're not a group of amateurs."

"I realize that y'all are highly trained professionals."

"As for me, I'm just a good ol' boy from Texas," Jack

told her. "I used to work for the DEA before I suffered a severe case of burnout."

"And the others?" she asked, genuinely interested, as she continued sipping her coffee.

"Sleeping beauty over there—" Jack inclined his head toward Matt O'Brien, who relaxed nearby, his eyes closed, his breathing soft and even "—is a former cowboy."

"Is he from Texas, too?"

Jack chuckled. "No, ma'am, he wasn't that kind of cowboy. Pretty boy Matt used to be a member of the Air Force's Green Hornets Squadron. He'll be piloting the chopper that'll take us into Grant Cullen territory."

"Oh, I see." Maggie studied the long, lean Matt, who was, by anyone's standards, a devastatingly handsome man.

Jack glanced at the big, six-foot-four bear of a man who sat across from Matt, his blue-gray eyes riveted to the pages inside a file folder that Ellen Denby had handed him when they'd first boarded the jet. "Then there's Hunter Whitelaw, a Georgia boy and an army man who was part of the *publicly unacknowledged* Delta Force."

"Mmm… I have heard of the Delta Force," Maggie said. "I thought it might not actually exist, except in the movies."

"Oh, it exists," Jack said, then turned his attention to the Native American standing at Egan's side. "Our ace tracker and wilderness expert is Joe Ornelas. He used to be a Navajo policeman."

"Yes, Egan told me that Mr. Ornelas would be our guide."

Finally, as she finished the last drops of coffee, Maggie's gaze settled on the tall, quiet man who sat alone, apart from the others. She had noticed that he'd said very little to anyone since the agents had boarded the plane. He, too, seemed immersed in reading the contents of a file folder.

"That's Wolfe," Jack told her. "David Wolfe. Don't know anything about him…except that Sam Dundee, who owns our agency, personally hired him. Unfriendly cuss. Stays to himself. Doesn't socialize. But he's an expert marksman. He can shoot a gnat off a horse's as—er…a horse's ear from a mile away."

"I suppose a talent like that could come in handy, couldn't it? Especially on an assignment that requires…" Maggie swallowed the lump in her throat. When they went in to rescue Bent, there was bound to be shooting. Probably a lot of shooting. And someone might get killed. One of these men. Or one of Grant Cullen's soldiers. Or even Egan or Bent.

"Try not to think about what's going to happen," Jack said, his voice low and soft and soothing, as he took the empty coffee mug from Maggie's unsteady hand. "Just concentrate on the fact that come this time tomorrow, you'll have your son back with you, all safe and sound."

"You're right. That's exactly what I must concentrate on, if I'm going to keep my sanity."

"Are you sure I can't get you something to eat?" Jack asked. "If you don't want a sandwich, let me get you one of those pastries and another cup of coffee."

"I'm fine, but thank you all the same."

Before Jack could respond, Ellen Denby approached and gave him a nod of dismissal. He patted Maggie's hand and offered her a weak smile. She responded with a fragile smile of her own, then turned to Ellen who quickly took the seat Jack had just vacated.

"How are you holding up?" Ellen asked, her voice naturally throaty and sexy.

"I'm all right."

"Sorry that I haven't had a chance for us to get better acquainted, but since we pulled this operation together pretty damn fast, we needed the time in flight to finish plotting our course of action.''

"I understand.''

"I know this is rough on you, Maggie, but you've got to realize how difficult this is for Egan.''

Maggie's head snapped up. She glared at Ellen. "If you're referring to the fact that he blames himself for the situation Bent's in, then yes, I do realize how difficult this is for him. But I think you should understand something, Ms. Denby. A part of me wants Egan to blame himself, because however irrational it may sound to you, I blame Egan. He should have told me about Grant Cullen when we…when… He should have told me fifteen years ago.''

"You're right, he should have,'' Ellen agreed. "And you should have told Egan that he had a son. The way I see it, there's more than enough blame to go around.''

"Yes, you're quite right.''

Ellen's gaze softened as she looked Maggie directly in the eye. "We're going to rescue Bent. You have to hold on to that thought.''

Maggie nodded. "How long have you known Egan?''

"Only since he came to work at the Dundee Agency,'' Ellen replied. "Why do you ask?''

Maggie nervously rubbed her fingertips up and down her thigh, her short, manicured nails scraping over the cotton knit fabric of her tan slacks. "Despite the fact that he is the father of my child, I really don't know anything about the man Egan is today. I suppose I thought that if you knew him well—''

"There isn't a special woman in his life. I know that for a fact.''

"I wasn't asking about his love life.''

"Yes, you were.'' Ellen's facial expression didn't alter

in the least. "You wouldn't be human if you weren't curious."

"That's all it is—just curiosity."

"Hmm-mmm. Well, Egan's life isn't exactly an open book. He's a fairly private man, but there's one thing all of us at Dundee's know about him—he's a very lonely man."

"Lonely?"

"Yes. Lonely in a way I can't even begin to describe. Egan is a good man, who does his job well. He's friendly with me and all the other agents, but he keeps everyone in his life at arm's length. He doesn't allow anyone to get too close."

"Because of Grant Cullen," Maggie said. "He's never allowed himself to have established friendships or committed relationships of any kind because Grant Cullen could have used anyone Egan cared for against him."

"Didn't take you long to figure that out, did it? You're a smart lady, Maggie, so you should understand that what Egan is going through right now is every bit as bad as what you're going through. Worse, if that's possible. And believe me, I do know that no one can love a child more than his mother."

Maggie clenched her teeth together in an effort not to cry. She hated the thought of showing such a feminine weakness in front of a tough-as-nails woman like Ellen Denby.

Ellen sat beside Maggie throughout the rest of the flight, occasionally engaging her in conversation, but mostly just offering her female companionship and comfort. Maggie realized that Ellen understood that a mother's love was incomparable to any other love, an emotion so strong and pure that since time immemorial, mothers have not only killed to protect their young, but they have often died to

protect them. Just as the males of the species have done to
protect their mates.

Why was Ellen so astute about the depth a mother's
love? Maggie wondered. Had she simply assumed this was
true or did she know firsthand?

When they arrived in Flagstaff, having landed at Pulliam
Airport, Ellen and all the agents, except Egan and Joe, left
in a rental car for a private airstrip, where, Maggie had been
told, they would inspect the helicopter Matt O'Brien would
use to take them within hiking distance of Cullen's hideaway before nightfall.

Egan hoisted Maggie's overnight bag, along with his
own, over his shoulder and led her to the parking deck
where a late-model SUV was waiting for them. Joe Ornelas
opened the unlocked vehicle, slipped his hand under the
floor mat on the driver's side and lifted a key. After they
stored their bags in the back, on top of a stack of provi-
sions, Egan settled Maggie in the front seat and took the
key from Joe, who climbed in the seat directly behind Maggie. Egan slid behind the wheel, started the engine and maneuvered the SUV out of the deck and onto the road leading
from the airport.

"We're about forty miles from Minerva," Joe said, as
he removed a map from the black leather briefcase he carried. "We take Interstate 40 toward Winslow, but we exit
off at Cedar Hills and then it's two-lane all the way in to
Minerva."

"Maggie, do you need to stop for anything before we
leave Flagstaff?" Egan asked, but didn't glance her way.

"No, I'm fine," she replied.

"Then we should be in Minerva in less than an hour."

Thirty-seven minutes later, they reached the downtown
area of a small, isolated town perched halfway up the

mountain. Time seemed to have stopped here sometime in the early twentieth century, Maggie thought, as she watched tree-lined Main Street unfold in front of her. The tallest structure in town appeared to be the two-story, corner brick that had apparently once housed a hotel. Glancing down alleyways, she noted the sidewalks turned into wide stretches of old asphalt and some weathered, wooden hitching posts remained intact, a reminder of a bygone era.

Joe pointed out Schmissrauter's Garage, a crumbling stucco building with an attached front porch constructed of unfinished logs. A couple of antique gas pumps stood out front on the cracked pavement. Silent sentinels of another time.

Egan drove on past the place where he was supposed to make contact with the person possessing the directions to Cullen's fort.

"Aren't we stopping?" Maggie asked.

"No," Egan said.

Egan pulled the SUV to a halt in front of the only restaurant in town. "We'll park here." Miss Fannie's was housed in a tin-roofed, clapboard house that hadn't seen a fresh coat of paint in two decades "You two go in and order dinner, while I walk over to the garage and take care of a little business."

Maggie grasped Egan's arm. "Isn't Joe going with you?"

"I can handle this alone," he told her, then glanced over his shoulder at Joe. "After we eat, we'll head out immediately. I want to be within five miles of Cullen's fort before we make camp tonight."

Joe only nodded, but the minute Egan exited the SUV, Joe jumped out and opened Maggie's door for her. After he helped her disembark, he escorted her into Miss Fannie's. The place reminded her of a little café in Parsons City where her father had taken her when she was a little girl for the best greasy hamburgers in the world. Oiled wooden floors, marred with wear. Bead-board ceilings from which rickety fans dangled. A long counter, with a row of round stools, the seats covered with cracked, faded red vinyl. Pete's Café hadn't existed, except in her memory for over thirty years, but this place brought her memories to life.

They seated themselves at a table near the door. A fat, middle-aged waitress with teeth as yellow as her bleached hair handed them each a well-worn menu.

"What'll it be folks?" the woman asked, eyeing them suspiciously.

"Why don't you order for all three of us, Maggie?" Joe suggested.

"You folks lost your way or something?" Their waitress scratched her head with the nub of the pencil she held in her hand. "We don't get many strangers in these parts."

"Mr. and Mrs. Cassidy are here in Arizona to do some hiking. They hired me as a guide," Joe explained.

"Where's her husband?" She inclined her head toward Maggie.

"At the garage," Joe said. "He'll be on over soon."

Nervously Maggie scanned the menu, all the while wondering if any of the other patrons in Miss Fannie's might be spies for Grant Cullen. The old coot at the counter, slurping down soup? Or the Native American couple at a back table? Or maybe the three men feasting on gravy-smothered fried steaks? Hadn't the possibility that one of Cullen's men could be watching them crossed Joe's mind? What if this whole town was under Cullen's control? *Stop it!* a strong-willed inner voice demanded. *You can't let your imagination run wild with you like that.*

"Three cheeseburgers, three orders of fries and three large colas, please," Maggie ordered, then looked to Joe for approval.

He smiled, and for the first time since she'd been in his presence, she realized what a beautiful man Joe Ornelas was. Not in the classically handsome way some men were, but in a bronze-sculpture way, with a muscular physique and a magnificent profile.

The waitress's sausage-link fingers clasped her pencil tightly as she hurriedly scribbled down their order. "We got some homemade apple pie. It's mighty good."

"All right. We'll take three pieces." Maggie handed her menu to the waitress and Joe followed suit.

Minutes ticked by. Neither she nor Joe bothered with making small talk. Maggie checked her watch continuously. Where was Egan? What was taking him so long? Had something gone wrong?

Fifteen minutes later, Joe got up and walked over to an old jukebox in the corner of the restaurant. He dropped in several coins, then selected the songs.

Three things occurred simultaneously. The waitress brought their order and placed the food on the table. Hank Williams's distinctive voice wailed the lyrics of "I'm So Lonesome, I Could Cry." And Egan Cassidy sat down beside Maggie.

She wanted to ask him what had happened, if everything was all right, but she didn't. Instead she said, "Did Bentley ever tell you about the hamburgers at Pete's Café?"

The edges of Egan's lips curved up in a hint of a smile. "Yeah, he sure did. Hamburgers. Cherry Cokes. Root beer floats. He said his old man used to take him there—take both of you there."

"This place reminds me of Pete's."

"We couldn't save Bentley." Egan laid his hand over

Maggie's where it rested atop the table. "But we are going
to save his namesake."

Maggie wished she could cry. Longed to weep until she
was spent. But the tears wouldn't come anymore. It was as
if fear had numbed her completely and dried up all her
tears.

"Let's eat." Egan picked up his burger, ketchup oozing
down the sides of the bun, and took a huge bite.

The food was greasy, but good. Unfortunately Maggie
had to force down what little she ate. She noticed that both
Egan and Joe left over half their burgers and fries untouched and all three of them did little more than taste the
pie.

Egan paid the bill, leaving the waitress a nice tip, and
the three of them used the rest rooms and changed into
their battle gear. Rugged outerwear and boots, suitable for
a horseback ride and eventually a hike in wilds of the Arizona mountains. Within ten minutes, they climbed into the
SUV and headed out of town on a dusty dirt road that led
higher into the mountains. No one spoke for a good ten
minutes.

"I told the guy at the garage that I had a guide who was
going part of the way with us," Egan said. "I'm sure he'll
report that bit of news to Cullen."

"But Cullen told you that we had to come alone, didn't
he?" Maggie watched as Egan's jaw tightened. "What if
he gets upset that we—"

"Don't worry," Egan said. "As long as you and I go in
alone, everything will be fine."

Maggie nodded. *Oh, please, God, let Egan be right about
Grant Cullen.*

"Remember, this is all a game to Cullen." Egan glanced
her way, then quickly returned his focus to the winding
road ahead of them. "He's trying to figure out what I'll do,

what I've got planned. He thinks he has me right where he
wants me, but at the same time, he'll wonder if we'll really
come in alone and whether or not I'll have a team waiting
to attack.''

''He'll be prepared, then,'' Maggie said. ''What's to stop
his men from gunning down the Dundee agents?''

''We have a secret weapon.'' Egan stole a quick glance
in the interior rearview mirror at Joe. ''A way to get in
Cullen's stronghold without storming the place. But even
with that advantage, this is a risky operation. I won't lie to
you, Maggie. Anything can happen when all hell breaks
loose. But the Dundee squad knows that their first priority
is to get you and Bent out safely.''

Grant Cullen ate the last bite of bloody steak, then
downed the last drops of Cabernet Sauvignon. With a wave
of his hand, he commanded that his wineglass be filled
again. Sawyer MacNamara obeyed instantly, then stepped
back, standing at attention and waiting. Waiting for *the general* to drink himself into a stupor. For the past month,
Sawyer had been assigned as one of Cullen's bodyguards.
He and two young idealistic morons rotated duty every
eight hours. He considered himself damn lucky to have
gotten this close to the commander in chief so quickly.
After all, he'd just been inducted into this secret order six
months ago.

Sawyer had realized immediately that Grant Cullen, although a highly intelligent man, was insane. Perhaps not
clinically insane, but insane by the average person's standards. The man had taken money he'd earned through a
lifetime of illegal dealings all over the world and built himself a fort high in the Arizona mountains. And once he had
completed his stockade, he had set about collecting himself

a small group of followers, whom he'd trained in warfare. Cullen's group called themselves the Ultimate Survivalists.

It had taken Sawyer months to even make contact with one of Cullen's men and another two months to persuade the man to introduce him to the general. He had memorized the manifesto Cullen had written and using it and the information he already had on Cullen, Sawyer had conned his way into the inner circle. Right where he wanted to be.

What his superior at the bureau had ordered him to do— only this morning via his cell phone—might well jeopardize nine months of undercover work. But what choice did he have? He had to follow orders, didn't he? Besides, a fourteen-year-old boy's life might well depend on his actions.

Maggie hadn't been on a horse in years. Not since she'd been a teenager and used to visit Aunt Sue and Uncle Jim on their farm. But the only way to reach Cullen's fort was by horseback or on foot, unless you could helicopter in the way the Dundee squad was going to do. But then Cullen wasn't keeping an eye on Ellen's agents the way he was them. Miles back, Joe and Egan had told her that someone was watching them, remaining a safe distance behind. They had surmised that one of Cullen's men had been in Minerva and had been following them.

Joe had found a fairly clear trail and they had followed it for several miles, winding slowly but surely higher and higher up the mountain. Lush ponderosa pines grew in profusion. Thick grass blanketed the ground like carpet in some areas, and towering boulders hovered around them from time to time. When the trail ran out, Joe made a new path, ever mindful of not only their safety, but the safety of the animals they rode. Maggie could tell quite easily that Joe had an affinity with the horses.

At sunset, they stopped to rest for a bit, and refilled their canteens with cool, clean water from a mountain spring. She heard Joe and Egan talking in hushed tones as they checked the map again. Then Joe came over to her and took her hand in his.

"I will see you in the morning, Maggie."

"Are you leaving us already?" she asked, not wanting to see him go. Not wanting to be alone with Egan.

"I need to meet up with the others before nightfall," he told her. "You and Egan don't have much farther to go before you make camp. Whoever's following us needs to know that you and Egan are going the rest of the way alone. Doing it this way substantiates our story that Egan hired me as a guide."

"What if he follows you?" Maggie squeezed Joe's hand.

"I don't think he will, but if he does, I can easily lose him or I can— Anyway, we figure his orders were to stick with Egan and you."

Maggie realized that Joe had been about to say *or I can kill him.* How had her life come to this? she wondered. Climbing a mountain in Arizona, trying to reach a madman's fortress, joining forces with a highly trained squad of professionals who were all capable of killing. In the most horrible nightmare imaginable, she would never have dreamed that her son would be kidnapped, the pawn in some sick game of revenge.

You know how this all happened, a taunting inner voice said. *Fifteen years ago, you fell in love with a man you barely knew. You gave yourself to him, body and soul, and he left you pregnant with his child. But he didn't bother to tell you that by simply existing, your son would be in unspeakable danger.*

Maggie bid farewell to Joe, then she and Egan remounted and, leading the packhorse behind them, resumed their journey upward and onward—straight to hell.

Chapter 6

When the sun set in a blaze of color over the western slopes, the temperatures began dropping almost immediately. Egan dug into their supplies for their jackets before continuing the journey. He had hoped to be within five miles of Cullen's mountaintop fort before they would be forced to stop for the night, but he now realized that eight miles would be as close as they could get. It would soon be dark and he had to set up camp and get Maggie settled. Thank God Maggie was in good physical condition and had experience as an amateur hiker, otherwise this trip would have been far more difficult for her, and thus for him.

Tonight might well be the last night of his life. He knew that fact only too well. Tomorrow he would meet the enemy, accept the challenge and fight a battle that had been in the making for twenty-eight years. But his life didn't matter. He had no qualms about dying to save his son or in laying down his life to keep Maggie safe.

Sweet Maggie. The bravest woman he'd ever known. A

lesser woman, when confronted with similar circumstances, would have already broken under the strain. Oh, she had cracked a few times, splintered apart slightly, but she had somehow managed to hold herself together. She was being strong for Bent.

There were so many things he wanted to say to Maggie, so many things he needed to tell her. Tonight might be his last opportunity. Right before he had departed, Joe Ornelas had given Egan some advice.

Tell Maggie the truth. Tell her everything. She has a right to know.

Maggie did have a right to know, not only about the secret plans to rescue Bent, but about his backup plan and the inevitability of his own death. If anything went wrong, there was no way Cullen would allow him to live. Of course, Egan had no intention of giving up without the fight of his life, but if it came down to a choice between saving Bent's life and his coming out of this alive, there would be no question of which he would choose.

Twenty minutes later, with the fading sunlight almost gone, Egan selected a small, secluded clearing surrounded by towering trees. From the looks of the site, he figured that sometime in the past few months, someone—members of Cullen's Ultimate Survivalists group perhaps?—had used the spot. The clearing was man-made. Already the brush was beginning to reclaim the area. A stone circle that had once encompassed a campfire remained intact.

"We'll camp here," Egan told Maggie. "There's not much light left, so this will have to do."

She nodded agreement, then followed him when he dismounted. "Are we still being followed?" she whispered.

"I don't think so. I'm pretty sure that once he saw Joe leaving, he headed out, back to the fort, to report to Cullen."

Egan slid the rifle from its leather sheath and propped it against a nearby pine, then removed the saddles from his and Maggie's horses and dumped their gear on the ground.

"We'll set the horses free in the morning," he said. "We'll have to make the last eight miles or so on foot because most of it is a steep climb straight up and the horses will be of no use to us."

Again she nodded before falling into step beside Egan, as he strode toward the packhorse.

"Why don't you sit down over there—" he pointed to a small boulder protruding out of the ground "—and rest, while I get the tent set up."

"Why don't I help you instead?"

Egan snapped around to look at her. When he saw the determined set of her jaw and the fierceness in her eyes, he smiled. "Okay. Why don't you help me?"

Together they set up the two-person tent without any trouble. Three aluminum poles crisscrossed into a four-pole junction that suspended the canopy. The rainfly attached to the pole with snaps and the tent came equipped with extra-long stake-out loops.

"I'll leave the rifle with you," he told her. "If I remember correctly, you know how to handle a rifle, don't you?"

"Yes, I know how, but I haven't handled one in years. I used to go skeet shooting with Daddy and Bentley."

While Maggie spread out their featherweight sleeping bags inside the tent, Egan went in search of firewood. By the time he returned with enough wood to build a decent fire, Maggie had placed a blanket on the ground and sat cross-legged, staring up at the starry sky.

He hesitated at the edge of the clearing and watched her, instinctively realizing that she was praying. Pleading with God. Making a bargain with *the* higher power. Sending out positive thoughts into the vast universe. The serenity that encompassed her swept over him without warning, as if subconsciously she was sharing her hope with him. In that one instant, Egan dared to believe that the impossible was possible. Tomorrow he would save Bent, keep Maggie unharmed and escape with his life.

When he dumped the firewood and kindling twigs into the rock circle, Maggie tilted up her head and glanced at him. "Do you want something to eat or drink?" she asked. "We seem to have a week's supply of rations."

"Nothing for me." Kneeling, he arranged the pieces of dead tree limbs and the handful of sticks into a proper stack, then removed a lighter from his pocket and used it to ignite the dry kindling that would catch the logs afire and leave a warm, glowing fire.

"It's a beautiful night," Maggie said, her gaze returning to the heavens.

Egan sat beside her and looked up at the black sky littered with tiny, sparkling stars and a huge three-quarter moon. "Maggie, there are some things you need to know."

"Hmm-mmm." She continued staring up at the night sky. "About tomorrow?"

"About Grant Cullen. About the Dundee squad's secret weapon. About tomorrow…and about me."

He felt her stir beside him and when he turned to face her, she scooted far enough away from him that there was no chance their bodies would accidentally touch. But then she looked directly at him. Her gaze bold. Strong. Daring him.

He recognized the fear in her eyes and knew she was bracing herself for whatever he would tell her. For just an instant he seriously thought of letting the moment pass, of glossing over the facts in order to protect her. But he owed her nothing less than the truth. By not being completely honest with Maggie, the only person he'd be protecting would be himself.

"I thought you had already told me everything about Grant Cullen," she said. "Is there more?"

"Not about the past…about our past history. But there is more about the man himself. Who and what he is now."

"Oh."

Her lips formed a perfect oval. Moonlight glimmered in her hair, burnishing the rich mahogany with dark red highlights. A reflection of the campfire's flames danced in her brown eyes. Attracted to her beauty, tempted by the aura of unaffected sensuality that was a part of the woman, Egan's body reacted on a purely physical level.

"Cullen has been a mercenary most of his life," Egan said.

"Like you."

"Yeah, like me," he admitted. "But regardless of what I did, I always lived by my own moral code. Cullen has no morals. He amassed a fortune over the years by taking on jobs no one else would take. That's how he could afford to buy so much land and build his fort here in Arizona."

"Why would he want a fort?" Maggie asked.

"To house his army and rule his little kingdom." Egan settled his open palms over his knees. "Cullen heads up a group he refers to as the Ultimate Survivalists. Our government suspects Cullen's little band of merry men are responsible for several bombings over the past few years that have resulted in numerous deaths."

"My God!"

"What I'm about to tell you is strictly confidential."

Maggie nodded, understanding.

"About six months ago, an FBI agent went undercover and joined the Ultimate Survivalists. Recently he's become one of Cullen's bodyguards."

"The secret weapon!" Maggie said. "An inside man."

"Yeah, something like that." Egan flexed his shoulder muscles, trying to relax them. Tension coiled inside him like a rattler preparing to attack. "Before dawn, this federal agent will unlock a secret passageway that leads up into Cullen's fort. The Dundee squad will be inside and already in place when you and I arrive."

"Why would this FBI agent help us? And how did you know about this undercover man? I don't understand any of this. How have y'all been communicating with him?"

"Cellular phones that use a scrambling security frequency is our means of communication. We know about the inside man because the Dundee Agency has some contacts, at pretty high levels, within all the government agencies. You need to remember that seventy-five percent of our agents are either former government agents or were members of various elite military groups."

"Then why aren't government agents handling this raid?"

"They're involved," Egan said. "They've been waiting for a reason to storm Cullen's fort and clean out that vipers nest. We've made a bargain with them—they allow us to get Bent out safely and we let them use Bent's kidnapping as their reason to attack the Ultimate Survivalists."

"Now, let me get this straight—the Dundee Agency is working with the government, using Bent's kidnapping and our rescue attempt as a means to destroy Grant Cullen. Is that right?"

Even before she shot up off the blanket and her cold stare pierced daggers into him, it wasn't difficult for Egan to see that Maggie was angry. No, more than angry. She was furious.

"How could you, Egan? How could you! Our son's life is at stake, and you've turned this rescue into an all-out war with Grant Cullen.'' Enraged, she stomped away from the campfire.

Ah, hell, he'd done it now, Egan thought. This is what happens when you're totally honest with a woman. They misinterpret, they misunderstand and they overreact.

''Maggie!'' He jumped up and followed her.

The closer he got to her, the faster she ran, until he had no choice—for her safety—but to chase her and tackle her down to the ground. She fought him at first, but when he pinned her hands over her head and trapped her body between his spread legs, she ceased struggling and stared up into his face. Moonlight glistened off her tears. Egan's gut clenched tightly. Dammit! He had hurt Maggie again. It was as if everything he said and everything he did caused her pain.

''Will you listen to me?'' he pleaded.

''Do I have a choice?'' Her chest rose and fell in undulating rhythm as she panted, her breath quick and ragged.

''This whole deal is one of 'you scratch our back, we scratch yours.' We need them and they need us.''

''Don't you lie to me, Egan Cassidy. Not when it concerns my son's life.''

''You may not believe me, but I've never lied to you, Maggie. And I'm not lying now. Without help, our chances of rescuing Bent wouldn't be good. The truth of the matter is that Cullen plans to kill Bent and you and then me. And I figure he intends to make my agony last as long as possible—maybe for days.''

''I—I'm not sure I understand.''

Egan felt the fury inside Maggie's tense body begin to subside, ever so slowly. ''Cullen wants to torture Bent—'' Egan pressed his cheek to Maggie's when she gasped ''—and you. He probably intends to rape you and make me watch.'' Egan pulled Maggie up into a sitting position, his bent knees on either side of her, and wrapped her in his arms. "That's what kind of man we're dealing with."

Maggie sat there on the ground, enfolded in Egan's embrace and didn't say a word as she trembled uncontrollably.

"I'm using whatever means necessary to prevent any harm from coming to you or Bent. And if that meant blackmailing the president, I'd do it." Egan lifted Maggie to her feet. "This ground is cold, honey. Come on, let's get back to the fire."

She walked unsteadily at his side, supported by his tight grip around her waist. They returned to the blanket and sat together, Egan holding her close.

"By joining forces with the FBI, I'm not putting Bent in more danger," Egan explained. "What we're doing is giving us a better chance of saving him. That's the only reason I agreed to the arrangement."

"What's going to happen in the morning, when you and I arrive at the fort?" With the rage completely drained from her, Maggie's voice returned to a calm, controlled tone.

"The plan is for the Dundee agents and the government boys to take Cullen's little army off guard, once you and I are inside to distract Cullen. He'll be expecting an attack only from the outside, so the element of surprise will be on our side."

"How can you predict what will happen?" she asked. "Something could go wrong. Bent could be caught in the middle of—"

Egan tightened his hold on Maggie. "Trust me to make sure Bent is safe. I promise you that my top priority is to get the two of you out of Cullen's clutches and make sure he's never a threat to either of you again."

"But—"

Egan pressed his index finger over her lips, silencing her. Ah, Maggie. Maggie, my love. Always so inquisitive, so

headstrong and determined. A lady who knew her own
mind and wouldn't be pacified by half-truths.

"There is nothing I won't do to save Bent's life," Egan
promised, then clasped her face with his hands, leaned forward and kissed her forehead. "I'll do whatever is necessary." Grasping her hands, he urged her to her feet. "We
have a big day tomorrow. Why don't you get some rest,
even if you can't sleep?"

"You're right. I am tired." Without saying another word
or giving him a backward glance, Maggie stood, walked
away from him and crawled inside the tent.

Egan sat alone on the blanket. Nocturnal animal sounds
echoed in the stillness. An owl's eerily mournful hoots. A
predatory cat's distant cry. Insects sang their unique songs,
blending together in an arthropodan serenade. With the forest all around him and the dark heavens above, Egan felt
encompassed by nature. He had been alone most of his life,
but he had never felt as lonely as he did at this precise
moment. Maggie had withdrawn from him, leaving an emptiness inside him that he couldn't explain.

If this was his last night on earth, he didn't want to spend
it alone. He needed human comfort. A kind word. A gentle
touch. The feel of a loving woman in his arms. If he went
to Maggie, if he asked for solace, would she turn him
away?

Maggie removed her boots and set them aside, then unzipped her sleeping bag and slid her legs inside the folds.
Trying to relax, she closed her eyes and listened to the
rhythm of her heart as she breathed in and out. In and out.

Rest, she told herself. Rest. You have to be at your physical and mental best in the morning. Tomorrow is the single
most important day of your life. By day's end tomorrow,

you and Bent will be home in Alabama. And this nightmare will be behind you.

But what about Egan? a concerned inner voice asked.

Yes, what about Egan? Egan, Bent's father. Egan, the man she had once loved with mindless passion. Egan, the person who would risk anything—including his own life—to save their son.

Maggie's eyelids flew open. Her heartbeat accelerated. With trembling fingers, she unzipped her sleeping bag and scrambled from its confinement.

Oh, dear God! It can't be true. It can't be.

With a blinding moment of gut-wrenching insight, Maggie realized a horrifying truth. Egan had every intention of sacrificing his life to save Bent. Despite a surprise attack from the Dundee squad, Egan couldn't be certain that Cullen wouldn't have time to strike, wouldn't have time to kill Bent. Now she understood Egan's backup plan—the one he hadn't mentioned.

"Oh, Egan!" she cried.

With adrenaline rushing through her body, she raced out of the tent in search of Egan. She halted, momentarily hesitating when she saw him standing only a few feet away, his gaze fixed on the sky. Armed with the truth—the deadly reality of what tomorrow might bring—Maggie faced her feelings honestly, for the first time in many years. Despite the fact that he had rejected her, left her pregnant and never returned, she still had deep feelings for Egan Cassidy. And she still wanted him in a way she'd never wanted another man. She knew her feelings weren't logical—hell, they never had been where Egan was concerned. But love wasn't supposed to make sense, was it? At least not the wild, all-consuming type of love that she and Egan had shared.

Tomorrow could bring death to Egan. And to her. For each of them were equally prepared to sacrifice themselves

for their child. Tonight might well be their last night together.

In her sock feet, Maggie flew toward Egan, her heart
beating erratically. Her mind filled with thoughts of one
final shared intimacy. Her body yearning to celebrate life,
to grasp the pleasure and savor it for as long as possible.

"Egan!"

Turning when she called his name, Egan moved toward
her, his arms open to catch her. She flung herself at him.
Her arms circled his waist, clinging to him, hugging him,
whimpering his name. Grasping her shoulders, he shook her
gently.

"What's wrong, Maggie? What is it?"

She looked up at him, tears pooling in her eyes, her
mouth open on a gasping sigh. "I know," she said. "I
know."

Forking his fingers through her hair, which hung loosely
around her shoulders, Egan clutched the back of her head
with his open palm. "What do you know?"

Tears trickled down her cheeks, around her nose and
over her lips. "I know what you're planning to do, and I
love you for being willing to...to..."

He understood then that she had figured out his backup
plan, if it came to a choice between letting Cullen kill Bent
and in dying himself. "Maggie...I—"

He swept his hands down her arms and then up to cup
her face and stare into her eyes. Her expression spoke
volumes. All her emotions showed plainly on her face.
Compassion and passion. Fear. Gratitude. Hope and hope-
lessness. And love. God, was it possible that Maggie still
cared about him?

"Once this is all over, I won't ever let anything or anyone hurt you again, Maggie. Not even me. I swear!"

She nodded her understanding, her face wet with tears. "Make love to me tonight. Now."

While there's still time. Before we walk straight into hell tomorrow, knowing one or both of us may die. Neither of them verbally expressed what they both thought, what each of them silently acknowledged.

Egan shut his eyes. Tremors racked his body. Like a precious gift from heaven, her invitation touched his heart and opened up the emotions he had kept buried for fifteen long, lonely years. Maggie was the only woman he had ever allowed himself to truly care about, but he had ended things with her abruptly, thinking that by doing so he was protecting her.

His kiss took her breath away. Tender passion. Barely contained hunger, tempered by loving consideration. She opened herself to him, taking pleasure in the taste and smell of him. In the sound of his ragged breath. The feel of his hard body beneath her fingertips. The rasp of his beard and mustache against her skin.

The whole world faded into oblivion, ceasing to exist. Only she and Egan and the compulsion to come together as one existed in their private universe. A man. A woman. And a primeval instinct that thousands of years of civilization had left unchanged.

With his mouth clinging, his teeth nipping, Egan swung Maggie up into his arms and headed toward their tent. She draped her arm around his neck, giving herself to him, surrendering to the desperate need that rode them both so relentlessly.

Inside the tent, closed off from the outside elements, warm and secure, Egan and Maggie knelt on their knees and faced each other. Only the light from a gas lantern illuminated the cosy interior as Egan reached out and slid Maggie's jacket from her shoulders and down her arms.

She shucked off the lightweight coat, letting it drop to her side before she responded by removing Egan's jacket.

Her fingers shook when she undid the first button on his heavy cotton shirt. She hadn't been with a man since her divorce from Gil. Her sexual experience was limited to two men. Everything she knew about passion and mindless pleasure, she had learned from Egan. The anticipation of experiencing once again the earth-shattering loving she had known only with Egan filled Maggie with longing. She practically ripped his shirt from his body, leaving his broad chest bare. He was older, his chest hair dusted with gray, but his body appeared as toned and hard as it had been fifteen years ago.

Egan unbuttoned Maggie's shirt and tossed it aside, leaving only her bra standing between him and the sight of her breasts. He pressed the center front catch of her bra and the plastic mechanism popped open. Dropping his palms over her shoulders, he hooked each index finger under the straps and glided the bit of satin down her arms.

"My body isn't the same as it was when I was twenty-three," she said. "I'm thirty-eight now and I've carried and given birth to a child."

"My child."

Maggie shivered, even before his hands cupped and lifted her breasts. His touch ignited shards of tingling awareness within the very core of her femininity.

"You're more beautiful now," he said, his voice a rugged moan as his thumbs raked over her pebble-hard nipples.

"So—so are you."

It was the passion talking and they both knew it. They saw each other through a rosy haze of lust and longing. And a need to make these last sweet moments together as perfect as possible. Now was not the time for brutal honesty or harsh reality.

Egan dragged her up against him, crushing her breasts against his chest, rubbing their bodies together as they sighed and moaned with the pleasure of flesh on flesh. Holding her to him, his sex throbbing, his heartbeat roaring in his ears, he consumed her mouth. She clung to him, returning in equal measure the intensity of his kiss. As their tongues dueled, he tumbled her onto her open sleeping bag and came down over her, grinding his arousal into her mound.

Sighing with pleasure, she lifted her hips and thrust upward. "I want you so."

Lifting himself onto his knees, straddling her hips, Egan worked furiously to unsnap and unzip her jeans. He slid his hands beneath her, grasped the waistband and dragged her jeans down her hips and legs. After pulling them over her feet, he threw them to his side and concentrated on the white lace panties that hid her lush red curls from his view.

Maggie unbuckled Egan's belt and slid it through the loops on his jeans, then undid the snap and zipper. Not waiting to remove his pants, she slipped her hand inside and caressed the hardness covered by his briefs. Egan groaned deep in his throat, then covered her hand with his and urged her to continue fondling him.

Rising just enough to be able to kiss his chest, Maggie began a sensual assault that soon had Egan begging her to stop. He grabbed her by the back of the neck and pulled her marauding lips and seductive tongue away from his body.

"I can't take much more of this, Maggie, my love."

She smiled at him, savoring the triumph of unnerving him completely. "Want me to stop?"

"Yeah. Maybe in a hundred years."

He held her at bay until he could get rid of his boots and jeans. Then when nothing stood between them except her panties and his briefs, he placed her hand back where it had been and put his in the corresponding spot on her body. As he began to rub, so did she. And when he inched his fingers inside the leg-band of her panties, she inserted her fingers beneath the leg-band of his briefs. Her fingers curled around his erection. His fingers parted her moist feminine folds and sought her throbbing kernel.

After petting her until she wriggled and moaned, Egan urged her panties down her hips. Maggie maneuvered her legs so that he could remove her underwear. He inserted two fingers up and into her. She gasped when he invaded her, the sensation electrifying as he added the strumming of his thumb over her pulsating nub.

She yanked on the waistband of his briefs, tugging them downward by slow degrees. The minute he helped her remove them, she circled him with her hand. Pumping rhythmically, her soft hand stiffened his sex to the rock-hard stage.

Lowering his head, Egan captured one tight nipple in his mouth and suckled her greedily. And all the while his talented fingers worked their magic between her legs. Within minutes her body clenched his fingers and her nub swelled. She squirmed against his hand, seeking fulfillment. He gave her what she wanted, increasing the tempo and pressure until she cried out and shuddered with release. While the aftershocks of her climax rippled over her nerve endings, Egan shoved her onto her back and plunged into her. Deeply. Completely.

Maggie draped her arms over his shoulders, wrapped her legs around his hips and sought his mouth with hers. His kisses were wet and wild, a frenzy of tongue and lips and teeth. She met him thrust for pounding thrust. Giving and taking. Loving and being loved.

And just as his pace doubled until he was jackhammering

into her, Maggie reached the pinnacle a second time. Fireworks exploded inside her body, sending her soaring. Her completion ignited his. His body tensed. Then with several quick, stabbing jabs, delving deeply, he jetted his release into her receptive body.

The animal roar that he uttered echoed inside the small tent. Maggie covered his face with kisses and wept with a joy she hadn't known since the last time Egan had loved her.

Egan eased his big body to her side and wrapped her in his arms. He kissed her forehead. Her eyelids. Her nose. And then her lips.

"Thank you," he said, his voice only a whisper.

"Oh, Egan. Don't thank me," she snuggled against him as close as she could get. "I wanted you every bit as much as you wanted me."

"It's always been that way between us, hasn't it? So much hunger and passion."

And love, she thought. *Heaven help me, I've always loved you!*

Chapter 7

The heavy metal door creaked as Sawyer eased it open. He made a quick check around and behind him to make sure no one else had heard. He'd been a hundred percent sure that no one saw him enter the stairwell that led to the subterranean vault, two levels below the fort. But it always paid to be extra careful, especially when so many people's lives depended on it.

Grant Cullen had planned this escape hatch as a means to freedom, the tunnel leading a quarter of a mile away and opening in the forest. He had installed the underground passage, just in case he ever needed it. Cullen might have other alternate ways to escape the fortress, but this was the only one Sawyer had learned of during his time with the Ultimate Survivalists. The general's paranoia kept him ever diligent. Always on the lookout for enemies, real and imagined.

In a whispered voice, Sawyer called, "All clear."

The first to appear, stepping out of the tunnel, was a

small guy, no taller than five-six. But the minute the Dundee agent's face and body came into full view, Sawyer realized this was no *he* but a *she*.

"I'm Denby," she said, then moved aside to allow room for her men to enter.

For just a minute Sawyer couldn't take his eyes off Ellen Denby. He'd heard about her, of course. Who hadn't? The gorgeous, hard-as-nails CEO of the nation's top private security and investigation agency. The black BDU she wore did nothing to disguise the lush contours of her very feminine shape. Sawyer swallowed. Damn, she was a looker. When she caught him staring at her, she gave him an eat-dirt-and-die look.

Clearing his throat, Sawyer switched his attention to the four big men, all wearing SWAT BDUs. Their weapons of choice—MP5 submachine guns and AK-47 rifles.

"Our pilot is with the chopper," Ellen said. "As soon as we get the kid, Ornelas and Whitelaw will take him out of here. Once the boy is safely on board, the rest of us will have ten minutes—tops—to clear out of this hellhole. What happens to Cullen and his followers after that is up to you G-men."

"What about Cassidy and the boy's mother?" Sawyer asked.

"The plans are for the mother to go with the boy. Cassidy will be on his own. He's going after Cullen, if we don't get him first."

Morning came too soon. Reality reappeared with the dawn. As daylight slowly spread across the eastern horizon, Egan enveloped Maggie in his arms and held her. His face was buried against her breasts. Her chin rested on the top of his head. They had made love again only moments ago.

Slow, sweet, desperate love. Each knowing what lay ahead of them.

"We need to get going soon," he told her. "It's nearly eight miles on foot to reach Cullen's fort."

"I'll do my best not to slow us down," she said. "I walk three or four days a week, most of the time. And I can usually make four miles in less than an hour."

"We'll move at your pace. The trek will tire us some, but we don't need to be totally exhausted when we get there."

Maggie speared her fingers through Egan's salt-and-pepper hair, grasped his head and titled it backward so that she could see his face. "If we—" She cleared her throat. "If we all three come out of this alive—Bent and you and me—I want you to get to know your son. He's a wonderful boy. And he's so much like you."

Egan eased up into a sitting position, bringing Maggie with him. "I want the opportunity to get to know Bent, but how do you think he'll feel about me? After all these years, he probably believes I don't give a damn about him."

"What you're doing today proves that theory wrong, doesn't it? He's a smart boy. He'll know." Maggie brushed her lips over Egan's. A gentle kiss. "No matter what happens, I'm glad we had this time together."

He caressed her cheek. "Me, too, Maggie, my love. Me, too."

Maggie cherished the hope that the rescue attempt would come off without any problems. She would not allow herself to even think about the worst-case scenario—that she and Egan and Bent could all die. She clung to the dream of a happily ever after for the three of them. But that was all it was—a dream. And probably a foolish one at that. There was a good chance that even if Bent and she made it out alive, Egan wouldn't. And if he did somehow survive, that didn't mean he'd become a part of their lives on a permanent basis. How would Bent react to a father he'd never known, a man he refused to discuss with her? And would it be possible for the three of them to actually become a family? Or would the anger and pain from the past and the sheer terror of Bent's kidnapping form a wedge that would forever keep them apart?

Maggie sought Egan's lips, longing for one final kiss. She had never been in love with anyone else, not even Gil. Egan had been the true love of her life, and after being with him again last night, she realized that there would never be anyone else for her. But sometimes love wasn't enough. Not unless the bond was equally strong for both partners. How did Egan truly feel about her? He hadn't told her that he loved her. Not in the past. Not in the present.

Within half an hour, they had dressed, eaten and taken down the tent. Morning sunshine spread quickly, lighting the sky and illuminating the forest thicket that surrounded them. Egan stashed their equipment behind a boulder, freed their horses and held out his hand to Maggie.

"Ready?"

She nodded.

"No matter what happens, concentrate on only one thing—saving Bent. Don't even think about me." He grabbed her shoulders. "Do you understand?"

"Yes, I understand."

When he noted the stricken expression on her face, he ran his hands up and down her arms, then released her. "This isn't a suicide mission for me. I have every intention of coming out alive. But I'm prepared to die, if that's what it takes."

The look in her eyes said it all and said it far more eloquently than words could have. Egan had never wanted to live as badly as he did now. Now that he knew Maggie still cared. Now that he knew he had a son.

"Let's go," he told her.

"You lead. I'll follow."

Today was the day he had been waiting for all these years. The day Egan Cassidy would suffer the torment of the damned. Grant's head ached slightly. He had consumed a little too much wine last night. But why not? He'd had every reason to celebrate. Later today, he would celebrate even more. And Egan would be present for the event! Ah, the games he would play with them. The fun he would have. He would keep most of his soldiers on guard, preparing for the inevitable attack. But he could spare a dozen or so to witness the game playing. He would take more pleasure in the proceedings if he had an audience present. An audience of devoted followers.

A smile curved Grant's lips as he thought about making both father and son watch while he enjoyed himself with Maggie. Egan's Maggie. The mother of his son.

He had no intention of killing his captives quickly or painlessly. The joy would be in their suffering. The real pleasure would come from listening to their pitiful cries for mercy.

Even in his most vivid fantasies, revenge had never been this incredibly perfect. He'd never dared hope that out there somewhere Egan had loved a woman and fathered a child.

Grant laughed, the sound echoing in the stillness of his bedchamber. *Good things come to those who wait,* he thought.

He rose from the bed, naked and aroused.

After the first four miles, Maggie and Egan took a five-minute break. Hiking up a mountainside took more stamina than a fast-paced walk in the park, but Maggie had held her own. He was proud of her. A Southern lady through and through, with breeding, education and a keen intelligence, she impressed him even more now than she had fifteen years ago.

He had never fallen so hard, so fast, as he had for the twenty-three-year-old Maggie. She had represented the unobtainable. She was everything he'd ever wanted—and more. He'd had no right to take her, but when she'd come to him willingly, happily, offering him her heart and her body, he had been unable to refuse her. Not fifteen years ago. Not last night.

There had never been another woman—before or after Maggie—who had meant as much to him. No one else had been unforgettable. Only Maggie had remained a part of him, a memory he hadn't been able to erase. All those old feelings had resurfaced last night. That gut-wrenching hunger. That animalistic need to mate. That emotional yearning. He wanted her now, more than ever. And deserved her even less.

"Thirsty?" Egan asked.

"Yes," she replied.

He uncapped the canteen and they shared the tepid water. With weak smiles and looks of understanding exchanged, they resumed their journey. Three and a half miles later, Grant Cullen's towering rock and wood fortress appeared before them, like a giant monster emerging from the bowels of the earth.

Maggie skidded to a halt when they were within ten yards of the massive entrance gates. She grabbed Egan's hand. "I'm scared."

He squeezed her hand. "I know. So am I."

Hand-in-hand, they approached the gates. As if by magic, the nine-foot-high metal gates swung open and a six-man guard quickly surrounded them. The men wore tan uniforms, the insignia of the Ultimate Survivalists organization attached to their jacket sleeves and emblazoned just above the bill of the their caps: a crossed black rifle and a red sword, on a field of white.

A stocky young man, apparently the officer in charge, issued orders for the *guests* to be searched. Egan tensed at the thought of one of these militant idiots touching Maggie, but he held his tongue and his temper. When Maggie's gaze caught his, he nodded, signaling her not to protest.

First they were asked to remove their jackets, which the soldiers searched and then returned. The searches were thorough, but quick. And despite the flush that stained Maggie's cheeks, she appeared unaffected. With her head held high and her backbone stiff, she remained silent.

"The general is expecting you," the young officer said. "I'm Colonel Sherman. If you'll come this way, please."

"Where is my son?" Maggie demanded.

Without looking directly at Maggie, Colonel Sherman said, "I'll bring your son to you when the general requests his presence in the grand hall."

Egan gave Maggie a nod and the two of them fell into step with their captors. When they entered the compound, Egan noted the flurry of activity. He counted two and a half dozen soldiers preparing for battle. Expecting and thus preparing for an attack from the outside. Apparently Cullen had figured that Egan wouldn't come alone. But what Cullen hadn't counted on was a federal agent named Sawyer MacNamara.

Sherman led Maggie and Egan into a massive round room filled with benches. A large dais had been placed in the center, directly beneath a circular skylight. What was this place? Egan wondered. A meeting hall? A place of worship? An enormous, intricately carved throne sat in the middle of the podium. Of course, this was the hub of the fortress, the *grand hall* Sawyer had mentioned as the place where Cullen would bring Bent for the showdown.

Egan's stomach knotted as realization dawned. This was Cullen's throne room, where he held court. This was the place he had chosen to come face-to-face with his longtime enemy. Cullen would want an audience to watch while he brought Egan to his knees—figuratively and literally. That meant part of his little army would be summoned to the grand hall to act as witnesses. While the feds kept Cullen's troops busy with their frontal attack, the Dundee agents could concentrate on this area.

The thought of bowing and scraping to that bastard sickened Egan, but he would do whatever he had to do. He had to make sure everything was timed perfectly, even if it meant waiting and enduring some humiliation. Nothing could go wrong. Absolutely nothing. Bent's life depended upon precise action.

The man who had introduced himself as Colonel Sherman motioned to one of the front benches. "Sit here and wait."

"I want to know where Bent is! Where is my son and how is he?" Maggie glared viciously at the colonel.

"Your son is quite safe, Ms. Douglas," Sherman said. "He's unharmed."

"Where's Cullen?" Egan asked.

"I'm here, Cassidy." The voice came from the doorway.

Egan and Maggie whirled around just in time to see the general make his grand entrance. Wearing an ostentatious uniform, as gaudy as any movie star dictator, Grant Cullen marched into the arena. Flanked by an honor guard carrying rifles, the madman smiled fiendishly, as he saluted Egan.

Time had taken a toll on Cullen, but Egan suspected the evil within him had aged the man far more than the passing years. Although his hair was gray and his face heavily wrinkled, his body seemed to still be hard and thickly muscled.

"My old comrade, we meet again," Cullen said, then with a wave of his hand dismissed his guard. They fell away from him, but remained in two separate lines of three, awaiting his next command. He leaned over and whispered something to Colonel Sherman, who clicked his heels, saluted and left the room.

Boys, Egan thought. A bunch of boy soldiers. Not a one in the lot over twenty-five. Easily brainwashed youths, seeking a charismatic leader. Well, they'd found one in Cullen. But they had also signed their own death warrants by following a devil doomed to his own particular hell.

"We're here, as you requested," Egan said. "Maggie and I. Now, we want you to hold up your end of the bargain and release Bent."

"Ah, yes, Bentley Tyson Douglas…a fine young man. Reminds me a great deal of you, Cassidy. He's got your grit. You'd be proud of him. He pretty much told me to go to hell."

Maggie shoved her fist against her mouth in an effort to mask her frightened gasp. In his peripheral vision, Egan caught a glimpse of the terror in Maggie's eyes. Don't unravel now, he wanted to tell her. That's what Cullen wants. He will feed on our fear and our anger.

"No need to worry, Ms. Douglas," Cullen said, his smile widening. "I haven't harmed a hair on your son's head, despite the fact that he hasn't appreciated my hospitality. Bent has been under the watchful eye of my most valued soldier, Colonel Sherman."

"Where is Bent?" Maggie asked.

"I've sent for him," Cullen told her. "You'll see him shortly. Until then, please be seated. Both of you."

Egan took the suggestion as a cordial command. Grasping Maggie's arm, he pulled her down beside him on the front pew. "So, what now?"

"We wait." Cullen climbed the three steps up onto the dais and took his place on the majestic throne. "And while we wait, we can either talk over old times or we can discuss the present. Which do you prefer?"

"I prefer not to talk to you at all," Egan said. "I prefer that you allow Maggie and Bent to go free and that I stay here for the two of us to settle this between ourselves."

Cullen's boisterous laughter echoed off the walls. "So, you haven't lost your sense of humor. Not yet." His gaze settled on Maggie. His lips twisted into a vicious smirk. "But you will. You will. You didn't trust me to keep my word any more than I trusted you to keep yours."

"Are you saying that you aren't going to let Bent and Maggie go free?" Egan asked, knowing the answer only too well, but playing the game by Cullen's rules.

"And are you telling me that there isn't a group of agents on their way here, prepared to attack my fortress? Want to tell me when they're arriving? This morning? This afternoon?"

Maggie shuffled at his side. Without looking at her, he dropped his hand to the bench between them, palm open and down, in a *stay calm* gesture. Then he focused his attention on Cullen. "You said for us to come alone. With Bent's life at stake, would I lie to you?"

"Yeah, sure you would. And I told you that I'd let the boy and his mother go free, didn't I? Looks like we're both a couple of liars."

Marching through two double-wide doorways, uniformed soldiers began assembling. Egan scanned the room, counting bodies. Two dozen, give or take. Thirty-some-odd men in the outer courtyard preparing for an attack and half that number congregating for Cullen's upcoming stage show.

All in all, possibly fifty men. A small army, but an army all the same. Personally trained by Cullen, a shrewd professional. Soldiers equipped with up-to-date weapons. But from what the feds had found out about this operation, Egan's guess was that half the troops were green recruits, still being trained. And if he knew Cullen—and he did— the trained soldiers were the ones preparing for attack and the unseasoned ones were right here in the grand hall.

Good. That meant the Dundee squad might be outnumbered, but they would be dealing with amateurs. The odds in their favor just improved.

"Well, there's the young man of the hour." Cullen grinned as he held out his hand in a gesture to draw everyone's attention to the middle aisle.

"Bent!" Maggie came halfway to her feet.

Egan jerked her back down and gave her a disapproving frown. Tears gathered in the corners of her eyes as she twisted her head just enough to catch a glimpse, over Egan's shoulder, of her son.

Egan inclined his head slightly, in order to take his first look at Maggie's child. The boy was no longer a boy, but a young man. Tall, lean and handsome. A bit gangly in the way most fourteen-year-old boys are. Thick black hair, the color Egan's own hair had been before the gray set in. And dark gray eyes. Cassidy eyes. Like Egan's and Egan's father's. Looking at Bent was like looking into a mirror and seeing himself at that age. Except his son was better looking, having inherited a touch of glamour from Maggie that softened his features just a bit.

Bent walked down the aisle, head high, shoulders squared. He was probably scared out of his mind, but he didn't show it. *Never let them see you sweat, son!*

Egan's heart filled with pride at the sight of the child Maggie had given him. And he ached with a fear akin to none he'd ever known. He had already decided that he would gladly forfeit his life to save Bent's, and seeing his son only reinforced that resolve a thousand times over.

"Would you like to hug your son, Ms. Douglas?" Cullen asked. "And talk to him for a few minutes? Before we proceed with more important matters."

Maggie glanced at Egan, who nodded. "Yes," she said. "I'd very much like to hug my son."

Colonel Sherman walked Bent up the steps and onto the dais, halting him a good eight feet to Cullen's left.

Cullen motioned to Maggie. "Come up here."

Maggie stood on unsteady legs, trying to keep her composure and not allow Grant Cullen the satisfaction of seeing her fall apart. After taking a deep breath and saying a quick, silent prayer, she hurried up onto the dais. The moment she reached Bent, she wrapped her arms around him and hugged him fiercely.

She wanted to never let him go. If only she could pick him up and hold him, the way she'd done when he was a little boy. If only she could carry him out of this prison and flee with him to safety. This tall, proud young man was her baby. If anything happened to him, she wouldn't want to go on living.

"Are you all right?" she asked, her voice low.

"I'm fine."

"Some men are going to rescue you," Maggie whispered. "They're friends of your father's. When they arrive, go with them and do whatever they tell you to do."

Cullen snapped his fingers. "Enough! Say your good-byes."

"Mama?" Bent looked to Maggie for an explanation.

"I love you," she said.

"I love you, too, Mama."

Colonel Sherman grabbed Bent's arm and hauled him

over to one of two poles that ran from the floor to the ceiling on each side of the dais. As if preparing Bent for a firing squad execution, Sherman draped Bent's hands behind the pole and secured them with rope. Then he wrapped a length of rope around the boy's chest and looped it together behind the post.

"What are you doing?" Maggie cried.

"Bring Ms. Douglas to me," Cullen ordered.

When Sherman grabbed her, she struggled at first, but when her gaze met Egan's, she stopped fighting and went with the young colonel. He shoved her down at Cullen's feet, then pulled a dog collar and leash from the pocket of his jacket. After attaching the collar to Maggie's neck, he handed the leash to Cullen.

Egan balled his hands into tight fists. Every protective instinct he possessed ordered him to attack. But now was not the time. Not yet. He glanced casually at his watch. Thirteen minutes. He had to keep Maggie and Bent alive for thirteen more minutes. And if he'd guessed correctly about Cullen's intentions, his old enemy had planned the next couple of hours to consist of only pregame preparations. Setting the stage for the big show.

But once the feds attacked, Cullen would immediately step things up and put the deadly game into high gear. He no doubt believed his army could hold off an attack, mainly due to the almost impenetrable location of his mountainside fort and due even more to his own illogical, cocky self-assurance. The man thought he was invincible. He had probably planned for endless hours of torture, perhaps even days, despite the fact that he was well aware of an imminent attack.

Cullen stood, jerked on Maggie's leash and yanked her to her feet. "Have you ever played Russian roulette, Ms. Douglas?"

"No." Maggie gulped the word, as emotion lodged in her throat.

She had promised Egan that she could handle this, that she could be strong and brave. That she wouldn't break. He had promised her that he would save Bent. She had to hold on to that promise. She had to believe that he could fulfill his pledge to save their child.

"Well, we're going to play a little game of it now," Cullen told her, then motioned for a young soldier, who rose out of the audience and came forward to do his master's bidding.

Cullen snapped his fingers and Sherman produced a revolver, which he handed to the young soldier. "This could all be over quickly, without any suffering. I'm willing to let fate be the judge of whether we end this now or we enjoy ourselves for a few more hours."

Maggie held her breath. What was this madman going to do? she wondered. *God, help us!*

"Hold the gun to your temple," Cullen ordered the soldier, who obeyed without question. "Now, pull the trigger."

Maggie gasped. The soldier did as he'd been told. A distinct click reverberated in the hushed stillness of the arena. Cullen snatched the weapon from the boy's hand, then patted him on the back. "Well done."

Cullen dragged Maggie with him as he headed toward Egan. He held the gun to Egan's temple, a wicked smile on his lips. Maggie trembled from head to toe. She closed her eyes and pleaded to God to intervene. *Another loud click.* Breathing a sigh of relief, she slumped her shoulders and said a quick prayer of thanks.

How much longer until the attack? a frightened voice within Maggie's mind demanded. Cullen's games had only just begun and already she was on the verge of hysteria.

The Dundee agents were supposed to already be inside the fortress and federal agents were supposed to be on their way here. What were they waiting for? *Help us, now!*

Cullen's laughter echoed inside Maggie's head. When he drew in the chain leash, bringing her closer and closer to him, she cringed. Holding the gun to her temple, he leaned over and kissed her cheek. Her instincts told her to scratch his eyes out, to kick and claw. But she did nothing. Her breathing grew ragged when she felt the cold steel of the gun barrel against her skin.

"I hope there isn't a bullet with your name on it, Maggie. I do have such delicious plans for you."

"Wait!" Egan yelled.

Cullen's lazy glance in Egan's direction chilled Maggie to the bone.

"Wait for what?" Cullen asked.

"I'll take Maggie's turn," Egan said.

"Do you hear that?" Cullen rubbed the tip of the gun barrel around in circles on Maggie's temple. "Isn't that gallant? What do you say, Maggie, do you want Egan to take your turn?"

"No, I—" Maggie said.

"Yes, dammit, yes!" Egan said.

"Well, we have quite a quandary, don't we?" Cullen's self-satisfied smile etched his face with deep laugh lines. He snapped his fingers. "I have the perfect solution. We'll let Bent take his mother's turn."

"No!" Maggie and Egan screamed in unison.

Egan checked his watch. Five minutes. Five freaking minutes! The moment the attack began, Cullen would assume he had everything under control. He'd probably be in no hurry to dismiss his audience, but if he allowed his military training to rule his actions, he'd order these soldiers to join their comrades on the front line. But whether the Dundee squad had to face a handful of Cullen's men or an even two dozen, they knew what had to be done.

Egan had to play for time. And he had to get Maggie away from Cullen before the Dundee squad made their move. Once Cullen realized what was happening, he'd kill Maggie instantly and go for Bent next.

"Such devoted parents," Cullen said snidely. "Aren't you a lucky boy."

Cullen hauled Maggie with him across the dais to where Bent stood shackled to the pole. When he laid the gun against Bent's cheek, Maggie keened loudly. Cullen smiled at her. "*Tsk-tsk.* Mustn't get so upset. After all the odds are in his favor. There really is only one bullet in this gun."

"I'll take my turn," Maggie pleaded. "And I'll take Bent's turn. Please let me take my son's turn!"

"You're too eager," Cullen told her. "Besides, using the boy will make this so much more painful for Cassidy. He'll not only die a thousand deaths waiting for the sound of the gun to fire, but he'll be in agony watching you suffer."

"You're a monster!" Maggie lunged at Cullen, knocking him off balance enough so that he lost his tight grip on the revolver.

Colonel Sherman jumped to the rescue, snatching the gun off the floor the minute it landed. Cullen jerked Maggie's leash, pulling her close, then pressed his nose against hers. "I like spirit in a woman. It makes the conquest all the sweeter."

"Leave my mother alone!" Bent yelled.

"Ah, the protective son heard from." Cullen handed Maggie's leash to Sherman and took the gun from him. "Walk Maggie over to stand by her lover. They can watch together."

The young colonel dragged Maggie off the dais so

quickly that she almost lost her footing, but she somehow managed to remain on her feet. The moment Sherman shoved her up against Egan, she gritted her teeth and whispered to Egan, "Do something!"

Egan checked his watch. One minute and counting.

"Hang on, Maggie. Hang on," he said, his voice a low rumble.

Cullen held the revolver to Bent's temple. "Any last words?"

"Yeah," Bent said. "Go to hell!"

My baby. My baby. Oh, Bent! The silent cries shrieked from Maggie's heart.

A barrage of artillery bombarded the fortress. A loud explosion shook the very foundation of Cullen's hideaway. Egan suspected that Cullen's private helicopter had just gone up in smoke. The boy soldiers in the audience mumbled loudly as they jumped to their feet. Egan grasped one of Maggie's trembling hands.

Cullen eased the gun away from Bent's head and smiled at Egan.

"By the time they blast their way into here, you'll all be dead and I'll be long gone."

"You seem awfully sure," Egan shouted over the roar of nearby artillery fire.

"I am," Cullen said, then turned to Colonel Sherman. "Take all but half a dozen men. They'll be needed out there—" Cullen inclined his head toward the doorway. "Report back to me when you've assessed the situation."

"Yes, sir!"

Sherman followed orders, leaving behind six soldiers, who spread out around the room, their rifles ready.

"If Cassidy makes a move, shoot him," Cullen said, then motioned to Maggie. "Come here."

Maggie didn't budge.

"You can buy some time for yourself, as well as your son and Egan, if you cooperate," he told her. "I had hoped we'd have more time, but I won't need more than a few minutes to—"

"Don't you touch her!" Bent cried. "Don't you dare—"

"Shut up!" Cullen slapped Bent with the back of his hand.

Maggie moaned when she saw the trickle of blood oozing from Bent's bursted lip.

Cullen stomped off the dais, heading straight toward Maggie. She stood frozen to the spot, waiting, counting the seconds. Before he was halfway to her, the doors flew open and five black-clad commandos stormed the inner sanctum. Taken off guard, the boy soldiers didn't react immediately. Cullen yelled for them to fire.

Egan shoved Maggie to the floor and quickly covered her body with his as bullets whizzed overhead.

"Kill the boy!" Cullen shouted.

"No!" Maggie screamed.

Chapter 8

Egan held Maggie down, knowing that if he let her go, she would run headlong into the middle of the gunfire between Cullen's soldiers and the Dundee squad. Her maternal instincts had shifted into overdrive. Her only thoughts were of protecting her child. But her panic could get her killed and interfere with Bent's rescue. Egan had no choice but to subdue her. She struggled to free herself, crying, begging him to help Bent before it was too late.

"Joe and Hunter will take care of Bent," he told her, praying he could get through to her in her panicked state of mind. "He's their first priority." How did he make her understand that Bent's best chance of survival rested in the hands of the two Dundee agents and that neither he nor she could get to Bent in time?

Maggie trembled, shudders racking her body. Egan grabbed her and rolled them under the nearest bench. Hot metal zoomed all around them as the sound of repetitive shooting became deafening. After endless moments of intense warfare, a deadly silence prevailed.

"Cassidy!" a loud female voice shouted.

"Stay put," Egan told Maggie, then scooted out from under the bench just enough to see Ellen Denby scanning the room, while Wolfe and Jack Parker kept her covered. Egan lifted his arm and signaled to Ellen.

The moment Ellen noted his location, she held out a handgun and with effortless ease tossed the Glock to Egan. He caught the weapon in midair. After quickly checking the magazine, he chambered a round.

"We've got Bent!" Joe Ornelas shouted.

"Get him out of here!" Ellen ordered.

Egan caught a glimpse of Bent, flanked by Joe Ornelas and Hunter Whitelaw, as they took him out of immediate harm's way.

Maggie grasped Egan's shirtfront. "Bent's safe?"

Maggie's teardrops hit his hand—the hand that held the 9-mm. "Yeah, honey, Bent's safe." He didn't bother qualifying his statement, explaining that the squad had to get Bent out of the fortress before he would be truly safe. Or that the only way to obtain Bent's safety one hundred percent now and in the future was to eliminate Cullen permanently.

"Room's cleared," Ellen said. "Let's get moving while we can."

"We have to get out of here," Egan told Maggie. "I'm going to remove this damn dog collar from your neck—" he unsnapped the catch "—and then we're going to ease out from underneath this bench and make a run for the doors on the right. Stay with me. Understand?"

"Yes," she managed to reply, her voice shaky as Egan removed the collar and tossed it aside.

When Egan and Maggie reached the hallway, Ellen

Denby, an MP5 in her hands, motioned for them to wait.
Three Survivalists charged up the hallway, shooting repeatedly, as if they thought firepower alone could protect
them. Bullets splintered wood and sent shards of concrete
flying. Overconfident as only the young and inexperienced
could be, they walked right into the ambush. The threesome
wouldn't know what hit them, Egan thought.

From their vantage points on either side of the curved
corridor, Parker aimed his AK-47 and Wolfe did the same.
The blasts reverberated down the hallway as they took out
all three of Cullen's soldiers. Parker waved an all clear.
Ellen nodded to Egan, who clutched Maggie's arm and
shoved her into motion. Guiding her around the dead bodies, Egan urged Maggie forward, as Ellen covered them
from the rear.

While they hurried down the corridor, ever mindful of
the unknown waiting around each turn, Egan felt proud of
Maggie. Not only was she keeping pace with them, but
once she'd known Bent was safe, she had kept her composure during the maelstrom of battle. Maggie didn't pos-
sess Ellen's training, expertise or hard-ass attitude, but in
her own way she was every bit as brave and strong.

"Where's Cullen?" Egan asked.

"Two seconds after we showed up and he realized he
couldn't shoot at Bent without risking his own life, he made
a hasty exit out a back entrance of the throne room," Ellen
said.

"Think he'll try the escape tunnel?" Parker asked.

"Don't think so." Egan's breathing remained even as he
raced along the hallway. "My bet is he hasn't figured out
exactly what happened. Until he does, he'll keep fighting."

Occasionally checking the rear for any sign of the enemy, Ellen kept pace with the others. Suddenly Wolfe
stopped and dropped. As he did, a bullet zinged over him,

piercing the wall at the exact level his head had been a millisecond before. Just as the lone shooter came into view, Wolfe took him out with one fatal head shot.

"Time's a-wasting, boys and girls," Parker said, his Texas accent decidedly distinctive at the moment. "Once Joe and Hunter have Bent aboard the chopper, O'Brien will wait exactly ten minutes—if he can—and then they're gone and so is our transportation out of Cullen's private little hell."

"We'll make it," Ellen said. "We're nearly to the stairs. Too bad we can't take a chance on the elevator, but we don't dare risk getting caught with nowhere to run."

Within minutes, the five of them were in the stairwell headed to the subterranean level. But they had two flights to descend before reaching their goal. Their stomping boots clanged the metal steps as they scurried ever downward. The stairwell remained clear all the way to the third level. Apparently Cullen hadn't yet figured out how the Dundee squad had gained access to his fortress, Egan thought. But it was only a matter of time before he put two and two together and realized he had a traitor in his midst—someone who had allowed the intruders entrance through the secret tunnel.

Every good commando knew that you had to get in, do your job and get the hell out before the enemy knew what had hit them. Egan grunted. Maybe, just maybe they were going to make it out alive—all of them.

When they reached the vault, deep within the mountain, Parker and Wolfe took the lead, followed by Egan and Maggie. Ellen brought up the rear. Things are going too good, Egan decided. There hadn't been a hitch in the operation. Bent was probably already aboard the chopper and within minutes they would be joining him. The feds were keeping Cullen's troops busy. But where exactly was Cullen? Egan's gut instincts told him that that wily bastard would have a few tricks up his sleeve, even after a surprise attack. But what sort of tricks? And when would he strike?

As they emerged from the tunnel, the bright daylight momentarily blinded them, but within seconds Egan's eyesight returned. In the distance he could hear the roar of the chopper's motor and as he scanned the area, he noted the whirlwind effect blowing through the trees and shrubs. They congregated just outside the tunnel—Egan, Maggie, Wolfe, Parker and Ellen.

"What are we waiting for?" Parker asked. "Let's get the hell out of here."

"Take Maggie with you," Egan told Ellen.

Maggie balked. "What do you mean—"

"I have to find Cullen," Egan said. "Go with Ellen."

"You can't stay here!" Maggie grasped Egan's shirtfront. "I'm not leaving you here. You're coming with us!"

Just as Egan started to shove Maggie away, Wolfe let out an earsplitting warrior's yell, warning them of danger. A good twenty-five feet above them, perched on an overhang, Winn Sherman manned a machine gun. Grant Cullen stood at his side.

No time to think, only to react. Egan dragged Maggie with him as he headed for the closest cover behind a massive boulder near the heavily wooded area to the south. Ellen and Parker dropped and rolled toward Wolfe, who had already made a mad dash and a leap into a gully at the edge of a pathway leading to the chopper. Wolfe, Parker and Denby aimed their weapons.

Rapid machine-gun fire peppered the ground, snapped off spindly tree limbs and chipped off chunks from the boulder. Egan surveyed the situation quickly and realized he and Maggie were cut off from escape, trapped between the wilderness and the fortress.

The three Dundee agents returned fire, but were at a great disadvantage. Egan realized that the smartest thing for them to do was get to the chopper as fast as possible. He had wanted Maggie to go with them, but it didn't look as if that was possible now. After checking the time, Egan realized that O'Brien would be taking off in two minutes, with or without the others.

Get your men aboard that chopper, Denby! Egan's mind issued the order. Ellen would take care of things on her end, and it would be up to Egan to handle things here. He knew that he and Maggie had only one chance to survive.

While the machine gun riddled the boulder, Egan grasped Maggie's chin. She stared at him, a look of sheer terror in her eyes. "We can't make it to the chopper," he told her. "And I won't risk your life letting you stay here until I can eliminate Cullen."

"You were going to stay here and kill him, weren't you, even if it meant dying yourself?"

"Plans have changed," he said. "Eliminating Cullen will have to wait. Right now, getting you to safety is far more important."

The whine of the chopper's engine reached an earsplitting roar as the motors revved. The aircraft lifted, hovering above them. A force of strong air whipped over the towering trees and the resonance of the helicopter's rotating blades hummed noisily. A steady stream of gunfire blasted from the machine gun nest, preventing the chopper from getting anywhere near Egan and Maggie. They were, for all intents and purposes, cut off from any hope of a rescue.

Within minutes the chopper disappeared over the mountain ridge. Egan glanced up at the overhang where Sherman had manned the machine gun. Sunlight glinted off the powerful weapon, but no shooter was in sight. That probably meant Sherman and Cullen had realized Egan and Maggie hadn't escaped with the squad and were preparing to search for them.

"We have to get moving," Egan told Maggie. "There's a good chance they'll be following us, so we're going to have to move fast and keep going as long as possible."

She nodded, her head bobbing repeatedly, fear widening her eyes. They crawled away from the boulder and into the nearby brush, then Egan jerked her up behind a stand of tall ponderosa pines. He checked the area all around them. North. South. East. And west.

"We can't go down the mountain the way we came in, so there's no hope of getting to our supplies. Cullen knows the route we took coming here," Egan explained. "And I don't think there's a chance we could get through to the feds, without getting caught in the cross fire and this battle could go on until nightfall. Maybe longer. Cullen will come after us. Our only choice is to find our way back to civilization and contact Ellen." Gazing into Maggie's eyes he saw weariness, uncertainty and understanding. And a fear she could not hide. "I won't lie to you. It'll be rough going. We don't have a compass or supplies of any kind, including food and water. If we don't find a town before night, we'll have no shelter."

"What other choice do we have?" she asked.

"The only other choices we have are to risk getting gunned down by either Cullen's soldiers or being accidentally shot by the feds if we cross over into the war zone." Egan took a deep breath. "Or we can give ourselves up to Cullen."

Maggie shook her head. "Tell me how Cullen and Sherman got away, if the feds have the fortress surrounded?"

"Undoubtedly he had more than one escape hatch."

"He left his men there to fight and die, didn't he?"

"Yeah. That's exactly what he did. I just hope those poor

stupid boys don't fight to the death. While they're giving their lives for the Ultimate Survivalists cause, their glorious leader will be tracking you and me.''

"He and Sherman will have rifles, maybe even submachine guns, won't they?"

"I have this pistol." He showed her the Glock. "I've got seventeen rounds and I don't intend to waste one shot. Now, come on. Let's get going. Our goal is to stay at least one step ahead of them and if we're lucky, we'll lose them.''

Egan knew the odds, but he was willing to accept those fifty-fifty odds and bet he and Maggie could come out of this the winners. Just the fact that Bent was safe put them ahead in the game already.

He might not know this country as well as Cullen did, but he had survived in the wilderness more than once and he'd put his skills up against Cullen's any day of the week. He had to make sure to cover his tracks, to take the unexpected path, to do the illogical. Cullen was the type of man who would become easily frustrated if confused. And Egan meant to confuse the hell out of the son of a bitch!

"Why did you go off and leave them?" Bent Douglas demanded in a tone that reminded Ellen of Egan Cassidy's ferocious growl. "How could you have—"

Hunter Whitelaw laid his bear-paw of a hand on Bent's shoulder. "There's no way they could have made it to the chopper from where they were. Not without being shot down by that machine gun. We couldn't get to them and they couldn't get to us."

"Our orders were to take you away and keep you safe, no matter what else went down," Ellen said.

"Whose orders?" Bent asked.

"Your father's," Ellen replied.

Bent searched Ellen's face. "Who are you people and what does Egan Cassidy have to do with what happened to me? That man, that General Cullen, knew my father, didn't he? He was using me as bait to bring Egan Cassidy to him."

"Cassidy is a former mercenary," Ellen said. "He worked freelance for the CIA several years before he retired. A couple of years ago, he came to work for us. The Dundee Private Security and Investigation Agency in Atlanta. There's been bad blood between Grant Cullen and your father for a long time, but I'll let Egan explain the details to you."

"Then you believe he and my mother will be all right?"

Hunter squeezed Bent's shoulder. Ellen wished she could tell the boy what he wanted to hear and for just a moment she considered lying to him. But she owed Egan's son the truth, even if she did choose to put a positive spin on it.

"I believe that if any man can find a way out of that situation and bring your mother back to you, then Egan Cassidy can."

"Isn't there anything you can do?" Bent asked. "Can't you go back and help them?"

"There's no way to know for sure where they went," Ellen said. "That's a big mountain down there."

"Then what are you going to do?" Bent glared at Ellen.

"I'm going to take you to Flagstaff and wait there for Egan to contact us. Ornelas and Whitelaw—" she nodded first toward one and then toward the other "—are going to be your personal bodyguards."

"Why do I need bodyguards if the man who kidnapped me is still back at the fort?"

"Because Cullen heads up a group called the Ultimate Survivalists and we have no idea how far-reaching this group is or if Cullen has issued orders to harm you." Ellen hated being brutally honest, but these circumstances called for nothing less. Bent wasn't a child. He was a young man of fourteen. He would be safer armed with the knowledge that his life might still be in danger.

What a freaking mess to be in, Ellen thought. If Cassidy didn't make it through, if he and Maggie didn't survive, then the Dundee agents would have an orphan on their hands. And if Cassidy didn't take care of Cullen, Bent's life would remain in danger. There was only one solution to this problem.

Grant Cullen had to die. And Egan Cassidy had to live.

Winn Sherman loaded a backpack onto the young soldier, then draped a rifle over his shoulder. "We're ready, sir."

"The men have their orders," Cullen said. "They'll hold the fort as long as possible to give us time to escape and then they'll surrender."

"We'd better get going," Sherman suggested. "Cassidy and the woman already have an hour's head start."

"Not to worry." Cullen grinned as he petted the sub-machine gun he held, then knelt to caress MacArthur and Patton. "Where can they go except down the mountain? If we don't catch them on the way down, we'll catch them at the bottom. This game isn't over until I win. And that can't happen until Cassidy, his son and his woman are all dead."

Maggie and Egan had been hiking at a hard, steady pace for over three and a half hours, a grueling journey to put as much distance as possible between them and their pursuers. Egan had used every method he knew to throw their searchers off track, including choosing a destination on the far side of the mountain that would prolong their descent. He hoped Cullen would assume he would choose the quickest and easiest way.

Egan had rushed Maggie, forcing her into an uncomfortable pace, wanting them to reach water for two reasons. First, they were both hot, tired and thirsty. One of the greatest dangers to survival was dehydration. And second, despite his best efforts, it was possible that Cullen might pick up their trail. But if they could follow a streambed for several miles, they could improve their odds of escaping completely.

"Listen!" Egan shouted. "Do you hear it?"

"A waterfall?" Maggie asked.

"And where there's a waterfall in these mountains, there's usually a streambed. Come on. Follow me."

Maggie's lungs burned, her calf muscles quivered and her back ached. She wanted nothing more than to lie down and rest. And never get up again. But instead, she tagged after Egan like an obedient puppy. Doing her best to keep up, she made her way behind Egan through a narrow passage that led them down into a steep gorge. Towering walls of jagged rock closed in around them, waiting to rip and tear their clothes and skin. Gravel slipped beneath their feet, often showering in a rockslide to the bottom of the gorge.

When Egan reached level ground, he grasped Maggie's hand and led her into a box canyon, deep within the mountain. Sheer walls of stone rose up a good two hundred feet. Three-fourths in the middle of the granite wall, a spray of pummeling water spouted forth and jetted in a twelve-foot fall to the pond, which created a meandering stream that disappeared around the bend.

"Just a little farther and we can take a longer rest," Egan told her. "But we can stop here for a few minutes."

Maggie dropped to her knees, not caring that the rocky terrain of the streambed ate into her jeans. Cupping her hands, she swooped up cool, crystal-clear water and brought it to her lips. Nothing had ever tasted as sweet. After drinking several handfuls, she lifted another and splashed the water in her face.

Egan drank his fill from the stream, then doused his head into the creek. Rising up onto his feet, he waited for Maggie to stand, and when she didn't, he grabbed her arm and jerked her up beside him.

"I think we're safe from Cullen. At least temporarily. He'll have a damn hard time finding us." Egan swiped flyaway strands of Maggie's hair from her face. A warm flush brightened her cheeks a shade darker than the sunburn on her nose and forehead. "You've got the beginning of a sunburn." He tapped the tip of her nose.

"It's this darn peaches-and-cream complexion of mine," she said, a faint smile curving the corners of her mouth.

"Sorry we don't have anything you can use to protect that beautiful skin of yours." He caressed her cheek. "But I'm afraid we have more immediate and essential problems to concern us."

"I assume you mean other than escaping from Cullen."

"Shelter," he told her. "Come night, we'll need a safe place to sleep."

"What about food?"

"If necessary, we could live for weeks without food, but only days without water."

"Anything else I should worry about?" she asked.

"Let me do the worrying for both of us." When she frowned, her forehead wrinkling and her eyes narrowing into a don't-try-to-placate-me glare, Egan gave her a gentle shove. "Let's get moving. We'll rest farther upstream. I promise."

Knowing that her child was safe, Maggie could face anything that came her way. And she had no doubts that she

was in good hands with Egan. Nodding agreement, her
frown turned into a halfhearted smile.

"That's my Maggie."

She had no idea where they were. All she knew was that
they hadn't reached civilization and hadn't seen any sign
of human life all day. Egan had backtracked and zigzagged
and by his own admission, taken them miles out of their
way, all in an effort to throw Cullen off track. Once Egan
had felt reasonably certain they had circumvented Cullen's
search, they took frequent rest stops, for which Maggie was
eternally grateful.

The sun sank low on the western horizon, melting into
a rotund crescent pool of golden orange. The terrain spread
across the rocky ground to a dense stand of pine and spruce
trees. A lichen that Egan had told her was called "Old
Man's Beard" dangled from the branches of many of the
spruce trees. Farther along the mountainside, white aspens
grew in profusion and New Mexican locust flowers hovered
around their trunks.

Night was fast approaching and they had yet to find shelter. The last rays of sunlight shot across the horizon, creating a red and purple hued display in the sky. The temperature had already begun to drop. Maggie shivered.

"Even when we stop for the night, we can't risk a fire,"
Egan said. "I'm sorry."

"What are we going to do, huddle under a tree?"

"Maybe. But I keep hoping we'll run across a cave."

"Yeah, sure." Maggie's stomach growled. "And while
you're hoping, hope for a bowl of chili and some corn
bread."

"What's the matter, didn't you like the nuts and berries
I found for us?" he asked teasingly.

"I know we won't starve without food for quite some

time, but subsisting on sour berries and bitter nuts that even a squirrel wouldn't touch could definitely affect my normally sunny disposition.''

"Then tomorrow I'll see if I can't find you more edible fare.''

"How about bacon and eggs?'' Maggie sighed. "I suppose I should be more concerned about where we're spending the night than about what we'll have for breakfast.''

Perhaps she should consider it odd that they could joke at a time like this, but somehow, with Egan and her, the jovial comradery seemed perfectly natural. After all, not only was their son safe with the Dundee agents, but they themselves had escaped death more than once today. Despite the threat of Cullen's pursuit, she felt lucky. Lucky to be alive and lucky to be with Egan. She knew, in her heart, that if anyone could get them to safety, he could.

But once Egan reunited her with Bent, what would happen then? an inner voice asked. But she knew the answer. He would hunt down Cullen, face his worst enemy and destroy him. Or be destroyed!

"I think I've found an economy suite for us.'' Egan clutched Maggie's shoulders and maneuvered her around to stand in front of him. "Take a look. It doesn't provide the security and total privacy of a cave, but it allows us a great view of the stars.''

At the foot of a rocky embankment littered with brush and wildflowers, Maggie spotted Egan's discovery—an odd-shaped boulder, with an overhanging lip curved like the letter *C*. It wasn't a cave, she thought, but it was the next best thing.

"I'm sorry that I haven't been able to find a better place for us to spend the night, but the overhang will provide a modicum of shelter and the jagged cliff wall surrounding it will add to the feel of privacy.''

"Looks like Motel Heaven to me." Maggie offered him a weary, but appreciative smile. "How do we get down there?"

"We climb down," he said.

"I was afraid that's what you'd say."

"Not wimping out on me at this late stage are you, Maggie mine?"

"You lead, I'll follow," she repeated the words that had now become a litany.

"Just what I wanted to hear." Egan flashed her a brilliant smile. "A woman who knows how to take orders."

"We'll head back to Minerva," Cullen said. "There's not much daylight left, so call and have someone meet us before dark."

"Yes, sir," Colonel Sherman said.

Winn Sherman instantly obeyed the general. He made a quick phone call, while young Lieutenant Shatz handed Cullen a canteen of water. Cullen drank his fill, then motioned to Shatz. The lieutenant removed a bowl from his backpack and filled it with water from his own canteen. Cullen led his rottweilers to the tepid liquid and then handed their reins to Shatz.

"Where the hell is he?" Cullen fumed. "He's led us on a merry chase, but if Cassidy thinks he's outsmarted me, he'd better think again. He may have gotten away this time. But our organization has eyes and ears everywhere in this part of the state. Once he shows up, we'll take care of him." Cullen stroked the submachine gun in his hand.

Winn would follow General Cullen to hell and back for the cause. But tracking down Egan Cassidy and Maggie Douglas had nothing to do with the Ultimate Survivalists. This was a personal vendetta in which the general had involved his soldiers. Winn couldn't stop thinking about the men back at the fort. All those who had died and all those who would be arrested. A bunch of fine young men—boys he had helped train. But he didn't dare question Grant Cullen's authority.

The general had promised that once Cassidy and his woman were eliminated, he would regroup and recruit new soldiers. The cause would rise from the ashes more powerful and more glorious than ever.

That's all that mattered to Winn. The Ultimate Survivalists. So when the time came, he would be at his master's side, to hunt down and kill Egan Cassidy.

Chapter 9

The oddly shaped boulder curved over them like a canopy, giving them some protection from the elements. Even though the breeze that rustled through the treetops didn't touch them, the falling temperature chilled them. Egan finished the mattress of branches, moss and leaves he had built, row after row, to cover the cold ground.

"Lie down," he told Maggie. "And turn toward the boulder."

With exhaustion claiming her body and mind, Maggie gladly complied with his command. Although the cushion beneath her lacked the comfort of her bed at home, Maggie's weary body appreciated the luxury of simply lying down and relaxing. The aromatic evergreen boughs filled the night air with their fresh, woodsy scent.

Egan lifted the small branches he had stripped from nearby spruce trees and dragged them with him as he eased down beside Maggie, his chest to her back. He removed the pistol he'd worn secured by his belt and set it within his reach. Once in place, their bodies lying spoon fashion, he rearranged the branches, covering Maggie and himself from ankles to shoulders as he completed their survival bed.

"Is your back exposed?" Maggie asked. "Are you cold?"

"I'm fine, honey. How about you?"

"I never thought a bed of sticks and leaves would feel so heavenly. Or smell so good." Her soft sigh transformed into a deep yawn. "I don't think there's a muscle in my body that isn't aching. Even my hair aches."

He nuzzled her hair, then kissed her head. "Your hair smells like sunshine."

A tiny giggle hung in her throat. "I can't decide if that was a sweet thing for you to say or just downright silly."

"I'd prefer for you to think it was romantic."

"It was," she told him. "But then you always were a romantic. Always said just the right words, always did just the right thing. Inside that warrior's body, you have the heart and soul of a poet."

Egan chuckled. "You think so, do you?"

"I know so."

A languid silence, a soul-felt weariness equal to the debility of their bodies, shrouded them. Long-ago memories invaded their thoughts. A week out of time, when they had been lovers. Tender words spoken in the quiet moments after lovemaking. Earthy, erotic phrases whispered in the heat of passion. Gentle strokes. Flesh against flesh. A joining of hearts and bodies. And souls.

A child, created in those sweet, unforgettable moments when nothing and no one had existed except the two of them.

Egan splayed his hand across her belly. "I wish I could have been with you when you were carrying Bent."

Maggie placed her hand over his. "I wanted you there with me. I needed you." She shuddered ever so slightly.

"Can you ever forgive me for what I did? And for putting you and Bent at risk? I never intended to hurt you. I would rather have died than to have harmed you in any way."

She snuggled against him, loving the feel of his big body draped around her, warming her, protecting her. "Our romance…our love affair was as much my doing as yours."

"But you weren't the one harboring deadly secrets," he said. "I was the one who had no right to become emotionally involved, to chance creating a child. I knew I couldn't fall in love and marry and have children. Cullen was always breathing down my neck. Just waiting for the opportunity to use a woman—or a child—against me."

"Oh, Egan." Maggie gulped down the tears that threatened her. "How terribly unfair life has been to you. And all because you exposed that monster for what he was…for what he still is."

"Don't think about Cullen." Egan lifted his head enough so that he could kiss her cheek. Her jaw. The spot below her ear. "I'll make sure he's never a threat to you or Bent again."

Maggie understood what Egan was telling her, that he would have to face his enemy and destroy him. The gentle side of Maggie's nature abhorred the thought of Egan killing another human being. But the protective, maternal instincts that were equally a part of her nature wanted Grant Cullen dead.

"Do you think someone will explain the situation to Bent?" Maggie asked. "He must be awfully confused. I hope—" her voice cracked with emotion. "I know he's fourteen, but he's still just a little boy in so many ways."

"Ellen will give him an explanation," Egan said. "Probably the condensed version, but enough so that he won't wonder why Cullen kidnapped him. And she'll assure him that I'll get you safely back to him." Egan caressed Maggie's belly, his hand moving in wide circles from waist to thighs. "Tell me about my son. Please."

Maggie breathed deeply, then exhaled on a long, slow sigh. "You saw him today. Don't you think he resembles you a great deal?"

"He's my spitting image," Egan agreed. "Except he's prettier than I ever was. Got that from you. That natural glamour."

"He inherited your adventurous streak. Sometimes his fearlessness scares me to death. You know what a cautious person I am." Except when it came to loving Egan, she thought. Then she was totally reckless and took enormous risks. In the past. But what about now? She had given him her body, freely, lovingly, last night. But could she truly take a life-altering chance and give her heart to this man? Was he capable of living a normal life? Without danger and excitement? Without adventure and risk?

"He's a good kid, though, isn't he?" Egan asked.

"Oh, yes. Bent is a really good kid. He's kind and considerate and loving. And he's always been my little man." Tears gathered in Maggie's eyes. "I suppose he somehow felt that he had to take care of me because his father wasn't… Even when I was married to Gil, Bent looked out for me. If Gil and I ever argued, Bent was always ready to come to my defense."

"If it hadn't been for me…if I hadn't shown up in your life, you'd have married Gil and lived happily ever after." Egan clutched Maggie to him, a purely possessive gesture. "And Bent would have been his son, not mine. I really screwed things up for you, didn't I?"

Maggie wriggled around, reversing her position and

shedding several shielding branches in the process, until she lay facing Egan. The glimmering moonlight cast shadows across their bodies and allowed her to see the dark silhouette of Egan's face. She burrowed her head against the side of his neck and wrapped her arm around his waist.

"I don't know how my life would have turned out if you'd never been a part of it," she said, her soft voice laced with emotion. "But no one, least of all Gil, could have given me a son half as wonderful as Bent."

"Ah, Maggie. Sweet Maggie mine."

His lips sought and found hers in the darkness. Tender passion.

A soothing balm to Egan's wounded soul. An unspoken confession from Maggie's heart. When the kiss ended, they held each other, seeking warmth and comfort.

"Bent was a big baby. Nine pounds and ten ounces. And twenty-two inches long," Maggie said. "And man did he have an appetite." She laughed. "He still has a ravenous appetite. I can't fill him up. We can finish dinner and within two hours, he's back in the kitchen fixing himself a couple of sandwiches and getting another helping of dessert."

"He's a big boy. Close to six feet. Right?"

"Right. And he's healthy and intelligent and good at sports. Baseball and softball are his favorites. You should see his collection of baseball cards. If we traded them in, we could afford to send him to college from the proceeds."

"What's he interested in doing with his life? I mean, when he finishes high school?"

"Well, his future plans change on a fairly regular basis. One month his plans are to get a baseball scholarship and eventually play in the major leagues. Then another month, he talks about being a psychiatrist and helping people like his uncle Bentley. Several times he's mentioned he might like a military career, but when he sees that his talking about being a professional soldier upsets me, he changes the subject.''

"When this is all over...when Cullen is no longer a threat—'' Egan paused. His voice lowered and softened. "I know I don't deserve it, but I'd very much like the opportunity to get to know my son, to be a part of his life.''

Maggie's heartbeat accelerated. Did she want Egan in her life on a permanent basis? Could they build a relationship on passion? Or on their shared parenthood? Egan was asking to be a part of Bent's life, not a part of hers, she reminded herself. But didn't the one include the other?

"I won't try to keep you and Bent apart,'' she said. "Now that you are aware of his existence, whatever relationship you form with Bent will be up to you and him.''

"Does he hate me? If you've told him that I deserted you when you were pregnant, then he must—''

"He doesn't hate you. But he doesn't know you.'' Maggie reverted to her original position, turning her back on Egan. "You'll have to earn his trust and his friendship.''

"You don't have any objections?''

"Why should I? You *are* his father.''

Egan laid his hand over Maggie's waist and pulled her body closer until they were once again nestled snugly together. "Thank you,'' he whispered.

Swirling mists surrounded Maggie, like mountaintop fog, thick and damp and grayish white. Egan was with her, his big, hard body hovering over her, his lips seeking, his sex probing. The ecstasy of their joining splintered through her body, sending waves of pleasure into every fiber of her being.

Suddenly Egan was gone and she was alone. So alone. Her hand settled over her swollen belly. No, not alone. Egan had left her with his child. The man she loved was lost to her forever, but she had his baby, growing inside her. Safe. Secure.

And then Bent lay in his mother's arm, tiny and sweet-smelling, as only infants can be. She held him to her breast and his eager little mouth latched on greedily. If only Egan were here. If only he could see his son. Egan! her heart cried. Please, come back.

From out of nowhere Grant Cullen appeared and wrenched Bent from Maggie's arms. He kicked her aside when she tried to fight him. He held Bent by the back of his little cotton pajamas and dangled him over the edge of a fiery precipice. She begged and pleaded and bargained with the inhuman devil, but all he did was laugh at her. Shrill, maniacal screeches.

Maggie tried to move, tried to reach out for Bent, but she found herself bound and gagged, rendered helpless to defend her baby.

Egan! Help us, Egan! Help us!

But Egan was not there. He wasn't going to come to their aid. He wasn't going to save Bent.

Cullen released his hold on Bent and his round, little body began a headlong fall into the volcanic depths.

No! Maggie screamed. Egan!

She woke with a start, Egan hovering over her, shaking her gently. She stared up at his dark silhouette and for one brief moment was lost between the nightmare and reality.

"Maggie, honey, what's wrong? You were screaming and saying my name."

She sat up and scooted away from him, then gulped down air as she tried to take control of her wild thoughts and frazzled nerves. "Dream," she said. "No, not a dream. A nightmare. Bent was…Bent was a baby and Cullen took him from me and—"

Egan laid two fingers over Maggie's lips, silencing her.

"It's all over. Bent is safe. Cullen will never get near him again."

"Oh, Egan, I kept calling for you. I needed you. We needed you and you weren't there. You didn't help us. Bent...Bent—" Maggie sucked in quick, harsh breaths. "Cullen threw Bent into a fiery hole. My baby. My baby! And you weren't there. Where were you, Egan? Why didn't you help us?"

Shedding the blanket of branches, Egan reached out for Maggie. She fought him as he jerked her into his arms, but he held her, allowing her to struggle and cry and vent her anger. She fought like a madwoman until she exhausted herself and fell limply against Egan. He encompassed her within his embrace and stroked her back tenderly.

Maggie lifted her arms, twining them around Egan's neck. "You didn't come back." Clinging to him, she sobbed quietly.

Egan's heart ached with a desperate need to console Maggie, but he knew only too well that he was powerless to ease her pain. All he could do was hold her, protect her and continue reassuring her. She had lived through hell, through a mother's darkest, most twisted and evil nightmare. What had he expected, that Bent's kidnapping would leave no scars on her kind, gentle soul?

Losing track of time, he held Maggie until she finally fell asleep in his arms. He wriggled around, easing Maggie along with him, until he could lean against the rock wall of the boulder. As she slept soundly, he prayed her sleep would remain undisturbed.

Her dream—her nightmare—had revealed her heart's fears, her repressed memories. But he understood the depth of her hatred and anger—both directed at him. Fifteen years ago when he had left her, he had thought he was doing the right thing. He had truly believed he was protecting her.

But he hadn't known about the child. God, how she must
have hated him for leaving her pregnant! How long had she
waited for him to return? How many years had she spent
expecting him to come back to her and claim his son?

You didn't come back. Her accusatory words echoed inside his head. She had waited for years. And when she'd
given up hope, she had married Gil. He realized now what
he'd done to Maggie and why, even if she loved him, she
would never be able to forgive him.

He had left her without giving her the true reason and
by doing so had given her false hopes. And by not telling
her about the threat Grant Cullen posed, he had put both
Maggie's life and their son's life in danger.

Oh, Maggie, my love, you didn't deserve the hand fate
dealt you. You deserve a better man, one who has never
broken your heart and shattered your life.

I will never hurt you again. I promise.

Maggie awoke slowly, leisurely, stretching out on the
survival bed. As her mind begin to clear, she remembered
where she was. She searched the bed for any sign of her
companion. He wasn't there!

"Egan!"

Remnants of her nightmare remained clearly in her mind,
as did her furious struggle with Egan when he'd tried to
calm her. What had she said to him? Try to remember,
Maggie. Try to remember!

Egan approached the boulder, his hands filled with edible
berries and nuts. "Were you calling for me? I'd gone out
to collect our breakfast."

He knelt in front of her and held out his harvest. "If we
could build a fire, I'd catch some fish. But to be on the safe
side—"

"Do you think Cullen is still following us?"

"Maybe. I don't think so, but we can't afford to take any chances."

"How much longer will we be wandering in the wilderness? Shouldn't we be close to finding a town by now?"

"Hold out your hands," he instructed. "Let's eat and then we can wash up in the stream and—"

"How much longer?" Her exasperated expression added strength to her demand.

"I should have you back in civilization by nightfall."

She held out her hands. He dumped half the nuts and berries into her open palms. Their gazes met and locked. Maggie's eyes questioned him, but he wasn't quite sure what she was asking.

"Unless I've read my directions wrong, going by the sun and the growth signs of the trees and the location of the stars last night, we can head that way—" he indicated with his index finger "—this morning and be reasonably sure we're going northwest. If we don't run into any trouble, and don't take too many rest stops—"

"What sort of trouble?"

"I wasn't referring to Cullen," he told her, then picked out several berries and popped them into his mouth.

"Egan, about last night…about my nightmare—"

"You don't have to explain," he said. "Having a crazy, mixed-up dream about Bent being in danger from Cullen was perfectly normal, after what happened at the fort. And wanting to beat the hell out of me was just as normal. After all, I'm the reason Bent was kidnapped and you and he were almost killed."

"I'm sorry about the way I reacted." She wanted to reach out and touch him, to tell him that she didn't blame him. She knew he had saved her life and Bent's.

"My feud with Cullen put our son's life in danger. That

was my fault. You have nothing to be sorry about. I'm the one with all the regrets, the one who's at fault.''

"You saved us."

"I saved you from a danger that I had created." He rose to his feet, turned his back to her and stomped toward the stand of evergreens.

What was he thinking? Maggie wondered. How did he truly feel about her? About his son? He had done what any honorable man would have done—whatever was necessary to protect his child and that child's mother. He'd made it perfectly clear that he wanted a relationship with Bent, but that didn't necessarily mean she was included, did it? She had fooled herself once, when she'd been younger and much more naive about men and about love. She had thought because Egan had made love to her that he loved her and would want her to be his wife. She wouldn't make that mistake again. She could not allow herself to assume anything when it came to Egan Cassidy's emotions.

Hurriedly Maggie picked out the berries, held them in one hand and tossed the nuts to the ground. Filling her mouth with the sour fruit, she munched and then swallowed. Nourishment was nourishment, she told herself. She certainly wasn't going to starve to death.

She rose to her feet, then brushed green spruce needles from her clothes. "I need to…er…to…you know." She cleared her throat. "Then I'll be ready to leave."

"Yeah, sure. Go ahead. I'll wait here for you and then we'll head toward the stream. We can clean up, drink our fill and then be on our way."

She didn't like this tension between them, but how could she defuse it? Her nightmare had somehow created a wall between them—an invisible barrier formed from her anger and fear and his guilt and regret.

Maggie scurried into the wooded area to relieve herself,

then returned hurriedly and placed a smile on her face as she approached Egan. All she could do now was reach out to him with warmth and pleasantness. But would he accept her cordiality, after she had furiously attacked him last night?

"Ready," she said.

Without a smile, he inclined his head and gestured for her to follow him. Her heart ached. She wanted to beg him not to shut her out this way, not to close down his emotions and pretend he didn't care. *Maybe he doesn't care,* an inner voice nagged. *Maybe he'll be glad to see the last of you. No, you're wrong! He does care. He does.*

Egan purposefully slowed his gait, allowing Maggie to keep pace. He had pushed her yesterday, out of necessity, but today he could go easy on her. If Cullen hadn't caught up with them by now, the odds were that he'd given up and was at this very minute plotting a way to find them before they left Arizona.

But surely Cullen knew that he would come after him, that since he had kidnapped Bent, there would be no place he could hide. And Egan had no intention of sending Maggie and Bent home. Not until Cullen was no longer a threat to them. He'd find a safe place for them. A secret sanctuary. And once Cullen had been eliminated, he would take Maggie and her son home where they could resume their normal life. And if Bent wanted him to be a part of that life, he would do everything within his power to build a relationship with the boy. But he would make no demands on Maggie, no requests. He would never do anything to hurt her—not ever again.

He couldn't bear to think about the way she had cried out for him, the way she'd said, *you didn't come back.* She had suffered enough at his hands. Asking for forgiveness would never be enough. He couldn't give her back those lost years of waiting and hoping for a man who hadn't returned. He couldn't undo the past. But he could protect her now—protect her from him.

Ellen Denby punched the End button on her cellular phone and slid the phone into her vest pocket. "That was Sawyer MacNamara. The siege at Cullen's fort is over. Thirty-five Ultimate Survivalists surrendered this morning, but Grant Cullen and Winn Sherman weren't among the captured."

"So, Cullen's escaped," Hunter Whitelaw said.

"Bastard's tracking Egan." Joe Ornelas slammed his big fist down on the table, rattling their breakfast dishes.

"Maybe," Ellen said, casting a glance at Bent Douglas, who lay on the sofa in their Flagstaff hotel suite, his hands crossed under his head. He hadn't moved a muscle, but she sensed that he was listening to every word they said. "If Egan hasn't shown up by tonight, we'll see if we can't get a search party organized. Maybe the feds can spare MacNamara and he can arrange for a few local boys to help out."

"Do y'all think something has happened to my mother and...er...Mr. Cassidy?" Bent asked.

"Not really," Ellen assured him. "I'd lay odds that Cassidy will show up by nightfall. He's taken his own sweet time coming down off the mountain because he's been outfoxing Cullen."

"But if they don't contact you by—"

Bent's question ended abruptly when Ellen's cellular phone rang again. Both Dundee agents, as well as Bent, focused their attention on Ellen, each holding their breath, waiting for word on Egan and Maggie.

"Denby here." Ellen's eyes narrowed. Her forehead wrinkled. "Damn. Yeah, sure thing, Sam. I'll leave Wolfe with Joe and Hunter until things are settled here. Jack and Matt and I will take the Dundee jet back to Atlanta ASAP.'' Ellen returned her cell phone to her vest pocket.

''What's going on?'' Hunter asked.

''A new case that demands my personal attention,'' Ellen explained. ''Joe, you and Hunter will continue to act as Bent's personal bodyguards, until…well, until Egan tells you otherwise. When our man Cassidy is no longer AWOL and has figured out how he plans to proceed, I can spare Wolfe for a few more days. He's told me that he wants to help Egan track down Cullen.''

Grant Cullen, wearing a silk robe, emerged from the bathroom and hailed Lieutenant Shatz with a wave of his hand. ''You may bring in my breakfast now.''

''Yes, sir.''

The young man hurried out of the bedroom and returned within minutes, carrying a silver tray. After placing the tray on the small table in front of the windows, he removed the domed lid to reveal a plate of pork chops and scrambled eggs. Steam rose from a cup of black coffee at the side of the plate.

Cullen tightened the silk cord belt around his waist, eased out a chair and sat down at the table. ''Is Colonel Sherman back yet?''

''Yes, sir, he returned about five minutes ago.''

''Ask him to come in, please. I want a full report.''

''Yes, sir.''

Winn Sherman, dressed in civilian attire, marched into his superior's bedroom, halted in front of him, clicked his heels and saluted.

''What did you find out?'' Cullen speared one pork chop with his knife, then sliced it into small pieces.

"The soldiers at the fort surrendered this morning and were taken into custody."

"Did you make arrangements for lawyers?" Cullen placed a piece of meat in his mouth and chewed.

"Yes, sir. And I made some phone calls, to certain loyal supporters and have found out that Cassidy's fellow Dundee agents are staying in Flagstaff. Apparently Cassidy and Ms. Douglas haven't shown up, yet."

"That means they're still in the mountains." Cullen lifted his coffee cup. "No doubt he thinks he's outsmarted me. But I'm the smart one. Tucked away here in my little house in Minerva, where the citizenry will keep my whereabouts a secret, I can rest and make plans for our next confrontation."

"What if Cassidy takes the woman and boy back to Alabama?"

"If that happens, we'll follow. In a few days. But knowing Cassidy as I do, I'm sure he'll send them somewhere he thinks is safe and then he'll try to track me down. I'll just have to make sure I get to him before he gets to me."

Chapter 10

Towering cottonwoods dotted the landscape, blending in with the junipers, pines and blackjack oaks. Enormous saguaros, their fat, prickly arms reaching skyward, grew throughout the thick brush. Clusters of prickly pear cactuses pushed up through the rocky ground. During Egan and Maggie's journey down a winding track along the mountain wall, dark storm clouds gathered overhead, blocking out the sun and forecasting rain. The wind picked up, swaying treetops and whistling around craggy boulders.

When Egan changed directions, heading up a rock-studded path, Maggie balked. "Where are you going?"

"In case it's slipped your notice, the bottom is fixing to fall out," he said, casting his gaze at the swirling gray clouds. "We need to find some kind of shelter before we get caught in a downpour."

"And just where do you think we'll find any shelter out here in the middle of nowhere?" She planted her hands on her hips and glared at him.

"If I'm not mistaken, this weed-infested path could lead to an abandoned mine or a ghost town or maybe just a couple of old shacks. From the Arizona maps I studied and the data I read, there are numerous places throughout the mountains in this state that were left to the elements when mines played out."

As her gaze lingered on the gloomy sky, Maggie noted two buzzards hovering high above them. An uneasy shudder racked her body. "I'd settle for a damp cave right now."

"Yeah, so would I. I don't relish the idea of our being swept away in a spring rain." He motioned for her to follow him.

As if to encourage Maggie's cooperation, a clap of thunder boomed in the distance. She gasped and jumped simultaneously. "I'm coming. I'm coming."

As the intervals between thunder claps and lightning flashes shortened, Egan's search for shelter escalated. He placed Maggie in front of him, knowing that he had to let her set the pace or he would force her into an unmerciful march. The farther they climbed, the wider the pathway. Egan became convinced that this had once been a road. And roads always led somewhere, didn't they?

Maggie's unnerving screech halted Egan immediately. "What's wrong?" He jerked the Glock from where he'd stuffed it under his belt and rushed to her side just in time to see a coyote dash across the road. "Good God, woman, you scared me to death over a coyote?"

"I'm sorry," she said sarcastically. "But the thing startled me. It just came out of nowhere."

"And now it's gone. So there's nothing to be afraid of." He returned the pistol to its nest at his back, then reached over and patted Maggie on the shoulder. "I didn't mean to snap at you."

"And I didn't mean to overreact. I guess we can both be forgiven for being nervous and on edge."

Tiny droplets splattered onto Maggie and Egan and pitted the dirt pathway at their feet. Egan grabbed Maggie's hand.

"Come on, honey. We'd better head into the woods. The tree branches should provide some protection. At least it's better than nothing."

Within minutes the feisty wind increased, picking up dead leaves and scattered debris and sending them whirling around in the air. Thunder drummed. Lightning crackled. And a heavy downpour soaked the earth.

Egan and Maggie ran into a wooded area, just off the road. Breathless, their bodies dripping with moisture, they stopped beneath a large sheltering grove of trees. Egan gently shoved Maggie back against the trunk of a cottonwood and shielded her body with his.

Their breaths mingled as he pressed his forehead to hers. She closed her eyes and listened. Listened to the rain. Listened to her thumping heartbeat. With his chest pushing against her damp breasts, her already peaked nipples responded by tightening even more and tingling with awareness. How could she possibly be sexually aroused at a time like this? she wondered. Wet, tired and on the run. *With Egan.* His presence alone excited her. Now as much as it had in the past. The aura of strength and danger that surrounded him possessed aphrodisiacal powers.

Maggie's lips parted on an indrawn breath. Aligning their lower bodies so that his erection nestled between the apex of her thighs, Egan covered her mouth with his. Hot and wet and wild, they shared a kiss that left them both breathless and yearning for more.

"I can hardly take you here and now!" he said, his words a harsh curse. "What is it about you, Maggie mine, that makes me lose my head whenever I'm around you?"

She didn't respond. There were no words to describe the way she felt or explain the unexplainable. The chemistry between them couldn't be denied. A look. A touch. A kiss. An explosion of the senses.

As the rain seeped between the branches, dripping down onto Egan's head and back, reality momentarily returned. His gaze searched past Maggie, through the trees and beyond the grove. At first he thought his imagination was playing tricks on him. He blinked a couple of times. But what he'd thought might be a mirage was still there. About a hundred yards above the wooded area, a stone building with a rusted roof awaited them.

"Let's go." Egan dragged Maggie out from under the canopy of trees.

As the rain pelted her relentlessly, Maggie swiped the moisture from her face. "Where are we going?" Has he lost his mind? she wondered.

"Look straight ahead," he told her.

"It's a house!" she cried.

"It's a shack," he corrected. "But even if the roof is leaking, it'll provide better shelter for us."

By the time they reached the small rock building, they were soaked to the skin. Maggie barely had time to notice the crumbling rock wall that jutted out from either side of the abandoned hovel before Egan shoved open the creaking wooden door and propelled her into the dark, dank belly of the one-room dump. Signifying countless years of neglect, strong mustiness and a faint malodorous scent assailed her senses. Bending over double as she fought to catch her breath, droplets cascaded off her body and puddled around her feet. When Egan pushed the door closed, the rusted hinges squealed and the bottom edge of the door scraped along the dirt floor.

With her breathing returning to normal and her eyesight

adjusting to the dim interior, lit only from daylight passing through two small, high windows, Maggie took note of her surroundings. Several cobweb-draped bottles perched in one windowsill. A dust-coated wooden table and chairs, along with an ancient wood-burning stove, created a kitchen nook on one side of the room, while a simple metal bed, without a mattress, and a rickety wooden chest provided what had once been the sleeping quarters. Tiny streams of rain leaked through holes in the old tin roof, pitter-pattering onto the rusted iron bedstead, dripping down on the center of the table and boring little pools into the packed-dirt floor. Maggie's nose crinkled when she saw the dried pellets littering the floor here and there, reminders of non-human inhabitants.

"Be it ever so humble," Egan said.

"I think humble is an overestimation."

He shook his head, shooting a shower of raindrops all around him. "At least we're out of the rain."

"More or less." Maggie eyed the numerous areas where the leaking roof allowed the rain inside the house.

Egan pulled out a chair from the table and sat, then crossed one leg over the other and proceeded to remove his boots. "Better than a cave, don't you think?"

"Much," she agreed, then slumped down in the chair opposite him and mimicked his actions. After taking off her boots and wet socks, she rubbed her aching feet. "I've got blisters on the bottom of my feet."

"Are they bad?" He removed the pistol, laid it on the table and immediately scooted his chair around the table and grabbed both of Maggie's feet.

"What are you doing?"

"I'd think it's obvious. I'm seeing for myself how bad your blisters are."

When she tried to jerk her feet out of his grasp, his big

hands circled her ankles and placed her feet in his lap. Egan grinned at her. She tried to frown, but instead the corners of her mouth lifted into a hint of a smile.

He studied the tiny blister on the underside of her right foot, then inspected the larger blister on the pad of her left foot. As she watched, he pulled one foot between his legs, setting the heel directly against his sex. After lifting her other leg up so that her foot was even with his chest, he ran caressing fingers over, under and around, being careful to avoid the blister.

"What—" she cleared her throat "—what are you doing?"

"Inspecting your blisters."

"Oh."

He lifted his gaze from her long, slender feet to her big brown eyes. "If I could build a fire, our clothes would dry faster and we'd dry out faster, too."

"But you can't build a fire," she said.

"There's more than one kind of fire." Egan slid his hand beneath the hem of Maggie's jeans, his touch tender and seductive as he petted her ankle. And all the while he maintained eye contact with her.

"Is there...more than one kind of fire?" She sucked in a deep, unsteady breath, knowing that if he continued touching her, she would soon be begging him to make love to her.

Her twitching toes patted against his erection. His wicked grin widened as his eyes lowered to her breasts. Her clearly outlined nipples strained against the wet material of her chambray shirt.

"Oh, yes, there is most definitely more than one kind of fire," he said.

Egan lifted her right leg and then her left, placing them on either side of his hips. Immediately he reached over and hauled her out of her chair and onto his lap. As her bottom settled onto his thighs and her mound softened against his erection, her toes grazed the dirt floor as she straddled him.

"Every time I touch you, a fire ignites inside me. Instantaneous combustion," he said. "Something beyond my control. Believe me, sweet Maggie, I can't help responding to you the way I do."

"I know." She wrapped her arms around him and laid her head on his shoulder. With her lips brushing his neck, she whimpered, "It's the same with me. I can't stop myself from wanting you. Only you. I've never felt this way with anyone else."

He lifted her head from his shoulder and cupped her chin between his thumb and index finger. "And I have never felt this way with anyone else."

When his lips touched hers, her feminine core squeezed tight as tingling sparks of desire radiated upward and outward through her body. Alive with sensations, she responded to every stimulus. The taste of his tongue mating with hers. The feel of his beard and mustache gently scratching her skin. The smell of his purely masculine scent.

Egan ended the kiss, leaving them both breathless, aroused and aching. He buried his face against her breasts and nuzzled her. His mouth sought and found a beaded nipple, covered it and suckled her through the wet cloth of her shirt. Maggie keened deep in her throat, tossing back her hair, which glistened with raindrops, as Egan slid his hand beneath the waistband and down inside her jeans and panties. He caressed her hip. Her warm, wet lips traveled over his neck and up to his ear. She nibbled on his earlobe.

Egan grasped her bottom with one hand and clutched the back of her neck with the other. Lust wound tightly inside

him, hardening his sex and urging him to take what he
wanted.

"Stop me now, Maggie, or there will be no turning
back."

She responded by unbuttoning his shirt and exposing his
chest. The moment she ran her fingers through his chest
hair, he unbelted, unsnapped and unzipped her jeans in
rapid succession. Standing, Maggie allowed him to remove
her jeans and panties. He cupped her buttocks and nuzzled
her belly, then hurriedly undid the fly of his jeans and freed
his sex.

Maggie trembled with longing, her body aching for release. She glanced down at him for just a second before he
impaled her, dragging her down and onto his shaft. That
momentary glimpse of him, big and hard and ready, excited
every feminine instinct within her.

Hot and wet and swollen with desire, her sheath surrounded him tightly. He held her in place for a heart-
pounding minute, letting her body adjust to his. And then
he lifted her hips, almost removing his sex from within her,
before burying himself deeply with one surging thrust.

Her voice crying out with the pleasure of their joining
echoed in the hushed stillness of the deserted cabin. Outside
the rain continued drenching the earth. Lightning crackled
across the sky and thunder shook the broken windowpanes.

Once he had taken her completely, he removed her
jacket. Then he unbuttoned her shirt, spread it apart and
unhooked her bra. With the utmost tenderness, he attacked
first one breast and then the other. When his mouth tugged
on her nipple, powerful, titillating fissions exploded inside
her.

With his mouth at her breast, he placed his hands under
her bottom, lifting her. "Ride me," he demanded, as his
fingers bit into her naked hips.

She quickly set the rhythm, beginning with a slow, seductive dance. In and out. Up and down. Leisurely enjoying each stroke. As tension coiled tighter and tighter, Maggie accelerated the pace.

"That's it," Egan mouthed the words against her breast. "Harder and faster!"

With a frenzied desire pushing her, Maggie gave herself over to the primitive needs of her body and of his. Egan took control, clutching her hips and pumping into her with deep, hard lunges that soon had her moaning with pleasure. Her release hit her with the force of a raging storm. She shuddered when an overwhelming climax claimed her. Egan accelerated his thrusts to a frantic tempo. He came apart, unraveling at the speed of light as he jetted into her, all the while deep groans erupted from his throat.

While aftershocks rippled along their nerve endings and Maggie's body quivered with supersensitivity to his touch, they clung to each other, their breaths labored, their skin sticky with perspiration.

His sex remained inside her. He didn't want to disengage his body from hers. At this moment she was still a part of him. When he stroked her back with his fingertips, she shuddered. Oh, how he loved the fact that she was so easily aroused and that even after fulfillment, she could be receptive to renewed passion. At his age, once was usually more than enough to satisfy him—with any other woman. But with Maggie, once would never be enough.

She was his only as long as she needed him. Once the threat of Grant Cullen's existence was removed, Egan would have to let her go. She deserved to have her sane and sensible life in Alabama restored. It was what she wanted—what he wanted for her. But until that time came, he intended to store up as many perfect memories as possible. Enough to last the rest of his life.

Maggie rubbed her smooth cheek against his beard-rough cheek. "Listen. It's still raining. We could be stuck here for hours."

"So we could." Egan lifted her up and off his lap, disengaging their connection. When she stood on wobbly legs, he reached out to steady her.

Maggie possessed a woman's body. Lush, full, rounded. Egan's gaze traveled the length of her form, from wild, mahogany hair hanging in damp curling strands across her back and over her shoulders to the dark, fiery triangle at the apex of her legs. And oh, those legs. Those long, luscious legs. Remembering the way she had mounted him, straddling him as they made love, his sex twitched with renewed vigor.

"Wish that bed had a mattress," he said. "I feel like taking a long nap."

She stared pointedly at his unzipped jeans. "Are you sure you feel like taking a nap? From where I'm standing, it looks like you might have something else in mind besides sleeping."

"Nah," he teased her. "That's just wishful thinking on your part. Remember, honey, I'm an old man, and you just wore me out."

"Did I indeed?"

Maggie inched backward, far enough so that he couldn't touch her without getting up out of the chair. Then she removed her open shirt and unhooked bra and tossed them onto the table. Naked, humming with sexual energy and hungry for dessert to follow the banquet she had shared with Egan only minutes earlier, Maggie stretched her arms over her head and lifted her hair atop her head. Closing her eyes, she let her hair tumble slowly, seductively, through her fingers, parting it in the back and tossing it forward so that the strands rested on the rise of her breasts.

Egan licked his lips, then swallowed hard. Maggie was as much in the grips of this madness as he, as completely controlled by the sexual urges of her body as he was dominated by his. Only once before had he allowed passion to overrule every rational thought—a never-to-be-forgotten week with Maggie. Fifteen years ago.

He had used protection then, every time, except the first time, when they'd both been wild with need. But now, he had made love to Maggie for the second time—without a condom. What if she became pregnant again?

Some selfish demon inside him hoped for that impossible dream. If Maggie were pregnant with his child...

"It's getting hot in here," Maggie said, as she rubbed the sweat from her neck with the palm of her hand, her fingers coming to rest inches above the indention between her full breasts.

She was tempting him, playing the seductress. Years ago, she had been like this—a spirited, hungry wanton, insatiable in her desire for him. She evoked every protective, possessive, primevally male instinct within him. All that was feminine about her summoned all that was masculine about him.

"We could go outside and cool off in the rain," he suggested and laughed when he noted the surprised look on her face.

"Cool water might douse that fire I see beginning to burn in you." She glanced meaningfully at his semierect sex.

Egan rose to his feet, shucked off his jacket and shirt, stripped out of his jeans and nodded his head toward the back door. "Why don't we find out?"

He grabbed her hand as he walked past her. She followed him across the room, knowing at that precise moment she would follow this man anywhere. The door creaked and groaned as he forced it open. A cool mist blew into the interior, spraying their naked bodies. Without a word of warning, Egan tugged Maggie up against him and then pulled her through the door and out onto the back porch. Rain splattered down over them, washing through the partially dilapidated tin roof.

"Oh!" Maggie gulped as rainwater cooled her heated body.

"Are you still hot?" he asked, rubbing his chest against her breasts, teasing her.

"My skin is just warm now, but inside, I'm still hot."

"How hot are you, Maggie, my love?"

With his arm around her waist, he led her off the porch and out into the yard. A four-foot stone fence, crumbled to the ground in several sections, encircled what had once been a private spot. Tiny, pink wild roses wove up and around the wall nearest the house. Ankle-high weeds dotted the rocky earth. Like two children, carefree and happy, they danced in the rain, their bodies drenched, their desires escalating.

Maggie watched Egan, a man like no other. Entranced by the essence of his masculinity, she couldn't take her eyes off him. Tall and lean, every ounce of muscle superbly toned. Coated with moisture, his graying chest hair curled into tight rings, as did the darker hair that dusted his arms and legs. His sex, still aroused, beckoned her touch. Unable to resist the temptation, she reached out and ran a fingertip over the smooth, bulbous head, which reacted with a hefty jerk. When she circled him with her hand, he groaned. When she set her hand into motion, every muscle in his big body tensed.

"You're killing me, honey." He grabbed her hand to stop its movement.

"That wasn't my intention." She released him, but

inched her hand up and over his belly, around his waist and back down to palm one tight buttock.

Manacling the wrist of her other hand, he hauled her up against him. She gasped when their wet bodies collided. "What was your intention?" he asked.

She rubbed herself against him, pressing the intimate parts of their bodies together. "Being out here is like stepping under a giant shower, isn't it?"

Egan laughed. "If you want me primed and ready for action again, then we'd better get out of this rain."

She pulled away from him and raced toward the porch. When Egan caught her, he whirled her around and instantly shoved her gently up against the exterior wall of the house. She reached out, intending to put her arms around his neck and draw him into her embrace. But he escaped her clutches by dropping to his knees. The moment he buried his face against her belly and wrapped his arms around her hips, Maggie quivered like a willow in the wind.

His lips dotted kisses from waist to thigh, then nuzzled her damp, red curls. As his hand slid between her legs, she braced herself by planting one hand on his shoulder. She threaded the fingers of her other hand through his hair and gripped his head. His fingers probed, delved and stroked. Maggie's body tightened around those caressing fingers. After he had urged her thighs farther apart and had prepared her with his fingertips, he held her legs separated enough to allow his mouth to take charge.

Smoldering hot sensations blazed up from her depths, spreading quickly through her body, setting her afire. Maggie's knees liquefied and began to give way, spreading her legs even farther apart. While Egan slid one big hand behind her to cup her bottom and support her, his other hand reached up to encompass her left breast.

Pleasure almost too intense to bear claimed her, shatter-

ing her composure and tossing her headlong into fulfillment. Before the last convulsion racked Maggie's body,
Egan lifted her just enough to accommodate a quick, hard
thrust, embedding himself to the hilt. Her legs curled
around his hips. Her buttocks pressed against the smooth,
wet surface of the stone wall.

They mated there on the porch, their hunger for each
other without bounds. Giving and taking in equal amounts,
they shared a mutual gratification. And when Egan roared
as fulfillment drained every ounce of strength from his
body, Maggie toppled over the edge, spiraling out of control.

She slid her legs down his hips, placed her feet on the
floor and slumped against him. Keeping her wedged between his body and the wall, Egan dipped his head and
found her lips.

"If I lived a thousand years, I could never get enough
of you," he murmured, then kissed her with the conviction
of his words.

Chapter 11

Tinkling raindrops dripped off the edge of the tin roof. Afternoon sunshine glutted the interior with abundant illumination, washing over the dingy walls and floor, reflecting off the metal bedstead and revealing the shabbiness of their rock house refuge. Maggie pulled on her socks, their cool dampness soothing to her blisters. After lifting one of her boots from the floor, she glanced sideways toward the open front door. Egan waited in the doorway, his back to her, his wide shoulders almost touching either side of the rotting wooden frame.

Maggie supposed she could lie to herself about what had happened between them. She could blame Egan. She could pretend that he had seduced her. But what good would lying to herself do? None! The truth of the matter was that she had wanted Egan. She always had and probably always would. Before meeting him fifteen years ago, she had laughed at the thought that loving someone could become a *fever in your blood.* But that's exactly what her feelings for Egan were. A fever in her blood. An incurable fever.

What had happened between them—what always happened between them—was by mutual consent. But accepting that fact didn't help Maggie much right now. She found it easy enough to lose her head, to throw caution to the wind and become a wild woman in Egan's arms. But the difficult part came afterward. Once their insatiable hunger had been temporarily fed and she was thinking straight. That's when doubt and fear and a hint of regret came into play.

Why was it that with Gil, a man who had loved her, made a commitment to her and even adopted her child, she had never been able to feel such mindless passion? Somehow with Egan, a temporary lover who had never made her any promises beyond the moment, she had found an incomparable ecstasy.

"Are you about ready?" Egan asked, glancing back over his shoulder.

She looked away, down at her feet, deliberately avoiding prolonged eye contact. "Yes. Just a couple of minutes more." Hurriedly she slipped into her boots. After tying the laces, she stood, brushed her hands down the sides of her damp jeans and headed for the front door.

Suddenly in her peripheral vision, Maggie noticed something moving across the floor only a few inches from her feet. Silently gliding. Slithering. Then she heard the deadly rattle. A snake! A rattlesnake! The minute her mind registered the danger, Maggie let out a bloodcurdling scream. Instinctive fear. A totally emotional reaction.

Instantly Egan reached for the pistol, whirled around and saw the stricken look on Maggie's face. His gaze followed her line of vision down to where the rattler curled, preparing to attack. He aimed the 9-mm and with one precisely aimed shot blew the reptile in two.

As the gunshot echoed in Maggie's ears, she rushed toward Egan. He hauled her up to his side and walked her out of the cabin and into the sunlight. Slightly breathless, her heart hammering madly, Maggie gazed into Egan's eyes. And there it was—that protective, possessive, caring look that told her she was his woman. He had always stared at her that way, since the first moment he saw her.

"I'm sorry I screamed," she said. "I know I overreacted again. I could have just told you the snake was there, without getting hysterical."

"It's okay." He stroked her back, letting his hand linger between her shoulder blades. "After what you've been through the past couple of days, you deserved at least one good scream."

"I suppose I did." A nervous giggle caught in her throat.

His fingertips inched their way upward and wound around the back of her neck. "Do we need to talk about what happened?"

"With the snake?" *Don't be a ninny,* an inner voice scolded. *You know he's not referring to the incident with the snake.*

"Maggie... I don't want to hurt you. Not ever again. I never meant for my actions to cause you harm in the past."

"You didn't make me any promises back then and you haven't made me any now." But I want you to, she silently pleaded. I want you to promise to love me and be with me the rest of our lives.

"You might not believe this, but I'm usually very much in control of myself and my actions. Except with you. I can't seem to keep my hands off you."

The giggle trapped inside her escaped, tittering from her throat. "You're taking the blame for something that is equally my fault. If what happened between us today ends up causing me any pain or creating any problems in my life, then I'll deal with it.''

"Alone? The way you dealt with Bent?" He caressed her neck.

"Bent wasn't a problem. He was a blessing." Maggie pulled away from Egan. "I've regretted many things in my life, but having Bent isn't one of them."

"I should have been there for you...and for my son." Egan stuffed his hands into the front pockets of his jeans in an effort not to grab Maggie and kiss the breath out of her. "Do you think it's too late for me to form some sort of relationship with Bent?"

Maggie sighed deeply. "I honestly don't know. Ten years ago, you definitely could have formed a bond with him. Even five years ago. But he isn't a child anymore. He's very much his own man. I'd like nothing better than for him to accept you as his father and for the two of you... All I know is that I'll encourage him to give you a chance."

"That's more than I deserve from you, after—"

She pressed an index finger over his lips, silencing him. "How about you get me back to civilization so we can see our son? I'm going to hug him so hard he'll turn beet red with embarrassment. But I don't care."

Egan cupped his hand over hers, kissed her finger and clasped her hand in his. "Let's head out." He led her away from the hut that had protected them from the rainstorm and toward the overgrown, winding pathway down the mountain. "As soon as we get to a phone, I'll contact Joe and Hunter and have them bring Bent to you as quickly as possible."

"And then we'll all go home to Alabama," she said.

Egan squeezed her hand, then halted abruptly. "Eventually."

"What do you mean—eventually?"

He released her hand and looked her square in the eye. "Until I find Cullen and eliminate him, you and Bent won't be safe back in Alabama. I plan to send you somewhere safe, someplace that Cullen knows nothing about. Joe and Hunter will stay with y'all until—"

"Until you either kill Cullen or he kills you!" Maggie whirled around and walked several feet away from Egan. With her arms crossed over her chest, she sucked in air, trying desperately not to cry.

"Maggie."

When he came up behind her and placed his hands on her shoulders, she shrugged off his embrace and refused to face him. "Don't tell me that there isn't a possibility that he'll kill you and not the other way around. And don't try to explain that this is something you have to do, that you can't leave it to the FBI to track him down and arrest him."

Egan allowed his hands to hover over her shoulders for a second or two before balling them into tight fists. "You and Bent will never be safe as long as Cullen is alive. If I thought his vendetta against me would end if he were arrested and sent to prison, then, yes, maybe I'd leave him to the authorities. But that's not the way this thing is going to play out. Not when your life and Bent's are at risk."

Maggie eased around slowly and brought her gaze up from the pathway at her feet to make direct eye contact with Egan. "I really don't have a choice, do I? I'll have to do as you ask. Bent and I both will." She took a tentative step toward Egan, but stopped herself before she reached him. "You don't think you have a choice either, do you?"

"No, honey, I don't. Not when it's either go after Cullen or allow him to come after us."

"And when Cullen has been…eliminated?" she asked.

"Then you and Bent can go home."

"And you?"

"Me? I'll come for a visit and see if my son is willing to let me be a part of his life." *And you, Maggie, my love, will you let me be a part of your life, too? Could we ever move beyond the past? Could you ever forget the kind of life I've lived and forgive me of all my sins?*

Two and a half hours later, the afternoon sun low on the western horizon, Egan and Maggie entered the outskirts of Stonyford, Arizona. Population 1,895. A *has-been* little town that appeared to have been around since the late nineteenth century. Although a few vehicles meandered up and down Main Street and across Medicine Bow Avenue, the only other paved street, most of the downtown area seemed deserted.

"Bet there's no chance this place has a hotel," Maggie said. "I doubt there's even a pay telephone available."

"Wrong on both counts," Egan corrected, his gaze focused up Main Street to the intersection with the town's lone traffic light. "That sign reads Stonyford Hotel—" He nodded to the right. "And over there—" he nodded left "—at that service station, is a pay phone."

"Will wonders never cease."

Maggie's legs ached and the blisters on her feet were now raw and burning. Despite sharing a rain bath with Egan earlier that afternoon, she felt grimy after two days in the wilderness.

"The sign painted on the front window of the hotel says Café." As if on cue, Egan's stomach growled. "Hope that place is still in business."

"Call Joe and Hunter first," Maggie said. "Then we can check out the hotel and café."

When they passed the barber shop, an elderly, white-haired cowboy, boots on his feet and a Stetson on his head, emerged. "Howdy, folks. You two look lost. Do you need some help?"

"As a matter of fact, we do," Egan said. "My wife and I—" he smiled at Maggie "—got lost up in the mountains and we need to contact some friends to come pick us up."

The grizzly old man pursed his thin lips. "Hmph! I don't understand you young folks hiking off into the mountains without a guide. There's bears and snakes and coyotes in the hills. And some of the roughest wilderness in this here United States." He looked Maggie up and down. "If I had me a wife like her, I'd keep her home and not drag her all over God's green earth."

"Believe me, Mr....er...Mr....?" Maggie bestowed her most endearing smile on the old man.

"Butram, ma'am. Ed Butram." He quickly removed his Stetson, lifted his shoulders and stood a good inch taller.

"Well, Mr. Butram, believe me when I tell you that this is my last trip into the mountains." Maggie laid her hand on Ed's arm. "Our son is staying with friends in Flagstaff and I know he's terribly worried about us. We need to call him as soon as possible to let him know we're all right."

"After we use that pay phone—" Egan inclined his head in the direction of the service station "—we were planning to check out the hotel and café."

"Can't use the phone over at Hamm's," Ed told them.

"Why not?" Maggie asked.

"Been out of order for the past two years." Ed chuckled. "Didn't nobody ever use it anyway. But the hotel has a phone you can use."

"Then the hotel is open?" Egan asked.

"What about the café?" Maggie's stomach rumbled.

"Why don't you two come along with me," Ed suggested as he stepped off the sidewalk and into the street. "Me and my sister, Corrie, own the hotel. Don't get many customers, so we closed off most of the rooms. But we keep a few cleaned and aired-out.''

''May we use the phone?'' Egan asked. ''We'll reimburse you when our friends arrive with some money.''

''Of course you can use the phone.'' Ed motioned for them to follow him. ''I'm afraid the café closed five years ago, but I'll get Corrie to rustle you up something while you call your boy.''

''This is so nice of you, Mr. Butram.'' Maggie kept in step with their host. When she glanced over her shoulder at Egan, who stayed a few feet behind, she noticed him surveying the town, as if he were searching for something—or someone. Did he honestly think Grant Cullen might be lurking around the corner?

''My pleasure, Mrs....'' Ed laughed. ''Don't think you mentioned your name.''

''Smith,'' Egan said.

''Jones,'' Maggie said.

Ed stopped, scratched his head and gave Maggie a puzzled look. ''Which is it, Smith or Jones?''

''Both,'' Maggie told him. ''My maiden name, which I retained after my marriage, is Jones. And my husband is Mr. Smith.'' Maggie's tense glare warned Egan to just go along with her explanation.

''What a darn fool thing for a woman to do,'' Ed said, then grumbled incoherently to himself. He gave Egan a sharp, disapproving look. ''Son, if I was you, I'd make this gal use my name.'' When the thought struck him, Ed cursed. ''I'll be damned. What name does your boy use?''

''Smith,'' Maggie and Egan said in unison.

Ed smiled, seemingly satisfied with their answer. ''Come along and make your phone call. I'll see if I can get Corrie away from that fool talk show she watches on TV every afternoon. Maybe you two could go on that show and tell folks why you go by two different last names after being married…how long did you say you'd been married?''

"Fifteen years," Maggie said as they followed Ed into the hotel foyer.

The entry had all the charm of an old lodge, with animal heads mounted on the wall and wooden beams crisscrossing the ceiling. Fresh paint hadn't touched the tan walls in years. Wear and tear had removed whatever veneer the hardwood floors might once have possessed.

"Phone's in there." Ed motioned toward an open doorway to a room that Maggie guessed served as the hotel office. "Just make yourselves at home and I'll go tell Corrie that we got guests."

"Thank you." Maggie kept smiling until Ed disappeared down the long, dimly lit hallway, then she swerved around and followed Egan. "Wait up, will you?"

Catching up with Egan just as he lifted the telephone receiver, she grabbed his hand. "Will it be safe to bring Bent here?"

Egan nodded. "Bent will be as safe here as in Flagstaff. As long as Cullen is alive you're both in danger, no matter where you are. Bent will have Joe, Hunter and Wolfe with him on the trip and once he's here, he'll have four of us protecting him."

"Five," she corrected. "Don't forget that I'd die to protect him, just as you would."

When a keening series of peeps reminded Egan that he still held the telephone receiver in his hand, he returned it to the base. "Look, Maggie, I know how much you want to see Bent and the risk is minimal in bringing him here, since Cullen has no idea where we are. We're getting out of here first thing in the morning to take you and Bent somewhere for safekeeping until…"

"Where are we going?"

"Somewhere close by, if possible. I'm counting on Joe knowing a safe place, maybe even on the Navajo reservation. If that's the case, then we'll be heading east anyway and it's best for the guys to bring Bent to us since we're already farther west than Flagstaff."

"I'll be so glad when this is all over and we're safe. All of us."

"Yeah, honey, me, too." He caressed her cheek. "Now, do you want to talk to your son?"

"Most definitely."

Waiting impatiently while he dialed, she patted her foot on the floor. When Egan glanced down at her dancing foot, she held it still and offered him an okay-I'm-nervous-so-shoot-me look.

"Joe? Yeah, Egan here. Maggie and I are safe and sound in some wide-place-in-the-road town called Stonyford, at the town's only hotel. Right on Main Street."

"Tell him I want to talk to Bent." Maggie tugged on Egan's arm.

"Maggie's anxious to talk to her son, but first I need to discuss something with Ellen."

As Egan eased his hip down on the edge of the desk, Maggie noted the frown on his face and wondered what was wrong.

"Okay. Let me talk to Wolfe then."

"Where's Ellen?" Maggie asked.

"She had to go back to Atlanta. An emergency," he explained.

"When can I—"

"Yeah, Wolfe, I'm going to need a safe place for Maggie and Bent to stay while I tend to business. And I'll want Joe and Hunter to remain with them for as long as it takes."

Maggie waited and waited while Egan's discussion continued. She listened halfheartedly, wishing he'd finish his business and let her talk to Bent. Finally she heard Egan say, "Put Bent on the phone."

He handed her the receiver, which she grabbed. "Hello, Bent?"

"Hi, Mama. Are you all right?"

"I'm fine, now that I hear your voice. Are you all right, sweetie?"

"I'm okay. Just worried about you. But now that I know you're safe and we can go home, everything will be all right, won't it?"

"Listen, Bent." Maggie hesitated, took a calming breath and started again. "We can't go home. Not right away."

"Why not?"

"The man who kidnapped you hasn't been caught and as long as he's free, he poses a danger to you and me."

"Because that General Cullen hates Egan Cassidy. All of this is his fault. My being kidnapped and our almost getting killed."

"Bent, sweetheart, this isn't Egan's fault."

"Yes, it is, and you know it! Don't try to defend him."

"All right. I won't. We don't need to settle this right now. Just cooperate with Mr. Ornelas and Mr. Whitelaw because whatever they do, it's for your safety."

"I understand. I'm not some dumb kid."

"I know you're not, sweetie. Now, listen, the Dundee agents are going to bring you here…to me. Tonight."

"Will I have to see *him?*"

She knew he was referring to Egan. "Yes, Bent, you will." She hadn't expected so much hostility from Bent, focused entirely on Egan. Although they had seldom discussed his father, Maggie wondered if all these years Bent had harbored hatred for a man he didn't even know. If he did, was it her fault?

"Well, don't expect me to be glad about it," Bent said. "He nearly got us both killed."

"I love you," she told her son, changing the subject. "I can hardly wait to see you."

"Yeah, me, too, Mama."

"See you very soon."

Maggie handed the receiver back to Egan. He eased it down on the cradle and glanced at Maggie.

"I take it that my son is none too happy with me right now." Egan rose to his feet. "I suppose expecting him to understand was wishful thinking on my part."

Maggie curled her fingers over Egan's forearm. "You can win him over. It may take time and a great deal of effort on your part, but Bent needs a father. He needs you. And whether he knows it or not, he wants you in his life."

"I'd like to believe that." Egan covered Maggie's hand with his. "But knowing that you and he are safe and that Cullen can never threaten either of you again, will be enough for me. I don't have the right to expect anything more."

"Oh, Egan, that's not—"

Ed poked his head around the door. "Got grub in the kitchen waiting on you. Corrie warmed up some chicken stew in the microwave and sliced some chocolate cake. I put on a fresh pot of coffee, too."

"Oh, Mr. Butram, that sounds wonderful." Maggie slipped her hand from beneath Egan's.

"After you eat, I'll show you upstairs to your room," Ed said. "Just one bathroom on the second floor is in operating order, but there's a big ol' tub and the shower works just fine."

"I don't suppose there's a chance you might find us some clean clothes?" Egan asked.

Ed inspected Egan's and Maggie's soiled, tattered attire.

"Corrie's shorter and rounder than you—" he eyed Maggie "—but I reckon you can tighten the belt on a pair of her jeans." Ed surveyed Egan from head to toe. "Now, you big fellow, pose a problem. Wouldn't none of my clothes fit you." He snapped his fingers as an idea struck him. "My nephew, Preston, is about your size. I think he might've left some things here. He comes for a visit a couple of times a year. I'll check with Corrie."

"We can't thank you…and Corrie…enough for you hospitality." Maggie patted Ed on the arm. "We spoke with our son and our friends. They'll be coming here sometime tonight. Do you have a couple of more rooms available?"

"Sure thing, little lady."

Maggie studied herself in the tall, narrow mirror attached to the back of the bathroom door. Corrie's jeans weren't a bad fit, only one size too large and the legs were a bit short. And where the plump, large-breasted Corrie would have filled out the blue chambray shirt, Maggie wore it like a minitent. But for once in her life, she really didn't care how she looked. She was clean, well-fed and she and Bent were safe. Within an hour or less, she'd see her son, be able to touch him and hold him and reassure herself that he was all right.

After slipping into Corrie's socks and putting on her own dirty boots, Maggie gathered up the damp towels and her filthy clothes. Ed had told her to just place the items in the wicker basket outside the bathroom door, so she followed instructions and dumped them on top of Egan's discarded apparel. He had come upstairs first to bathe, while she'd helped Corrie clean up the supper dishes.

Maggie opened the door to *their* bedroom. Egan lay stretched out atop the jacquard-style coverlet on the four-poster tester bed. His boots rested by the nightstand and his pistol lay on top, beside the lamp. Corrie's son's jeans fit Egan snugly, outlining the shape of his long, lean legs. The borrowed plaid shirt hung open from collar to hem, exposing his chest.

"When Bent arrives, you'll have to move to another bedroom." Maggie hovered in the doorway.

"I take it that our son wouldn't approve of our sharing a room." Egan smiled halfheartedly. "No problem. I'll share with Wolfe."

Maggie entered the room, but steered clear of the bed. She knew only too well that a partially undressed Egan might prove to be too much temptation. "Where do you suppose Joe and Hunter will take us in the morning?"

"You can be sure that it will be somewhere they can keep you and Bent safe." With his palms cupping the back of his head, which rested on two pillows, Egan gazed up at the ceiling. "Is Bent going to stir up a fuss about not getting to go home right away?"

Maggie sat in one of two overstuffed armchairs that flanked the double windows overlooking Main Street. The floral print material was slightly discolored and worn on the arms, but the thick padding afforded her a comfortable seat.

"He isn't pleased, but he'll cooperate. Bent's stubborn and sometimes headstrong, but he's very smart. He'll understand that staying in hiding is necessary."

"They should get here soon." Egan glanced quickly in Maggie's direction, then returned his gaze to the ceiling. "Should I make an effort to talk to Bent tonight or should I let it wait until—"

"Talk to him tonight." Maggie rubbed her neck and shoulders.

"What should I say to him?"

"Tell him the truth about what happened between you

and Grant Cullen. The first step in forming a relationship with Bent will be making him understand that his kidnapping and the danger we're in now isn't your fault.''

"But it is my fault.'' Egan sat up, pivoted slowly and scooted to the edge of the bed.

"It isn't! You're blaming yourself for something that is Grant Cullen's doing. You have no control over his actions. You never did.''

"I could have told you about Cullen fifteen years ago.''

"Yes, you could have,'' she agreed. "And I could have told you about Bent years ago, too. But you didn't and I didn't. So, if any of this is your fault, it's my fault, too.''

"Don't be ridiculous, Maggie. You're completely innocent of—''

"No, I'm not. Bent is the only innocent party. You made a mistake in not telling me about Cullen. And I made a mistake in not telling you about your son. But Cullen is the person who is at fault for ruining your life and putting Bent and me in danger.''

Egan rose to his feet, but hesitated before venturing closer to Maggie. "You're the most understanding person I know. You realize that Cullen's pursuit of revenge has ruined my life.''

Maggie's gaze locked with Egan's and for one endless moment, time stopped. Unspoken confessions passed between them. Unfulfilled hopes and dreams became a common thought. Heartfelt longing for what had been lost and could never be recaptured united them in mourning.

"Oh, Egan. My poor Egan.'' Teardrops gathered in her eyes as she held open her arms.

Drawn to her loving kindness, Egan crossed the room and knelt in front of her. She wrapped her arms across his back as he laid his head in her lap. With gentle fingers threading through his hair, she caressed his head.

Outside the last rays of sunlight faded. Dark shadows fell across the room. The sound of a car horn came from somewhere up the street. Egan didn't move. Barely breathed. A tender quiet cocooned them. Maggie had never felt more connected to—more a part of—anyone than she did Egan at that precise moment. Earlier today their bodies had mated, giving and receiving pleasure. And now their hearts joined, sharing sympathy and concern and deep understanding.

"Howdy. This here is Corrie Nesbitt, up in Stonyford. You remember me, Mr. Baker?"

"I'm afraid I don't. How can I help you, Mrs. Nesbitt?"

"Well, you stayed at my hotel when you was covering that story about the Johnson boy who fell down in the mine shaft and—"

"Oh, yes, I remember you now," Travis Baker said.

"You told me then that if anything else interesting ever happened up our way, I was to give you a call."

"Absolutely. I did tell you that, didn't I? Has something interesting happened *up your way?*"

"Is your TV station still paying out a hundred dollars for a news tip?" Corrie asked.

"Yes, ma'am, we sure are."

"All right then, I might have a story for you."

"I'm listening."

"Well, late this afternoon a man and a woman—they call themselves Mr. Smith and Ms. Jones—they come wandering into town looking like death warmed over, if you know what I mean."

"Strangers?" Travis Baker asked.

"Yes sirree. They said they'd been lost up in the mountains and they sure looked it. But I'm telling you, that even though they're both just as nice as they can be, there's more to their story than meets the eye. Might make a great human interest story for your viewers, if they'd tell you the details on camera.''

"Where are they now, this Mr. Smith and Ms. Jones?"

"Upstairs in one of our rooms," Corrie said. "They told Ed that they was married and had a son. Some friends is supposed to be bringing the boy and coming here tonight."

"Mrs. Nesbitt—"

"Call me Corrie."

"All right, Corrie, do you think these folks are criminals?"

Corrie harrumphed. "I didn't say that. I just figure there might be an interesting story here and I could make myself a hundred dollars."

"I'll tell you what, if you can keep them there overnight, I'll drive down first thing in the morning with a cameraman and see what Mr. Smith and Ms. Jones have to say for themselves."

"And you'll bring my money?"

Travis chuckled. "Yes, ma'am. I'll give you the money, if I actually get an interesting story."

Chapter 12

The Dundee agents arrived in Stonyford around eight-thirty. If the situation hadn't been so dead serious, Egan would have found it amusing. Corrie Nesbitt peeked out from a front window, her large, round eyes bulging with surprise and suspicion when she saw the men emerge from their car. Ed Butram stood just inside the hotel entrance, his arms crossed over his thin chest and a look of concerned curiosity on his weathered face.

Hunter Whitelaw got out of the car first, his big, bearlike body moving with amazing agility for a man so large. He scanned the area, then threw up his hand in greeting to Egan and Maggie, who stood side by side on the walk in front of the hotel. Egan nodded. Maggie smiled weakly.

Joe Ornelas emerged from the other side of the back seat, scanned the area and said something to the driver of the vehicle, David Wolfe.

"Your friend there is an Indian, ain't he?" Ed Butram asked.

"Navajo," Egan replied.

"Thought as much."

Hunter motioned to the other back seat occupant and Bent Douglas appeared. Tall, lean and good-looking. Egan's hands curled into loose fists and his heart swelled with pride at the sight of his son. His son! But the boy hated him. And who could blame him?

With Hunter and Joe flanking Bent, the three of them approached. Maggie ran down the sidewalk and into the street. Bent started to run to her, but was refrained by Hunter's big hand on his shoulder. The minute Maggie reached her son, she flung her arms around him and enveloped him in a smothering hug. Bent wrapped his arms around his mother and returned her fierce hug. Then Maggie grabbed his face between her hands and covered it with kisses.

Tears streamed down her cheeks as she stepped back, grasped Bent's hands and just stood there on the street looking at him. Egan ached with emotion. The love Maggie and Bent shared was a precious thing—something he wasn't a part of.

Don't ask for too much, Egan reminded himself. Maggie is safe. Bent is safe. And he was going to make sure they stayed safe always. He realized that he might never be allowed to become a part of their lives on a permanent basis, but knowing that Cullen could never threaten them again would have to be enough.

Who was he kidding? He wanted more. He wanted it all. Maggie. Bent. A normal life. But what were the odds that it could happen for him? Could Maggie ever truly trust him enough to give him a second chance? And was it possible for his son to forgive him? Would Bent ever allow him to be a real father to him?

Egan stepped aside as Maggie and Bent approached the

hotel, Joe and Hunter guarding them. Maggie paused momentarily as they passed, her gaze locking with Egan's. But Bent looked straight ahead, not even acknowledging Egan's existence.

"Your boy don't seem none too glad to see you," Ed Butram commented, then tossed a chew of tobacco into his mouth and went inside the hotel.

Ed was right about that, Egan thought. His son sure as hell wasn't glad to see him. But how could he blame Bent? After all, the boy had just lived through the most traumatic experience of his life—and he blamed Egan.

Wolfe pulled the car around into the alley, then returned to the hotel entrance, where Egan waited for him.

"Any problems?" Wolfe asked.

Egan stared into the man's eyes—a light, earthy green, a direct contrast to his dark skin. "No problems. Not even a hint of Cullen. Any word on what happened to him?"

"None," Wolfe said. "But then you didn't expect he'd make his location known, did you? He's hidden away somewhere safe and sound, waiting to find out where you are before he makes a move."

"I want Maggie and Bent to be taken someplace safe, somewhere they can be guarded day and night, until I've taken care of Cullen."

Wolfe eased up beside Egan. The man's movements mimicked a sleek panther. Perfectly coordinated. Deadly quiet.

"Ornelas's cousin, J.T. Blackwood, who used to be a Dundee agent, owns a ranch in New Mexico. He plans to take Maggie and Bent there. Either he or Whitelaw will be with them at all times and Blackwood's ranch hands will provide extra protection, as will Blackwood himself. And Maggie won't feel so alone with Blackwood's wife and sister around."

"First thing in the morning, we'll leave," Egan said. "Are you heading back to Atlanta or will you be going to New Mexico first?"

"Neither," Wolfe told him. "I'm going with you."

Egan snapped his head around and glared at Wolfe. "What do you mean you're going with me?"

"We discussed things, before Ellen left, and we decided that apprehending Cullen is a two-man job."

"This isn't a Dundee matter," Egan said. "This is a personal matter and I don't want to involve anyone else. I'll take care of Cullen by myself."

"You need an accomplice. Someone who isn't personally involved. Someone who can think rationally."

Egan chuckled. "You know I'm going to kill the bastard, don't you?"

"If we can bring him in alive—"

"Not an option!"

"The kidnapping charges alone would put him in prison for the rest of his life," Wolfe said. "If we can do this legally, you'd never have to explain to Maggie or to your son why—"

"I doubt my son will ever give me the chance to explain anything. And Maggie already understands."

Wolfe shrugged his wide shoulders. "However you decide to handle this, consider me your shadow until it's finished."

"Who decided that you'd get this assignment?" Egan didn't know David Wolfe very well. He suspected that no one did. Except maybe Sam Dundee, the big boss who had hired him.

"I volunteered."

Wolfe's facial expression didn't alter, but Egan noted a slight change in his eyes. Those damn pale eyes were spooky. Like the eyes of some predatory animal.

"So you enjoy suicide missions, do you?" Egan suspected he'd just learned something about the mysterious David Wolfe. Maybe the man didn't have a death wish, but the prospect of dying certainly didn't worry him.

When Wolfe made no reply, Egan slapped him on the back. The man tensed visibly. Egan let his hand fall away, then turned toward the hotel entrance. "Maggie wants me to talk to Bent tonight. She thinks he'll listen to what I have to say."

"Perhaps he will," Wolfe said. "But if you expect too much, you will be disappointed."

"I don't expect anything," Egan told him, then mumbled to himself, "I don't deserve anything."

Maggie sat beside Bent on the edge of the twin bed in the room Ed had assigned to her son. The old man had seemed to understand that their circumstances weren't normal and didn't question them. But Corrie's nosiness bothered Maggie slightly. The woman was as sweet as she could be and was truly friendly, but she possessed an abundance of curiosity that prompted her to ask too many questions.

Maggie glanced at Joe Ornelas who stood guard at the door. "Mr. Ornelas, would you mind if I had a few minutes alone with my son?"

"No, ma'am. I understand. I'll be right outside the door."

"Thank you."

The minute Joe closed the door behind him, Maggie took Bent's hand in hers and squeezed tightly. She had never realized how much she'd taken life for granted—the normal, everyday events like eating and sleeping and working. After coming so close to losing Bent, she would forever be aware of how quickly the most important things in your life can be taken from you. In the blink of an eye.

"Are you really all right?" she asked.

"Yeah, Mama, I'm really all right."

When Bent smiled at her, she saw Egan's smile. Looking at Bent now, she realized how very much he was his father's son. Not only did Egan deserve a chance to know their child, but Bent deserved a chance to know his father. She had to find a way to convince Bent that Egan was worthy of a second chance.

"I want you to do something for me," Maggie said.

"What?"

"I want you to talk to your father."

Bent jerked his hand from Maggie's grasp, shot up off the bed and paced around the room. "I don't have a father. Gil Douglas might have adopted me and called himself my father, but he was never anything but a temporary stepfather. And Egan Cassidy might have provided the sperm that helped create me, but he isn't my father. He's a stranger who walked out on my mother and never looked back. He's a man whose association with the scum of the earth put your life and mine in danger."

"Grant Cullen is a madman who has ruined Egan's life. He sought revenge against Egan because Egan had once exposed him as the evil man he was—the evil man he still is."

Maggie watched her son pacing, like a trapped animal on the verge of thrusting himself against the unbendable bars of the cage that bound him. Even though Bent had assured her that he was all right, she knew better. A rage that badly needed venting boiled inside her son. He was angry with Egan. With Cullen. And perhaps even with her. How could she help Bent? What could she do to ease his pain?

"Talk to Egan," she said.

"I don't want to talk to him."

"Perhaps you don't want to talk to him, but you need to hear what he has to say." Maggie rose from the bed, walked across the room and placed her hand on her son's shoulder. "Do this for me, Bent. Let Egan explain to you about his relationship with Cullen. I think once you know the truth, you won't blame your father for what happened."

Bent covered Maggie's hand with his own and looked directly into her eyes. "Okay. I'll listen to what he has to say. But only because it's what you want."

"Thank you, darling." She kissed his cheek. "I'll tell Mr. Ornelas to go get Egan and let him know you're ready to see him."

Egan wondered what sort of magic Maggie had performed to persuade their son to talk to him. Whatever means she'd used, he was grateful. But he was nervous. And scared. He didn't kid himself. He knew this might be the only chance he'd ever have with his son. What if he said the wrong thing? What if he misjudged, misstepped, misunderstood? So much was riding on this one conversation. He couldn't blow this opportunity.

God, help me!

Hunter sat in a straight-back chair outside the room. When Egan and Joe approached he nodded. "Maggie's still in there with him."

"He may want her there when we talk," Egan said.

Joe knocked on the door. "I've brought Egan with me."

Within seconds the door swung open. Maggie stood there alone. Then she stepped out into the hallway, leaving the door open behind her. Egan glanced into the room and saw Bent standing at the windows that overlooked the back alley. The boy stood ramrod straight, as if he had an iron bar attached to his spine.

"He's very hostile," Maggie said softly. "He's on the verge of exploding, so if he lashes out at you—"

"If he needs to vent his anger, I'm tough enough to take it." When Egan reached out to touch Maggie, she side-stepped him and he realized that their son's resentment stood between them, a barrier as potentially dangerous to their future together as Grant Cullen's existence was to their lives.

Egan entered the room, but halted just as he crossed the threshold. He glanced over his shoulder and looked at Maggie who waited in the hall. "Aren't you coming in with me?"

"No," she replied. "You and Bent need to be alone for this conversation."

Egan nodded. Maggie closed the door, shutting him inside the room with a young, raging bull, who was ready, willing and able to attack with the least provocation.

"Bent?"

The boy stiffened. "Yes, sir?"

"Your mother said that you've agreed to talk to me."

"I'll listen to whatever you have to say, only because my mother asked me to hear you out."

"Fair enough."

Bent whirled around, his steely gray eyes narrowed, his cheeks flushed and his big, manly hands clenching and un-clenching with nervous energy. "Fair? What the hell would you know about fair? Was it fair that you got my mother pregnant and left her? Was it fair that she's had to raise me all by herself? Was it fair that because you've spent your life associating with a bunch of fanatics and lunatics that one of them kidnapped me and put my mother through hell?"

The blast of Bent's venomous anger bombarded Egan, making direct hits to his already overburdened conscience.

Guilt piled upon guilt, weighing him down with regret. "You're right. None of it was fair. Not to you. Not to your mother. And whether you believe it or not, none of it was fair to me, either."

Bent glared at Egan, his gaze surveying his father from head to toe. "Every time Mama looks at me she must see you. If I were her, I'd hate me."

"Maggie loves you more than anything," Egan said.

"I know! My mother is the best. She's a good person who deserved a lot better than you ever gave her."

"Don't you think I know that?" Egan held out his hands, the expression beseeching his son for understanding.

"How could you have taken advantage of her the way you did?"

"Is that what Maggie told you?" Egan asked. "Did she say that I had taken—"

"Gil told me."

"Gil?"

"Yeah, Gil. You know, the guy my mother was engaged to marry when you showed up in her life and screwed up everything." Bent's hands shook; his chin quivered. "If it hadn't been for you, Gil Douglas would have been my real father. They'd have gotten married, had me and they'd still be together. But no, you had to ruin things. Gil told me how you used your friendship with my uncle Bentley to worm your way into Mama's heart—and into her bed!"

"Gil Douglas had no right to tell you anything about my relationship with Maggie. All you've heard is the opinion of a man who hated me because—"

"Because you stole his fiancée right out from under his nose!"

"Because your mother fell in love with me." Egan closed his eyes momentarily as the memory of that last night with Maggie washed over his consciousness. *I love you, Egan. I love you so much.* How many times during the past fifteen years had he heard that sweet voice echoing inside his head?

"But you didn't love her—you used her." Bent sneered at his father, a look of pure contempt on his handsome face.

Admit the truth. Don't lie to your son, Egan's conscience warned him. "I never meant to hurt Maggie. I didn't mean to use her. You're a little young to understand what happens between a man and a woman—"

"I know all about sex. You needed a woman, so you took advantage of my mother because she was infatuated with you."

"It wasn't like that, Bent. I swear to you that Maggie was never just some woman to me. I cared about her. I still care. About her and about you."

"Yeah, well, where were you fourteen years ago when I was born? Where was all that caring then?"

Egan took a tentative step in Bent's direction, but halted immediately when he noticed the stricken look on his son's face. The boy was scared to death that Egan might touch him, but Egan knew better than to tread on thin ice. If he even tried to place a hand on Bent's shoulder, the boy was likely to fly into a panicked rage.

Egan sat down in the only chair in the room, a wingback that had definitely seen better days. Once seated, he noted the slight relaxation in Bent's shoulders.

"When I was eighteen, I got drafted and wound up in Vietnam," Egan said, trying to keep his voice calm and unemotional. "To make a long story short, I met your uncle Bentley when he saved my life. We became friends then and remained friends as long as he lived. Bentley Tyson was probably the only real friend I've ever had."

"And you repaid his friendship by getting his little sister pregnant just a few weeks after his funeral."

Bent hovered over Egan, his hands knotted into fists. Egan knew that the boy was itching to hit him.

"If you want to hit me, son, then go ahead and do it." Egan lifted his chin and looked up at Bent. "Otherwise, give it a rest until you know the whole story."

Bent fumed. He clenched his jaw, clamped his teeth and snorted as his breathing grew fast and hard. Keening, he closed his eyes, wheeled around and stomped across the room. Egan waited, not saying a word.

With his back still to his father, Bent said, "Go ahead. I'm listening."

"While I was in Nam, I was captured and spent nearly a year in a Vietcong POW camp." Egan paused, not wanting to remember those days and yet never truly able to forget. "That's where I met Grant Cullen. I survived. But most of the men didn't survive…because of Cullen. He betrayed his country and his fellow soldiers. He traded information for favors and he also exposed a planned escape that cost a lot of men their lives. So, when I got the chance, I turned him in for what he'd done and a captured Vietcong major backed up my story. Cullen's West Point training and his family's position didn't help him much when the truth came out. Cullen's career was over. His wife left him and took their daughter. His father disowned him. And he blamed me for all his misfortunes."

"He blamed you for something that was his own fault?" Bent turned and faced Egan. "He hated you because you'd told the truth about what he did?"

"He swore that he'd never let me have any peace, that he would watch and wait until the day came when I had something that meant everything to me and then he would take it away."

"But that was how many years ago? Twenty-five? Thirty? Are you telling me that he's been keeping tabs on you all these years, waiting for a chance to hurt you the way he thinks you hurt him?''

Egan nodded. ''I could never allow anyone to be more than a casual part of my life. I couldn't love a woman and get married. I couldn't have any children. I couldn't even spend more than a few days at a time with friends. Anyone who cared about me ran a risk and it wasn't a risk I was willing to let anyone take.''

Bent's shoulders slumped, his whole body relaxing. ''Then why did you get involved with my mother?''

''I didn't mean for it to happen,'' Egan said as he scooted to the edge of the chair. ''But Maggie was...different. She was special. I tried damn hard to resist the way I felt about her, the way I knew she felt about me.'' *But loving her was the sweetest thing I've ever known,* he longed to say, but didn't. *I wanted her as I'd never wanted anything or anyone, before or since. And I still want her, now more than ever.* ''I didn't want to leave her. I swear to you that if I'd thought I had a choice, I'd have stayed with Maggie forever.''

''You left because you didn't want Cullen to know about her, so that he couldn't use her to get to you.''

Egan saw the realization dawn in Bent's eyes. His son knew the truth now. Was he mature enough to accept and understand?

''I should have told Maggie about Cullen.'' Egan dropped his hands between his legs and twined his fingers together as he gazed down at the floor. ''But I had no idea she was pregnant. If I'd known...''

''If you'd known, then what?'' Bent asked eagerly.

''I'd have made damn sure that you and Maggie were safe.''

''How did Cullen find out about us...about me?'' Bent asked.

"A private detective somehow unearthed my credit card records that showed I paid for flowers that were sent to Bentley's grave each year. From there, the detective did a little more digging and discovered that Maggie had a child and that I was listed on his birth certificate as the father."

"And once he found out about me..." Bent walked across the room and stood directly in front of Egan. "I understand. Like Mama said, it wasn't your fault that Cullen kidnapped me. And I guess I owe you my life, don't I?" Bent grunted. "So what happens now? What's to keep Cullen from coming after Mama and me again?"

"Me," Egan said. "I'm what's going to keep him from ever getting anywhere near you and Maggie."

"How are you going to stop him?"

"You don't need to worry about that. All you have to do is cooperate with Joe and Hunter and let them do their job as your and Maggie's bodyguards, until I take care of Cullen."

"You're going to kill him, aren't you?"

Egan didn't know how to respond to Bent's direct question. What would his son say if he admitted that he had no intention of allowing Grant Cullen to live?

"If necessary," Egan admitted and sought his son's eyes for a reaction.

Bent nodded, then glanced away as if he couldn't quite accept the truth. "It won't be the first time that you've killed someone, will it? You were a soldier in Vietnam and then you were a mercenary."

"It wasn't the life I would have willingly chosen. I did what I had to do. Most people have choices. My choices were limited."

"After...after Cullen is *eliminated*," Bent continued, "then Mama and I can go home, back to our normal life. Right?"

"Right."

"What about you?" Bent asked.

"What about me?"

"Will you go back to Atlanta, to your normal life?"

"That depends," Egan said. "On you and your mother."

"Do you really still care about her?" Bent shuffled his feet nervously.

"Yes, I still care."

"What about Mama? Do you think she still cares about you?"

"You'll have to ask her," Egan said.

"You'd better not ever hurt her again." Bent glowered at his father, his stance boldly aggressive. "She's got me now and I won't let you or anybody else hurt her."

"I'm glad you love your mother and that you want to protect her, but you don't have to protect her from me."

"If she doesn't want you to be a part of her life, then that's fine with me," Bent said. "I don't need you. I'm practically a man now. What do I need with a father? So when Mama and I go home, you'd better just go on back to Atlanta and leave us alone."

"If that's what you and Maggie want, then that's what I'll do."

"If Mama says it's all right for you to come back to Parsons City with us—for a visit—then that's okay, too. But only if it's what she wants."

"All right. We're in agreement." Egan held out his hand. "We'll leave the decision up to Maggie. We'll both abide by whatever she decides."

Bent stared at his father's hand for several minutes, then reluctantly accepted it in a hardy handshake. It took all of Egan's willpower not to jerk the boy forward and into his arms. This was his son, his and Maggie's child. And he'd never held this boy when he'd been a baby, never rocked him, never cared for him when he'd been sick. Bent had grown into a fine young man without ever having known the love and support of his father. Despite what Maggie had said, maybe Bent didn't need him, but Egan knew one thing for sure and certain—he needed Bent.

Now that he knew he had a son, there was no way he could ever walk away and leave him. More than anything, he wanted a second chance. A chance to make things right with Bent, to try to become a father to his son.

He held Bent's hand in his a little longer than necessary, until finally Bent pulled free and stood there staring at Egan.

"In case I don't get the chance to tell you tomorrow before you and Maggie leave, I want you to know that I'm proud you're my son and I'm sorry that I haven't been around since you were born."

A fine mist formed over Bent's eyes. He cleared his throat. "I guess we'd better let Mama know that everything's cleared up now and I understand why things happened the way they did." Bent headed for the door.

"Bent?"

"Yeah?" He glanced over his shoulder.

"Thanks."

Bent nodded, then opened the door and called out to his mother. Maggie came to the door, then glanced back and forth from father to son.

"Is everything all right?" she asked.

"Yes," Bent said. "Egan told me all about Grant Cullen and why he's been trying to find a way to get revenge all these years. I understand, so you can stop worrying. I don't blame Egan for what happened."

Maggie sighed with relief. "Good. I'm glad."

Egan crossed the room, stopped at Maggie's side and turned to Bent. "I'll see you both in the morning."

When Egan left the room, Maggie called out to him. She smiled at Bent. "I'll be right back. I need to speak to Egan for just a minute."

"Sure," Bent said. "Just hurry back. Okay?"

Maggie nodded, then rushed out into the hallway to catch Egan. He seemed intent upon escaping, so she ran down the corridor and grabbed his arm.

"I thought everything was all right between you and Bent," she said. "He understands now and he doesn't blame you for what happened with Grant Cullen. Right?"

Egan placed his hand over hers where she gripped his shirt. "Bent is a boy trying very hard to act like a man. He does understand about my relationship with Cullen and he even understands why I left you fifteen years ago." Egan tapped the side of his forehead with his index finger. "He understands with his mind. But in here—" Egan pounded his fist over his heart "—he's a little boy who can't forgive me for hurting his mama and for not being there for you and him all these years."

"Oh, Egan, give him time. Once he gets to know you—"

Egan grabbed Maggie's shoulders. "Is that what you want? Do you really want me to become a part of Bent's life…a part of your life? Our son has made it very clear to me that unless you're willing to give me a second chance, he doesn't want to have a thing to do with me."

"I see. So, you're saying that Bent expects us to come as a package deal. If you take the son, you have to take the mama, too."

"Your son loves you and doesn't want to see you get hurt." Egan eased his hands down Maggie's arms, grasped her wrists and then released her. "So, you think about things while I'm gone. And when I come to the Blackwood Ranch to let you know that y'all are safe from Cullen, you can tell me what the future holds for us."

"Egan, I—"

By placing his index finger over her lips, he silenced her. "Don't make a rash decision. Take your time. Whatever you decide will affect all three of us, for the rest of our lives."

Chapter 13

With the bedspread wrapped around her, Maggie sat by the windows that overlooked Stonyford's Main Street and watched the predawn sky. She had spent several hours with Bent last night and finally came to the conclusion that despite his lingering resentment of Egan, her son both wanted and needed his father in his life. But before that could happen, Bent and she would have to come to terms not only with the kidnapping, but with how Egan handled putting Grant Cullen out of commission. Permanently.

The world was a violent place—always had been and probably always would be. But living in Parsons City, Alabama, she had been able to shield Bent from a great deal of life's true ugliness. If Egan became a part of their lives, would he be able to leave behind that kill-or-be-killed lifestyle he had led for so many years? Could he survive without the adrenaline rush of danger and excitement on which he'd fed most of his adult life? Even if he were willing to

try settling down to a normal life, would he grow bored
and eventually leave them?

In her heart, Maggie knew that if Egan's venture into
their lives turned out to be only temporary, she and Bent
would be better off without him. She had survived when
she'd lost Egan the first time, but what would happen if
she lost him a second time? And what about Bent? How
would having his father desert him, once they had bonded,
affect him?

Maggie drew her feet up onto the chair and clutched the
edges of the spread where it crossed her chest. A tiny chill
trickled along her nerve endings. She had fallen in love
with Egan all over again and there was no use denying the
truth. Perhaps in the deepest recesses of her heart, she had
never stopped loving him. Poor fool that she was! She was
doomed to be a one-man woman and there really wasn't
anything she could do about it.

Egan wanted her, desired her greatly and couldn't seem
to get enough of their lovemaking. But did he love her?
Had he ever loved her? *I cared for you,* she remembered
him saying. Caring wasn't love. So, would Egan make a
commitment to her in order to become a father to Bent?
Was he willing to take the package deal, even without loving her?

The door to Maggie's room creaked slightly as it opened
ever so slowly. A thin thread of light from the hallway fell
across the floor like a pale line of paint. Maggie's senses
heightened. Her nerves came to full alert. *You're safe,* she
reminded herself. Egan and Wolfe were in the room next
to hers. Joe Ornelas slept in the bed beside Bent, just across
the hall. And Hunter Whitelaw kept a vigil outside in the
corridor.

The moment the door opened farther, she recognized
Egan's silhouette. Undoubtedly he was as restless as she,

as unable to sleep. They would say goodbye later today and go their separate ways. She and Bent into seclusion. Egan on a quest to find and destroy the threat to their lives. Had Egan been thinking about the possibility that, this time, he wouldn't come back alive? After all, he had survived a lifetime of constant danger. And together they had saved Bent and escaped Cullen's wrath. Did that mean Egan's luck had finally run out? What if instead of him eliminating Cullen, it was the other way around?

"Come in," Maggie said, her voice not much more than a whisper.

Egan walked into the dark room, illuminated only by the moonlight, and quietly closed the door behind him. "I just wanted to check on you. To make sure—"

"You've checked on Bent, too, haven't you?" she asked.

"Yes." Egan stood just inside the doorway, his breathing slow and steady.

"And he was sleeping?"

"Soundly."

"You've come to say goodbye, haven't you?"

"Maggie, I knew you were awake," he admitted. "I've been listening to you stirring around in here for the past hour."

"I've been thinking about us," she told him. "About what might happen to you when you go after Cullen."

Egan didn't move. He simply stood there in the darkness and waited. Maggie knew she would have to make the first move, extend an invitation, before he would come to her. At that very moment he was exerting superhuman control in order to keep his hands off her. She knew this as surely as she knew that in less than an hour the sun would rise in the east. The electrifying chemistry between them radiated an intense energy that drew them together, like a magnet and metal, one incapable of resisting the other.

"I don't want you to worry about me," Egan said, his voice low, as if he didn't want to be overheard. "I know what I'm doing. And I'm not going alone. Wolfe will be with me."

"I'm glad you won't be alone."

"Once this is over…once Cullen is no longer a threat, I'd like to try to find a way to make amends to you and Bent."

Maggie rose from the overstuffed chair, bringing the bedspread up with her as she stood. The edge of the jacquard-style print coverlet dragged behind her as she glided silently across the wooden floor. Transparent gilded moonbeams burnished her hair with gold, deepening the rich red into a dark mahogany. Egan swallowed hard. His body hardened instantly.

He had given himself a dozen good reasons why he should open Maggie's door, but all of the excuses had been lies. The only truth was that he knew they would say goodbye in a few hours and he couldn't bear the thought of not making love to her one final time.

Before she reached Egan, Maggie dropped the spread from around her shoulders. The soft cotton throw cascaded down her hips and legs and pooled around her feet on the floor. She stepped over the puddle of material and came to him, wearing only a pair of slightly oversize panties and an equally oversize, unbuttoned shirt.

Even in the dim light, he could make out the swell of her partially exposed breasts and the long, silky length of her gorgeous legs.

"Are you sure?" he asked, praying that she wouldn't change her mind. Not now. Not when he ached with such a desperate need to be inside her.

"I'm sure." She grasped the front edges of her borrowed

shirt and opened it fully, then slid it off her shoulders, over her arms and down her back.

Egan held his breath.

She let the shirt drop from her fingers and join the coverlet on the floor. With several slow, tormenting steps she made her way to him, then stopped directly in front of him and reached up to touch his bare chest. He let out the breath he'd been holding.

He touched her shoulders, his fingers grazing her skin with the lightness of feathers. Soft, sweet, slow. Tantalizing. Moments ticked by as his tender strokes inflamed her. Touching, but just barely. Across her shoulder, up her neck, over her chin, down her neck and across her other shoulder. Just when she thought she couldn't bear it unless he touched her more intimately, his fingertips glided over and around her breasts, but deliberately avoided her nipples.

Maggie drew in a sharp breath when he finally circled her nipples, but never touched them. Moaning deep in her throat, the sound a muted plea for him to end her torment, Maggie gripped his biceps. Egan lowered his head until his mouth hovered over the center of one breast. He flicked out his tongue and just barely brushed her nipple.

Maggie bit down on her lip to keep from screaming with the pure pleasure of that fleeting touch. As she held him tightly by the arms, he repeated the torture several times and then turned his attention to her other breast.

She rose on tiptoes, tossed back her head and gasped softly. Hurriedly, Egan divested himself of his jeans and then hooked his thumbs under the elastic of Maggie's baggy cotton panties. As soon as they were both naked, he walked her backward and toppled her over and into the center of the bed. He came down over her, straddling her hips. She gazed up at him with such desire in her eyes that he thought he'd lose it right then and there. But he was going to give her pleasure and that meant waiting. Waiting until she was begging him to take her.

He took his sex and began rubbing it against her kernel, tempting and teasing until she bucked her hips up, asking for more. But he continued the movements, slow and maddening, building the tension inside her.

"Oh, please, Egan. Please."

"Not yet."

After agonizing moments of torture, repeatedly petting her body with his, he finally eased the very tip inside her. When she tried to thrust upward to take more, he halted her.

Covering her face and neck with sweet, little pecks, Egan eased in and out a few inches, but he refused her pleas to bury himself inside her. She writhed beneath him, mumbling incoherent phrases. He covered her lips with his and lunged his tongue into her open mouth. She closed her lips around his tongue, trapping him, sucking greedily. The kiss deepened, expanded, becoming a parody of the most intimate of sexual acts.

Maggie grabbed Egan's taut buttocks and brought his body down as she lifted up to meet him. She had taken all the teasing she could endure. She wanted every inch of him. Now!

Egan obliged her—at long last. He thrust into her, deeply, completely. She trapped a scream in her throat. A scream of intense pleasure. And then the mating dance began in earnest. Hard, deep plunges that brought each of them closer and closer to the ultimate climax, to the perfect conclusion.

Maggie's entire body tensed as it reached the moment of fulfillment. One final stroke of Egan's sex and she shattered into a million fragments of quivering pleasure. Her release triggered his and he followed her, headlong, into an earth-shattering completion.

Their bodies damp with perspiration, their breathing ragged, they held each other while the aftershocks rippled through them and strength-robbing satiation claimed them thoroughly.

"General Cullen," Winn Sherman called out as he knocked loudly on Cullen's bedroom door. "Wake up, sir, and turn on your television."

"What the hell!" Cullen roused from sleep, angry for being disturbed, but knowing that Winn wouldn't have bothered him without good reason. He fumbled his fingers across the top of the nightstand, searching for the remote. The moment he found it, he hit the Power button.

"What channel?" Cullen demanded.

Winn called out the channel number. Cullen punched in the number as he sat up in bed. On screen, a pretty-boy reporter with an irritatingly phony smile stood in the middle of a street in some local town nearby. Cullen thought all small towns shared a likeness, especially those out here in the west.

After turning up the sound, he called out to Winn, "What's going on? Why did you want me to see this?"

"May I come in, sir?"

"Get me some coffee first."

"Yes, sir. But listen to what that reporter is saying."

Cullen turned up the sound and listened.

"We're here in Stonyford," the pretty boy said. "We have a report that a man and a woman walked out of the mountains yesterday, after spending days being lost in the wilderness. We're told that Mr. Smith and Ms. Jones are still inside the Stonyford Hotel and will be emerging shortly to speak to us about their harrowing ordeal."

Cullen shot out of bed and grabbed his silk robe. "Well, I'll be damned."

The reporter's name—Travis Baker—flashed across the screen. Travis pointed his handheld microphone toward a plump, elderly woman with a shock of curly gray hair and set of bright blue eyes.

"This is Mrs. Corrie Nesbitt, the proprietor of the hotel, where the couple is staying. What do you know about this Mr. Smith and Ms. Jones?"

"Don't know much," Corrie said. "He's a good-looking man, with a beard and mustache, about forty-five and she's a tall redhead, a few years younger. My brother, Ed Butram, ran across them when they first showed up here after spending a couple of days lost up there in the mountains. They was a couple of sorry-looking folks, I'll tell you. Dirty, hungry and tired."

"Did they share any of the details about their wilderness adventure with you?" Travis asked. "Did they explain how they got lost and what they were doing in the mountains without a guide?"

"Nope. They seem nice enough, but I say there's more to them than meets the eye." Corrie harrumphed loudly. "Three real slick-looking characters showed up here last night with a boy that Mr. Smith and Ms. Jones claim is their son. They all spent the night and are in there right now eating breakfast."

Travis pulled the microphone away from Corrie who had reached out to grab it. "Folks, stay with us. After this message from our sponsors, we will, hopefully, be granted an interview with the mysterious couple Mrs. Nesbitt just told us about."

Winn Sherman entered Cullen's bedroom, a mug of black coffee in his hand. "Here you are, sir."

Cullen muted the sound on the television, took the ceramic mug from Winn and sat on the edge of the bed. "You can run, but you can't hide." Cullen chuckled, then sipped his coffee.

"Do you think Mr. Smith and Ms. Jones are Cassidy and Maggie Douglas?" Winn asked.

"Oh, I'd lay odds that's exactly who they are. Some old hag even described them. A bearded man, about forty-five and a tall, redheaded woman."

"What a stroke of luck."

"Divine intervention," Cullen said. "The Almighty pointing the way for me." He sipped more coffee. "Find out how far Stonyford is from here and round up some good men. There's four of them, not counting the boy and the woman. With a dozen of us, we triple our odds."

"I know where Stonyford is. It's about twenty-five minutes from here, if we take the road around the mountain, and about forty-minutes if we go the main highway."

"As soon as Cassidy finds out that a reporter is on his heels, he'll get out of town as quickly as possible." Cullen placed his mug on the nightstand, then scratched his chin. "He'll figure there's a chance I saw the TV report or that one of my supporters did, so he'll be in a hurry to get his woman and his kid to safety."

"That means he'll probably head for the main highway. I suggest that we try to cut them off while they're still on the back road leading out of Stonyford."

"I agree. We need to set things in motion immediately."

"Yes, sir!" Winn clicked his heels and saluted.

"What the hell is going on out there?" Hunter Whitelaw roared, his deep baritone voice booming as he glanced out the window. "Looks like a TV reporter and a couple of cameramen. And Mrs. Nesbitt is being interviewed."

"Damn! That's all we need," Joe Ornelas said. "How

did they find out about you two?'' He glanced across the room to where Maggie and Egan stood in the corner, talking quietly.

"Knowing Corrie, she probably called that Travis Baker and told him about our wilderness survivors showing up yesterday, hoping she'd collect that hundred dollars they give away for news tips," Ed Butram explained.

"I suggest we head out as soon as possible," Wolfe said. "And preferably by a back entrance."

"I want y'all to take Maggie and Bent and leave immediately," Egan said. "I'll arrange for transportation for myself and—"

Maggie clutched Egan's arm. "No. You said that you weren't going alone, that Wolfe was going with you."

"I'll go with him to find Cullen once you and your son are in safekeeping," Wolfe reassured her, then quickly turned his attention to Ed Butram. "Do you have a car, Mr. Butram?"

"Got an old pickup," he replied.

"Would you be willing to rent or maybe even sell us that truck?" Wolfe asked.

"Ain't worth selling. It's fifteen years old and needs a new coat of paint," Ed said.

"How does it run?" Egan asked.

"Runs just fine. I keep it tuned up. Me and Corrie go into Flagstaff ever now and then."

"How much will you take for it?" Egan asked.

"Whatever you think's a fair amount."

"I'll write you out a check," Wolfe said. "By the way, where is your truck?"

"Out back." Ed hitched his thumb toward the rear of the hotel. "You'll need the registration and the keys."

"What are y'all planning?" Maggie asked when Ed left the room.

"We're planning on getting you and your son to safety," Wolfe said. "I'll contact Sawyer MacNamara and let him know that Cullen might be aware of our location. There's a good chance we'll need some backup."

"You think Cullen will definitely come after us, don't you?" She spoke to Wolfe, but her gaze rested on Egan.

"Better to play it safe than sorry," Hunter commented. "If Cullen's got some Ultimate Survivalists sympathizers, then he could put together a small army to come after us."

"You and Bent will go in the car with Wolfe, Joe and Hunter," Egan said. "I will follow closely behind in Ed Butram's truck, until we reach the Navajo reservation." And if we encounter Cullen and any of his followers, I can hold them off until the others take you and Bent to safety, Egan thought.

"Once we're on the reservation, we'll be able to make sure no one is following us," Joe said. "I'll call ahead and have J.T. bring along some of his ranch hands and meet us."

"What if General Cullen tries to stop us?" Bent's cold glare confronted Egan. "If he knows where we are, he could be on his way here right now."

"Maybe we'll get lucky and that won't happen," Egan said. "But if he does come after us, you can be sure we'll protect you and your mother. That's one of the reasons Wolfe is going to contact the FBI. Believe me, they want Cullen almost as much as I do." Egan laid his hand on Bent's shoulder. "Whatever happens, son, I know you'll watch out for your mother."

"You can count on it," Bent said.

"Do you know how to use a gun, Bent?" Hunter asked.

"No!" Maggie cried. "He doesn't know anything about guns."

"Aim and shoot," Hunter said. "If a target is close

enough, you're bound to hit something. It might become necessary for you and Bent to be armed."

"I'm not sure I could—" Maggie cringed.

"If it meant saving Bent's life, could you?" Egan asked her.

She nodded, then said, "Yes. Yes, I could and would do anything to save Bent."

"You already know how to use a rifle, but just as a precaution, it's probably a good idea to give you and Bent a quick lesson in how to use a handgun," Egan told her.

With his chin held high and his broad shoulders squared, Bent walked straight up to Egan. "Give me a gun and show me how to use it."

While Ed Butram joined his sister on the street, distracting Travis Baker with his version of how he "come upon" Mr. Smith and Ms. Jones yesterday, Stonyford's visitors made their escape. Wolfe had made arrangements with Sawyer MacNamara for federal agents to meet them en route, but Egan couldn't help wishing that they already had backup. Of course, there was no way to know if Cullen had seen the newscast or if someone might have relayed the information to him. But Egan had no doubt that Cullen would learn that he and Maggie had been in Stonyford. He just prayed he could get Maggie and Bent to safety before Cullen caught up with them.

Ed Butram's rusty, dilapidated, old truck chugged along, keeping up with the sleek, black sedan Wolfe maneuvered around the mountain curves. Every instinct Egan possessed sensed danger, but he wasn't sure if his concern for Maggie and their son had somehow altered his usually perfect perception. Did he sense immediate danger simply because he feared for Maggie and Bent?

Ed had told them that if they stayed on the old mountain

road they would eventually connect with a state highway, which would lead them to Interstate 40 and then it would be a straight shot to Gallup.

Once they made it to the interstate, the feds would escort them to the Navajo reservation and block any attempts Cullen might make to overtake them. After Maggie and Bent were safely hidden on the Blackwood Ranch, Egan and Wolfe would be free to pursue Cullen. They weren't bound by the law the way the federal agents were and could use whatever means necessary to stop Cullen—dead in his tracks.

As they descended the mountain, the two-lane road winding ever downward, sometimes at unnervingly steep angles, glimpses of wide valleys came into view. Foxtail grass, yellow-white in the morning sun, grew thickly across the wide vistas near the lake at the foot of the mountain. Dirt trails, cutting off the main road, led into the deep woods. They had passed at least half a dozen of those secluded lanes, and each time they passed one, Egan's heartbeat accelerated. A vehicle could easily hide and wait.

Surely they would reach the state highway soon, Egan thought as he checked his watch. Twenty minutes from Stonyford and so far, they hadn't seen another vehicle on the road. *Let's keep it that way!*

Straight ahead a narrow bridge crossed the East Fork of Pine Wood Creek. A dense stand of evergreens surrounded them, like giant sentinels towering into the sky. Just past the bridge the road turned sharply, concealing whatever lay around the bend. And they had just passed another of those damn little trails that led off into the woods.

The hairs on Egan's neck stood up. A warning chill shivered along his spine. He started to blow the truck's horn to caution Wolfe, but apparently something had forewarned

Wolfe. The sedan slowed to a halt just this side of the bridge.

Egan rolled down the driver's side window and listened. The truck's and the car's engines droned steadily. The only other sound was the hum of nature. A breeze high in the treetops. Leaves rustling. Squirrels chattering. Water flowing. Egan ran his hand over the smooth surface of the rifle Wolfe had given him before their departure, then he removed the pistol from his holster and laid it between his legs. He shifted gears and backed the truck off onto the side of the road. If danger was headed in their direction, he didn't want the truck to stand between the sedan and an escape route.

With a wave of his arm, Egan signaled Wolfe to proceed, knowing full well he didn't have to tell the man to do so with the utmost caution. The minute the sedan drove onto the bridge, a Hummer appeared, maneuvering hurriedly around the bend and into full view.

Egan's heart stopped for one split second before he grabbed the rifle and took aim from the passenger side window. The sedan reversed quickly, sending the vehicle onto the road alongside Egan's truck.

"Head back to Stonyford," Egan yelled. "I'll hold them off here."

The back door of the sedan flew open and Hunter Whitelaw jumped out, rifle in hand. "I'll stay here and help you."

"No!" Egan hollered. "Go with them. Now!"

With only a moment's hesitation, Hunter got back in the sedan and slammed the door. But before Wolfe could turn the car around, shots rang out from across the bridge and several bullets lodged in the car's front tires.

Two sport utility vehicles emerged from one of the half-hidden dirt side roads. Egan immediately recognized the man driving the lead SUV. Grant Cullen, a sickening grin plastered on his face, gunned the vehicle's gas pedal and flew around the Hummer, then came to a screeching halt on the bridge.

Dammit all! A hefty, fear-induced adrenaline rush flooded Egan's body. He'd known this was going to happen. In his gut. He had sensed the inevitability of this moment. He and Cullen face-to-face once again—with Maggie and Bent witnesses to the final showdown.

Chapter 14

Realizing exactly what was happening, Maggie followed
Wolfe's orders without question. They had been ambushed
by Grant Cullen and a group of his followers. With Joe and
Hunter shielding Maggie and Bent with their bodies, they
exited the sedan and made a mad dash into the ditch. Egan
and Wolfe covered them with a barrage of gunfire that kept
the Survivalists occupied.

At least a dozen armed men, not including Cullen and
Winn Sherman, poured out of the Hummer and the two
sports utility vehicles. A small army in comparison to the
four Dundee agents. Fear pumped through Maggie's system
as her mind assimilated the situation. This scenic mountain
road had suddenly turned into a war zone and she and her
son were trapped between the two warring factions. No,
that wasn't precisely accurate. She and her son were more
than innocent bystanders—they were a part of this battle,
their lives at stake because they were important to Egan
Cassidy.

Hunter motioned to Egan, who was separated from them by a good twenty-five feet. The two men exchanged some sort of hand signals that Maggie didn't comprehend.

Then Joe Ornelas inched his way over to Maggie. "You and Bent will stay here with Wolfe. I'm going to give you and Bent each weapons, so that if it becomes necessary—"

"I understand," she said, then accepted the 9-mm handgun from Joe.

"Hunter and I are going to make our way around behind them, while Egan and Wolfe keep their attention focused over here," Joe told her.

Hunter handed Bent his pistol, a twin to Joe's weapon, and shoved several extra clips into the pocket of Bent's jacket. "The more firepower the better, to distract Cullen's bunch. You're too far away to actually hit anybody, but they'll know we've got four shooters over here. Think you can do it?"

"Yeah, I can do it," Bent said confidently. "And so can Mama." He glance at Maggie. "Can't you?"

"Yes, of course I can." Maggie's heart lurched with an uneasiness that had nothing to do with the danger surrounding them. There was a look of excitement, of heady anticipation in her son's eyes and that look frightened her more than anything else. She had always known that the adventurous streak ran deep and wide in Bent, but until recently she had been able to curb his danger-seeking tendencies. Now, faced with a life-threatening situation, Bent became his father's son, in every sense of the word.

The gun in Maggie's hand felt alien to her, a weight she would prefer to toss aside. But she knew what she had to do. Joe gave her quick instructions, just as Hunter explained the basics to Bent. And all the while, Egan and Wolfe exchanged gunfire with the Survivalists troops. The noise distracted Maggie, but she tried to blot it out and concentrate on the task at hand.

Lying flat on her belly up against the side of the ditch, she looked across the bridge and immediately saw two men drop to the ground, casualties of Wolfe's expertise. The gunfire intensified when Joe and Hunter disappeared. Bent aimed and fired. Repeatedly. It was as if he'd been born with that gun in his hand, Maggie thought and cringed.

You can do this, she told herself. The first time she fired the weapon, every nerve in her body reacted. Holding back her urge to scream, she fired a second time.

Maggie lost track of the passing minutes as she continued firing the pistol. Her vision focused across the bridge where, one-by-one, the Survivalists began dropping like flies. That's when she realized Joe and Hunter had accomplished their goal. In a flurry of desperate activity, the few remaining troops piled into the Hummer. They're retreating, she thought. That must mean we've won the battle.

The Hummer backed up, turned around and headed in the direction from which it had come. Two lone men remained, one behind the wheel of each SUV. Even at this distance, she recognized Cullen in one vehicle and Colonel Sherman in the other. Within minutes, the two vehicles mimicked the Hummer's withdrawal. Maggie dropped the pistol to the ground. Her hands shook. Her heart raced. Nausea rose in her throat.

The roar of the old truck's engine caught Maggie's immediate attention. Egan! What was he doing? Where was he going? Ed Butram's rust-bucket pickup crossed the bridge, flying around and through the dead and wounded Survivalists.

"Where is he going?" Maggie asked Wolfe.

"Where do you think?"

"After Cullen."

"He can't let Cullen escape," Wolfe said. "You must know that."

Out of nowhere Hunter and Joe appeared. A bright red stain covered Hunter's shoulder.

"You're hurt," Maggie gasped.

"Bullet went straight through," Hunter said. "Looks worse than it is."

"Let's change those tires," Joe said. "So we can get the hell out of here. Egan just might need a little help."

"I'll give you a hand," Bent said and followed Joe around to the sedan's trunk.

"I'll help them," Wolfe told Hunter. "You get in touch with MacNamara and see where our backup is."

While Hunter used his cellular phone, Maggie paced the side of the road, nervous energy turning her into a jittery mess. She didn't know whether to cry, laugh hysterically or simply scream until she was hoarse. How could Egan face Cullen, Winn Sherman and at least four other men alone? He was terribly outnumbered. One against six were suicidal odds. But she understood Egan's reasoning. All that mattered to him was eliminating Cullen. Even if it cost him his own life in the process.

Egan saw Cullen's SUV directly ahead. The dark blue vehicle flew around a deadly curve. Egan floored the old pickup and within minutes caught up to his enemy. Cullen glanced back in the rearview mirror. His gaze wild. His features hard. Egan saw the fear on Cullen's face reflected in the mirror. Neither the Hummer nor the other SUV were within sight. Undoubtedly Sherman and the survivors had only one thing on their minds—escape.

Let them go, Egan thought. All that mattered to him was catching Cullen. And when he did...

With another hairpin curve just ahead, Egan squeezed all

the juice out of the old truck that it had in it, then rammed Cullen's SUV in the rear. Cullen bounded back, switching lanes as they neared the sharp loop. His vehicle skidded off the side of the road, shooting loose gravel in every direction and stirring up a whirlwind of dust.

Egan pulled the pickup alongside the SUV and they began a deadly game, using their vehicles as weapons. Back and forth. Ramming. Crashing. Metal crunching. Rubber burning. Sparks flying.

Cullen got ahead of Egan, the newer vehicle having a slight advantage. But within minutes Egan drew up along side the SUV, this time the truck on the wrong side of the road, near the mountain's edge. Once again, Egan instigated the crunching dance between his truck and the sports utility vehicle Cullen drove.

In a maneuver Egan hadn't been expecting, Cullen slowed down, whipped the SUV sideways and lunged, full-force, into the side of the pickup. Before Egan had a chance to do more than register what had happened, Cullen repeated the process, this time sending the old truck off the road. The back wheels dangled over the precipice, a rocky gorge far below the road. Just as Egan eased across the seat and opened the passenger's side door, Cullen took a shot at him. The bullet barely missed, embedding itself in the seat.

Damn! Egan thought. *I have to get out of this truck before it topples over the side and winds up at the bottom.* He checked to see if there was any space in which to maneuver on the other side. There wasn't. Less than six inches of level ground. The truck creaked and swayed. No choice! It had to be jump now or be swept over the cliff and down into the deep ravine, along with the truck.

Egan grabbed the rifle, flung open the driver's side door and bailed out, bracing himself for the downward lunge.

He rolled over the steep embankment, the huge jagged rocks ripping through his clothes and slicing into the exposed skin of his hands and face. After tumbling a good fifteen feet and losing his rifle in the process, he landed on a smooth boulder sticking out from the side of the mountain.

Every muscle in his body ached and he was pretty sure he had cracked a few ribs. Just as he checked his holster for his gun, he heard the tumbling crash of the old truck and looked up just in time to see it somersaulting past him down into the gorge a good fifty feet below where he rested on the ledge.

No doubt Cullen would be coming for him, so he'd better get on his feet. But that simple task proved more difficult than he'd thought. Pain sliced through his side when he tried to stand. Not only did his ribs hurt like hell, but a piercing ache radiated from his left thigh. When he glanced down, he saw a jagged rock sliver sticking out of his thigh. After casting his gaze upward, checking for Cullen, Egan used both hands to remove the thin slice of rock from his leg. Blood seeped from the wide, deep gash.

Keeping one eye open for Cullen, Egan ripped off a strip of material from the hem of his shirt and used it as a makeshift tourniquet to bind his thigh and slow the flow of blood.

Suddenly a loud boom vibrated the earth. Egan glanced down into the gorge. An explosion ripped through the old truck, shooting flames and swirls of smoke into the sky.

Despite the pain, Egan forced himself to stand and then to move. Just as he took shelter behind a crumbling rock formation, dotted with scrub grass and scraggily brush, Grant Cullen appeared at the top of the ridge. The moment Cullen saw Egan, he took aim and fired. The bullet splintered fragments from the rock formation and ricocheted off, hitting the nearby boulder. Egan got in a couple of shots, both landing just shy of their target.

"Too bad you didn't die, Cassidy," Cullen shouted. "Too bad for you, that is. I'm going to enjoy killing you slowly."

"I don't see it that way," Egan said. "Looks like a fair fight to me. We're both armed."

"Yeah, but I didn't just get banged up the way you did." Cullen's maniacal laughter echoed off the canyon walls.

Egan kept watch, using his pistol sparingly, waiting for Cullen to get within range. He had ten bullets left in this clip and then he'd be out of ammunition. He figured Cullen was equally armed. Maybe Cullen had another clip, but Egan figured it would be back in the SUV. Egan watched and waited as Cullen made his way down off the roadway, using every available rock formation and tree as cover on his descent.

When Cullen hid behind a parallel cluster of rocks, Egan waited for the gun battle to begin. He didn't have long to wait. Cullen fired several times, not even coming close to hitting his target. Egan assumed that Cullen had to be frustrated, wanting so badly to kill him and yet unable to reach him.

What were the odds, Egan wondered, that Cullen's men would return before either the Dundee agents or the FBI arrived? If Cullen's men came back, the chances of him killing Cullen instead of the other way around were slim to none. And if the feds showed up before he'd taken care of Cullen, then they would arrest him and his fate would be in the hands of the justice system. Egan didn't like those odds. For every criminal doing time, there were half a dozen walking around free. They'd gotten off on some technicality or another. He couldn't risk allowing Cullen to live. If he did, Maggie and Bent would never be safe.

"Looks like we're in a Mexican standoff, doesn't it?" Egan called loudly. "What do you say we end this here and now? The better man walks away alive."

"What are you suggesting?" Cullen asked.

"We both throw out our guns and meet face-to-face," Egan replied. "A couple of old soldiers in hand-to-hand combat. That is unless you're afraid I can whip your butt."

"It'd take a tougher son of a bitch than you to whip my butt, Cassidy." Cullen tossed his weapon out onto the steep incline that separated the two rock formations. "Now, you, Cassidy. I trust you to keep your word."

Egan knew there was a possibility that Cullen had another weapon on him, so he'd have to be careful. But it was a chance he had to take. He threw his Glock out on the ground so that Cullen could see it. "Now, who comes out first?"

Cullen emerged from behind the rocks, indeed an old soldier, but one in superb physical condition for his age. Motioning with his hand, he said, "Come on out, Cassidy. Let's find out who the better man is."

Ever cautious, Egan eased out from the protection of the rocks. Prepared to drop and roll if Cullen produced another gun, Egan took several tentative steps forward. Ignoring the pain in his leg and ribs, he faced his opponent.

"You look a little worse for wear, old buddy," Cullen taunted.

"Just a few scratches. Nothing to keep me from ripping you limb from limb."

Motioning again, Cullen grinned. "You want me? Come get me."

The two warriors circled each other, each wary. Suddenly Cullen whipped out a knife from the sheath strapped to his leg, then brandished the shiny blade in Egan's face.

"You didn't honestly think I'll give you an even chance, did you?" Cullen smirked, then lunged toward Egan.

Egan sidestepped the attack, then swerved around and braced himself for the next assault. Cullen recovered quickly and moved in again, jabbing repeatedly as he drew closer and closer. Attack. Avoid. Attack. Avoid. Suddenly Egan lost his balance when he slid across a section of loose gravel. He went down on his wounded knee. The pain spread outward from the cut and raced through his whole body. Cullen took that moment to swoop down, hoping for a kill. Despite great discomfort, Egan whirled sideways, deflecting the direct stab. The knife ripped through his shirt and sliced across his shoulder. Blood seeped through the material, creating a large red oval.

Realizing that now was the time, the exact moment to make his move, when Cullen felt all-powerful, Egan rammed into him, disregarding the threat of the deadly knife. Taken off guard, Cullen bounced backward from the direct blow. Egan wrestled his opponent to the ground and grabbed the hand that held the knife. Struggling fiercely, the two men rolled around on the rocky ground, each battling for supremacy.

Tossing Cullen onto his back, Egan manacled his wrist, then lifted his hand and repeatedly knocked it against the hard earth until Cullen's hand opened and the knife fell out. The two exchanged repeated blows as they tossed and tumbled downward, landing with brutal force on top of the protruding boulder. Their combat intensified. Cullen knocked Egan within an inch of the edge, then dove toward him in an effort to knock him off into the deep gorge.

Just as Cullen thought he was about to land the fatal blow, Egan counteracted with a last-minute maneuver of his own. Cullen cried out when he realized that he and not Egan would be flying through the air in a downward spiral, free-falling to the jagged rocks below. Dropping to his death.

Egan saw the realization on Cullen's face the very second he careened over the edge. Shock. Disbelief. And resignation, as if he were glad the battle was finally over, regardless of the outcome.

Cullen's continuous, bloodcurdling shriek echoed in Egan's ears long after Cullen's body had landed in a broken heap fifty feet below, inside the canyon. Egan stood on the boulder and looked down at death. The death of fear. The death of a wasted life. The final chapter written in blood.

As he made his way up the mountainside, his legs unsteady, Egan heard the approach of a vehicle. Damn! He turned to search for his Glock where it still lay on the ground, a few feet from Cullen's Ruger. Just as he reached for the pistol, he heard Joe Ornelas calling his name.

"Egan? Where the hell are you?"

"Down here!" Egan cried out.

"Where's Cullen?"

"Dead!"

Within minutes, Wolfe and Joe Ornelas made their way down the mountainside. Just as they flanked Egan and lifted his arms, one around each of their shoulders, Egan glanced up to the edge of the roadway. Maggie and Bent stood there together, mother and son side by side. Alive. Unharmed. Free from fear now and forever.

Maggie had insisted that Egan return home to Alabama with Bent and her to recuperate. After an overnight stay in the Flagstaff hospital, Egan had checked himself out, against doctor's orders. Hunter Whitelaw had stayed on several days, until his wound had begun to heal, then he had flown back to Atlanta, just as Joe and Wolfe had done. Once Maggie took charge, Egan had given in and allowed her to boss him around. If truth be told, he kind of liked having Maggie clucking over him like a mother hen. But Bent didn't seem to approve. Not of Egan living in his home nor of his mother giving Egan a great deal of TLC.

Egan had been ensconced on the soft leather sofa in Maggie's den most of the time during the three days since they'd arrived in Parsons City. Bent had returned to school immediately upon their return and the boy avoided Egan in the evenings. Three days of indulgent care and Egan was climbing the walls. He was unaccustomed to lying around doing nothing and being waited on hand and foot.

"Lunch is ready," Maggie called from the doorway.

Egan glanced up to see her standing there, a tray in her hand. "I can come to the table. You don't have to keep treating me as if I were an invalid."

"I know you're not an invalid." She brought the tray to him. "But you're recovering from five broken ribs, a deep cut in your thigh that required twenty stitches and a knife wound on your shoulder that required thirty-five stitches. And you left the hospital before you were supposed to."

"I'm not used to be mollycoddled."

Maggie eased her hand behind his back to help him sit up straight, then she fluffed his pillows and rearranged them for him.

"You're acting worse than Bent does when he gets sick," Maggie scolded. "Why is it that you can't just relax and enjoying letting someone else take care of you?"

Egan inspected his noonday meal. Homemade vegetable soup. A grilled cheese sandwich. And a large slice of Maggie's apple pie. What did he tell her—that he could easily get used to this kind of treatment? That he loved having her fuss over him, but he didn't dare let himself become accustomed to it.

This was a temporary arrangement. A visit with his son

until he was fully recovered. That had been Maggie's reasoning when she'd insisted he come home with them. At the time he'd been too physically weak and too soul-weary to argue with her.

Egan nodded toward the overstuffed, plaid armchair beside the sofa. "Sit down, Maggie. We need to talk."

"About what?" She rubbed her hands together nervously.

"Sit," he said.

She sat on the edge of the chair, placed her hands in her lap and sighed. "I'm sitting. So what do you want to talk about?"

"About you and me and Bent. About my staying here to recuperate."

"You're not leaving!" Maggie shot to her feet.

"Please, sit back down, honey. No, I'm not leaving today or even tomorrow. But you and I know that sooner or later, I'll have to go. Bent has made it perfectly clear that he doesn't want me here. He's not going to give me a chance, no matter how much you and I want him to."

"You've been here three days," she said. "That's hardly enough time. You and Bent are still strangers to each other."

"Do you honestly think that if I stay here a week or a month or even six months, Bent will come around?" Egan rubbed his forehead. "He can't even stand to be in the same room with me. He hasn't said ten words to me since—"

"You are staying here until you're fully recovered. You haven't given Bent an opportunity to get to know you." Maggie eased down and sat on the coffee table in front of the sofa, then reached out and took Egan's hand in hers. "I'm asking you to stay. For your own sake as much as Bent's. You need your son in your life as much as he needs you."

"You actually care about how I feel, don't you? After all I've put you through, you're willing to forgive me and help me win my son's affection. You, Maggie Tyson…Douglas, are one hell of a woman."

"Yes, I know." A soft, delicate smile curved her lips. "Bent will be home early today because he took his last final exam," Maggie explained. "I told him this morning that I expected him to spend the afternoon with us."

"And just what do you have planned?"

"I thought we'd go to the river and take the boat out. We could even stay overnight at our cottage down there. Bent loves the river and you could soak up some fresh air and sunshine."

"Sounds like a nice plan, but what if Bent doesn't want to—"

"He's already promised me."

"What did you do, twist his arm?"

"I asked him to do it as a favor to me," she admitted. "Now, you eat your lunch, while I go pack a few things for our little excursion."

Before Maggie reached the hallway, she heard the back door open.

"Bent?"

"Yeah, Mama, it's me. And wait till you see who I've got with me."

When Maggie entered the kitchen, she stopped dead in her tracks. There beside the refrigerator that Bent had opened searching for a cola stood her ex-husband.

"Hi, Mag," Gil Douglas said.

"What are you doing here?" she asked.

"I called him," Bent said. "I thought if anyone could talk sense to you and make you see what a mistake it is letting that man—" Bent nodded in the direction of the den "—back into your life, it would be Dad."

"Bent, you had no right to involve Gil in our affairs."

"Maggie, the boy is just worried about you," Gil said. "And since when don't I have a right to be concerned about my son?"

"Oh, he's your son, now, is he? Funny thing that you suddenly remember you have a son, just when Bent's biological father comes into his life." Maggie huffed loudly. "You haven't been a father to Bent since our divorce. You weren't even concerned enough about him when he was kidnapped to come here, so why is it that you can take off time from work to drop by and tell me how to run my life?"

"See, I told you that she wouldn't listen to me," Gil said to Bent. "She has a blind spot when it comes to Cassidy. She can't see him for who he is—a hired killer who used her and dumped her. He couldn't care less about her...or about you."

"Mama, listen to him, will you?"

"What I don't understand," Maggie said, "is why you're listening to him."

"Why shouldn't he listen to me?" Gil took a stand there beside Bent, two unlikely allies. "I was around the first time Egan Cassidy stormed into your life and nearly destroyed you. I don't want to see it happen a second time. The first time he wrecked our relationship. This time he'll wreck your relationship with Bent. Is that what you want?"

"How dare you! You have no right—"

"Legally, I'm Bent's father, so that gives me a right."

"I want you to leave," Maggie said. "All you're doing is stirring up trouble. Why, Gil? Have you been waiting fifteen years to pay me back for loving another man more than I could have ever loved you?"

"See?" Gil pointed a finger at Maggie, then glanced at

Bent's stricken face. "I told you that she's still in love with him."

"Damn you, Gil Douglas!" Maggie screamed. "Get out of my house!"

The door leading into the hallway swung open. Egan Cassidy filled the doorway. "I think I heard Maggie ask you to leave."

"It's been a long time, Cassidy," Gil said. "But I see you haven't changed. You just walked in here and took over again, didn't you? Well, you might be able to manipulate Maggie, but you have no power over *my* son. Bent knows what kind of man you are."

"Maybe so," Egan said. "But my guess is that he knows what kind of man you are, too."

"Please, Gil, just go. Now." Maggie looked at her ex-husband pleadingly.

"If Dad goes, I go," Bent said.

"What?" Maggie glared at Bent, shocked by his outburst.

"You heard him, didn't you?" Gil smirked. "Bent wants me to stay, but he wants Cassidy to go. So, what's it going to be, Maggie? Do you choose your son or your lover?"

"Why you slimy, jealous-hearted, backstabbing..." Maggie fumed. Of all the problems she had anticipated in trying to unite Bent and Egan, this one hadn't even entered her mind. During their marriage, Gil had tried to be a father to Bent, but he'd failed miserably. And since their divorce, Gil hadn't really been a part of their lives. But here he was, big as life, playing the role of protective parent.

"You're leaving right this minute." Maggie marched across the kitchen and pointed her index finger right into Gil's face. "And don't you ever come back, without an invitation from me."

"I told you that if Dad leaves, I leave," Bent repeated his threat.

"Pack a bag and meet me in the car," Gil said, then turned to Maggie. "I'll have him call you when we get to Nashville."

"He's not going anywhere with you," Maggie said.

"He's not a child," Gil reminded her. "He has a right to—"

Egan sauntered across the room, heading toward Gil. Gil backed out of the kitchen and onto the screened-in porch. Egan went after him. Bent followed both men outside, as did Maggie.

"I'll wait in the car for you, Bent," Gil said.

"Bent won't be going with you." Egan's voice possessed a dangerous undertone. "So, there's no point in your waiting for him."

When Bent flew past Maggie, heading toward Gil, Egan reached out and clamped his big hand down on Bent's shoulder. "You can leave with this man and break your mother's heart. Is that what you want?"

"I want to get away from you!" Bent shouted.

"You can run away from me, if that's really what you want to do, but nothing is going to change the fact that Gil Douglas isn't your father. I am. Like it or not, you are my son, not his. You look like me. You talk like me. You even walk like me."

"I don't want to be your son. Do you hear me?" Bent jerked out of Egan's hold. "You don't love my mother and you don't love me. You never wanted to be a part of our lives. You weren't here for us when we needed you. And when you finally showed up, it was only because some lunatic who hated you had kidnapped me!"

"Oh, Bent," Maggie cried. "I thought you understood

why Egan left me, why he stayed away. It wasn't because he wanted to."

"You say that I don't love your mother or you," Egan said. "You're wrong on both counts. I loved your mother. That's the reason I left her. I didn't have the right to love her. And you...Bent...son...you have no idea what you mean to me or how much I love you."

Tears welled up in Bent's eyes. "I don't believe you."

"What do I have to do to prove it to you?" Egan asked.

Bent's chin trembled. "I told you that I don't believe you. There's nothing you can do to prove it to me."

"Why don't you stick around and give me a chance? That's all I want. That's all your mother is asking of us— of you and me. That we give ourselves a chance to get to know each other. Do you think she's asking for too much?"

"Bent, don't listen to him." Gil Douglas glanced anxiously back and forth from Bent to Egan. "You know you can't trust him."

"Maybe you're right," Bent said. "Maybe I can't trust him. But I know one thing for sure and that's that the one person who really loves me is Mama. Not you, Gil." Bent glared at his adoptive father, then he focused his hard gaze on Egan. "And not you, either." He turned to Maggie. "I won't leave, Mama. I shouldn't have called Gil and got him involved in our problems. I acted like a stupid kid. I really am sorry."

Maggie opened her arms and Bent ran to her. Egan marched toward Gil Douglas, who made a hasty retreat to the driveway. Egan followed, catching up with Gil just as he opened his car door.

Egan grasped Gil's shoulder and whirled Gil around to face him. "I believe in giving a man fair warning. You stay in Nashville and take care of your woman and your child. That woman—" Egan nodded at the house "—is mine.

She always has been and she always will be. And that boy is my son. Mine. Not yours.''

"You have no right to either of them. Not after the way you—"

Egan tightened his hold on Gil's shoulder. "I gave up Maggie, and unknowingly gave up my son, to protect them from a monster. But that monster no longer exists and I'm free to claim what's mine. Neither Bent nor Maggie may ever be able to forgive me or allow me to be a permanent part of their lives, but I plan to do everything I can to persuade them that I deserve a second chance!''

Egan released Gil's shoulder and stepped aside. Gil jumped in his car, started the engine and sped out of the driveway. When Egan turned to go back to the house, he saw Maggie and Bent standing at the backyard gate. Waiting. Waiting for him.

Chapter 15

During his two months of recuperation, Egan had taken full advantage of his time with Maggie and Bent. He had realized early on that although Maggie would allow him to have a relationship with Bent no matter what happened between him and her, Egan could never have Maggie without a relationship with Bent. And he wanted them both. Unfortunately winning Bent over had turned out to be a formidable task. His son distrusted him and seemed to be testing him at every turn. But in all fairness, Egan had to admit that Bent was trying. Mostly to pacify Maggie. But Egan would gladly take whatever he could get, whatever Bent was willing to give.

He and Maggie were walking on eggshells around Bent, both of them doing whatever they could to bring the three of them together as a family. Since school was out, they spent every weekend at the river, swimming, boating and soaking up the fresh air and sunshine. During the week they ate breakfast and dinner together and often Egan and Bent went into town at lunch to join Maggie for sandwiches at Rare Finds. And last week they had taken a family vacation to the Gulf Coast, staying at the Grand Hotel in Point Clear.

Egan's relationship with Bent had improved, but they still had a long way to go to ever truly be father and son. Right now they were friendly acquaintances. The situation with Maggie and him was a different matter, but in its own way just as difficult to handle. He wanted to ask Maggie to marry him, but until Bent truly accepted him, marriage was out of the question. And until he and Maggie were in a committed relationship, they could hardly carry on an affair right under their disapproving son's nose. And disapprove he did!

Days went fairly smoothly since Maggie was gone for eight hours. But nights were hell. He was sleeping in the guest bedroom down the hall from Maggie and every time they tried pulling off a midnight tryst, Bent interrupted them. Nothing like having your fourteen-year-old son as a strict chaperone. Egan knew that Maggie was as frustrated as he. The sexual tension between them had just about reached the explosion point.

Egan had taken to writing at night and had just finished a new collection of Nage Styon verses. He would dedicate this book to Maggie and Bent.

Egan lifted the pages from the desk and bound them together with a metal clip. He did all his work in longhand, never using a typewriter or a computer. He had driven into town this morning and made three copies. One to send his editor. One for Maggie and one for Bent.

He carried the copies downstairs with him and placed them on the kitchen counter before he went outside and fired up the grill. He planned to have steaks ready when Maggie came home. He liked taking care of her, doing things that pleased her. By the way she glowed when he showed her the smallest amount of attention, he'd learned that it had been a very long time since anyone had made her feel special. If given the chance, Egan wanted to spend the rest of his life making Maggie feel like the most special woman in the world. And that's exactly what she was—to him and to Bent.

"Hey, you got time for a little one-on-one?" Bent bounced the basketball on the driveway, then tossed it into the net attached to the garage.

"When did you get home?" Egan smiled at his son.

"Chris dropped me off about ten minutes ago," Bent said.

"I didn't know Chris was old enough—"

"You're as bad as Mama checking up on me and my friends." Bent's expression didn't soften, but he spoke the words in a lighthearted manner. "Chris has his learner's permit and his big brother was in the car. Satisfied?"

Egan nodded. "Let me get the fire started in the grill, then I'll shoot hoops with you until it's time to put on the steaks."

Thirty minutes later, a hot and sweaty father and son took a break. Bent went into the kitchen and came back with individual bottles of water. He tossed one to Egan, then sat opposite him in a wicker chair on the back porch.

"I...er...I was wondering if you might want to play in a softball game with me Saturday," Bent said, then took a big swig of water, deliberately avoiding making eye contact.

"I didn't know you were on a team," Egan said.

"This is a special tournament sponsored by Chris's church." Bent gazed out across the backyard. "It's a charity thing."

"Sure, I'd be happy to play softball with you. But I have

to warn you that I haven't played in years. I'm pretty rusty.''

"Ah, that won't matter." Bent shrugged. "All the other dads probably won't be very good anyway. None of them are in as good a shape as you."

For a split second Egan's heart stopped. *All the other dads. All the other dads?* This was the closest Bent had come to recognizing Egan as his father. Did his son even realize what he'd said?

"So, what is it, a combination teens and old men's game?" Egan asked jokingly.

"Yeah, something like that." Bent downed the rest of his water in one long giant swallow, then crushed the empty plastic bottle. He got up, went outside and tossed the bottle into the garbage. "Hey, I think the grill's ready for those steaks."

Egan nodded, then went inside and took the marinated steaks from the refrigerator. When he opened the lid of the grill and laid the steaks on the rack above the smoldering coals, Bent came up beside him.

"That softball tournament...it's a 'Father and Son' thing," Bent admitted. "I thought it would make Mama happy if we did something like that together."

Egan closed the lid on the steaks, then cleared his throat. "Yeah, you're right. I think it would make Maggie happy." Taking a chance, praying that Bent wouldn't reject him, Egan laid his hand on Bent's shoulder. "I have to admit that it makes me happy, too."

Bent grinned. Egan's stomach knotted. This was the first genuine smile his son had given him. And it had taken only two months of diligent work to earn that smile.

Relaxing in her recliner in the den, an unread novel in her hand, Maggie watched her two guys sitting side by side on the sofa. They laughed and shouted and shoved or punched each other occasionally while they watched the Atlanta Braves game on television. Seeing Bent and Egan together this way was the answer to many prayers. After two months of cautious courtesy toward his father, Bent had finally let down the walls around his emotions and was making a real effort to allow Egan into his life.

Now, if only her overprotective son would give her permission to open her arms and her heart to Egan. Until the man she loved had come back into her life, she hadn't been overly concerned about not having had sex in years. But now that Egan had reawakened the sensual woman within her, this self-imposed celibacy was killing her. Every night she lay alone in her bed, thinking about Egan. He slept just down the hall. A one-minute walk. But it might as well have been a thousand miles. Bent had been more observant and disapproving than her own father would have been.

The telephone rang, jarring Maggie from her thoughts. She reached over and picked up the portable phone, then took note of the Caller ID number. Atlanta. The Dundee Agency. Maggie's heartbeat accelerated. Ellen had contacted Egan weekly the first month, but she hadn't phoned in weeks now.

Maggie answered on the third ring. "Hello."

"Maggie, this is Ellen Denby. How are you?"

"We're fine. How about you?"

"Doing okay." Ellen paused. "I hate to bother y'all, but I'm afraid something has come up and we're going to need Egan to make a trip to Chicago."

"Oh, I see."

"Is he around somewhere?"

"Yes. He's right here. He and Bent are watching a baseball game on TV." Maggie held the phone out to Egan, who was looking at her questioningly. "It's Ellen Denby."

Egan got up, reached out and took the phone. "Hi, there. What's up?"

"Remember the Marler case you worked on six months ago?" Ellen sighed. "Well, that case has come to trial. The assistant district attorney says he needs you to testify on Sybil Marler's behalf day after tomorrow and he wants to consult with you beforehand."

"That means I'll have to fly to Chicago in the morning," Egan said. "How about faxing the particulars of the case to my hotel room once I get there. I need to refresh my memory on a few points."

"Just remember that Sybil's husband is out on bail and he made some awfully ugly threats against you."

"I can handle Doyce Marler," Egan said. "The man's a pip-squeak."

"He's a pip-squeak who gets his kicks by beating his wife and kids. A guy like that is capable of killing."

"If anyone gets killed, it won't be me," Egan assured Ellen. "I'd like nothing better than the opportunity to beat the hell out that SOB."

"After your trip to Chicago, will you be coming back to Atlanta?" Ellen asked. "Or do you plan to retire and take up residence in Alabama permanently?"

"Depends," Egan replied. "We've still got things to work out."

"Good luck. Call me when you get to Chicago."

"Thanks. And you'll be hearing from me."

When Egan laid the phone on the coffee table, he noticed that Bent had moved across the room and now stood at Maggie's side. Mother and son stared at him, looks of concern on their faces.

"That was Ellen," Egan said. "I have to fly to Chicago tomorrow to testify in a case I worked on six months ago."

"I thought you weren't going back to work at Dundee's,'' Bent said. ''You told us that you were thinking about retiring. You made us believe that you wanted to stay here with us.''

''I do want to stay here with you and Maggie.'' Egan's stomach tightened with apprehension. ''This trip shouldn't last more than a few days.''

''Isn't there some way you can get out of going?'' Bent asked. ''Can't somebody else testify?''

''I'm afraid not. This was my case and I'm the one with the firsthand information.''

''After Chicago, you'll go back to Atlanta, won't you?'' Bent's face flushed. He curled his hands into tight fists. ''You've had your little family reunion, but things are getting pretty dull around here, aren't they?''

''No, son, that's not true.'' Egan held out his hand in a plea for understanding. ''This is just a quick trip. I'll come right back.''

Bent turned to his mother. ''You told me that if I gave him a chance, that if I'd let him be a father to me, he wouldn't leave us. Well, it looks like you were wrong. Again!''

''Bentley Tyson Douglas!'' Maggie glowered at her son. ''You're acting like a child. You're being totally unreasonable. Egan isn't leaving us for good.'' She turned to Egan. ''Tell him! Make him understand.''

''Yeah, Egan, make me understand.'' Bent walked over to his father and looked him square in the eye.

''Do you honestly think that I'd walk away from you and your mother and not come back?''

''Yeah, that's exactly what I think. You did it before, so what's to stop you from doing it again. This trip to Chicago is just an excuse so you can leave without having to explain that the quiet life in Parsons City isn't what you wanted.''

''Bent...son...'' When Egan tried to put his hand on

Bent's shoulder, the boy sidestepped him. "What can I say or do to prove to you that I'm telling you the truth?"

"Don't go to Chicago!"

Egan's shoulders slumped. "I have to go. If I don't testify, a criminal could go free."

"Well, if you leave, don't bother to come back!" Bent yelled. "Ever!"

When Bent stormed out of the den, Egan started to go after him, but Maggie rushed over and grabbed Egan's arm. "Don't. He's not going to listen to you. I know he's acting irrationally, but right now his emotions are in charge. He's convinced himself that you're leaving us and I don't think you'll be able to persuade him otherwise."

Egan grabbed Maggie's shoulder. "You know I'm coming back, don't you?"

Maggie's chin quivered. "Yes, if you tell me that you're coming back to us, then I believe you. But even if you come back, I'm afraid all the progress you've made with Bent these past two months may have been destroyed."

Egan wiped away a lone tear as it trickled down Maggie's cheek. "I'm going to pack and leave tonight." He pulled Maggie into his arms. "But when I come back—and I will be back as soon as I possibly can—I'll fix things with Bent. I promise."

Two hours later, Maggie waited alone at the foot of the stairs as Egan came down with his suitcase in hand. After telling her that he'd be back when *that man* left, Bent had gone for a walk.

Egan set his suitcase by the front door, then lifted Maggie's hand into his and gave her the manuscript pages for his latest volume of poetry. "This is for you. And for Bent."

Maggie glanced down at the title page. *Silence* by Nage Styon. She flipped to the second page and read the dedication. *To the love of my life, Maggie, and to Bent, the wonderful son she gave me.*

"Oh, Egan." Gripping the manuscript tightly, she flung her arms around him and laid her head on his chest. "Thank you."

"You knew, didn't you? You've known all along that I was Nage Styon."

"Yes, I've known ever since I bought the first volume of your poetry. If the name hadn't given you away, then the sentiments of your verses would have. I saw my brother Bentley in every line."

"I left Bent a copy upstairs in his room." Egan kissed Maggie, deeply and passionately, then released her and picked up his suitcase. "I'll be back, Maggie mine. And that's a promise you can take to the bank."

Maggie had been baking for four days. She had frozen cakes and pies and cookies—enough to feed an army for months. Despite what nagging fears remained in her heart, leftovers from the past, she kept telling herself repeatedly that Egan would come back to them. He had called every night, but Bent had refused to speak to him. Their son had been sulking ever since Egan left. If she didn't understand that Bent was acting out of fear and hurt, she would have already given him a tongue-lashing. But she did understand. He had just begun to trust Egan, just barely opened up to his father, when Egan had been called away. Although Bent's reaction might seem irrational to anyone else, she knew why her son had overreacted. He was beginning to love Egan and that love made him vulnerable.

Bent bounded into the kitchen, softball glove in hand. "The game starts in an hour and he's not here. I told you he wouldn't come back."

Maggie wiped her hands off on the towel, removed her

gingham apron and laid it on the counter. "Something must have come up to delay him."

"Why do you keep defending him? Get it through your head, Mama, he's not coming back."

"I don't intend to argue with you." Maggie picked up her bag from the table, hung the straps over her shoulder and then retrieved her car keys from a side pouch. "I'm ready to go."

"Yeah, me, too."

Forty-five minutes later, Maggie sat beside Janice De-weese in the stands at the Parsons City Athletic Park. She had been so sure Egan would keep his promise and make it back to town in time for the game. If he didn't show up, there was no way Bent would ever forgive him.

What if he isn't coming back? an insecure inner voice taunted her. What if Bent's right and Egan has decided that he can't live a quiet, simple life?

"Bent keeps looking around for Egan," Janice said. "He might have told you he doesn't think his father will show up, but he's sure hoping he will."

"I'm hoping he will, too," Maggie admitted. "I keep telling myself that something unavoidable came up."

"But you're having some doubts, aren't you?"

"It's just my insecurity. I know that Egan cares for me and that he wants a life with Bent and me."

"Then why isn't he here?" Janice asked.

"He'll be here. I just know he will." Maggie had to trust her heart, even if that heart had led her astray once before—fifteen years ago. Circumstances were different. Grant Cullen no longer posed a threat. Unlike years ago, Egan had made promises this time. Promises to her and to Bent.

The stands were filled with families. Mothers, brothers and sisters. Grandparents. Aunts and uncles. And groups of fathers and sons comprised the teams. But one father was missing. Bent's father.

She watched Bent as he tossed a ball back and forth with his friend Chris, whose father was present. Suddenly Bent missed the catch. The ball fell to the ground. Bent walked off the field and headed toward the entrance gates. Maggie pivoted slightly and glanced over her shoulder, following her son's journey. That's when she saw Egan. Wearing blue jeans and red T-shirt, identical to Bent's outfit, Egan stood just inside the park entrance.

Maggie's heart leaped into her throat. Tears misted her eyes. Egan laid his hand on his son's shoulder and together they joined the other players on the field. The coach tossed Egan a ball cap. After putting on the cap, he glanced up and scanned the crowd. When he spotted Maggie, he lifted his hand and waved. She stood up, tears streaming down her face, and blew him a kiss.

Egan lifted the sponge and ran it over Maggie's back. The scented bubbles dripped off the sponge onto his hand. After he scrubbed her back, he pulled her between his spread legs. Her buttocks nestled against his groin. She rested her head on his shoulder as he wrapped his arms around her. With tender caresses, he stroked her breasts, paying special attention to her nipples. When she moaned and rubbed her behind against his arousal, he slid his wet hands down over her tummy and slipped them between her thighs, separating her legs. With the fingers of one hand lifted to a breast and the fingers of the other hand occupied below, Egan teased her until she was breathless.

"Relax, honey, and let it happen," Egan whispered in her ear.

Obeying his command, she allowed his talented fingers to pleasure her. When fulfillment claimed her, shudders racking her body, Maggie cried out. Once the aftershocks subsided, Egan stood, water and bubbles dripping from his big body, and got out of the Jacuzzi tub in Maggie's bathroom. After tying a towel around his waist, he offered her his hand, then lifted her up and out of the tub. He wrapped a large, fluffy towel around her and dried her with slow, sensuous pats. Maggie grabbed her silk robe from the hook on the back of the door, slipped her arms through the sleeves and tied the belt.

Egan led her into her bedroom and over to the bed. After loosening her belt, he spread her robe apart to reveal her beautiful body. She smiled wickedly at him and snatched away his towel.

"Lady, you're asking for trouble," he said.

"Trouble's what I want, big boy." She looked directly at his erection.

"Then trouble is exactly what you're going to get."

He shoved her down on the bed and stood there gazing at her. Lifting her right foot, she stroked his hip, then inched her foot around so that her toes could tap against his sex.

"I'm glad Bent spent the night with Chris so that his parents could work off a little bottled-up tension," Maggie said. "These past two months without making love have been the longest two months of my life."

Egan parted her legs and walked between them, then lifted her hips. With one fast, deep lunge, he entered her. She sighed with pleasure, then straddled his waist with her legs and opened herself completely to his plunder.

"It'll take me years to make up for lost time," he told her.

"Then we shouldn't waste any time, should we?"

They made love with all the passion, all the hunger, all the longing that they had been forced to deny for so many weeks. They shared simultaneous climaxes that rocked them to the core of their bodies.

Sated and happy beyond their wildest dreams, they lay together in Maggie's bed, the night still young and the future spread out ahead of them like a golden dream waiting to be fulfilled.

Maggie held up her left hand and stared at the shimmering amethyst-and-diamond engagement ring Egan had bought while he'd been in Chicago. "I can't believe you remembered that my birthstone is an amethyst." She wriggled around, freeing her arm trapped between them, braced herself on one elbow and leaned across Egan's chest. "I love this ring. It's beautiful. But with all these diamonds it must have cost you a small fortune. I would have been happy with something less expensive."

Egan rose up and kissed her on the nose, then lifted his hand to thread his fingers through the damp, tangled mass of her hair. "I've got more money than I can spend in one lifetime, so let me enjoy myself and spend it on you and Bent."

"Hmm-mmm. I had no idea I was marrying a millionaire," she teased.

"You're marrying a man who loves you more than anything in this world and is grateful that you're giving him a chance to spend the rest of his life proving it to you."

"So while you're proving your love to me, what do you intend to do to keep yourself occupied when I'm working? You could always be a househusband."

"I'm going to write more Nage Styon poetry and I just might try my hand at writing a novel. Maybe a murder mystery."

"Hmm-mmm. Uh, Egan?"

"Huh?" He idly caressed her naked hip.

She snuggled as close to him as possible, then forked

her fingers through his chest hair. "Let's get married next week."

"Suits me just fine, but why the big hurry? I thought you women liked months to plan these big shindigs."

"I don't want a big wedding. I'd like something simple. Just you, me, Bent and Janice."

"I want whatever you want, honey. You know that, don't you?"

"Uh-huh. Does that total acceptance extend to *anything* I want?" She looked at him coyly and smiled.

"I'd give you anything in the world you wanted, if I could."

"How about another child?" She nuzzled his chin with her nose.

"You want a baby?"

"I want your baby. And this time, I want you to be with me, every step of the way."

"I can't believe…" As Egan rose into a sitting position, he eased Maggie up with him until she sat on his lap. "I'd be more than happy to oblige and feel blessed if you were to get pregnant. But honey, I'm forty-seven. The equipment still works, but I can't guarantee—"

She pressed her index finger against his lips. "Your equipment works just fine. As a matter of fact…I'm pretty sure that I'm already pregnant."

"What?"

"A little over two months pregnant," she admitted. "I took a home pregnancy test this morning and it came out positive."

"Oh, Maggie, honey. How the hell did I get so lucky?" He smothered her with kisses, then suddenly stopped. His mouth fell open; his jaw went slack. "What are you going to say to Bent? Do you think he'll be upset?"

"I'm going to say, 'You know that baby sister you always wanted when you were a little boy...'"

Egan laughed as he pulled Maggie down on top of him. "I love you, Maggie mine."

"And I love you, Egan."

Epilogue

Christmas at the Cassidy home was an incomparable event. The aroma of cinnamon wafted from the kitchen mingling with the scent of fresh evergreen throughout the house. Twinkling white lights adorned the eight-foot tree, draped the mantels in the living and dining rooms and set aflame the small shrubbery that lined the brick walkway. Red-and-green plaid ribbon laced over and under windows and doors, and huge bows graced every present stacked under the tree.

Shrill squeals and the sound of little feet bouncing up and down alerted Maggie that Bentley Tyson Cassidy had arrived. She checked the sugar cookies in the oven, wiped her hands on the towel and then rushed out of the kitchen and down the hallway. There in the foyer stood her eighteen-year-old son, home from the University of Alabama.

Red-haired, three-year-old Melanie clung to one of Bent's legs and her identical twin sister, Melinda, clung to the other. Egan reached down and lifted first one and then the other daughter away from their beloved big brother. Father and son stood side by side, each six-three and broad-shouldered, although Egan possessed the bulk of a mature man while Bent still retained the lankiness of youth.

"Mama!" Bent hurried toward Maggie, lifted her off her feet and whirled her around and around, then set her back on the floor. "The house looks wonderful and boy, something sure smells good."

"Cookies," Melinda said.

"Sugar cookies," Melanie clarified.

"Come on you two little demons. Y'all can help Mommy in the kitchen." Maggie gathered up the twins and herded them down the hallway. "Lunch will be ready soon," she called back to her men. "Put your bag in your room, Bent, then by the time you and your father wash up, I'll have chicken and dumplings on the table."

After picking up Bent's suitcase, Egan draped his arm around his son's shoulder. "It's good to have you here. Your mama's had a difficult time adjusting to your living away from home."

"Mama has, huh?" Bent grinned. "And you haven't missed me, have you, Dad?"

Egan chuckled. "Actually, Maggie's been handling your being gone better than I have. I guess I'll never feel as if I've had enough time with you."

"Yeah, I know what you mean," Bent said. "My little sisters are lucky that you've had the chance to be a part of their lives from the beginning." Bent hugged his father. "But I'm lucky that you didn't give up on me, considering what a stubborn mule I was before you and Mama got married."

"I would never have given up on you," Egan said. "And I'm the lucky one to have you and the girls and Maggie. She's given me a life I never thought I could have."

Fifteen minutes later, the Cassidy family gathered around the kitchen table for their noontime meal. After the twins said a prayer of thanks simultaneously, Maggie glanced across the table at her husband. Egan smiled at her and her stomach did a quivering little flip-flop. She mouthed the words "I love you" and he returned the silent gesture.

"What ya doing, Mama?" Melanie asked, her mouth half-full of dumplings.

"She and Daddy are making faces at each other," Melinda said. "They're always making kissie faces."

"That's because our mother and father love each other," Bent told his little sisters, then spread out both arms, reached over from where he sat between them and ruffled their silky red curls.

"And they love us, too," Melanie added. "Me and her—" she pointed to her sister "—and you." She pointed at Bent.

Everyone laughed. Joy in abundance filled Maggie's heart. She had everything she'd ever wanted—and more. So much more. Three beautiful, healthy children. A happy, contented husband who worshiped the ground she walked on. And the life she'd dreamed of since the first moment Egan Cassidy had walked into her life.

* * * * *

Beverly Barton has a new novel, coming in
Sensation in September 2006.

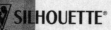

0506/23a

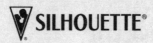
▼ SILHOUETTE®

SPECIAL EDITION™

THE ULTIMATE TEXAS BACHELOR
by Cathy Gillen Thacker

The McCabes

After his reality TV romance finishes, Brad McCabe swears off all women. But Lainey Carrington could be just the woman to change his mind. Although she's at his ranch under false pretences...

THE SUGAR HOUSE by Christine Flynn

Going Home

Emmy Larkin believed that Jack Travers' father had betrayed her father. But successful, handsome Jack wanted to make things right when confronted by this lovely, fiercely independent woman...

WANTED: ONE FATHER
by Penny Richards

Single dad Max Murdock needed a quiet place to write and a baby-sitter for his baby girl. Zoe Barlow could help with both. It was a perfect match, but were irresistible Zoe and her three impish boys the perfect family?

Don't miss out!
On sale from 19th May 2006

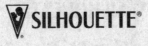

ALL HE EVER WANTED
by Allison Leigh

Montana

When young Erik fell down a mine shaft, he was saved by brave and beautiful Faith Taylor. Faith was amazed by the feelings Erik's handsome father, Cameron, awoke. But was Cam ready to find a new happiness?

PLAYING WITH FIRE by Arlene James

Lucky in Love

Struggling hairstylist Valerie Blunt had a lot on her mind —well, mainly the infuriatingly attractive Fire Marshal Ian Keene. Ian set Valerie alight whenever he was near...

BECAUSE A HUSBAND IS FOREVER
by Marie Ferrarella

The Cameo

Talk show host Dakota Delaney agreed to allow bodyguard Ian Russell to shadow her. But she hadn't counted on the constant battling or that he would want to take hold of her safety—and her heart.

0506/51

SILHOUETTE®
Desire™ 2 in 1

A MAN APART by Joan Hohl

Notorious charmer Justin Grainger wasn't planning on settling down, but a week of unbridled passion with sexy Hannah Deturk just wasn't enough. He was going to have to rethink his plans and incorporate a baby, too!

HOT TO THE TOUCH by Jennifer Greene

Fox Lockwood was suffering and no doctor could cure him. Enter Phoebe Schneider – a masseuse specialising in soothing infants. But Fox was a fully grown adult male, who wanted their relationship to take a more personal turn...

RULES OF ATTRACTION by Susan Crosby

Behind Closed Doors

PI Quinn Gerard was following a suspect, but the sexy bombshell turned out to be her twin sister, Claire. Could Quinn convince Claire to bend the rules and give in to their mutual attraction?

SCANDALOUS PASSION by Emilie Rose

Phoebe Drew feared intimate photos of her and her first love, Carter Jones, would affect her grandfather. So she went to Carter for help in finding them. But digging up the past also uncovered long-hidden passion.

THE RUGGED LONER by Bronwyn Jameson

Princes of the Outback

Australian widower Tomas Carlisle was stunned to learn that he had to father a child to inherit a cattle empire. Making a deal with friend Angelina Mori seemed the perfect solution – until their passion escalated.

AT YOUR SERVICE by Amy Jo Cousins

Runaway heiress Grace Haley donned an apron and posed as a waitress. She found herself sparring with her gorgeous new boss Christopher Tyler, wondering how he would react if he knew her secret.

On sale from 19th May 2006

Visit our website at www.silhouette.co.uk

SILHOUETTE®

INTRIGUE™

ROCKY MOUNTAIN MYSTERY
by Cassie Miles

Colorado Crime Consultants

Even though five years had passed since his sister's unsolved
murder, investigative reporter David Cross refused to give up
his quest for justice. Now that the perpetrator had emerged to
set his sights on David's colleague, could he protect the brainy
beauty – *and* beat the deranged killer at his own game?

OFFICIAL DUTY by Doreen Roberts

Cowboy Cops

Ginny Matthews's past had just caught up with her when the
man she loved and left twelve years ago knocked on her door
and told her that her foster parents had been murdered. Sheriff
Cully Black wanted Ginny back where she belonged – under his
protection and in his arms. But with a killer poised to strike
again, how long would this second chance last?

HARD EVIDENCE by Susan Peterson

Lipstick Ltd

Killan Cray was in really hot water. The street-smart sleuth
had returned home only to find herself face-to-face with Jack
O'Brien, the ex who had horribly betrayed her. But now that
someone was relentlessly stalking Killan, she had to out her
trust in the man she'd always loved…before it was too late.

SHADOWS ON THE LAKE by Leona Karr

Eclipse

Single mother Courtney Collins wanted to spend a relaxing
summer with her reclusive aunt. Instead she found herself
immersed in an unimaginable nightmare when her aunt's
obsession with her infant son went too far. Businessman Neil
Ellsworth would do anything to protect Courtney and her child,
but the danger they face may be too deadly to stop…

On sale from 19th May 2006

www.silhouette.co.uk